THE LAST SUNSET: AFTERLIFE

I0676498

A Novel Written By

REECE HEWITT

Ark House Press
PO Box 1722, Port Orchard, WA 98366 USA
PO Box 1321, Mona Vale NSW 1660 Australia
PO Box 318 334, West Harbour, Auckland 0661 New Zealand
arkhousepress.com

Cataloguing in Publication Data:
Title: The Last Sunset Afterlife
ISBN: 978-0-6487607-7-1
Subjects: Fiction, Christian
Other Authors/Contributors: Hewitt, Reece

Cover Design: Jeremy Hay
Layout by initiateagency.com

DISCLAIMER

This is a work of fiction. Names, characters, businesses, places, events and incidents are either the products of the author's imagination or used in a fictitious manner. Any resemblance to actual persons, living or dead, or actual events is purely coincidental.

I would like to expressly convey to you (the reader) that were I to accidentally offend anyone due to the content contained in this book it is entirely unintentional of me to do so. Verses quoted from the Bible are often out of context, and I have no theological qualifications. I have provided references to where you can read the rest of the surrounding material should the reader wish to.

Thanks to:

God

Everyone who reads this book

Cover art:

Jeremy Hay

I hope you enjoy the read!

- Reece Hewitt

TABLE OF CONTENTS

CHAPTER 1:

THE DAY AFTER

A faint, steady beeping sound was interrupted by an occasional cough and quiet talking from down the hallway. The smell of disinfectant lingered in the air. Zack felt the stitches pinch in his chest as he breathed. The early morning sunlight had just begun to peek through the curtains. He awoke with a jolt in his hospital bed. He tilted his head to the side and vomited all over his freshly changed bed sheets.

"No, no, no," he spluttered after wiping his mouth on his sleeve.

Zack held his head in his hands, quivering slightly. His mind was still in turmoil after his apocalyptic vision of the future. The realisation that it was all real, was still yet to sink in.

He looked around to see the only other patient in the room was still sleeping. Zack saw Father Andrews was not in his bed on the far side of the room. Zack reasoned he must have gone to the toilet. He tried to remember all they talked about the previous night before he fell asleep. Zack's shoulder felt damp as the vomit started to soak through his hospital gown.

"Just great!"

He fumbled around his bedside table for the button to call the nurse. He pressed it and watched the light turn green. He began to think about all that had happened, all that he must do.

"Rough night?"

The patient in the bed opposite his sat up and rubbed his eyes.

"Yeah, uh, sorry,"

The middle-aged man reached for his bedside table and put on his glasses.

"No problem. It looks like you've been through a lot," he began to scratch the cast on his leg.

"You could say that."

Zack's mind started to wander. He wanted to spend a few hours talking to Father Andrews. He had so many questions flying through his mind.

"Car accident too?"

"Huh?"

"It looks like you're pretty beaten up over there. Did a truck hit you?"

"Oh me, no, gunshot wound."

"You don't say! You're luckier than most."

"Yeah."

"I got hit by a car, messed up my leg pretty bad, I don't think I'll be back on my bike for weeks."

"Sorry to hear that."

"What's with all that screaming if you don't mind me asking?"

"What screaming?"

"You don't remember? The nurses came in a few times the night to try and calm you down. You seemed, pretty out of it."

Zack struggled to recall much of anything from the previous night's sleep. He still felt groggy with the mixture of pain relief drugs he was on. His headache was starting to return.

"Uh, sorry, no."

Zack leaned slowly towards the tissue box on the small table next to his bed. A sharp pain shot up through his chest and rebuked him. He felt like he had just been kicked in the chest by a horse.

"Hey, take it easy there; the nurse will be here soon."

Zack nodded.

His face screwed up until eventually the pain subsided a little.

"So what did you dream about?"

"I don't remember much. Uh, or you from yesterday?"

"They rolled me in about ten last night; you were already asleep then. I'm Bernard. Nice to meet you."

"Oh. I'm Zack"

"Have a think; I'm sure you'll be able to remember something. I heard it's very therapeutic to talk through dreams that cause discomfort."

"Is that so?"

"Yip, scientifically proven they say. Let's give it a try, I'll tell you all about my dreams last night, and then you tell me yours."

Bernard then proceeded to explain in detail a dream he had about going fishing on a deep lake. He explained how he caught a large fish, and it bit him on the same leg that was now in a cast.

Zack struggled to listen. He had more important things to think about.

"…and then I woke up."

Bernard looked over to Zack with an expectant look on his face.

More vomit soaked into Zack's bedding and he wondered where the nurse was.

"Your turn friend," Bernard looked genuinely interested.

Zack held his head; his headache was getting worse. He pressed the call button a few times. "Upon reflection, I suppose the fish in my dream is the car that hit me, and maybe the fishing rod is my subconscious telling me it was partially my fault. I could've been watching more closely."

"Yeah, maybe," Zack did his best his conceal his lack of interest in Bernard's dream.

Zack took a deep breath, and his chest began to sting again.

"Ok, Zack, tell me about your dream before you forget it all. I know some days I have a vivid dream, really life-like, but later in the day I can't remember much at all." Bernard said, smiling.

"Yeah" Zack wiped his vomit with the corner of his blankets

unsuccessfully.

"The nurse is probably just doing her rounds, she won't be far away," Bernard assured.

Zack could hear movement down the hallway, but he couldn't see any nurses.

Bernard looked back at him, waiting for Zack to speak.

Zack was tired and sore all over; he closed his eyes slowly. The morning sunlight began to feel too bright.

"I know it can't be easy for you with those injuries, come on, it'll pass the time. Just tell me anything you remember," Bernard offered.

"I remember lots of people dying; it was horrible. I'm not sure I want to talk about it."

"Understandable! Sounds more intense than my fishing dream already. Just go on at your own pace."

"I remember a tidal wave and darkness everywhere."

Bernard nodded for him to continue.

"I don't really know where to begin, I guess, demons started killing everyone. And I tried to fight back as best I could."

"A classic struggle between good and evil, that's common. What else?"

Zack pressed the call button again. He could not escape the smell, and yearned for a shower.

"Angels too, we held up in a Church, weapons, blessings, lots of people fighting with me…"

Bernard nodded again.

"Evil creatures everywhere, many of my friends died…"

"Do you know when these events take place?"

"When?"

Zack remembered that his vision felt like a few years of real life. He wondered if that's what he meant. His chest hurt.

"I dunno, a couple of years, I guess."

"OK good, do you know where the relics are?"

Zack's heart began to beat faster. The hair on the back of Zack's neck stood up.

"I didn't mention any relics…"

"Oh my mistake, go on."

Zack now had an unnerving feeling about Bernard. He seemed like he knew something that he was not letting on. He began to feel like he was being interrogated.

"Sorry, I need to rest."

"Oh, that's fine. I hope you feel better soon. I'll be here if you want to chat."

Zack rolled over in his bed and tried to avoid the vomit pooling on his sheets.

A few uneasy moments passed before Zack heard someone walking up the hallway towards his room.

"Oh, what a mess. I'll be back with a fresh set of sheets. Everything else OK?"

Zack nodded to the nurse as she walked out again. Zack wondered where Father Andrews was. He thought he would be back by now. He thought of asking Bernard but did not want to open another conversation.

A small team of nurses returned with more bedding and cleaning supplies.

"Take it nice and slowly," one nurse suggested.

A pained gasp escaped Zack's lungs as they transferred him to a clean bed. Pain erupted through his entire body. He closed his eyes and focused on breathing. One of the nurses adjusted his IV line, and he fell asleep once there was a lull in the pain.

A few hours passed, and Zack awoke with a mind fogged with medication. He could not get comfortable, but he did not want to move too much either. Bernard began talking to him, but Zack did not comprehend much of what he said. He closed his eyes and slept uneasily for a few more hours.

"How are you feeling Mr Michaels?" A nurse with a friendly smile asked as she stood over him.

Zack managed a nod. He opened his eyes and watched as she checked him over.

"Are you feeling at ease?"

Zack nodded again.

"Tell me who helps you in the future."

Zack swallowed a lump in his throat, and his eyes widened.

"What?" he muttered.

"Tell me now, it's Ok," the nurse peered into his eyes, trying to assess his level of alertness.

Zack felt confused. He closed his eyes and pretended to fall asleep. He desperately wanted to escape but was unable to.

"Stay with me."

The nurse held him by the shoulders and shook him.

Zack could not help but let a profanity slip as the pain gripped him again.

"Now you're beginning to understand Mr Michaels. Tell me what we want to know, and then you can go back to sleep and pretend none of this ever happened."

Zack looked to the other side of the bed to see Bernard standing over him too.

"Tell us and the pain stops," he said coldly.

The nurse adjusted his IV line again, and he began to feel more awake, His dulled sense of pain started to sharpen. Zack murmured with pain as he looked around the room. He noticed the door was shut and a bed had been moved to block it.

"What do you want?"

"Tell us about the relics, now!" the nurse brushed her black hair from her face as she spoke. Zack would have found her quite attractive if she was not torturing him. Zack thought they must have been talking about the relics Bishop Kephas used in his vision. But how could they even know about that?

"Who are you? Get away from me!" Zack began to struggle, but Bernard quickly held him down. More pain washed over him.

Zack let out a wail and scrunched his face up. He could not understand why all this was happening to him; he was just a nobody. He felt helpless and alone. It was too much for him.

"God, please!" Zack prayed.

"He's not here," the nurse scoffed.

Zack drew in a deep breath and closed his eyes. He tried to remember all he had been through. Memories of the battles he had fought and his friends filled his mind. He searched for his resolve and found it.

He opened his eyes once more and looked into his oppressor's eyes.

"No."

The nurse slapped him across the face. His face stung, and his headache roared into life once more.

"Tell us when the sky darkens," Bernard commanded.

Zack shook his head slightly with his mouth tightly closed. Bernard pulled out his cell-phone and tapped a few buttons. Immediately, the fire alarm in the hospital started blaring. Zack's headache became worse. The nurse then nodded at Bernard, who slapped Zack on his chest directly on his tender wound. Zack screamed aloud in agony at the top of his lungs.

Bernard smiled.

Between desperate breaths, Zack cried out with all he could for help. But it was useless with the fire alarm drowning out his cries. Zack heard a commotion outside, but no one tried the door to his room.

"You will tell us all you know," the nurse stated.

Zack writhed in his bed and struggled to get his breathing back under control.

Bernard raised his arm again, ready for another slap.

"OK, OK…" Zack relented.

The nurse smiled smugly.

"Check the hallway while I record this," Bernard said while he prepared his phone.

The nurse went over to the door and peered through the glass panel down the hallway.

"Interview with subject 'P-7-M'. Start at the beginning and don't leave anything out." Bernard held his phone near Zack.

Zack began to utter words in a barely audible voice.

"Speak up!" Bernard demanded.

Zack just glared at him as he held his chest. He continued talking as he was. Bernard held his phone right up to Zack's mouth.

Zack lurched forward and bit down as hard as he could into Bernard's finger. Blood filled his mouth. Bernard yelled and quickly wrenched his hand away, dropping his phone in the process. Zack spat Bernard's blood from his mouth.

"Did you record that OK?" Zack managed a smile despite injuring himself further in the process.

"Why you little…" Bernard flew into a tirade of foul insults.

Bernard's fist flew into Zack's face but was held back by the nurse before delivering a second blow.

"Not like that, Bernard. We're not savages."

"Shut your face Rachel, or I'll wipe your smile off next," Bernard spat in reply.

'We knew this could happen. Let's move straight to using the worm,"

Zack was still reeling from the punch but his ears pricked up at the word 'worm'.

"OK fine, I guess that'll save us some time."

Bernard grabbed some sheets from an empty bed and used them to tie Zacks hands down at his sides. In Zack's state, he could do little to stop him. Rachel retrieved a small bag from under Bernard's bed and returned to Zack. She pulled the blankets off him and ripped his gown open to expose his chest. Then she drew out two small jars from the bag and opened the first one muttering to herself as she went. The first jar contained a blood-like liquid. Zack heard some dark words of an evil incantation. Rachel grabbed the other jar and scooped out a pale looking paste. A pungent aroma filled the room. It smelt like a mixture of herbs and decomposing flesh. She drew a circle with it on Zack's chest.

"…you will become worm fodder!" she concluded as she poured the other jar into the circle she had made. Zack could do nothing but look on in horror. For a moment, nothing happened. Then slowly, a reaction started between the two substances. They started to sizzle and burned into his exposed skin. Zack desperately tried to wriggle free with no success. Bernard held his arms down.

"You're insane!"

"You'll have first-hand knowledge of insanity soon enough, boy!"

Bernard began to laugh and pointed at Zack's chest.

"It's starting already!"

The liquid began to bubble and froth up, causing Zack much pain in the process. As it congealed, it began to take form. Zack started to panic. Before his very eyes, he saw a Bloodworm take shape on his stomach. As the bubbles expired, the evil creature began to wriggle. Zack screamed as loud as he could. Bernard chuckled. Then the fire alarm stopped, instantly spawning concerned looks on Rachel and Bernard's faces.

"They can't have shut it off yet!" Bernard yelled as he picked up his phone from the floor.

"It doesn't matter. We gotta finish and get out of here," Rachel replied.

Zack screamed for help with all his might. Bernard rushed over and delivered several quick jabs into his face. Zack's head was driven back into his pillow, and he struggled to stay conscious. Bernard stuffed a wad of blankets into Zack's bleeding mouth and clamped his hands over his face.

"Hurry!"

"I can't hurry it any more than you can Bernie, just keep him quiet!"
Rachel peered through the window into the hallway.

Zack's swollen eyes stained the image into his mind of the Bloodworm burrowing into his flesh. Unable to breathe and pain reaching a new height, he fell into unconsciousness.

Uncounted hours passed until at last Zack awoke with a scream. When he opened his eyes, Rachel and Bernard were long gone, and everything in the room looked undisturbed. A panicked patient on the far side of the room repeatedly pushed the button to call the nurse.

"The nurses are on the way," she said, still flustered from Zack's sudden outburst.

Zack continued screaming as he clawed away his sheets and gown. His chest wound bandages were soaked in blood, but no evidence of a bloodworm remained. He ripped off the bandage and patted his chest and stomach down over and over.

"Stop!" a blonde-haired nurse yelled as she rushed into the room.

Zack flinched as he saw her approach but unclenched his fist when he saw it was not Rachel.

"Susan! Get in here!" she yelled into the hallway as she tried to stop him.

"It's OK, just calm down. You're in Brakenside Hospital; I'm Lyn your nurse, please leave your bandages alone."

Zack grabbed once more at his stomach, this time pulling some of his stitches and causing them to bleed again. Zack desperately loosed a garbled explanation of Rachel and Bernard's attack on him. Lyn held Zacks bloody hands away from his wound and listened as best she could.

Susan, the senior nurse on duty, hurried in with a syringe in her hand and promptly jabbed it into Zack's arm. He quickly relaxed and lay back into his pillow. Zack's breathing became more rhythmic, and he began to calm down. His eyelids became increasingly heavy. He tried to stay awake and listen as best he could as the nurses continued to work on him.

"He claims another patient attacked him, and there was a nurse named Rachel. This guy sure has some really vivid dreams."

Zack struggled but did not succeed with opening his eyes with the sedative flowing through his system.

They continued talking as if he was already asleep.

"Yes, poor lad, I heard his yelling in the early hours of this morning."

"Understandable if you survive a gunshot like that I suppose."

"Yes, it's amazing he's still alive."

Zack started to doubt his sanity when another nurse walked in.

"Was his face bruised like that yesterday?"

Zack couldn't help but lose consciousness again.

Zack slept fitfully through the night and woke early the next day. His mouth was very dry, and he struggled to swallow. He began to lean towards his side table for a glass of water but quickly stopped. The pain in his chest today was crippling. His head ached all over. He felt the call button remote near his right hand and pressed it over and over.

"Just relax, you're in the hospital," the patient opposite Zack assured him. She looked nervous, expecting him at any moment to start screaming again.

Zack closed his eyes for a moment then heard the door open. Lyn came in, followed by two police officers. They explained that they had looked into his case but did not find Rachel or Bernard in the hospital computer system or on any of the security cameras. Zack headache felt worse. He struggled to remember any more details.

"Fire alarm?"

"Yes sorry about that, we had a temporary malfunction yesterday. It's been resolved now," Lyn explained.

The three reassured Zack that everything was OK. One of the police officers suggested he may have slipped and hit his head while sleepwalking.

"It's more common than most people realise," she said reasonably.

Zack didn't feel like arguing. After a few more questions, the police officers left. Zack began to wonder if he had been all another nightmare.

"Can I get you anything?" Lyn asked with genuine concern on her face.

"Where's Father Andrews gone?" Zack pointed to the freshly changed empty bed where he had been.

"Oh, he checked himself out. He said he had something urgent to deal with. He did mention that he left you a note. Didn't you get it?"

Zack looked around for a note but found nothing.

"I guess not."

"Your parents are here to see you. Just press the button if you need me," Lyn said with a smile.

Zack returned the smile as she left.

Zack's parents came into see him as soon the nurse left the room. Jess and Roger Michaels brought with them a bunch of flowers and relieved faces when they saw their son was awake. Jess swooped in for a very careful hug. Zack tried to hide the wince of pain he felt. His father noticed and patted him on the shoulder instead.

"Good to see you son."

"You too, Dad."

Zack's mother blinked back tears of relief and smiled at them both.

"Graham let us know what happened. We've been so worried, but the doctors say you're doing so well."

"Just rest, son, you'll be OK."

"Yeah. I'll try."

They sat with him for a few hours. It became clear that Zack was not up for extended conversation just yet. They went to leave, and from the chatter in the hallway, Zack assumed his friends had arrived.

Zack had just relaxed back into his bed as the door opened again and his friends walked in.

"Are you OK buddy?" Graham asked as he rushed to his side. Beth and Mindy followed close behind.

"I'm OK I guess," Zack replied weakly.

His friends detailed everything that had been going on. Zack smiled and nodded through as much of the conversation as he could until he could no longer keep his eyes open. He felt utterly drained.

"We'll be back later, rest up Zack," Mindy said as they quietly left the room.

Zack spent the next several months in the hospital gradually recovering from his injuries. Stanley from Zack's work came to visit a few times and explained that Gold Star Security Services would continue to pay his wages while he was in recovery. The incident at the bank had generated a lot of media coverage, and Gold Star handled it well. His friends would often visit, and they would spend some time talking and playing board games.

Eventually, Zack had healed enough that he could leave the hospital and returned home to his flat with Graham. He slept a lot and continued with a wide range of pain medications. He was now able to do everyday things like wash himself and walk short distances without assistance. There was not any precedence from recovering from what should have been a fatal gunshot, so his friends and family did not push him too hard. Zack still felt tired all the time. He spent the majority of his time on the couch watching television.

· · ·

Jenson Bickles was your average white-collar businessman in a large corporate who worked on the twenty-fifth floor of a high rise in a large city. He spent most of his day somewhere between his desk and the several meeting rooms in the building. Today did not seem any different to routine as cleared his emails.

"Hey Jenson, in my office now," Jenson's boss Daniel hollered across the floor. It was rarely a good omen.

"Coming sir," Jenson quickly made his way across the floor, dodging glances from his co-workers.

Daniel returned to his desk and sat down as Jenson neared the door.

"Close it behind ya."

Jenson nodded and sat down in the chair opposite him.

"Look, Jenson; I'm going to get right to the point. I'm in a bit of a pickle, and I'm hoping you're going to be able to help me out."

"Yes, sir, what is it?"

"My caseload has far exceeded what I'm capable of for some time, and I'm under pressure to deliver from the higher-ups. I'm going to ask you to take on some extra work..."

At this point, Jenson was certain he would be spending yet more overtime at work. Over the past few months, everyone seemed to have more work to do and even tighter timelines. There had been subtle hints that people who failed to meet their targets would be let go. He had reasoned with himself up until now that this was just temporary.

"...but this time, it'll be off the books..."

Jenson immediately sat up and took notice. Daniel was a very strict man; he even audited the teabag consumption when he deemed that it was getting 'excessive'. Daniel ran his fingers through the remaining hair on his head. It looked like he was loathed to ask for help. He reluctantly continued.

"…I have a very special portfolio that I want you to take care of for me. It will be a higher priority than anything else. Regardless of all the other margin targets I keep demanding uptdates on. This is what really needs to get done. Understand?"

Jenson nodded his understanding. But he had no idea what was being asked of him yet.

"We have a client that is running some serious projects, and I want to you manage funds for them. It's pretty similar work to that project from last quarter with the acquisitions and property deals."

"I remember it."

"Good. They'll need monthly updates in-person to ensure all is going to plan. I can't emphasise this enough. Do not, I repeat, do not miss a single meeting. I don't care if your whole family is in a serious car accident, you go to the meeting, understand?"

Jenson nodded again. He was not used to Daniel placing one client on such a pedestal; he was normally all about the numbers, not names.

"Your first meeting will be tonight, drop whatever you're currently on and start preparing now. I've made a start on this month's report; you'll just have to clean up around the edges."

"Yes, sir."

"What shall I tell Tanya if she asks what I'm doing?"

"Stupid woman. Always sticking her nose in where it doesn't belong. Just tell her to come to see me."

Daniel scrawled on a scrap of paper an address for an Italian restaurant downtown. It included the booth to sit at and what meal to order.

"Can you remember this?"

"Yes, sir,"

"No, don't 'yes sir' me. Can you really remember this?" Daniel shoved the note closer to his face."

"I will remember."

"Good. Now eat it,"

"What?" A nervous smile spread across Jenson's face, unsure if this was some joke.

"Eat this note and never speak to anyone about this. Ever. Or you'll wish you were dead." Daniel stared at him as he spoke with utter seriousness.

Jenson took it and slowly drew it towards his mouth. He quickly wondered what his chances would be to get another job away from his crazy boss.

"Oh, and after each meeting, as long as you perform as expected, you'll get an extra thirty percent deposited into an account of your choosing."

Jenson swallowed the scrap of paper as if it was coated in honey.

"Yes, sir."

"Good, now get out."

Jenson stood to leave.

"I'll know if you stuff this up, Jenson. For your sake, make sure it's your best work."

"I will, sir, thank you."

Jenson returned to his desk and began his new work.

. . .

Months later, Beth and Graham were in the kitchen of Graham and Zack's flat making lunch.

"So, I was thinking about getting our own place like we talked about…" Beth looked over at Graham before continuing. "…I was thinking soon. Zack's mobile again. We could find something nearby,"

Graham sighed as he struggled with this decision again.

"I'm not sure it's the right time. You know I want to, it's just…"

"You realise there may not ever be a perfect time, right?"

"I know."

"And?"

"You know I want to, that place we looked at a few weeks ago would've been perfect."

"The one that's no longer available?"

"Yeah, I know I said I'd talk to Zack, but, well…"

"Are you OK babe?" Beth asked as she saw Graham slice up way too much cheese for their sandwiches.

"Oh, whoops yeah I'm fine. I'm just at a loss as to what to do about Zack."

"Oh? Did some more results come in?" Beth looked over at Zack mindlessly watching television, oblivious to their conversation.

"No, physically he's fine. But I don't know how to put it; it seems like my best friend died that day," he started to slice up even more cheese.

Beth walked around the table and held him.

"What do you mean?"

"Well, I know he's been through a lot…" Graham lowered his voice.

"…and I get that he has to recover and all that. But he just doesn't seem to be his old self. He sleeps all the time, and all he ever does is watch stupid television. He barely talks to me. It's like he's just running on auto-pilot. And I wonder how many of all those drugs he really needs."

Beth nodded. She would often come over to see Graham and Zack would barely even notice that she was there. All she got today was a 'hello' which he did not even move his eyes from the television to say.

"The doctors did say it would take time."

"I know, I know, I just, well, I don't know."

Beth thought for a moment.

"I know! Let's get him out of the house, a change of scenery and fresh air would do him good."

"I agree with you, but I've asked and asked, but he just says he's too tired. I think the only time he leaves the house is when I take him to his checkups."

"It's nearly been a year, hasn't it? let's take him out for the day, that's bound to raise his morale."

"It's worth a shot, I guess."

They walked into the lounge, and Graham offered Zack a sandwich.

"Here you go, Zack."

"Thanks."

Beth told Zack of their idea of a day out to celebrate.

Zack chewed his sandwich as she spoke.

"No thanks."

"But, we didn't even choose where to go yet? There's bound to be somewhere you'd like to go."

Zack chewed as he looked for his pill bottle next to his chair. He popped a pill with a drink of water.

"Nah, I'm good," Zack replied, his eyes returning to the television.

Graham looked at Beth in a told-you-so kind of way. She motioned him to help her out.

"Zack, we're just trying to help. Surely, you need to do more than watch television all day, every day. Perhaps we could go to that museum, or maybe just walk around a park?" Graham attempted.

Zack was looking tired and put his sandwich down.

"Would you like to go to the beach we all went to a few years back?" Beth offered

Zack had closed his eyes.

"Zack?"

He had successfully escaped another conversation with a nap.

Beth took Graham by the arm and led him into the kitchen.

"OK, that does it…" Beth began as she explained her plan to help Zack.

"Brilliant," Graham replied when she had finished.

They both smiled.

A few weeks later Zack's phone beeped to remind him of his appointment with his Doctor.

"Graham, can you drive me today?" Zack asked from the couch.

"Yeah sure buddy, I'll be back to pick you up at four-thirty."

"Oh? I thought it was at eleven like last time?"

"No, they changed it to three-thirty, remember?"

"Oh OK," he said, popping another pill.

Zack ached all the time, despite his friends best intentions and his doctors suggestions, he was sure he still needed every bit of medicinal relief he could get. He felt like he had just finished running a marathon all of the time. His head would not stop aching.

After Zack had finished at the doctors' offices, he walked his way slowly down to the car park. As he got there, he saw Graham parking his car.

"Hey Zacky!" Mindy waved out the window of the back seat.

He returned the wave with a puzzled yet glad expression on his face. Graham, Beth and Mindy got out of the car and walked over. Graham handed over a small object covered in wrapping paper.

"What's all this?" Zack asked.

"Congratulations man, it's been a year that you've been out of the hospital!"

Zack unwrapped a self-help book on healing after trauma.

"Thank you," he said flatly.

Graham continued.

"We've decided it's time for you to enter the world once again, and we're taking you out to dinner!"

"A year already?"

"Well, it's actually next week sometime, but you get the idea. We're all delighted to have you still with us."

Zack smiled, and after some weak resistance, he hopped in, and they drove to a local restaurant.

"I'm getting the lasagne for sure" Mindy decided.

She looked beautiful tonight, and Zack tried not to stare. He had not yet announced his love for her and did not have a good reason why not.

"Oh good choice," Beth said as she looked over her menu.

"Would you like to share a pizza with me, Zack?" Graham asked.

Zack looked over his options a final time.

"Yeah sounds good," he replied, as he popped another pill.

Zack and Graham had nearly finished their pizza, and the four friends were having a most enjoyable night in each other's company. Graham had just finished imitating one of his co-workers with a silly expression on his face and managed to choke on a chunk of chicken from his pizza.

"Are you OK?" Zack leant over to Graham just as the piece came flying out of his mouth and hit Zack in the face. Graham erupted in laughter followed by Zack and the girls. After they had all caught their breath, Zack realised he had somehow split sauce down his shirt in the process and made his way slowly to the bathroom. His chest was hurting again, and he wondered if he laughed too much. Upon his return, he asked politely to be taken home. His friends suggested alternatives unsuccessfully.

The following day Graham decided it was time to talk to Zack. They were eating breakfast together when Graham spoke up.

"So is everything OK with you, Zack?"

"Yeah," Zack said vacantly.

He looked like he was settling in for yet another day in front of the television.

"I mean really, are you alright?" Graham put his cutlery down and looked at Zack.

"I'm OK" he replied, not looking away from the TV.

"Maybe you should go outside today?" Graham suggested.

"Nah," Zack replied.

Graham was not sure how to help his best friend. He understood that he needed to heal, but it seemed like Zack had no interest in helping himself. He was receiving his full pay from Gold Star as generous support to help him get well. It did not provide Zack with a huge incentive to rush back to work.

"I'm here if you wanna talk Zack. You know that, right?"

"Yeah."

Graham sighed.

"Well, I gotta go to work now. I'll catch you later."

"Bye."

. . .

Elsewhere, Jenson was sitting in a restaurant booth by the window alone. He had ordered the meal prescribed as usual and was waiting for his contact to arrive. He did not expect much from this meeting if it was to be anything like the previous ones. They normally ended with a cancellation text message from an anonymous number saying that his attendance was no longer required. Initially, this had worried Jenson, but when the money arrived in his account, he had assumed all was up to standard. Daniel had not mentioned anything to him, and Jenson did not want to bring it up unnecessarily. Jenson was just about to get up and leave when a large man sat down in his booth opposite him.

"Oh hi, I'm Jenson."

The large man nodded without introducing himself.

"Have you ordered yet?"

"Yes, they said it's on the way."

"Good, I'm starving."

Just then, the waiter came by with a spaghetti dish. He was about to place it down in front of Jenson when the large man motioned that it was for him. Jenson had normally eaten it in the past meetings as he did not see the need for it to go to waste. He had stopped ordering anything for himself after no one showing up for the first few meetings.

"Bring me some wine too, will you?"

"I'll bring you the wine list, sir."

"Just bring me whatever is the most expensive stuff you have."

"Very good sir," the waiter replied as he walked off.

Jenson began to wonder just who this man was.

"Ah, just the way I like it," he said as he slowly chewed his pasta.

"You can call me, Pete…" he began with just enough delay to make Jenson think he just made up that name on the spot. "…I trust you have kept our funds in good order again this month?" he said after a few mouthfuls.

"Hi Pete, yes, I've exceeded returns for the third month in a row."

Jenson withdrew some papers from his briefcase and put them on the table. He spent the next half an hour detailing Pete's investments and estimates for next month.

Upon finishing his meal, Pete abruptly stood up and left.

. . .

One Sunday morning a few weeks later, Zack finally decided he would go for that walk. Partly because he thought it would do him some good, but mostly because of Graham's perseverance. Graham offered to go with him, but Zack said he would prefer to walk alone. He gradually made his way along the sidewalk through Brakenside. He was not in a hurry to get anywhere. There was a cold wind that felt like it went right through him. As Zack walked, he wondered how long he would need to be away for before he could return home.

Eventually, he walked past St. Thomas' church; it looked like a service was finishing up. The place had an eerie feeling of recognition.

Father Andrews walked up to Zack catching him by surprise.

"Oh Zack, it's great to see you. Walking about by yourself even. Why didn't you call?"

"Huh?" Zack looked confused

"Wait, did you get my note?"

"I don't remember getting any note."

"Ah, that explains it. Anyway, have you got some time free now?"

"I guess, why?"

"Great! follow me."

Father Andrews quickly turned and walked up the path to his office. As Zack followed, he could not help but notice how intact and clean everything looked. Echos from Zack's vision flickered on the edges of his mind. As they walked Father Andrews made a call on his cell-phone.

"Hi Kephas, you'll never guess who just strolled up alive and well."

Zack listened to one side of the conversation.

"Zack Michaels…That's right, yes. OK, great… See you soon."

Father Andrews turned to Zack as they entered his office.

"The Bishop will be with us shortly. We've got a lot to discuss."

"We do?"

Father Andrews looked back at him with a glimpse of concern on his face.

"Would you like something to eat? I'm starving."

"Yes, please."

They walked down the hallway to the kitchen and Father Andrews made them some sandwiches and retrieved some cupcakes from the pantry. They returned to his office and had just finished eating as Bishop Kephas walked in.

"Nice to meet you, Zack, I'm Kephas," he said as he held out his hand.

"Good to see you again Bishop," Zack said as he shook it.

"Again? Oh, I'm sorry, my memory is not the best."

"Oh no, it's not that, I knew you from before, well, I think I better explain…"

Zack began to talk about his vision but struggled to remember many details. Zack's head began to hurt. He remembered discussing with

Father Andrews that evening they talked in the hospital but now found it difficult.

"I remember lots of death and darkness."

"Please go on."

"Well, I remember you Bishop, and lots of people died."

Zack headache returned with full vigour. He held his hands up to the sides of his head.

"Sorry maybe we should do this another time," Zack suggested.

Both men shared a glance.

"Zackary Michaels, have you been attacked?" Kephas asked directly.

"Umm, No, I don't think so, I'm not sure."

"Do you think he could be?" Father Andrews asked Kephas quietly.

"We need to be sure," he replied.

"What's going on?"

"Please come with us right away. We just want to check something."

They all stood and walked directly to the back room of the Chapel.

As they walked in, Zack started to feel queasy.

"Urgh, I'm not feeling the best here. I think I need to go home."

"Please, Zack bear with us just for a few minutes," Kephas implored.

Zack started to feel dizzy and was helped into a chair.

"Please, can you hold this a moment," Father Andrews passed him a thick book.

As Zack held it, he felt a strong repulsion all over. He quivered and dropped it on the floor.

As he was trying to understand why, Bishop Kephas split some water from a small bottle on his arm.

"Hey!"

He felt a stinging sensation and promptly began coughing and dry reaching. His head hurt even more. The two holy men nodded to each other.

"Zack, my son, we believe that you are suffering from demonic oppression. We will need your cooperation, try and focus on the words we are saying."

Zack managed to nod.

"In nomis patris et filii et spiritus santci, in the name of the Father and the Son and the Holy Spirit…" they began.

The two men performed a spiritual deliverance for Zack, which consisted of multiple prayers, reading of scripture and the use of holy water. Zack did not remember much of it until he found himself vomiting up blood onto the floor. His mind immediately cleared, and his memories flooded back with full clarity. He felt like a great weight was lifted off him. He no longer felt lethargic. More so, he felt energised. He knew he had so much to prepare.

"Thank you, thank you. Sorry. I remember it all now. They put a Bloodworm in me."

"Are you sure? Father Andrews asked

"Certain, is that what I've vomited up?" Zack asked.

"Does your vomit look red to you?"

"Yes, of course, it's all bloody," Zack pointed, and to his amazement, the dark red colour faded before his eyes.

"What?!"

"It seems you have been given the gift of spiritual sight young Zack," Kephas observed.

Zack just sat motionless for a moment. His vomit now looked just like a recently chewed cupcake.

"Oh, I'm so sorry about the mess. Let me clean it up."

"That'd be great," Father Andrews said with a smile as he passed him some paper towels.

Zack's mind flooded with questions. He began to spit them out as fast as he could.

"Woah, let's start at the beginning. If you can, talk us through your vision." Kephas suggested.

The three discussed Zack's vision of the apocalyptic future at great length. They were both quite surprised upon hearing about Father Andrews death. Both of their faces continued to drop as Zack described how many people were lost. After Zack felt like he had described everything, he spent some more time answering their many questions. He then asked several questions of his own.

"I think we need to get Zack to Rome," Father Andrews suggested.

"I agree," Bishop Kephas added.

"What? Why?"

"That's where our Order is based; I think many lives could be saved worldwide if you can pass on the information that you've just told us. Thats where I went to when I left the hospital in a hurry."

Zack thought about it for a moment. Previously he had only thought about his local region. He quickly decided if he was going to save as many lives as he could, this would be a good way to do it.

"Ok, let's go."

"Allow us time to get things organised. Plus you need time to heal. We'll call you."

"Sounds good," Zack replied.

He walked out with a wave goodbye and made it to the street. He knew he had so much to do.

Graham got home from work and kicked off his shoes and walked into the lounge.

"Zack? Hey?" He was surprised to see the television turned off and no-one was home.

He grabbed his phone and sent Zack a text message. Almost immediately it beeped with a short response.

"I'm out, be home later."

Graham was glad Zack was finally off the couch and watched something of his own choosing for a change. He had leftovers for dinner alone and sent Zack another text. After a few minutes, he got another message.

"Still busy, don't wait up. I'll fill you in later."

Graham was surprised but tried not to worry about it. As he was typing a reply, Beth rang him, and they ended up chatting for a while.

"You'll never guess what happened today hun."

"Oh? More friction at work?"

"No, Zack left the house."

"Oh, that's great! good for him."

"And he's still not home; he said not to wait up."

"Really?"

"Yeah, I messaged him just now."

"I'll be right over," Beth replied with a big smile.

The next morning when Graham awoke, Zack was still not home. Graham checked his phone to find a message from Zack saying he would be back later. Graham decided he would try his best not to worry about it and rushed off to work. During the day he sent Zack a few more messages. But it was not until late the following day before Zack called Graham back.

"Hey sorry I've been busy. I'll tell you all about it tomorrow morning. I'll be home late tonight."

"Zack, are you OK? Do you want me to come and pick you up?"

"Nah, I'm good. I'm actually better than I have been in a long time."

"What's going on man?"

"I'll tell you all about it Graham; I just need a bit of time to finish up. I'll be back later."

"Ok sure," Graham replied, something in his voice reminded him of the Zack he knew growing up.

True to his word, Zack got home late that evening and went directly to bed. The next morning Graham walked out of his room to see Zack sitting at the kitchen table drawing in a notebook. As soon as he saw Graham, he collected up his pieces of paper and closed the book.

"What are you up to?"

"You'll see, have you got time free for me to show you something?" Zack asked.

"Yeah sure, I'm not working today. What did you want to show me?"

"Well it's not as ready as I'd like yet, but I suppose it might not ever be as ready as I hope."

"What is?"

"You'll see. Let's go for a drive after straight breakfast. Just promise me you'll keep an open mind, OK?"

"Sure thing. Zack, are you on some new meds?" Graham wondered.

"Nope. Honestly, I'm fine."

"Sure?"

"Yip. OK then. Eggs? I'll cook." Zack asked.

"You cook?"

"Yeah, I can you know."

"Prove it," Graham said, smiling.

"Deal!"

Zack shuffled his papers away and cooked breakfast.

Afterwards, they hopped into Graham's car and after a short trip arrived at a local storage company. Zack directed Graham where to park, directly in front of unit thirty-nine.

"You have your own storage garage? What for? I didn't think you were running out of space at our place."

Zack returned a knowing smile and pulled the keys from his pocket to unlock the roller door. He had pulled up about knee high before he stopped and turned to Graham.

"OK, before I show you what I've been up to promise that you'll hear me out before you freak out."

"Why would I freak out?"

"Just promise me."

"Sure thing."

"OK, follow me in."

Zack pulled up the door and waited for Graham to duck under. He rolled it shut after him, and after a brief moment of darkness, the lights flickered on.

Graham blinked in disbelief. He muttered an expletive under his breath.

"What is all of this? Are you mental?!"

"Hey, I told you not to freak out. OK, come here, and sit down."

Zack plopped Graham down in a small chair by a table at the side of the small room.

Graham stared at all the maps and drawings stuck up all over the walls. Racks of supplies of all different types were stacked up behind him. Stacks of paper littered the desk next to a small printer and laptop. Zack did not want to forget any part of his vision and recorded all the details about it that he could remember.

"This is where I've been remembering, recording, organising, reading and planning," Zack began.

Graham continued to look around but showed he was listening.

"I thought rather than try and piecemeal tell you details of everything I'd try and get everything all sorted, then brief you all."

"All?"

"Yeah, I plan to tell everyone I know once I'm all set up."

"Tell us what exactly?"

"I don't know why, or how, but I've seen things Graham, things that I feel like I've lived through. As real as I'm talking to you now. I can remember things as clearly as we had breakfast this morning."

Graham nodded slowly waiting for the punch line.

"OK, where to begin… God, he's real. Angels, Demons, all of it, it's all true. I need to prepare and try and save everyone I can from what's coming."

"What's that?"

"I've seen the world end as we know it. The collapse of civilisation and probably millions, maybe billions dead."

Zack was energised that he could finally tell someone about what he had been working on over the past few frantic days. He picked up a drawing he made of a Bloodworm,

"This is a bloodworm, oh and a Scarkin. And this is my attempt an Angel," Zack passed Graham a big pile of sketches from the table.

"...and I've been collecting supplies, simple stuff like water, food, medicine, clothes and cooking stuff," Zack turn Graham around in his chair to show him his stockpile.

'Oh, so you're like a Prepper now? I think I saw a documentary about those cra.... about people who stockpile everything," Graham narrowly avoiding saying 'crazy.'

"Kinda," Zack replied.

Graham picked up a large hammer which Zack had began etching scripture into.

"What's the writing for?"

"It's my first attempt at a sanctified weapon. With it, we'll be able to damage the demons."

"Oh right,"

Graham looked over to a sketch of a demon. He swung the hammer around as if he was fighting.

"This will certainly mess those creatures up. Oh! Call this one 'Face-smasher', no, 'Toothbreaker' yeah that's it."

Zack smiled.

"Yeah, that's the idea."

Graham put the hammer down and looked around.

He looked Zack in the eyes.

"So what sort of movie are you making? Like a horror sort of thing?"

"I'm not making a movie; I'm serious about all this."

Graham looked at him and smiled.

"Is this a prank or something? Are you recording me?"

"Nope. I'm dead serious."

"Really?"

"Yes."

Graham cocked his head to the side.

Zack nodded.

"Ok, then. I don't know what to say; this is pretty intense stuff Zack."

"Yeah, it is."

"Why you?"

"I feel like I have this drive inside me. I kinda feel like I was made to do this. If not me then who? Ya know?"

Zack remembered some scripture which captured just how he felt.

Isaiah 6
[8] Then I heard the voice of the Lord saying, "Whom shall I send? And who will go for us?"
And I said, "Here am I. Send me!"

They sat and talked for a few hours. Zack was relieved that Graham was still listening to him. He had half-expected him just to storm out thinking he was crazy.

The next day, Graham drove Zack, Beth and Mindy back to the storage unit. Zack explained his vision and his preparation as best he could to all of them. After a few awkward minutes of silence and nervous laughter, his friends seemed to be Ok with it all.

Graham caught several 'is-he-serious' faces from both Beth and Mindy. They did not exactly believe that the world was going to end as Zack had described but understood it was how Zack was dealing with being shot.

"I've heard some of the best artists used the traumatic experience of their lives to help with their paintings," Beth commented.

"It's great to see you out and about Zack," Mindy added.

"One other thing, I'm going to Rome," Zack declared.

CHAPTER 2:

ESCALATION

Shocked faces waited for an explanation.

"That's where the holy Order I mentioned are based. I need to find as many answers as I can. I won't be gone too long," Zack explained.

"Seriously? You've never even left the country before," Graham spoke what they were all thinking.

"I know I had a rush on getting my passport."

"Woah Zack…" Beth began.

"…Don't you think you should, I don't know, take things easy a bit first? You've only walked from your bed to the couch for a year, and now you're going overseas? It just seems a bit much."

"I understand your concern. And thank you, all of you. I know this must seem odd."

"Odd? Its a bit more than that," Graham interrupted.

"Look, I'm not going to be trekking up a mountain or anything; I know I'll need to build up my fitness and stuff."

"Are you sure about this?" Mindy asked

"Yes I am," Zack replied.

"Did the doctor start you on some new drugs?" Graham wondered aloud as he looked for Zack's pill bottle, which was never too far from him.

"No, I've actually eased off most of my meds."

Graham rolled his eyes.

"I'm not crazy, trust me I'll be fine."

A moment of silence passed as they all looked around at Zack's craziness piled up around them.

"Well if you can't beat 'em, join 'em as they say," Graham announced.

"Huh?"

"I have been building up my annual leave for a while now, and since it looks like you're convinced about this Zack, I'm going with you."

"Thanks Graham, but you really don't have to do that."

"Nope, it's final. I'm coming, so get used to it," he replied firmly.

Beth gave Graham an "I'm going to talk to you later" look.

"Well you two are definitely full of surprises," Beth said.

They talked for a while, then they left Zack to his crazy work.

"Sorry, I think I pushed him too hard, and now he's flipped his lid," Graham said as they hopped in his car.

"Surely he's just amped up at the moment. You don't think he'll actually go to Rome, do you?" Mindy asked.

"I don't know. He seemed pretty sure. However, if he ends up doing another sci-fi marathon on the couch this week instead, I'm OK with that too."

"I hope he's Ok," Mindy said.

"Yeah, me too," Beth added.

A few weeks later, much to everyone's surprise Zack and Graham were standing at the end of their driveway with their luggage packed. Beth and Mindy had come along to see them off.

Beth latched onto Graham with a big hug.

"I'm going to miss you," she said as she kissed him.

"Likewise, I'm sure we'll be back before you know it."

Mindy's phone beeped, and she looked down at the screen for a few moments.

"Is it?" Beth ran over excitedly, peering over her shoulder.

"Yes! I'm in, I'm in!" Mindy said with delight.

They hugged each other and danced around on the spot.

"What's up?" Zack asked.

"I got into the Doverton Nursing School!" Mindy exclaimed. "…I start in a few weeks!"

"Congratulations!"

"Good on you Mindy!"

"Yeah, that's brilliant!"

Zack knew she would be moving to Doverton and wondered how often he would get to see her. He wished he had spent more time with her since he left the hospital. He had spent every spare minute preparing, reading, crafting and more time with Father Andrews and Bishop Kephas than his friends.

A blue sedan drove up the road and slowly pulled into their driveway. Father Andrews got out and walked over to introduce himself. Graham was surprised he was not wearing some ornate robe. He looked just like a normal person in jeans and a brown jersey.

"Nice to meet you Priest, Sir," Graham said, extending his hand.

"Feel free to call me Douglas, if you'd prefer," Father Andrews said, smiling.

"I'm Graham. This is Beth and Mindy."

"Hello"

"Hi"

After a brief chat, they put their bags in the boot of the car and drove away.

"Everyone is leaving me," Beth said, barely audible.

"What was that?" Mindy asked

"Oh nothing, I hope they'll be OK."

"I'm sure they will be, from what Zack said it's almost like they are going to visit some old library. Not too much can go wrong there, right?"

"Yeah, you're right. Anyway, we should go out to celebrate!"

"Great idea, my treat."

"So we're really doing this huh?" Graham asked as they drove into the airport.

"Yeah, thanks again for coming with me Graham. You're the best."

"The very best," he replied with a smile.

"Remember that when we're checking out all the bars and restaurants."

"Oh I will,"

"I can show you a few good local spots if you like?" Father Andrews offered.

Graham had not thought a priest would go anywhere and imagined him always reading a Bible in a church somewhere.

"Yeah thanks," Zack replied.

They looked up to see a passenger jet coming into land; the dull roar could be heard over the radio. They parked in the car park building and pulled their bags out.

"Are you sure you've got everything Zack?" Graham asked.

Zack did a quick mental tally on what he packed. Mostly just clothes, toiletries and a few notebooks. He patted his pocket where he kept his passport.

"Yip all set. You too?"

They both nodded.

"OK, let's go," Father Andrews said as he locked the car.

After a short walk to the international terminal and checking their bags, they sat in a small cafe while they waited for their flight to be called.

"So what made you want to be a priest? I can't imagine they get many perks," Graham asked.

Father Andrews chuckled.

"Not in any traditional sense, what I like is that I really get to help people. I'm not just pleasing customers or shareholders. I get to be a part of a positive change in people's lives."

"Oh I didn't think about that, yeah job satisfaction is a big one. But what happens if you really feel like a beer or a big TV or a new car?"

"Well, just like you, if I feel like a beer, I drink one. I do get a small allowance that I can use. Not that I could buy a new car with it though. Though tell me, if you were able to live happily without all those things, would you really be missing out on anything?"

Graham paused for a moment as he thought about it.

"Yes!" he said with a big smile. "Isn't it hard praying all the time?"

Father Andrews recited one of his favourite quotes from scripture:

Romans 12
[12] Be joyful in hope, patient in affliction, faithful in prayer.

"…Faith seems to come easy to some; others have to work at it. And by others, I mean me," He replied with a smile.

The loudspeaker announced that their flight was ready to board and they made their way through the busy terminal. Zack could hardly believe he was about to leave the country. His mind was buzzing through all the parts of his vision that he could remember. He had been writing down everything he could ever since he had awoken from his drug and demon caused stupor. He quickly added a few more notes in his phone as they waited in line to board the aircraft.

"Boarding passes please," the flight attendant asked with a smile.

"Here you go."

They squeezed their way onboard and into their economy size seats.

"Ready?" Graham asked.

Zack nodded.

"Thanks again Graham, the next trip we have you can pick the destination OK?"

"Deal!" Graham picked up the travel magazine from the seat pocket and began to flick through it as he thought about where they should go next.

"How are you feeling Zack?" Father Andrews asked.

"I'm pretty much back to normal now, thanks. It still hurts when I take a big breath, but I'm no longer tired all the time, and my mind feels like the fog is gone."

"I'm glad to hear that."

"I'm off all my medication now too."

"Impressive."

Father Andrews pulled his Bible out of his bag. As he did so, Graham piped up.

"Haven't you finished reading it yet? Graham asked with a smile on his face.

"There is still a lot in here I have to learn. We show this world and the next what is important to us by what we spend our time on."

"I guess, I'll be watching a few of these movies," Graham replied.

"Oh, have they got that new shark movie?"

"Let me check... yes they have it."

"Great, I'll watch that one after my prayers," he said with a smile.

"What are you praying for?" Zack asked.

"All sorts of things really. For thanksgiving, people who I know are in need, my failings, for our safe and successful trip to name a few."

"Do you ever run out of things to pray for?"

"In those times I like to think of it like I'm praying now for struggles that may take place in the future."

Zack liked that idea and nodded in agreement.

"How are things with you anyway?"

"I'm well thank you; I'm very interested in what we can learn on this trip. I feel like for some reason it's of the utmost importance."

Zack nodded. It was so nice to talk to someone who didn't give off the 'I'm talking with a crazy person' vibe. Zack felt like he had a real responsibility for people around him because of his vision. He hoped he could live up the high expectations he set himself.

"Yeah me too."

The flight attendants reminded everyone of the safety features of the aircraft and Zack listened intently. He was the only one of the three that had not been on a large airliner before, and he was taking it all in. Zack tried to think of what he would do if the plane crashed. He was not sure his vision would really help him with that. He decided if it did, he would pray. He thought it best to pray anyway.

'God, please help our flight to go safely. Thanks. Amen.'

Hours later they touched down at the international airport in Rome, Italy. They were tired from the trip and slowly made their way through the terminal with the crowds of other passengers.

"I've arranged for a taxi into the city," Zack told Graham and Father Andrews as they picked up their bags at the carousel.

"Cool," Graham said as he looked around. He had never been to this part of Europe before and intended to remember all he could. He took out his phone and snapped a few pictures of a sculpture in the foyer.

They walked through the doors and looked for someone holding a sign with Zack's name on it. Moments later Zack pointed and they walked over.

"Ah Mister Michaels, allow me," the man holding the sign took one of Zack's bags and led them outside towards his vehicle.

"Welcome to Rome, my name is Jed; Please follow me."

"Hi Jed."

Zack stopped for a moment and looked around. It was late evening, and there was a gentle breeze with just enough chill to keep Zack alert. He felt very fatigued from the flight. The pick-up area was very busy as travellers from all over found their transport and made their way into Rome.

"C'mon," Graham said as they loaded their bags into the back of a white car.

The four men hopped into the taxi, and they drove into the city. Graham and Zack stared out the windows soaking it all in. Father Andrews pointed out a few sights as they passed. Jed commented on a couple more.

"Once we've unpacked, I thought we perhaps go for a short walk, and I can show you a few of the local attractions?" Father Andrews didn't seem to be affected by the long flight.

"Sounds good," Graham replied. Zack just felt like going to bed but remembered how much Graham loved travelling and seeing new places.

"We've don't have anything scheduled until lunchtime tomorrow so we can relax tomorrow morning," Father Andrews continued.

Zack nodded as he watched the streetlight lit roads whizzing past.

After navigating the surprisingly busy streets of the city, they pulled up to their hotel. Zack was immediately underwhelmed. It did resemble the pictures he had seen online, but it was far from impressive. Three tour buses were unloading in the entranceway to the hotel with tourists everywhere.

"We unload just next door," Jed declared as he pulled in to the two-story car park building next to the hotel. He drove slowly up to the top floor and pulled into the first free parking space.

Zack opened the car door and stepped out into the night air. He stretched and yawned. He saw a few men walking on the far side of the car park. The thin clouds wafted slowly above them. It was forecast to be a sunny day tomorrow. Jed passed Graham and Father Andrews their bags from the boot and walked over with Zack's bag.

"Worm fodder!" a strained voice hissed.

Zack turned around just as the blade entered his side. Jed was snarling in front of him holding the butterfly knife. Pain erupted throughout Zack's body. He began to scream. The knife twisted slightly as he yanked it out. Zack's hand automatically held the wound tightly. He could feel his fingers quickly warm as blood spilled through them.

His mind raced. Adrenaline surged. Yet, for a split-second, he just stood there.

"Help" Zack cried as he staggered back.

Jed's eyes were bulging as he made another lunge with his knife. Zack tried to fend off the incoming thrust, and the knife cut deep into his right forearm. Zack could hear a commotion on the opposite side of the car.

"DIE!" Jed screamed as he slashed wildly. He loosed a tirade of spittle and a mixture of words Zack didn't understand.

Zack fell backwards on to the concrete. The impact loosed a surge of blood from his side. Jed jumped down toward him and caught a kick in the face as Zack tried to scuttle backwards.

The glass shattered on the far side of the car and Zack could hear fighting.

"Scum!"

Graham appeared behind Jed and let loose a flurry of quick punches into him. Jed turned and slashed him across the arm. He followed up with a stab to the mid-section, but somehow Graham caught his hand on the way in and it only resulted in a shallow wound. They struggled over the knife with desperate punches and kicks flying in all directions.

Zack found himself get up and jump onto Jed's back, covering his face with his bloodied hands. He received an elbow to the stomach, and his grip was broken. Graham loosed a right hook which connected and broke Jed's nose. Desperate stabbing resulted in a few punctures to Graham's forearms and shoulder. Zack grabbed hold of Jed's arm, and the three fell to the ground. Zack got stabbed again in the process. His left arm now spat blood onto the concrete. Graham landed a few more punches, and Jed finally lost his knife.

Zack fumbled as he tried to grab the knife and it skidded underneath the car. Thankfully it was out of Jed's reach. Graham rose up and dropped his weight down with a swift jab. Jed's skull snapped backwards and bit into the curb. He began to go limp, and a pool of blood began to ooze out through his matted hair. Zack kicked himself free of him and tried to stand up. He felt a swell of dizziness and fell back onto the ground. He gripped his side, which was now soaked in his blood. Jed twitched unnaturally and his eyes half-closed. Graham stood as a man was thrown over the bonnet of the taxi and landed into the three.

"Are you OK?" Father Andrews ran to Zack and pulled him to his feet.

Zack just groaned.

Graham kicked and struggled his way free from the newest attacker. Who looked to have been struggling with a few injuries of his own.

"MAGGOTS!" He yelled, spitting blood from his broken teeth as he did so.

Zack, Graham and Father Andrews edged slowly back as the man scrambled to his feet. He pulled a grenade from his pocket.

"Crap," Father Andrews blurted.

The bloodied man pulled the pin and ran at them.

Father Andrews burst forward and revealed his martial skills by launching his boot up into his face with a swift kick. The grenade fell and bounced unexpectedly back towards the taxi.

The detonation threw everyone to the ground as shrapnel burst out in all directions. All of the car alarms in the building started blaring. Jed's internal organs were jellified by the pure concussive force. Not to mention all the enormous external damage. The second attacker was a little further away, but multiple fragments burrowed deep into his body. He died immediately. With the two attackers so kindly soaking up most of the explosion the three tourists only received deep gashes, significant hearing damage and complete disorientation.

Father Andrews clambered his way over to check on Graham who lay closer to him.

"Are you OK?" Father Andrews shouted over the din as he quickly surveyed his injuries.

Graham spat out a few swear words which aptly described their situation and nodded painfully.

Next, Father Andrews repeated the process with Zack. Zack coughed up some blood in response. On the far side of the car, the third attacker, which Father Andrews had also fought off, scrambled to his feet and ran away. Graham began to sit up but elected to bleed where he was.

"No, no, no," Father Andrews cried as he discovered the deep wound in Zack's side.

The blade had been driven deep into Zack's left kidney, and he had unknown internal bleeding. Father Andrews pulled off his jersey and jammed it into the wound. A cry of pain escaped Zack's lungs. Douglas grabbed his partially shredded bag pulled out a towel. Using a few shirts, he made an improvised bandage that kept the pressure on Zack's worst wound.

Douglas had earned his share of stab and shrapnel wounds too as he bled from various places, but for now, it seemed like they weren't stopping him. After he had managed to slow most of Zack's blood loss, he moved back to Graham and applied a similar technique. Lastly, he wrapped his own injuries with the remanets of his packed clothing. A local appeared on the staircase and expressed his shock in a foreign language then rushed over to help.

Douglas held his hand up to his ear and motioned a telephone. The man nodded and quickly dialled emergency services. Just as the car alarms finally started to shut off, Zack could hear sirens in the distance. He had begun shaking uncontrollably and even managed to vomit over himself.

Douglas was now lying down, holding his own injuries. More people had rushed in, and soon a crowd of people were doing their best to assist. Three ambulances and four police cars drove in shortly afterwards.

"Move aside," the ambulance officer commanded as he and three others made it over to the scene.

Zack soon felt a rush of pain relief medication flood into his veins. A pained cry caused him to look over to his friend. He saw Graham being lifted on to a stretcher. Police officers began to secure the scene. Before Zack realised he was in the back of the ambulance being rushed to the closest hospital. Zack kept a few memories of paramedics leaning over him but eventually lost consciousness.

Upon arrival at the hospital, the three injured men were rushed into the intensive care unit. Graham stabilised quickly and was given intravenous fluids to assist with recovery. Douglas needed four units of blood to replace what he had lost. After a few hours, the team of doctors were happy with his condition.

Zack was hurried into surgery, where many skilled hands managed to stop the internal bleeding before it was too late. Numerous doctors looked alarmed at the mess of scars on Zack's chest already. Both Graham and Father Andrews injuries were stitched up; thankfully they avoided permanent damage to any vital organs.

A few days later Zack awoke in the recovery room. He heard Graham and Father Andrews talking.

"I didn't know you were like a ninja-priest! You smashed those guys!"

"Thank you; you also did a good amount of smashing."

"But I don't get it, isn't it supposed to be love the neighbour or whatever? Not roundhouse kick your neighbour in the head?"

"You're absolutely right. And in any normal circumstance, you'd see me behave and teach exactly that. At the time, I believed my actions contributed to the least negative effects for all those concerned..."

"Don't get me wrong," Graham interrupted. "...those guys absolutely deserved it, and we owe you our lives. But they certainly did experience some pretty gnarly negative effects."

"Yes. I'm praying that our trip here will be able to save thousands of lives."

"Oh?"

"Oh great, I'm in a hospital again? What happened?" Zack asked as he battled with the drugs in his groggy mind.

"You're un-killable dude! That's what. And what the hell is this trip all about? I sure as hell didn't expect us to be attacked by a bunch of psychos."

"Sorry, I..."

"I lost the tip of my little finger even!" Graham held up a bandaged hand. Some of the shrapnel mangled the end of his left pinky finger beyond saving, and the doctors had to remove it just past the nail bed.

"...I can't think of what I actually use it for, but I kinda wanted to keep it anyway." Graham finished with a smile. His feigned anger dissolved into concern.

"Are you OK buddy?"

Zack nodded.

"You guys OK?"

"Yes"

"Yeah man."

"Who were those guys?"

"Nutjobs, that's who."

"Actually, I have a good idea of the organisation they are part of,"

Father Andrews began.

Expectant looks encouraged him to continue.

"This would now be the second attempt on your life."

"What?!"

Zack's mind lurched back to when he was last in hospital, and he narrowly avoided vomiting.

"Did you just say we have assassins after us? What sort of craziness is going on here?"

Father Andrews held up his hands in a placating manner.

"We'll go through everything, though perhaps not right now."

"Oh you're awake!" a nurse entered their room with a smile.

"...I'm glad to see you made it."

"Me too," Zack replied.

After a few minutes of checking his bandages and filling out his chart, she returned with some hospital food.

"Do you think we're supposed to eat it?" Graham asked, prodding his jelly after the nurse left the room.

Zack nodded with his mouth full.

"It's much better than the Brakenside stuff."

"My apologies, this isn't the cuisine I was hoping to show you both," Douglas offered, smiling.

After they had finished their meal, Father Andrews began to explain.

"While we're recovering I thought we could go into a few more details. But please be mindful this is not public knowledge, and we'll need to keep what we discuss here private. At least for now."

Graham leaned a little closer.

"I was hoping we'd have this conversation at my Orders office, but we're not going to make it there today so let's cover a few basics."

"You *are* a secret agent!" Graham declared with a grin.

Douglas returned a smile. "In a way, yes..."

Douglas described that he was a member of the Holy Order of Salt and Light. An organisation set up thousands of years ago, whose main goal was to protect humanity in the end times.

"We focus on spiritual warfare, but as you've seen, physical combat is necessary for rare situations."

Before there was time to ask questions, the door opened, and Bishop Kephas walked in carrying a small bag.

"Hello all, I came as soon as I could."

"Good to see you."

"I'm glad to see you're all in one piece."

"Not quite" Graham held up his finger.

Zack was relieved Graham was taking all of it so well.

"Well, at least you're all alive. From what I heard, things could have ended up quite differently."

"Douglas," Kephas began in a quiet voice. Zack was close enough that he could just make out what was said.

"There have been many other attacks; I think we need to get them in as soon as possible."

"How many?"

"I don't know yet; I've only just landed."

"Hey what's going on?" Graham asked.

"It's OK, Kephas I was just beginning to explain things.

"I'm sorry. You have all been through so much. You deserve to know what you've landed in to."

Zack remembered his vision.

"Were they members of the Sons of the Snake?"

Both priests looked at him as if he had just used the most profane language possible.

"Where did you learn that name?" Douglas asked.

"I remembered it from, before, well the future, or whatever."

"Ah yes, well I suspect you're right. They have been the cause of much suffering for hundreds of years."

"We should ask Eleazar," Douglas said to Kephas.

"Who?"

"The Cardinal Eleazar, he's the leader of our Order, and if anyone knows what's going on, it'll be him."

Kephas asked about their attack, and Douglas described all he could. It seemed that his memory was better than Zack's as he even detailed exactly what the attackers wore and their distinguishing features. It was like he had police training. Kephas listened and made some notes in his book. When he had finished the account, Douglas finished with

"…They knew we were coming; they must be very well connected. Their influence has spread far."

"Agreed, like a cancer," Kephas replied.

Kephas returned his book to his bag and stood to leave.

"Monica will be up shortly."

The door opened, and an attractive woman Zack's age came in. Her blonde hair was tightly platted on both sides meeting in a short ponytail at the back of her head.

"Perimeter is secure," she told Kephas.

She wore a long black coat in a similar style to the battle garb Zack remembered Kephas wearing in his vision. Zack watched her as she scanned the room. Their eyes met and he could not help but smile.

"It looks like they nearly got these ones," she said to Kephas.

Kephas nodded as she left the room.

"We'll be close by," he explained as they left.

"Thank you."

To the surprise of the doctors, several days later, the three were feeling well enough to leave the hospital. Douglas, Graham and Zack climbed into a taxi and drove across town. Zack's eyes rarely left the back of the drivers head.

"Check it out!" Graham pointed as they passed another landmark.

Zack turned too slowly and just missed it, whatever it was. His mind did not have room for tourist attractions right now. He was picturing what the world headquarters of the Order of Salt and Light would look like. He imagined them driving into the Vatican and pulling up in the front of a great fortress-like cathedral on a hill. There would be strong steel doors and probably patrolling guards.

"Here we are," the driver declared, snapping Zack out of his daydream.

Zack was immediately confused; they had not travelled far from the hospital at all. They were stopped in a side road of the back of the commercial district. Zack peered out the window to see a small two-story brick office. There were no signs or giant crosses on the roof.

"Is this it?" he asked Father Andrews.

"Yes, follow me," as said as he paid the driver.

They slowly extracted themselves from the car, wary of some tender wounds still healing.

Zack watched until the driver had driven down the road and around the corner. Not all the taxi drivers were lunatics it seemed.

"I was expecting something a little grander for some organisation that's been around for so long," Graham spoke what Zack was thinking.

"We try not to attract attention. And to be blunt, some don't see the 'end of the world club' being worth too much investment. But I assure you we have all we need," Father Andrews explained.

Another taxi drove up, and Kephas and Monica got out.

"Greetings Bishop, Hi Monica," Douglas said as they approached.

"Welcome to the Salt and Light Praetorium," a voice from behind them spoke.

Zack turned to see a little old man standing in the doorway.

"Eleazar, good to see you, my old friend."

Kephas walked over and hugged him.

"You look well," Father Andrews said.

Monica nodded reverently.

"And these must be our newest guests. Welcome. I am Cardinal

Eleazar Guntha. I look after things here."

Zack and Graham introduced themselves.

"Ah yes. Thank you for enduring so much to get here. Come in, come in. We can talk more inside."

He opened the door and led them into the foyer. It was entirely unremarkable, like that of a small office. He approached a door at the back and punched in code into the security lock. He held the door opened for them and Kephas lead them up the stairs. A faint scent of incense wafted down from somewhere upstairs. There were old looking portraits on the walls that Zack correctly assumed were saints.

At the top of the stairs, they walked through a hallway lined with books. There were hundreds of all different sizes and shapes. Towards the end, Zack could see a locked glass cabinet with some truly ancient books kept inside. Kephas lead them into a small dining area, and they sat down.

"The council will be ready for you shortly," Eleazar explained as he walked further down the hallway.

"So, what happens next?" Zack asked.

"The council will want to hear about your vision. The more detailed, the better. They will ask questions, some probably unexpected. You need not feel nervous." Douglas explained.

The four chatted for a short while, and then Eleazar returned. This time he wore a deep red ornate priestly robe and a distinctive hat.

"This way if you please," he gestured.

They followed him down another hallway and entered a large meeting room.

Two old men sat at a large table in the centre of the room. They too, were dressed in priestly attire. They stood up as the newcomers came in and took a seat at the table which was bare other than a jug of water and several glasses.

"This is Bishop Julius Anagwavar, and Bishop Emil Linnlock, we run the Ordeam Sal el Lux and report directly to the Pope..." Eleazar explained as he sat next to them.

They smiled and nodded in turn.

"...Our Order can trace its origins back when Jesus walked the earth. Anyone can read the many accounts of exorcisms described in the New Testament. Often, many neglect the battle with our unseen enemy. We have maintained just a small number of members throughout history, and for the most part, our actions go unnoticed. Except perhaps our contribution to the Battle of Lepanto. We the church militant, have a responsibility to..."

"...Protect the people in the end times?" Graham abbreviated.

"Well, yes, if you put it simply." Emil agreed.

Zack hoped that Graham would not interrupt further. He stared over at Graham. He hoped his look conveyed his intention. Graham returned an expression that was a mixture between 'What? He was prattling on and on' and 'OK fine I'll try and behave'.

Emil continued.

"Let's start with a prayer, In the name of the Father, and of the Son and the Holy Spirit, Amen. Dear Lord God. Thank you that despite all odds we've all made it here today. Thank you for your love and protection. Open our minds to your will. Help us with discernment and guide our actions. Help Zack remember all he can and empower us to save as many people as possible. Amen."

"Amen."

"If you please Zack, please recount all you can of your vision for us. Please add any details that you remember, even if you feel that they seem unimportant. If you're happy to, we'd like to record this session." Eleazar pointed to a small microphone set up on the table.

"Sure."

Over the next few hours, Zack relayed his vision of the end of the world to the three men. They made lots of notes and did not interrupt. Graham looked quite disturbed at several occasions as Zack unleashed more details than he had when talking about it previously. Zack lost his place a few times and would jump back and add something, but he did better than he expected. He noticed Monica listening intently with a grim look on her face.

As Zack came to a close, Kephas prompted some more details with a few questions.

The three council members spoke quietly to each other for a moment, and Zack drank the last of his glass of water.

Eleazar began.

"Thank you very much Zack for your recount. We understand this can be very difficult and you did an admirable job of relaying it to us. When you feel ready, we'd like to ask you a series of questions. Some may be uncomfortable to answer, but if you're willing, we would very much appreciate an honest answer. We are not judging you here."

"Yes OK."

Emil sorted his papers and began with his list of questions.

"Have you had any history with alcohol or drug abuse?"

"No"

"Have you ever used any prescription medicine for psychological reasons?"

"No"

Once Emil had finished the questions on his piece of paper, he motioned to Julius who began with his. These were directly related to his vision.

"When you awoke on the boat, did you feel like you were dreaming?"

"No, it felt real. I was convinced the events actually happened. It still feels like they did happen. I've never had any other experience even close to it."

"How long did you feel the vision went on for? Hours? Days?"

"It felt more like years. I'm not sure how many exactly, a few, less than five anyway."

Each time Julius would make a few notes as Zack answered, he gestured for Eleazar to continue.

He picked up his piece of paper with notes on it.

"Would you like some lunch?"

The last question surprised him.

"uh, yes please."

"Great, I'm starving."

They took a well-deserved break and enjoyed a simple lunch of bread and cheeses. Zack looked around and read a plaque on the wall.

John 1
5 *The light shines in the darkness, and the darkness has not overcome it.*

"We're ready to continue if you are Zack?" Eleazar asked.

Zack nodded, and they all walked back into the meeting room. The three Cardinals looked like that they had come to a decision.

"Normally, these things take a lot more time. But in light of the circumstances, and thanks to some earlier communications with Bishop Kephas and Father Andrews, and a lot of prayer, we have concluded that you've experienced a genuine vision from our Lord God."

Bishop Kephas and Father Andrews looked relieved and glad.

"Well, I knew that already..." Zack said quickly.

"Yes, thank you for your patience. Before recent years, we would rarely encounter a Prophet more than once in every decade. Now you're the twenty-seventh in the past few years."

"Wait. What?"

"You Zackary Michaels are a prophet of the Almighty God."

Graham looked at Zack; Zack looked back at him.

Graham burst into laughter, then as quickly as he could, he stopped himself.

"That can't be right? Can it? I'm not a holy person. I've made my share of mistakes."

"Well, officially you've entered the review process, and we should be using the word 'provisional' Prophet. But you get my meaning. And we're not saying that you're without fault. We have all fallen short or been stained by sin at some point. But being a Prophet is not about being perfect. It's about using the knowledge you've received from God for the betterment of others."

"Oh, so what do I do now?"

"That's the right question. We'll go into more details over the coming days. But to start with, pray, heal, train and prepare."

"Zack this is a hard road ahead of you..." Emil spoke up "...are you willing to proceed?"

Zack thought for a moment, as he remembered his vision.

"Yes, yes I am."

"I am so pleased to hear that. Let's say the St. Michaels prayer together." Emil passed out a prayer card.

Saint Michael Archangel, defend us in battle, be our protection against the wickedness and snares of the devil; may God rebuke him, we humbly pray; and do thou, O Prince of the heavenly host, by the power of God, cast into hell Satan and all the evil spirits who prowl through the world seeking the ruin of souls. Amen.

"When you're able, you'll need martial arts training," Julius added.

Graham looked a little shocked.

Zack nodded.

"Take this prayer card too. Keep it with you; recite it as often as you can. Memorise it into innermost self. The prayer was titled 'The seven seals of Christ'.

They spoke for a while longer and eventually stopped for the day. As they retired to the dining area, Monica approached.

"Let's break for afternoon tea."

"Are you able to sleep?" Monica asked him quietly as they ate.

Zack's nightmares entered the front of his mind.

"Mostly."

"I know what you're going through. I too experienced a vision with many similarities to yours."

"Oh?"

"Mine took place in my hometown too. So much death…" she drifted off momentarily.

"It was five years ago, but I can still remember it like it was yesterday."

"Oh really?"

"I was in what should have been a fatal car accident, but I woke up. In to what I later discovered was a vision."

"I'm sorry for you too then."

"Thanks, have you started preparing?"

Zack knew just what she meant.

"Only recently, I, I was sick for a long time."

"Yes I heard. They came after me too. I've survived three attempts so far."

Monica pulled the neck of her top down slightly to reveal a large scar. It went down further than Zack could politely look. Next, she rolled up her sleeves and exposed a large collection of scars on her forearms.

"Woah."

"We're the lucky ones you realise. Many of the other Prophets have been killed."

Zack felt the target on his back; it didn't feel good.

She looked him in the eyes with an intense stare.

"We have to survive. We have to save as many people as we possibly can."

Zack understood.

"Agreed."

Zack appreciated talking to someone who understood what he had been through.

Zack poured a glass of water for Emil who had walked over to them.

"How did you hurt it?" Zack said, pointing to Emil's left hand that was tightly bound in bandages.

"Oh this?" he lifted it closer, and Zack saw the bandages were covered in scripture.

"I've not actually injured my hand, but I've kept it wrapped tightly to prevent me from moving it. I've had it on for a few days now."

Zack looked confused.

"Why would you do that?"

"It's what we call a penitent binding. I use it to remind me how blessed I am. Have you ever lost something and didn't appreciate how good it was until it was gone?"

"Yeah"

"It's like that, and every time I go to use my left hand, I'm reminded to pray. I offer it up to God and am thankful. When my time of prayer has finished, I will take it off again."

"I think I understand…" Zack nodded.

They returned to the Praetorium every day during their stay in Rome. Zack absorbed all he could. Graham managed to find a great collection of tourist spots to visit whenever they were not working.

. . .

Jenson sat at his desk, with his mind utterly focused on his latest reports. For the past few months, he had been spending more and more of his time on his off-book work. Tanya was furious she had not been consulted, but as soon as Daniel spoke to her about it, she left Jenson alone. Only an occasional scowl remained. As many times as Jenson tried, he could not meet the profits demanded of him this month, and he was stressing. He tried every option he could think of. Recently he had completed some pretty risky deals just to meet his targets. Something he had told himself he would never do.

Jenson's wife Suzy's coldness had thawed a little when they moved into their new lavish townhouse. They had been avoiding each other for several months. Every convenience and luxury was now at Jenson's disposal. But now he was counting on that extra income. This month, despite his extensive skills and experience he was going to fall short.

The phone rang.

"Yes? You got it? Fantastic. Thanks, yeah, I'll send through the documents immediately."

Jenson's last-minute deal had come through in time. He totalled his profits again. It was not enough. He was short five percent. Jenson remembered Daniel's seriousness when he first began work on this project.

'Surely they can't expect me to hit these numbers in the current conditions' he thought to himself.

He knew others in his department had made some significant losses recently. Jenson knew he was the best in the building. If he couldn't do it, it just couldn't be done. Jenson looked at the time. He was tired. He took a deep breath.

"Close enough."

He completed his report and packed up.

An hour later, Jenson was sitting in his usual spot in the restaurant eating pasta. It was another meeting without Pete showing up. Jenson was glad. He would prefer not to see him this month of all months. He had only seen Pete a couple of times. But Jenson did not like him, though he wasn't quite sure why.

His mobile phone rang. 'Unknown Number' was displayed on the screen.

"Hello?" Jenson answered.

"You've failed," a voice on the other end said. It sounded like Pete, but Jenson was not sure.

"Hitting those numbers is just not possible right now, everyone is struggling, just…"

"Shut it. This can never happen again."

The line went dead.

Jenson slammed his phone down onto the table. Jenson knew this client had no idea about finance.

"Bad day?" the waitress asked as she came to clear away the empty plates.

She was regularly on shift for Jenson's monthly meetings. She was very attractive and smiled at him enough to make him wonder about seeing more of her. They would often chat.

"Hi Sandra, I just performed a miracle for my clients, and they hung up on me!"

"How rude."

"Yeah, But I'm sure they will come around. Anyway, the meal was delicious as usual, thank you."

"You're welcome," she returned a moment later carrying a glass of wine.

"On the house, free of charge on bad days," she smiled.

"Oh thank you, you didn't have to do that."

Sandra didn't hurry with clearing the plates away.

"How's your day been?"

"Good thanks, I'm just about to finish up actually."

"Oh yeah, any plans?"

"Maybe," she said, leaning over further than she needed to reach across the table.

Jenson decided he'd try his luck.

"Would you like to go out for a drink?"

"Yes, just give me a few minutes."

Sandra left with a smile.

Jenson smiled back, feeling great. He then realised he had just asked her out.

'What am I doing?'

'Doing more things he'd promised himself he'd never do,' his conscience replied.

He debated with himself if he should just leave. He knew he would have to return here in a month, and that would make things awkward. Sandra returned as he sat there. She wore a little black dress that showed off her alluring figure.

Jenson gulped.

"Let's go!" she said, taking his arm.

Before he knew it, they were at a local night club drinking cocktails. Jenson talked about his job, and Sandra really listened. It was evident that she was impressed by his high finance position. Jenson learned that she had a sick, elderly father and she was also a secretary in one of the nearby office blocks. They both enjoyed each other's company.

After a few hours, Jenson decided he had better go.

"I have work tom-morrow I gotta go," Jenson slurred

"You can't drive now silly," Sandra giggled

"I'll grab us a taxi then."

"OK, let's go."

She dragged him from the bar outside, and they quickly found a taxi.

Jenson watched as they drove past his expensive European imported car. He decided to worry about it later. His car had an alarm, and he had other things on his mind. They chatted and laughed as they were driven through the city. Jenson could not remember the last time he felt like someone really understood him as Sandra did. She laughed at every one of his jokes, and her smile seemed like just what he needed. The taxi stopped outside Sandra's apartment. She opened her door and pulled Jenson across the back seat out her door.

The sound of crunching metal and shattering glass filled the air as the taxi was shunted sideways. Jenson was thrown into the pavement and gravel bit into his face. As he rolled over, he saw Sandra laying on the pavement. Blood filled his mouth. He staggered to his feet to see a drunk had just driven his car into them. He looked at where he had been sitting a moment ago and realised how close he had just come to be being killed. The taxi driver was screaming profanity as he called the police. The drunk just sat in his car and took another swig from a bottle in a brown paper bag.

"Jenson!" Sandra yelled

"I'm OK, are you alright?"

She hurried over and used her jacket to wipe the blood from his face, scraping his wound in the process.

"What are you doing?"

Jenson snatched the jacket away.

Sandra did not appreciate being snapped at, and took a step back.

"Oh, I'm sorry Sandra,"

She nodded, but the mood of the evening had been killed. Jenson gave his details to the taxi driver, who was still screaming down his phone. Jenson walked Sandra to her door.

"Thanks Sandra, sorry about everything. I'll make it up to you."

She smiled in return and gave him a quick kiss on the forehead.

"Call me," she wrote her number on his hand.

Jenson walked away from the crash site as more people started to gather around. His face stung all over. He entered Sandra's number into his phone under the name of the restaurant.

A short time later, he got home to an empty house. He found a note from his wife on the kitchen table.

"Jenson, I've decided to go on that cruise with the girls. I knew you'd be too busy to come. See you in three weeks. Suzy."

Jenson crumpled the note up in his hand. Last time they discussed it, he thought he had made it pretty clear that it was a waste of money.

A few days later, Jenson was at work mulling over his newest monthly target. Actually, he was thinking about Sandra. He debated whether he should wait until next month before he saw her again. He did not want to wait. Jenson had been working on a big deal, and if it worked out, he would make the next three months targets with it alone. He had spent a lot of time on the phone to his latest client. They had needed a lot of convincing. This was expected when so much money was at stake. But Jenson was very good at his job. He also had lots of cultivated numbers and projections to back him up. Numbers were truth, weren't they?

Jenson checked his phone. No new messages. With all the hours he had been putting in at work for the past several months he had lost touch with most of his friends. Suzy had been more elusive than usual. He had only received one text message from her on the cruise.

"The weather is here is great."

He did not bother replying.

Jenson dialled Sandra.

"Hello?" she answered on the second ring.

"Hi, it's Jenson."

He could hear her smiling on the other end of the phone. He started smiling too.

. . .

Zack, Graham, Douglas and Kephas were on their flight back to Brakenside. Their trip did not go to plan, but Zack was glad he went. Graham was now convinced that Zack was not crazy after all. Slowly, all the talk of God and spirits seemed less strange to him.

Douglas had been praying quietly for over an hour. Kephas had just managed to fall asleep. Graham was watching the onboard movie. Zack was reading one of the many tomes he was privileged enough to borrow from the Praetorium. He decided he should start with the Bible. Zack flicked through the pages, unsure of how to begin. It was dauntingly large. He stopped on a page and read it.

Jeremiah 29
[11] For I know the plans I have for you," declares the LORD, *"plans to prosper you and not to harm you, plans to give you hope and a future. [12] Then you will call on me and come and pray to me, and I will listen to you. [13] You will seek me and find me when you seek me with all your heart.*

He began with the New Testament. After listening to others over the past few weeks, he thought he better learn about Jesus first then he would go back to read the Old Testament.

An hour later they had touched down at the airport and were in a taxi home to their flat. They had dropped off Douglas and Kephas on the way.
"What a trip man," Graham began.
"I know, right. Thanks so much for coming with me. I literally

wouldn't have made it without you."

"You're welcome. But next time I pick the destination deal?"

"Deal."

"And the next adventure won't have crazy psychos. Or as many books!"

Zack returned a smile.

Beth and Mindy were waiting in the driveway of their flat as they pulled in.

"Graham!" Beth swooped in and tied Graham up in a big hug as she proceeded to smother him with kisses.

"Gentle!" Graham managed as his injuries protested.

"Oh I'm sorry," she stood back and assessed him.

"You're right, I'm glad you didn't send me a photo of you, you look terrible," she jested. But behind her smile was concern.

"Hey!"

Zack climbed out of the car as Mindy approached.

After careful hugs all around, they walked inside.

"It sounded so scary. Are you really both OK?" Mindy asked.

"Yeah, thanks Mindy," Zack assured her.

They chatted for a few hours about their trip then went out for dinner.

The next day Zack started his training regime. He began with a long walk around the block. With his slowly healing injuries, it felt long at least. Over time, he slowly pushed himself into a jog then a run. After a few months of regular exercise, he was fit. He found the local mixed martial arts school and was delighted to see Malcolm teaching one of the classes. Zack felt like they were old buddies from his vision. But as Zack expected, Malcolm introduced himself as if they had never met.

Gold Star was happy to have him back at work, and he even got a framed picture hung in one of the hallways. Stanley said he would try and find him some more bank shifts in the next few weeks. He recommended that Zack should not push himself too hard too quickly.

Each day Zack continued with his reading. He had so much to get through, but he took it at his own pace trying to remember everything he read. Zack often made his own notes and short summaries of what he learned. Douglas and Kephas would visit once a week, and they would spend some time in prayer and study. They also made their own preparations. Zack slowly but surely felt like he was getting a grasp on it all. Zack felt a responsibility for the spiritual protection of those around him. He had no more time for television.

. . .

An elderly man lay quietly in his bed. His breathing was slow and pained. A cough startled others in the room.

"Grandfather, are you alright?"

Paul Otterman's granddaughter Elise brought over a glass of water. A small nod was the only reply. Paul's health had been deteriorating recently, and the small family had gathered for what the doctor predicted would be his last moments.

Elise offered the glass to his lips, but Paul lay his head back on the pillow and closed his eyes. He never opened them again. A few moments later, and it became clear he had died. The room filled with sobs and tears.

"He's gone to a better place," one said.

They read a prayer from Paul's Bible. It had been in his family for generations. Paul had used it regularly for years, but no-one wanted it now. Afterwards, they assembled in the lounge for afternoon tea. No-one felt like eating much.

An hour later, Paul's son Rex arrived. As he pushed his wheelchair up the small path to the front door, memories flooded back to him. He stopped. It was the first time he had been back in forty years. The last time he was here, he had left in an ambulance. When Rex was a young man, he fought with his drunken father and was thrown down the stairs. He had used a wheelchair ever since. True to a promise to himself, Rex only returned once he knew his father had died. Despite Paul giving up drinking and turning his life around, Rex never forgave him.

Rex drew in a deep breath and began to turn himself around.

"Dad!" Elise called from the window.

Rex heard her but continued on his way back to the road.

"Hold on Dad," Elise pleaded as she caught up to him.

"So he's gone then?"

"Yes, he…"

"Good."

Elise looked at him in a disapproving manner he knew well, but she relented.

"It's OK; I get it. But he's gone now, and you can finally let all that go."

Rex slapped the sides of his wheelchair.

"Can I?"

Elise sighed.

"The kids are inside. They'd love to see you. Please come in. I can't remember the last time we had so much family together."

Rex looked at his daughter for a moment. His love for her outweighed the feelings he had for his late father, for the moment.

"Fine, but I can't stay too long."

"Great! There's still lots of food left."

Despite his protests, Rex enjoyed spending time with his family. However, he made no effort to say goodbye to his father at the far end of the hallway.

After some encouragement, he promised to keep his daughter company on the long drive across the country back to her home. She had filled her car boot with Paul's possessions she wanted and given the rest away to the poor.

. . .

It was nearing the end of the month, and Jenson was at his desk late at night. He looked down at his totals. He was not going to make his target for the second month in a row. He had made it through last month without the extra cash, but it was tight. He was expecting that he would still get a partial payment. Especially considering all the extra hours he had put in. But he received nothing at all. Suzy had continued to spend on her cruise with her friends without a care in the world. Jenson muttered under his breath.

The phone rang.

"Hello?"

"Look, Jenson, we know what you're offering, and don't get me wrong; we know it's a good deal. It's just we need a bit more time to get through some resistances with the stakeholders. I'll give you a call next week."

"I understand, thanks Leroy. If there are any more details you need give me a call, day or night."

"OK. Cheers, bye."

Jenson kicked his desk, making heads on the far side of the office turn.

He felt sure they would sign on time. But now the deal would not land until next month. He was currently thirty-five percent short of his target. His phone beeped with another message from Sandra. They had been seeing each other more often over the past weeks. The latest message included a picture of what Sandra was and was not wearing. He packed up his files and left for her house.

Jenson walked up to the tall brick apartment building and pressed the button with Sandra's name next to it. A moment later, a buzzer sounded and he pulled the door open and headed to the elevator. Sandra was quite happy where she was living. But Jenson thought it was dirty and would avoid touching all the surfaces of the building he could. He stopped on the ninth floor and walked down the hallway to Sandra's place. He knocked quietly, and Sandra opened the door almost immediately.

"Hey sugar. Tough day? I made you dinner," she kissed him as he walked in, leaving his bag on the lounge floor.

"Yeah,"

Sandra's apartment was small but tidy. Jenson had previously had a few thought of buying her a bigger place somewhere nicer but had not verbalised anything yet. Jenson sat down at the small table as Sandra poured him some wine. She sat down opposite him as he realised he was starving. He took a deep breath and a gulp of wine and began to eat as he looked over at Sandra. For a moment, her beauty distracted him from the thoughts of missing another months target bouncing around his mind.

"Are you alright?" she asked, genuinely concerned.

Jenson was tempted to tell her everything.

"Some troubles at work…"

Sandra didn't look convinced and cocked her head.

"…I was stressed out for a moment. But I've got something in the works that will fix it." Jenson thought of the big deal he had nearly landed. He had some details to work through, but was confident that it would give him such a large cash injection he would be able to do whatever he liked.

"Can I help with anything?"

"You already have, this dinner is delicious, thank you."

"Oh, I got something for you," Jenson pulled a small card out of his wallet and handed it to her.

"What's this?"

"Open it," Jenson replied with a smile.

Sandra opened it and found an appointment card with her father's name on it.

"Thanks for the thought, but I can't afford to send Pa to a private hospital."

"You don't need to worry about all that; I've taken care of it."

"What?"

"He's got a full care treatment plan all set up. You just need to wheel him in there and they'll do the rest,"

She closed it and handed it back to him.

"I, I didn't ask for this. I can't accept,"

"You can…" he countered, passing it back.

"…It's non-refundable, plus I wanted to get you something special and I had to think of something better than a necklace."

Sandra was motionless for a moment reading Jenson's body language. She knew his mind was made up.

"Thank you," she spoke in a quiet voice as she wiped a tear starting to escape her eye.

"Oh, what's wrong? I wasn't trying to upset you," Jenson rushed over and put his arms around her.

"It's just, I, thank you. Really, I mean it. Thank you."

She took a few breaths as a giant smile spread across her face.

"Go on, give him a call" Jenson offered.

"Oh, I'll call him first thing tomorrow. He'll be asleep already. Besides I haven't had a chance to thank you properly yet…"

She approached him with a look in her eye that Jenson could not resist.

The following day, Jenson was at work sorting through his files as his phone rang. He did not recognise the number on the screen.

"Jenson speaking."

"You've failed us…"

"But…"

"We warned you, but you don't seem to understand. Let's clear that up right now."

The line went dead

"Moron!" Jenson spat as he dropped his phone on the table.

A burst of light from outside lit the window closest to him. Jenson walked over and looked down into the street to see a car on fire. In the car park building next to his office block. In a short moment, he realised it was his car. He always parked on the roof level closest to the stairs. He thought he saw a figure run into the stairwell, but he could not be sure.

"What the…"

Jenson dropped the files he was carrying and ran to the elevator. He furiously smashed the 'down' button until the elevator relented and let him travel slowly to the ground floor. He ran through the lobby and across the street. By now there was a growing group of onlookers assembled in the street watching the fire safely from street level. Jenson pushed through the crowd looking up at his prized possession, burning like unwanted trash. He could not believe they had torched his car. He spat profanity into the street along with some spittle.

"They're insane!"

His phone rang again.

"What?!"

There was a pause on the other end.

Jenson held his phone to his ear.

"Do you understand now?"

Jenson lost his cool; he proceeded to tell the voice on the other end exactly what he thought and where they could shove their project and monthly reports. After some horrified looks from people nearby and several breaths to calm down he began to listen again.

"Jenson?"

"What?!"

"Do you know what I'm looking at?"

Jenson answered with an array of foul words.

The voice waited for him to finish and calmly spoke.

"I'm looking at a picture of you and your mother…"

Jenson froze, his mother had passed away a few years before. He kept a photo of the two of them in his study at home.

"Jenson, it's burning…"

He hung up and ran down the street to the nearest taxi. He pushed a couple aside as they were about to hop in.

"Hey! What do you think you're doing?!" they protested.

Jenson ignored them and recited his address to the driver.

"I think they were…" the driver began.

"Five times your normal rate. Cash. As fast as you can! Now!" he commanded.

The driver turned to see the notes in Jenson's hand.

Wheels spun as the taxi launched out into the traffic, honking as it went. What seemed like an eternity later Jenson arrived on his street.

The flames lit up the neighbourhood as they approached. Jenson could hear sirens in the distance as he desperately peered out the window trying to see.

"Oh buddy it doesn't look good," the driver declared the obvious.

"Get me as close as you can," Jenson said, handing over the cash he promised.

He climbed out and ran a short distance to his driveway. As he came closer, he saw it was not his house that was on fire, just his detached garage. But the flames were getting very close to the house. With the fire as big as it was, there was nothing he could do but stand and watch it all burn. Many of the neighbours came out to watch. A couple spoke to him, but their words did not reach him.

His thoughts dwelled on all the items which he had not yet unpacked. It was all stored in his charred garage. Some of it was junk, and he would not be sad to see it go. But other boxes contained precious memories and sentimental items he could not replace, regardless of how much money he had.

Jenson's phone rang again.

"Do you understand now?" a voice spoke

Jenson was silent. He struggled to think how they could have pulled this off.

The voice then proceeded to list off several addresses in a row. Jenson recognised each one. All the addresses of his close family were mentioned.

"Now if you don't want to see them burn too, you'll meet your targets."

"OK." Jenson relented as the line went dead.

Three fire engines roared up the road, and firefighters swarmed the scene and got the blaze under control. The garage was now a wet, charred empty shell. The side of his house closest was blackened with the windows broken from the heat. There was untold smoke damage inside.

Jenson could not believe this was happening to him. He had a nice boring life, didn't he? He walked in and immediately, the stench of smoke hit him. He walked around the first floor of his house and was surprised much of it looked intact. He entered the kitchen to find a light coating of ash over everything. He climbed the stairs and found the bathroom in a similar state. He entered the bedroom and packed a small bag of clothes.

He called Sandra.

"Hey it's me, look can I stay at your place for a few days please?"

"Of course, what happened?"

"I'll tell you all about it soon."

"OK…"

Jenson returned to the street and called for a taxi.

While he waited, he checked his offshore bank accounts. Whatever was going on, Jenson was not interested in taking part any further. He had been covertly siphoning money from his employer over the past several years into his private nest egg. He was not expecting to use it so soon. In his mind, he had earned every cent. He had put some of his best work into his company, and he was merely paying himself what he was worth. However, this was a lot more over the years than what the Human Resources department allotted him.

A red zero balance starred back at him.

"Impossible!"

He logged in three times the same number was displayed. He checked the last few transactions. Jenson's mind started to spin. There was no way that they could have known about that. He was very careful in how he had manoeuvred the money around. His company had even passed a financial audit three years ago without incident. All the funds had been transferred to an account number he did not recognise.

Jenson spat on to the street in disgust. These guys were incredibly good. He wondered why they even needed him if they had the skills to empty him out.

The taxi pulled up, and he threw his bag into the backseat and climbed in. He recited Sandra's address and the vehicle pulled out onto the road. Jenson checked his standard bank accounts, and they looked normal. Or did they? He scanned through the many transactions which gave Jenson some indication of his wife's spending habits. Amongst them all was that same mysterious bank account number he had seen before. It was only a few hundred dollars leaving his account, but that got him thinking. He flicked back to his offshore accounts and did a quick mental total of the numbers. They had taken exactly how much he was short of his monthly target. Not a cent more or less.

Jenson was comfortable throwing around huge numbers during his work, but they seemed to take on a new significance when they impacted his personal cash. Normally a loss was a just a loss. Somewhere a shareholder would have noticed his portfolio drop a few points. But nothing impacted Jenson directly. This stung. Jenson was not used to risking his own money. He was too careful for that. Jenson wondered what he had got himself into.

The taxi stopped outside Sandra's place and the taxi driver turned around expectantly. Jenson opened his wallet and swiped his card.

"Thank you. Enjoy the rest of your night."

"Yeah," Jenson replied absently as he hopped out.

"Dammit," he yelled aloud.

He now remembered he had paid for Sandra's sick father's treatment with his credit card. Although it was a large amount, it was trivial next to the nest egg he had been preparing. Emphasis on 'had'. The thought flashed through his mind of calling the private hospital tomorrow morning and say there had been some sort of mistake. He was genuinely interested in Sandra but without his offshore funds, he needed to prioritise. He wondered how he would explain that, or any of it for that matter. Jenson hoped Sandra's father was sick enough to not need care for very long. To stack the deck in his favour, he decided that the hospital had just called him with some more details. He would explain to Sandra that his booking began in three months. That would save him significant funds and still keep Sandra happy.

A few weeks later, a very stressed Jenson got a call at work.

"Jenson?"

"Leroy, tell me the good news."

"Ha, you guessed it. It's official, we're on board. The paperwork should be coming through shortly."

"Brilliant! You've made the right decision Leroy. I appreciate the call. Thanks."

"I know you won't let us down. Thank you for coming to us with this one."

"You're most welcome."

"Thanks, we'll be in touch. Bye"

"Bye."

Jenson could not help but do a quick victory dance around his office. Heads turned from their desks and stared in his direction, but he did not care. Relief flooded over him. His collection of alternative options were not ideal, and now they did not matter. Jenson's profit surged upwards to an almost criminal amount. He was reminded again why he loved his job. He sent Sandra a message.

"It came through!!!!!!!!" He added a few smiley emojis on the end.

After a few moments, the rush began to subside, and he began planning how he would spend his money. He sat at his desk for a moment with his pen hovering over the piece of paper in front of him. He took a deep breath, signed it, then walked into his boss' office.

"Judy told me already Jenson, great work!" Daniel said with a smile.

"Thanks, I quit." Jenson handed over his signed resignation.

"What?"

"I want out Daniel, from the other thing too."

"Close the door!" Daniel demanded, standing up, his fury growing.

Jenson closed the door and sat down.

"I've had enough; those guys have problems. I'm done."

"They are not going to like that."

"I've settled this month two weeks ahead with significantly more than target. That should keep them off my back."

Jenson handed over another piece of paper, which Daniel's eyes widened as he read it.

"This is probably next month's target too! What the hell sort of deal did you land today?"

"My last one in this company Daniel," Jenson said firmly.

"Look, landing deals like this will allow me to revisit your salary Jenson. I mean, in a major way. I..."

"No, Daniel. Sorry I'm not interested."

Daniel thought for a moment.

"You going to work at S&R, aren't you?"

"Yes."

Daniel swore under his breath.

"Fine. If you've made up your mind. But I don't know what they'll say. I've never heard of anyone quitting before."

"Just tell them not to contact me again."

"That's not up to me."

"Bye Daniel." Jenson opened the door to walk out.

"Jenson?"

"Yeah,"

"We could've given you everything."

"Goodbye," he shut the door behind him.

Shortly afterwards, Jenson was clearing out his desk as the call he was hoping would not arrive did. This time the calling number was blocked.

"What do you want?" Jenson spoke curtly.

"Firstly to thank you..." an unfamiliar woman's voice replied. Jenson pulled the phone away from his ear for a moment and wondered if it was the people he thought it was.

"What happened to the other guy?"

"With your request to leave, I became aware that some things have been handled less than professionally. I will correct that, and he has been dealt with accordingly."

Jenson wondered exactly what that could mean, and as he thought, he unwittingly paused long enough for her to continue talking.

"Your significant contribution to the next month's targets also got my attention. You are obviously skilled, and we don't want to lose someone with your talent."

"I'm not interested."

"Twenty percent bonus just to hear me out. It'll be up to you after that. If you still want out, I'll adjust our standard procedures to let you leave, unfettered."

Jenson paused. He wrestled with his own decision to leave. He knew they would do something to try and keep him. But that was a large amount of money just to listen to a short conversation and say 'no'.

"So to confirm, I'm out either way."

"Yes. No more strings attached."

"What about the damage to my house?"

"Hear what I have to offer first, and then we can discuss the details."

"I get the money straight away?"

"Yes, we'll wire it to your account immediately after this call."

Jenson paused for a second.

"OK, I'm listening."

She spoke at length about an upcoming project they wanted him to manage.

Outside his office, the janitor heard "Double my current rate?!" as Jenson shut his door.

As the workday came to a close, Jenson was the last one left on the floor. He waved to the few employees who tried to get his attention as they left but continued talking on the phone. The janitor politely waited outside. Jenson opened his door as he hung up. He gathered his few personal effects from his desk and made his way to the elevator ignoring the janitor entirely.

After the janitor had emptied the rubbish bin and cleaned the glass, he wiped the desk down and noticed a pad with two words written on it:
'Project Groundswell'
Thinking nothing of it the janitor tore off the page and threw it in his rubbish bag.

. . .

It was a clear, crisp morning with only a few fluffy clouds high in the sky. Most people were still in bed or had not left their houses yet. Graham decided to join Zack on his morning run.

"I'm choosing our route," Graham declared as they set off down the road.

"Sure thing," Zack replied, who was getting bored of running the same track anyway.

They chatted for the first few blocks until they needed all of their lung capacity just to keep running.

After a few more blocks Graham made a turn that directed them closer to town. Zack started to guess what Graham was up to. A short time later, they arrived at Graham's favourite bakery.

"Man, I gotta have a quick rest," he said puffing.

"How convenient, we just happen to have a bakery nearby," Zack replied, smiling.

"Yeah, what a fluke," Graham returned the smile.

They jogged to the bakery and emerged a few minutes later with pies and drinks in hand. They sat at a wooden bench and bit into their hot pies.

"Ah! Ah! Hot!" Graham waved his mouth as he opened his can of drink.

Zack had just done the same and burnt the top of his mouth on a delicious but scorching hot mince pie. After a few swigs of cola, they felt better and chatted away in between bites of pie.

Graham was in the middle of explaining to Zack what had happened to him at work the previous day when Zack jumped up off the seat and sprinted across the road to an alleyway just behind a fast-food restaurant.

"Hey?!" Graham called.

A homeless man was rummaging through one of the rubbish bins and loading up his supermarket trolley filled with all sorts that he had found. It looked like Zack was running straight for him and he took a step back and put the trolley between him and Zack.

"Run for your life!" Zack screamed at him as he ran over.

The homeless man looked around, seeing no threat but Zack.

"No!"

Graham watched in horror as Zack drew a knife from his pocket as he bounded up the footpath on the far side of the road.

"Woah! Zack stop!" he began to run over to his crazed friend.

As the homeless man and Graham watched, Zack swung his short blade through thin air with deadly intent. He nearly lost his balance and made a flurry of repeated swings again after regaining his footing. Graham saw the murderous intent in Zack's eyes. The homeless man relaxed a little after seeing the crazy young man try and stab the morning breeze instead of him. He wheeled his supermarket trolley away.

"A little early to be on the hard stuff isn't it?" he called over his shoulder.

"Huh?!" A flood of confusion stained Zack's face as he now stood motionless.

"Are you OK?" Graham ran over to his friend and placed both hands on his shoulders.

He tried to get Zack to focus on him, and after a brief shake, Zack snapped out of it.

"What the hell are you doing Zack?!" Graham demanded

"Didn't you see it? Where did it go?" Zack spun around looking for his quarry.

"Dude, there's nothing here. What did you think you saw?"

"A demon was right where I'm standing. As clear as you are in front of me now."

"Where?"

"Well, then it just vanished."

"Zack…"

Zack quoted scripture in reply.

1 Peter 5

[8] Be alert and of sober mind. Your enemy the devil prowls around like a roaring lion looking for someone to devour. [9] Resist him, standing firm in the faith, because you know that the family of believers throughout the world is undergoing the same kind of sufferings.

"Sounds like you're way too sober to me!"

"I know, I know, it sounds mental. But I swear I just saw it. It was about to attack the homeless guy. I…"

Zack put his knife back in his pocket.

Graham looked around and was thankful no-one else had seen the event.

They walked across the road back to their pies.

"Why did you pack a knife for a run?"

"I was just being prepared."

"A little too prepared perhaps?"

"Yeah. Uh, Sorry. I don't know…"

"It's OK, no harm done. Let's just walk home huh?"

"Yeah OK."

Graham began to wonder what toll all of the recent events had taken on his friend.

In the following months, Zack saw a few more demons, seemingly unperceived to anyone but him. One he saw following a woman walking through a busy street as he travelled by in the bus. The surrounding people acted as if nothing was there. Thankfully, Zack didn't pull out his knife on the bus. He decided he would instead talk to Bishop Kephas about it.

Chapter 3:

Long weekend

One sunny Friday afternoon, Graham was driving Zack and Beth to Doverton from Brakenside. Zack was looking out the window from the backseat. Beth was trying to find something she liked on the radio. With the coming Monday being a public holiday they had decided it was a perfect time to visit Mindy.

Zack's mind was still buzzing with all the things he needed to prepare. He had made a spreadsheet which he constantly accessed on his phone. He recorded, categorised and budgeted his next steps to be in a better position with the end of the world looming sometime in the future.

They were cruising along the motorway as Zack saw a tow-truck winching a broken down vehicle off to the side of the road. Zack added some more notes about extra tools that would come in handy.

"Zack? Are you listening?" Beth repeated.

"Oh sorry, what?"

"Are you sure you want to go in to work on your day off?"

"Yeah, I've not been to the Doverton Gold Star offices before. Stanley works there now; I thought I'd pop in and say hello. After that, I'm going to shop for some more supplies. Then I'll meet you at Mindy's. You guys enjoy your romantic afternoon," he said with a smile. Graham chuckled.

"I've heard the museum is worth a trip just by itself. You're welcome to join us," Beth offered.

"Next time."

"OK, Mindy finishes work at five, so we'll see you then."

"Five, OK got it."

They made good time for the rest of the way into Doverton, eventually taking the off-ramp to the central business district. Tall glass high-rises stood proudly in all directions. Graham carefully manoeuvred his way through the busy streets and stopped at a pedestrian crossing on the street opposite Zack's destination.

"This OK Zack?"

"Great. Thanks. See you later."

Zack jumped out and made his way along the busy footpath. What seemed like hundreds of people were making their way up and down the street, busy with their own lives. Zack waited for the signal to cross the road and made his way into the Gold Star building lobby. It was modern with a giant artistic fountain in the foyer. The iconic Gold Star logo was fashioned out of metal and hung on the wall behind the reception counter. Numerous potted plants brightened the room with bright green leaves and an array of colourful flowers.

Zack thought to himself this must be where Gold Star takes big corporate clients to win their business. He smiled as he looked around, then walked up to reception desk.

"Hi," a cheery older woman greeted him as he approached.

"Hello, I'm here to see Stanley McGregor. He's on the ninth floor. I used to work with him in Brakenside."

Zack pulled out his Gold Star identification card as he spoke.

"Very well, please fill out the visitor register, and I'll give him a call."

"Thanks,"

After a moment the receptionist had Stanley on the line.

"Mr McGregor, this is Beverly from reception, you have a visitor....

yes, OK I'll send him up, bye."

"He said he'd meet you in his office. Take the first elevator to the ninth floor, on the far side of the floor, you'll see the staff kitchen his office is opposite that."

"OK, thanks,"

Zack walked up to the turn styles and swiped his ID card. He then followed two other people dressed in professional business attire into the lift. After pressing the button for his floor, he waited patiently as people got on and off during the way up. On the ninth floor, and tried to see where the kitchen area was. He saw a large open plan office floor filled with desks, computers and many staff going about their work. No-one paid him any attention. He started walking across the floor then spotted a few people congregating about a coffee machine on the far side. He found a set of offices and meeting rooms opposite with Stanley's name on one of the doors. He waited around for a few minutes expecting to see Stanley appear at any moment. His phone buzzed in his pocket with a new message.

"Sorry. 10 mins away."

Zack typed a reply to Stanley

"OK see you then."

He wandered around the staff kitchen area for a few moments before realising he needed to go to the toilet. Zack searched for the nearest restroom. As the urge grew with insistency, he spotted what he was looking for. He made his way past the kitchen and entered the men's restrooms and sat down in a cubicle. Zack wondered what he had eaten that did not agree with him as he pulled out his phone from his pocket.

Across town, Graham and Beth were hopping out of the car at the museum car park. Beth was still holding the museum pamphlet in her hand she had got weeks earlier when she had planned this trip.

"What should we visit first, Classical or the Modern art exhibit?" she asked.

Graham was happy to spend the afternoon with Beth but had much less enthusiasm when it came to art.

"Classical sounds good."

"Good idea, that way we can observe the pieces that potentially could have inspired the later ones."

"Yeah"

Beth was aware art was not Graham's passion but appreciated him making an effort.

"Perhaps we could stop in at the cafe afterwards?"

"Good idea."

Hand in hand, they walked towards the museum entrance.

. . .

Back in Brakenside, Bishop Kephas and Father Andrews were working in the Church gardens. Deon West and three others were also helping out. When one of the elderly members of the church died, she had left a small plot of land on the city outskirts to the church. It had been planted with potatoes and other vegetables each year since. Working with some of the community who were struggling with substance abuse, they regularly tended to their crop. Some of their produce was given to the local soup kitchen with the rest sold to local markets with the proceeds going to help the poor.

"Like this Bishop," Deon leaned down and with a skilful hand plucked out a weed roots and all.

"Got it," Kephas tried to repeat the procedure but was only half as successful.

"Better."

Deon walked over to check on the others. Lucy Tollman was an elderly lady who loved gardening and was happy to help out whenever work needed to be done. Today's pair of helpers had been rostered as part of their community service. The Brakenside Police Department had decided it was a great way to repay society.

Donny Ortenga was in his early twenties and had been convicted of reckless driving causing injury. Other than when he was behind the wheel, he was a polite individual and got along well with others.

"So Donny, how are you going?" Father Andrews asked.

"OK I guess, couldn't a tractor do this instead?"

Douglas smiled.

"Perhaps, but today it's up to us."

Donny nodded.

"I guess so."

"What are you going to do after this?"

"Probably go home, watch TV, see some friends tonight."

"That sounds good, what about after today?"

Donny started to wonder what he was getting at.

"Well I'm rostered to work on Tuesday, so from then I'll just be doing standard stuff."

"I see, what about after all of your days on earth are done?"

Donny thought something like this would likely appear in the conversation.

"I guess I'll die eventually then whatever it is after that."

"You're not sure what'll happen after you die?"

"Nope, I figured, I'm trying to live a good life, and if there's a God I'll go to Heaven."

"Oh, why would he let you into Heaven?"

"Well, why not? I've not killed anyone."

"I'm glad to hear that. But I think that's the mistake many people make. Including myself for many years."

"Oh?"

"It talks about the entry requirements to get to Heaven in the Bible. To get in, you have to be completely perfect. Not a single sin. Whether that be something small or large."

"Well, then no-one would get in?"

"Correct!"

"All of us have sinned in our lives, and the price of sin is eternal death."

Donny now was a bit lost, he thought he knew the general idea of what these people were about, but it seems this Priest was a bit different.

"That doesn't sound great…" Donny offered.

"Agreed. There's no way we can make it by ourselves. That's why Jesus had to die on a cross for our sins. You see, he's paid the price for us. We just need to believe. I like to think of it like this. On Earth we're running along, then death is like a large cliff in front of us. Alone, we just fall off. But Jesus is holding out his hand out to us. If we reach for him, he catches us and saves us from falling."

"Huh? I've not heard it put like that before."

"Thanks for listening Donny. It's my job after all," Father Andrews said with a smile.

Mike Wisley was nineteen and thought the world owed him a favour. He had burnt part of a fast-food restaurant sparked from a disagreement on how fresh the food should have been. He seemed angry all the time, and Father Andrews feared he could end up committing a more serious crime if he did not get enough support to change direction.

"Let's see if we can fill this wheelbarrow before afternoon tea time shall we?" Father Andrews offered.

Mike looked his way and made a meagre attempt to speed up his dismally slow efforts at pulling weeds.

"Well, that's a start," he said with a smile.

$\cdots$

Meanwhile, Jenson was wrapping up his presentation to the board of directors. The meeting room was quiet as everyone listened to him as he spoke.

"Thank you all for listening. Are there any questions?" Jenson asked.

The room of well-dressed businessmen was nodding, and there was a general vibe of agreement with what Jenson had proposed.

A balding man in a black suit spoke.

"How confident are you on the timeline?"

"I've spoken to our Eastern and Southern divisions already on this one. As long as they can supply by the end of the month, we can be very confident that delivery occurs as planned. I'm aware that timing is everything when it comes to an operation like this so I've factored in a buffer to allow for any unforeseen circumstances that may arise. We can do this."

"Good, good."

"OK Jenson, thanks for your work, we'll discuss and have an answer for you by early next week."

"Thank you."

They waited for him to leave the room before they began their discussions.

Jenson was enjoying his new role and was encouraged with how well his first presentation had gone. He began the walk back to his office.

. . .

On the far side of the world, in the early hours of the morning in a remote village, an elderly Nun was on her nightly walk. Sister Lee struggled to stay asleep with a relentless ache in her legs. She had found her only relief was from long walks which often occurred in the middle of the night. Lee would climb the small hill at the back of her residence into the native bush to pray. Using her trusty torchlight, she lit her way. The path was well used, and she could almost walk with her eyes closed if she had to. She reached the top of the hill and sat at the park bench to catch her breath. She rubbed her tired legs. The aches had already dulled. She was confident by the time she got back to bed, they would feel better. She knelt and began her nightly prayers. For some reason she could not shake a verse from her head she had read earlier in the day:

Ezekiel 7
⁷Doom has come upon you,
upon you who dwell in the land.
The time has come! The day is near!
There is panic, not joy, on the mountains.

After a short time, she stopped and stood up. Taking a deep breath of the cold night air, she could not shake a feeling of uneasiness. Something was different about tonight. Looking around did not yield any answers. She felt like someone was watching her. Admittedly she did not live in the safest place, but few criminals would bother a poor old nun.

"Hello?" she called out.

Her voice fell into emptiness and silence.

She knelt back down and continued with her prayer. She was finding it increasingly difficult to concentrate. Something she struggled with from time to time but tonight was on a whole other level. She stood again and walked around her immediate vicinity. Unnerved by a feeling she could not explain. She pulled her dressing gown tighter around her and knelt again.

"…Repent…"

The word seemed to echo quietly from nowhere. Her eyes darted around as she strained her ears to locate the sound.

"...Repent..."

The words felt a little louder this time. She started to recognise that it emanated in her very being. It was not merely acoustic sounds. It was something more, something deeper. Only twice in her life had Sister Lee heard the Word of God before, both times were not as clear as it was now. She bowed her head and prayed even more fervently.

"...REPENT..."

Her whole body resonated with the word. This was not just a part of a human-made language. Lee could sense the true meaning behind it as if this was the first truth she had ever experienced. She felt a call to stop all sinful behaviour and turn to God with all her heart. Nothing was lost in translation. Of the three languages she spoke fluently, each one formed the same meaning. The word itself seemed to be her true native tongue.

The earth shook as she fell onto her side into the soft, cool grass. The earth itself seemed to groan and quiver. The night sky flickered with flashes of colour. Auroras danced out from the edges of the sky to meet above her. It was beautiful, awe-inspiring yet terrible to behold. The sky cracked with thunder as lightning lit up the clouds. The clouds abruptly dissolved into nothingness and a clear sky of stars blazed down on her. Lee rolled onto her back and soaked in the truly spectacular sight.

. . .

Zack was still sitting in the toilet when he thought someone in the next stall was speaking to him. A brief moment passed as his mind struggled to make sense of it.

"...Repent..."

Zack's mind kicked into overdrive. The end of the world was starting, and he was stuck in a cubicle with his pants down! He quickly finished his business and stood up as the third Word of God boomed into his very core. The whole building shook violently, and he was thrown to the ground. Zack thought of all his supplies back in Brakenside. All his plans were based around him being in Brakenside when the end came.

"Idiot!" he reprimanded himself.

"We're gonna die!" a man screamed from somewhere at the other end of the restroom.

Zack's immediate thought which he did not voice was 'yeah probably.'

The building made disturbingly loud grinding sounds, which managed to drown out the screaming occupants. The fire alarm kicked in after a brief moment, blaring panic into the already frantic office workers. Zack tried to stand and slipped in the dirty water gushing out from broken pipes. His nose alerted him to the fact that water from the toilets had sloshed out on the floor.

Zack wished he had brought his Bible with him, and some of his knives, and armour and rations, and medical supplies. Any of it would have been great. Instead, he only had his clothes, wallet, keys, and cell phone. With that thought, he quickly noticed the 'No signal' message. His right hand went his chest and was relieved to feel the rosary beads around his neck under his T-shirt.

'Well, that's something at least…I mean, Thank you, Lord God. Thank you that I have my rosary with me. Guide me to help as many as I can. Amen.' he prayed.

The dreadful sounds of destruction seemed to hit him from every direction. He flew into the wall as the building lurched from side to side beneath him. Zack's body flooded his system with adrenaline. It was finally time to do what he was made for. He scrambled out of the cubicle and shouted to be heard above the fire alarm.

"Is there anyone hurt in here?"

"I'm here!" a voice called.

The building began to settle as Zack made his way over. A scared man came from the other end of the bathroom towards him.

"What do we do?" he yelled.

"Let's check on everyone else."

Zack walked past him, opening the toilet door as he went. A man burst in, holding back a mouth full of vomit. As the stench of the busted pipes hit him, he slipped on the floor and threw his lunch all over the place. A glance around the office floor entered Zacks mind as he struggled to comprehend that only moments ago was an ordinary office. The vomiting man wiped his mouth on his sleeve and pushed past him again as he rushed to the fire exit.

Zack soaked in the devastation. A crowd of people were rushing towards the fire exit, blocking the view to the left. The majority of the glass on the outside of the building had shattered, allowing a cool breeze to flow through the floor. The roof had collapsed with part of the floor above crushing those unlucky enough to be beneath it off to his right. It was dim as all the florescent lights had all gone out. The occasional fire sprinkler was spurting drips of water out over the mess. Desks had been thrown with their occupants in tow. Computers, cabinets and supplies had been jettisoned everywhere.

Beneath the fire alarm, Zack heard numerous screams of people crying out in pain. He tried to remember what he had studied from his first aid course.

'D.R.S.A.B.C.' he spoke aloud to himself.

"Help!" a desperate woman called from nearby. Her desk had toppled over onto her and was trapping her legs. Zack ran over and managed to pry it off her. Her legs were badly bruised, but she was able to walk.

"Thank you," she called as Zack moved off towards the next person. A man was nursing a large laceration on his leg. Grabbing a jacket from a nearby toppled chair, he offered it to him.

"Wrap it up to slow the blood loss."

The man nodded and with help, did just that.

"We need help over here!"

A pair of men were trying to lift some of the debris from the collapsed roof off someone trapped below. Zack made his way over through the carnage as best he could. He saw a pair of legs underneath the ceiling panels that had been scattered over the floor.

"We gotta lift this," a middle-aged man commanded, pointing to a large steel girder which looked like it belonged in the roof.

The three of them took hold as best they could and heaved it to one side. The man dug away to reveal a lifeless body with a very broken looking neck.

"No, no, no!" he muttered.

The building shook once more, nearly causing Zack to lose his balance.

"Barry, come on!" one of them called tugging at the others arm. He eventually succeeded in pulling him towards the crowd at the fire exit on the far side of the floor. There was a loud commotion as people were pushing to try and get to the stairs.

"Another one!" A lady in a fluoro vest yelled by one of the meeting rooms. Zack and a few others rushed over to help. The pair of people must have been in a meeting room moments before. They now lay in a mess of broken glass. One had already clearly died, but the other was only covered in deep cuts.

"Help me lift him out."

"OK"

The small group removed what glass they could and began to drag the injured man. An eruption of screaming protested his movement, and they stopped. A pool of blood began to seep out from underneath him as became quieter and paler. Those trying to help him did not know how to help, and in a few short moments, his chest stopped heaving, and then stopped moving altogether.

"He's gone?"

"Sorry, I…"

Two of the group stayed with the pair as the fluoro vested lady slowly stood and made her way around the floor searching for others. Zack followed her, but after their search, they did not find any more seriously injured people.

Abruptly the fire alarm stopped. The yelling and commotion seamlessly filled the void. There did not seem to be any progress in the stairwell and Zack made his way over to try and see what was happening. Numerous people were shouting and swearing at each other, with a few even beginning to throw punches. Zack peered through the crowd to see the stairway was crammed full. There was no way anyone would be making it onto the stairway from their floor.

"Move it! C'mon!" One large man was yelling into the stairwell.

Swearing and frustration were the only replies.

On each of the fifty other floors, people desperately tried to force their way into the stairwell. Beverly remained cowering under the large reception desk on the ground floor. Memories from an earthquake in her childhood had frozen her in place. The ground floor lobby quickly filled with people as the two other internal staircases disgorged panicked office workers.

"Over here!"

Zack turned to see a group of the crowd near the fire escape stairs had begun to rush down the internal staircase. Soon another surge of people rushed in their direction. Both exits were now blocked with people, and Zack had nowhere to go. He walked cautiously to the edge of the floor, looked out. The surrounding high-rise buildings looked to be in a similar state. They had shed their silvery skin of glass and now stood ugly and broken. Peering down to the street below, layers of broken glass and debris-covered everything. Zack shuddered to think of the hundreds of people who must have been cut to ribbons when that lethal shower of shards came down.

Zack swore under his breath.

"Zack!" a familiar voice called.

"Stanley, you're OK!" Zack smiled as he saw his former boss emerge from the crowd.

"I see you're in one piece too! I'd expect nothing less from someone as lucky as you. The stairs don't seem to be moving at all."

"I think I know why, have a look," Zack motioned him over to the edge of the floor.

Stanley surveyed the devastation.

"I was hoping that somehow it was just our building. It looks like everything in the CBD has been hit."

"Yeah, I haven't seen a single undamaged building."

"Good grief, look at the road. It's like it snowed glass down there."

"Yeah, I don't suppose there is any room for all the people trying to evacuate to go."

"What a mess."

"OK Zack, follow me. We gotta do something quickly."

. . .

Across town, Graham and Beth were caught in the crowd of people flooding out of the museum.

"I can't believe it!" Beth yelled over the sirens.

The fire alarm of the museum could still be heard amongst the many car alarms squealing from all around them.

"I don't think we've ever had earthquakes around here have we?"

"Not that I know of," Graham shouted back.

They had been herded to the evacuation point in the middle of the car park.

"Do you think this is all that stuff that Zack has been going on about?" Beth asked in a scared voice.

"I really hope not..." Graham also recalled Zack's recount of his vision. "... if it is, things are going to get a whole lot worse."

Graham looked around to see the surrounding buildings all in bad shape. The streets were crowded with bewildered people. Luckily for the museum-goers, they congregated in the large car park away from the fallen glass and debris.

"Let's head back to our car," Graham suggested.

"OK, I'll follow you,"

They weaved their way through the crowd occasionally passing somebody with minor cuts or bruises gained moments earlier. Some of the crowd had began to disperse in every direction, as people tried to go and help others or find their way home.

Loud shrieks cut through the commotion as a few people caught fire. Beth spun around to see something she could not immediately understand. There was a disturbance in the air above the crowd of people closest to the museum. It was dark, and it flickered with energy. It had scorched everything around it. She felt a wave of air pressure slam into her as the rift expanded.

"Beth!" Graham pulled her away from the onlookers.

"Whatever that is, it's not good."

They dodged their way through the crowd and made their way to their car. A deep guttural roar burst out from behind them. Beth could not help but turn to look. She saw a pair of large claws pierce through the strange black rift. They seemed to tear at the fabric of reality, pulled it apart and a moment later, a horrific beast was before them. Beth immediately thought of what Zack had previously struggled to describe as a Mortkin. A demon from the depths of Hell stood before them. The dark force behind it began to shrink and dull until it looked like a passing shadow, then the rift was gone.

A wave of cries erupted as the creature strode forth and began to cleave into the crowd with its long claws. Sprays of blood flew into the air showering panicked people struggling to flee.

Graham dragged Beth between the parked cars and screaming people. "Run!"

They clambered into their car at one end of the car park, and Graham started the engine. As they did so, many cars lurched forth from their parks and collided in a crunch of steel. Their car jolted to one side as the car next to them smacked into them, skidding against the car in front of it. Graham saw a few fleeing people fall as cars smashed their way forward as best they could.

"Hold on!"

Graham put their car into reverse, and they shot backwards through a chain-link fence.

"What the hell are you doing?!" Beth cried.

"Avoiding that hell-spawn that's what!"

They skidded across the small grass verge onto the street behind them. Bouncing over the footpath and curb, they hit the road with a jolt. Beth kept her eyes on the demon ripping through the people and cars. With the fence breached, people began to spill out of the car park running in all directions. Graham changed gear, and they burst forwards up on to the curb again and spun around back towards the road.

"Watch out!" Beth screamed.

A man came running through the nearby trees; Graham knocked him over as the side of the car slammed into him. Graham did not slow one bit but was thankful to see him pick himself up and keep moving, albeit it now only at a stagger. They sped down the road towards the closest intersection where Graham slammed on his brakes. It was too late; the roads were already choked to a halt. Their car skidded forwards over the broken glass and debris in the road and crunched itself to a stop against a parked car.

"Are you OK?"

"Yeah," Beth said, nursing a small cut to her head.

They peered back behind them and saw the demon stomp down the verge. Just as Graham was opening the door, another car careened into them followed shortly by a few more. A moment later they were trapped in on all sides by vehicles desperately trying to escape. Some of them kept their engines running, futilely revving their engines in an attempt to push their way through. Graham caught a glance of the lady in the car next to theirs.

"We're not going anywhere, lady!" Graham called out.

But she retained the crazed look on her face as she slammed her hands into the steering wheel.

"No!" Beth screamed as she saw the demon turn towards their direction. Both sides of their car were crushed up against other vehicles, and they could not open the doors. The demon approached the first car in the pile-up and punched its claws through the driver's window impaling the occupant. It ripped his body out and flung it out onto the road. It made a few steps; then the demon seemed to begin to struggle.

Dark energy gathered around it, and it progressively seemed to take hold of the creature. Beth and Graham looked on as a sphere of crackling sparks began to spin its way around it. The demon seemed to be trying to fight it but to no avail. It was lifted slightly from the ground as the sphere neared completion. Then the sphere began to shrink around it quickly. Bursts of demonic blood sprayed out on to the road below as it was compressed smaller and smaller. A moment later, the dark energy was a tiny ball that vanished from view. The demon was no more.

From the confines of their trapped car, Beth and Graham exchanged looks.

"What the…?" Graham began.

After a moment of shocked silence, Beth spoke

"Mindy and Zack! We have to find them."

"Yeah. Uh. I'm not sure how in all this craziness. But let's try. Um… Grab whatever seems useful from the car. I don't think we're going to be driving anywhere."

"OK, good thinking," Beth agreed as she rummaged through the glove box jamming a few items in her handbag.

Graham wound down his window and pulled himself out between the gap between their car and the next. The lady in her car on the other side finally stopped trying to drive through the traffic jam and turned her engine off.

"About time," Graham said to himself.

"Beth, honey, out through here," Graham sat on the roof of the parked car and beckoned Beth to follow.

"Help me."

After a moment of shuffling to the driver's seat, she wriggled her way out the window. They sat on the car roof for a moment as Graham put his arms around her.

"We're OK. We made it."

Beth snuggled into him.

"Thanks, I love you, you know that, right?"

"I love you too babe," he replied.

Graham surveyed their surroundings and tried to decide on their next move.

...

On the far side of the country, Rex slowly wheeled himself along the footpath. He had promised his daughter Elise that he would continue with his daily exercise. On any normal day, he did enjoy the fresh air. He was on his way to the supermarket when chaos broke out. He felt the earth rumble underneath him. Rex had heard the sound of squealing tires and crunching metal from multiple directions.

"What the?"

As he made his way down the street, he saw people running everywhere. Some had the look of terror on their faces. There were a few cars that sped down the road at dangerously fast speeds. Despite the feeling of fear he had growing inside him, he continued into town. He told himself everything would settle down by the time he got to town. At the far end of the street, he thought he saw a strange shape dash between some parked vehicles where all the screaming was coming from. But Rex could not make out what it was.

"What's going on?" he called as a few ran past him.

The woman running past was crying and did not stop to explain. The others ignored him completely. As he got to the end of the street, he could see the extent of the anarchy. The series of shops on either side of the road all had their glass windows smashed. Everywhere he looked people were looting. A few people were fighting in the street, and the sound of gunshots echoed from somewhere close by.

"Bloody madness!" he said to himself.

Rex decided that instead of pressing on to the supermarket, he would get just the necessities at the convenience store. As he wheeled past a women's clothing store, he saw a staff member empty the till of cash and run out the door. More people were running up and down the street with several bumping into him.

"Hey, watch it!"

"Shut it, old man!" one called back after knocking into him.

He continued as best he could through the people around him until he felt someone grab his wheelchair.

"Gimme that!" a gruff voice commanded from behind him.

Rex spun around as a young man punched him in the head and tipped him out onto the pavement. Pain rippled through him as he scraped his elbows and hands on the concrete.

"You piece of…" Rex hollered as he turned to see the man who took his chair run with it across the road. He had already loaded it up like his personal shopping trolley with obviously looted items. The offender narrowly missed a car as it sped down the road. Upon, reaching the curb, the earth shook again and he slipped over.

Rex looked on as if in slow motion as a car smashed into the man and his wheelchair. The impact left him lying face down on the road with a growing pool of blood oozing out from a wound on his head. The driver of the car quickly shifted into reverse and sped away out of sight. The people around Rex toppled over as the earth shook and a couple landed on him.

"Hey!"

"Watch it!"

Cries of fear filled the air as panicked people tried to scramble away. The earthquake caused further damage to the battered buildings, sending bricks crashing to the ground. Abruptly the shaking stopped, and those that fell on Rex left him unaided. He looked over to his wheelchair to see it bent and misshapen.

"Just great!" he spat.

"Excuse me?" he called to those rushing past him on the ground.

Nobody looked his way.

Rex's calls for help became more desperate as the crowd thinned out. But no-one stopped to help him.

He finally realised that he would have to make his own way and began to drag himself along the footpath. He had to this once or twice in his life before, but it was always just a short distance back to his chair. Everything all of a sudden seemed to be further away.

A couple of gunshots rang out from further down the road. It seemed that people had already begun to kill each other over the remaining goods. Rex persisted and eventually made it a short distance down the road to a convenience store. He was already puffing and did not want to think about the trip home.

"Just one bit at a time," he told himself.

A few people stepped over him as he made his way into the well-looted store. He had been to this store numerous times before, but none from his current perspective. The owners were always very accommodating and would help him with his shopping if he needed it. The small shop had several aisles stocked with food and other necessities. Rex shuffled along the floor and was immediately relieved that the polished floors were easier to move over that the footpath outside. He hoped that some food was within reach. He cursed not having full cupboards at home.

"Stupid!"

He could hear other people elsewhere in the store, grabbing items and making a mess in the process. Rex made his way down the first aisle.

"OK, this is our store now! Drop everything and get out!" a voice shouted from the doorway.

Rex heard a few men enter the shop.

"Hurry up!" one of them shouted impatiently.

The people at the back of the store begrudgingly left their trolley and cautiously made their way towards the door. Rex tried to move along a short distance silently.

"Hey! Do you think I'm stupid? Empty your coat!"

"Please, just a few cans?"

Rex heard the thud of a baseball bat and cries of pain and could picture what was happening. Several more impacts silenced the cries completely.

"No-one steals from me!"

Rex heard one of them declare as he caught his breath.

The men strolled into the store, assessing what was now theirs. Rex's heart started to beat faster.

"Hey!"

Rex heard the clattering of several items drop and the men sprinted towards the back of the store. Thankfully, they did not notice Rex on the floor as they sped past.

"Get him!"

"No please! I just…"

Rex heard whoever was at the back of the store fighting. After some frantic cries, some dull-sounding impacts made a splashing sound. After that, just the two men could be heard.

"Oh! Damn! Look at the mess you made!"

"Shut up! He deserved it."

Rex gulped and tried to drag himself back towards the door. He could hear the thugs making their way around the store. It would only be a matter of time before they found him. He scuffled around the end of the aisle and made his way passed the counter.

"Hey you! don't move!"

Rex froze, more out of fear than obedience.

He heard them rush to his position, and one of them kicked him over on to his back. Rex drew up his hands over his face. He saw one of them raise the blood-stained bat in his hands.

"Hold it!" the other called.

"What?"

"Don't kill him."

"Why not?"

"Damn, what's wrong with you man. Check his weedy little legs out. This guy is a cripple. Don't ever hit a cripple."

"But he's stealing from our shop man!"

Rex spoke up. "I have taken nothing, just let me go."

"See?"

"They all say that."

"True. Check him."

Rex got roughly pat down to check he had not stowed any food in his pockets. His wallet was pulled out, emptied then dropped back onto him.

"Consider this payment for entry."

"Fine," Rex agreed weakly.

"You're savage man."

"What? These are the times we're in."

"I guess."

One of them grabbed him by his legs and dragged him back outside to the footpath.

"Don't come back, you hear?"

Rex nodded and began the slow crawl home.

• • •

Moments earlier in Brakenside, Bishop Kephas and Father Andrews both stopped pulling weeds as they felt the word of God enter them.

"Come quickly!" Father Andrews called to their helpers.

The Bishop nodded, and they huddled together in the middle of the field.

"What the hell is going on?" Mike protested, just as the earth began to shake.

They hunkered down amongst the vegetables as Bishop Kephas prayed over them.

"Oh loving God, eternal Father protect and guide us in this time of trial. May our actions bring others closer to you…"

The Bishop fell to his knee as the ground under him shuddered. They kept praying until a few minutes after the shaking stopped.

"It's beginning," Father Andrews told the Bishop.

"I agree, we have to return to the city. The people there will need us," they both stood and beckoned to the others to follow them back to the vehicles. On the walk back, Mike veered towards his car.

"Mike, you'll want to stick with us during these times. We can explain on the way back," Father Andrews advised.

"They said I just had to help on the farm. They didn't say I had to listen to you all," Mike replied.

As they tried to convince Mike to stay, Lucy pointed up into the sky.

"Look!" She said in wonder.

They turned towards where she was pointing. It was the sun. Four dark spots had formed on it evenly spread out near its edges. They slowly grew in size, and their shape changed to form two flat sides. As they looked on, they converged towards the centre until only a cross shape remained. The earth was a little darker, as a result, like on a cloudy day. People all around the earth looked skywards and observed the same. In a few short minutes, the sun had become a cross for all to see. Father Andrews and Kephas both made the sign of the cross as they looked on in awe. They remembered what Zack had told them of his vision, the cross in the sky, and what was to come next.

"This is some apocalypse type thing for sure," Donny declared.

"Yes, yes it is." Father Andrews confirmed.

"It's exactly that." Bishop Kephas spoke as he turned his gaze to Mike.

"Well maybe I'll follow you just a little while," he admitted, trying not to show how unsettled he was.

Father Andrews, Bishop Kephas, Lucy and Donny hopped into Lucy's car drove down the long driveway and headed back towards town. Mike followed closely behind in his car with Deon.

"Where should we go?" Lucy asked, obviously scared, but trying hard to keep it together.

"Let's head to the Cathedral," Father Andrews directed.

Bishop Kephas nodded.

"Let's take it nice and slowly Lucy. I don't think it'll be the simple drive across town as it was this morning," he advised.

"Are we all going to die?" Donny asked with a stone-cold expression

"Yes, but hopefully not today..." Bishop Kephas said with a smile.

"... already we've been more blessed than many. That earthquake has probably devastated much of Brakenside."

"I'm gonna stick close to you guys," Donny added.

"Put your faith in the Lord God, and you will have the best ally of all."

"One more thing, did anyone else hear something earlier?" I mean like something unusual?"

"Repent," Lucy spoke as she kept her eyes forward.

"That was a Word from God himself..." Father Andrews explained. "...we only have to turn our hearts towards him and seek forgiveness for our sins, and we will be saved."

"It is a huge privilege and an honour to receive such a gift. You must try to understand as difficult as it will be. God loves you. More than you can fathom."

"You're saying that as if you know things will become harder?"

"They will."

Donny gulped.

· · ·

As Jenson walked back to his office, he heard the word of God calling him back. For a moment, he thought about changing his life's direction. But that moment passed all too quickly. The office threw him to the ground as the quake unleashed its great wrath. Jenson let loose a slew of abusive language as he hit the ground. He tried to regain his footing throughout, but it was not until it was over that he could make headway down the corridor. He checked his cell phone, but there was no signal. He opened a drawer and pulled out a satellite phone, he dialled a number by memory and held it to his ear and listened to the recorded looping message.

"All cells proceed as planned. All cells proceed as planned..."

After several hallways and an elevator trip to below ground level, he arrived at Operations. He approached the large security door, punched some numbers into the keypad then pressed the button next to it. A faint buzz was heard from inside. A moment later a face appeared at the tiny window in the door. After seeing Jenson's face, a small buzz was heard then the door opened.

"Report!" he called as he stomped inside.

The large room contained three people and a vast array of computers and monitors on one side. On the other, there was a kitchen, shower and several bunk beds. A middle-aged man in attire that looked like he had been wearing it all week quickly stood up.

"Backup power is so far unaffected. We've got massive outages in our network. Some have been restored already. Secondary communication channels are online."

"Good. Initiate Project Groundswell now."

"As another drill?"

"For real dammit. This is what we've been preparing for," Jenson slapped his hand down on the desk.

"Let's go! Timing is crucial."

"I'll prime the lines," the other man responded. He looked the most worn of the three.

"I'm ready on my end," a tired-looking young lady added.

They all watched the main monitor as a large map was displayed. Red lights were scattered all over it, with several gauges and numbers on the secondary screens.

"Armed?"

"One second. I'm double-checking a couple. OK, yes, all armed."

The three paused for a moment and looked to Jenson.

"Do it."

The three operators began typing furiously; executing the programs they had been working hard on for so long.

A moment passed, and they stopped and watched the screen with Jenson. Suddenly a huge number of lights turned green in the top quadrant. A split second later the other three quadrants followed. A number of red lights remained lit. After a brief effort at the keyboards again they did not change.

"Number 3381 is a no go."

"Same with the mine."

"Mine also."

"What's our effective percentage? Is that real-time?"

"Yes, that's live data. We're at 57.3%."

"That's well within our predictions. Better actually."

They tried to read how Jenson would react. He said nothing for a moment as he read the figures on the secondary monitors. He stood back, and a smile grew over his face.

"Great work team. I'm happy with this result. You should be proud."

"Yesss!" the tired man exclaimed as he spun around in his chair.

The other two exchanged high fives. There was a huge amount of relief on their faces.

Jenson shook each of their hands offering his congratulations.

"OK, export the results to my laptop then we can wrap this up."

One of the men opened a box from under the desk and plugged in a laptop. The other two began to disconnect a series of servers on the far wall. Progressively the auxiliary monitors blacked out.

"Come on!" Jenson hurried the man loading the laptop with files.

"Its nearly there," he promised.

He quickly double-checked the contents of a few folders then gave the nod.

"It's done."

Jenson took the laptop and confirmed he had what he needed.

"Great, thank you."

The other two began disconnecting the hard drives from the servers, putting them in a large plastic tub. Jenson opened a cupboard and pulled on a white plastic suit. One like you would expect to see in a cleanroom or hazardous materials lab. In a few moments, he had pulled it on. He returned to the cupboard and grabbed a headset. He stopped at the door and checked his watch.

"We'll be lifting off in exactly fourteen minutes."

"We're on it," one assured him as they opened the security door for him.

Jenson walked out with the laptop as the door was shut behind him. Jenson made his way down the long corridor.

The remaining three quickly collected the hard drives and pushed the bin to a corner of the room. The two men lifted the bin and tipped it into a steel drum. The three went to the cupboard and pulled on their plastic suits and grabbed their headsets. After they were dressed, they returned to the steel drum. In the ceiling above them was an air vent. A switch next to it was pressed, and the whir of an extractor fan could be heard.

"Would you like to do the honours?"

"Sure."

The woman opened a drawer and pulled out a box of matches. She lit one and used it to set the box alight. She tossed it into the drum. A whoosh of accelerant burst the contents into flames. The three watched the evidence of what they had done burn for a moment.

"Let's go."

They turned and attempted to open the door. But it did not move. Several more attempts yielded the same result. The keypad was unresponsive.

"Hurry, open it up!"

They pulled on the door handle with all of their strength. They checked every alternative. There was none. The woman began to cough as the room slowly began to fill with smoke.

"The fire!"

They ran back to the drum and looked up into the air vent, which should have been drawing the smoke outside. It did not. They tried the switch again and again. More spluttered coughing broke out amongst them.

"We gotta put it out!"

"Yeah, on it."

After a few panicked moments, they managed to smother the fire and eventually it went out. The woman replayed the numerous times they had practised this procedure without a hitch. One of the men was banging on the door. He yelled for help at the top of his lungs.

"Help the door is stuck! Let us out!"

The other man slumped to a sitting position on the ground.

"It's not stuck…" he began.

"What do you mean?" The yelling man stopped and faced him.

"Do you really think on today of all days, the door just happens to get stuck? No. They have finished with us. They are just tying up loose ends."

The woman tried to gulp down the lump in her throat. She did not want to believe him. She took a turn, yelling and banging on the door. Now both men sat on the ground beneath the smoke coughing. She gave up yelling and peered as best she could out the small window in the door down the hallway. Just at the very edge of what she could see was a small white object. It was the sleeve of a plastic suit that Jenson was wearing moments before.

"Jenson's left his suit in the hallway. You're right. We're not getting out of here."

The three coughed without speaking for a moment trying to understand their new predicament. They realised the new passports; the plane waiting for them at the private airport, the offshore bank accounts, was all a lie.

One man got up and kicked over a table.

"Calm down, it's no use."

"I'm not dying in here. Help me out here."

He bent the metal table leg back and forth several times until it broke off at the join.

"Let's crack that window," he said, pointing to the security door.

"We could rig up some coolant fans and extract the smoke. We have enough food here to work out a way out."

The woman's face lit up at the idea.

"That might just work."

Within moments they were working together again.

Down the corridor in a storage room, Jenson was watching their progress on a monitor. He had regretted taking his plastic suit off as early as he did. But it was extremely uncomfortable. The ruse had been working so well up until this point.

Jenson had always waited for them to open the door for him, leading them to believe that he could not have opened or locked the door any time he wished to. After another moment of viewing, he decided he had seen enough. However unlikely their plan of escape was, he needed to be sure. The risk of the three sharing what they knew was too great. He reached up to the handle near the ceiling and rotated it ninety degrees. There was a slight hiss as the pipe it was attached to vented gas into the room down the hall.

Inside the room, the three paused their efforts as they heard fans kick in above their heads.

"The fans are working again!" The woman exclaimed in delight.

They stopped and hugged each other, relieved that it was all just a big misunderstanding. They could feel the air moving in, and the smoke began to dissipate.

"The door's still stuck," one man said puzzled.

"It'll be OK, they..." the woman began, suddenly a bit dizzy and very tired.

"Take it easy, that smoke you inhaled before is probably... you know... its..."

The three collapsed against the back of the door together.

"I'm sure they'll have the door..."

A moment later, they had all lost consciousness and died shortly after that. Jenson disconnected the hard drive of the computer he was using and placed it in his laptop bag. He walked out into the hallway, sending a message with his satellite phone as he did so.

"Project Groundswell is underway as planned."

Another satellite phone beeped on the far side of the country as it received Jenson's message. His was lost amongst the hundreds of other messages just like it. The owner pulled it out and scrolled through the numerous projects declaring they were underway. Even more, flooded in as he did so. He smiled. His decades of planning and the investment of vast resources was finally beginning to pay off.

. . .

Sister Lee had remained kneeling for the past hour in desperate prayer. She eventually stood and decided she should get back, lest the others worry about her. As she walked her way down the hill, she looked off to the city far in the distance. Normally she could see a blur of lights and the motorway leading off to her right. Now, she had to squint to make out just a few scattered lights across the whole horizon. She felt like she would need every prayer she could muster for what lay ahead.

. . .

Graham looked around at the devastation around him. Cars were smashed into each other in all directions. Broken glass and debris littered the streets. People were running in all directions. All of the bright advertising signs had all gone black. A mixture of sirens, alarms and shouting saturated the air.

For once, people did not have all the information they could possibly desire at their fingertips. That alone frightened many. Feeble emergency procedures told people to go to the designated meeting point and await the all-clear. But that announcement never came.

"C'mon, Mindy's house is this way," Beth pointed.
Graham climbed down off the roof of the car.
"Shouldn't we go get Zack first?"
"We told him we'd meet him there. If I were him, I'd head to Mindy's

house. Anyway, of all the people in this city, he's probably the most equipped to deal with all this madness. Mindy will need our help more."

"Yeah, OK. Let's get to Mindy's, and hopefully, Zack will already be there."

. . .

Zack hurried across the floor following Stanley.

"Here take this," Stanley shoved an empty box into his hands.

"What for?"

"You'll see, follow me."

They made it to the far side of the floor, and Stanley opened up the kitchen cupboards. He swept their contents into the box he was carrying then swapped his box for Zacks. Next, he opened the refrigerator and did the same. Zack thought he understood until on the way across the floor, they ducked into an empty office.

"Close the door."

Stanley sat on the floor behind the desk. Zack watched for a moment as Stanley rummaged through the box from the freezer then open up a small lunch box. He proceeded to shove its contents into his mouth as quick as he could. Stanley was not a small man, and it looked like he had just fallen headfirst off the diet wagon.

"Dig in," he uttered in-between mouthfuls.

"What are you doing? Surely we need to share this out with everyone?" Zack demanded.

Stanley paused his feast for a moment and looked at Zack very seriously.

"Zack. Listen to me carefully. If you don't do exactly what I tell you, you'll die here."

"Oh really?!"

"Yes really. Do you know how many people in this building alone?

Hundreds! More in the building next to us, and many more throughout the city. You saw the street down there. It's completely lost. It'll take weeks or months to get to all the people probably trapped all over the damn place. Meanwhile, we're going to starve to death." Stanley took a swig from a bottle of drink. Zack looked on as he lost respect for the man.

"I for one, am not going to starve. You're a smart guy. Let's eat what we can of this; then we'll hit the other kitchens before people realise it's important."

"Stanley…"

Zack's retort was cut short by a frantic screaming. Zack turned to see the crowd near the stairs sprinting off wildly in all directions. Tripping over debris and scrambling away as best they could. Then his eyes stopped. His brain began to process what he saw. A large Mortkin was glutting itself in slaughter. It stood taller than the humans around it, and its long claws sliced deep gashes out of all those near it. Blood splashed onto the ceiling and surrounding remains of broken office furniture.

Zack's mind fought itself for a brief moment as he saw the terror on people's faces. They could see the demon too. Zack found himself beginning to run towards it. He coiled his rosary beads in his right hand. This was not like the ghostly visages that faded at his approach and caused him to doubt his sanity. It continued to lunge at the closest victims and impale whoever it could reach. The demon had a snarl that twisted almost into a grin, like it was enjoying itself. He spoke holy scripture aloud as he closed the distance.

Isaiah 12
² Surely God is my salvation;
I will trust and not be afraid.
The LORD, the LORD himself, is my strength and my defense;
he has become my salvation."

Zack's heart kicked into gear as he reached a full sprint between the fallen desks and escaping people. All of Zack's combat experience from his vision and his subsequent martial training was begging to be unleashed. A righteous fury rose up in him like an unstoppable eruption. The demon pulled his claws out from a dying person near its feet and shifted its gaze as Zack got closer.

Zack shouted the Rite of Banishment as he charged at the evil creature. "In nomine domini, ad quos eieci te ad inferum!"

The demon shuddered in disgust at the holy words. It was all the opening Zack needed. He jumped on to a desk then leapt forward with a rapid right jab. His punch connected with the Mortkin's head and it staggered backwards. Zack dropped down and fired a flurry of punches into its midsection and upper left thigh. Claws burst forth in retaliation as it buckled. A quick dodge and fend with a forearm limited their impact. Zack launched upwards with an uppercut that threw the demon off its feet and into the table behind it. Zack jumped onto it, raining down punches into its face. With a flick of his wrist, he loosened his rosary beads and brought them down around its neck. Zack twisted and ripped the demon's head from its body, throwing it on to the floor.

Zack drew a breath as he quickly scanned the floor for more foes. He saw only shocked people staring back at him in disbelief. A moment later, he checked on the closest victim who had already died. The surrounded people began to gather as screams rung out from the floor above them. Zack bolted towards the stairwell into the jam of people trying to get in.

"Move!" Zack yelled.

Upon seeing the demon-blood splattered warrior, they moved aside as quickly as they could. Inside the stairwell, people were packed in as tight as possible. Zack wriggled as best he could a few places closer to the handrail on the edge of the stairs. As he did so, a fresh surge of people from the above floor forced their way onto the stairs.

"I can kill it!" Zack cried as he struggled to move.

The man next to Zack stared him directly in the eyes and at once believed him. After all, he was the only one trying to go up the stairs.

"Help him, push him up" he called. Zack stood on the handrail of stairs and managed to push himself up. They lifted him upon their shoulders and Zack scuttled over people up onto the next level. Numerous people shrieked with complaint, which Zack ignored. Reaching the door, he slipped off the back of the last people in the crowd and fell to the ground. He jumped to his feet and searched for his foe. A few steps away, another large Mortkin had pinned an older lady to a desk. She was screaming with all the capacity she could muster.

Zack ran at the demon who seemed to be unaware of his assault until it was too late. Zack pounced on its back and repeatedly punched it in the back of the head with a holy beaded fist. It crumpled to his attack as he drove it into the floor.

"Are there any others?" Zack called to the floor of stunned onlookers who gave no actionable response.

"Demons! Are there more of them?"

Zack rushed to a man cowering by the queue to the stairs. He managed to shake his head but did not reply.

Zack returned to the stairwell. The people at the entrance made way for him and helped squeeze him in. Using the same strategy as before, he pushed himself up using the handrail and climbed over the people until he made it to the next floor. Zack scanned the floor but did not find any demons. After more troubles in the stairwell he did the same on the next two floors. By now it was clear to Zack that none of these people had seen any demons. They were alarmed at the recent earthquake, but they did not have the same terror in their eyes.

As he tried to return to try the stairwell to try the next floor up a large man held him back.

"You can wait in line like everybody else pal."

Zack saw he was ready to fight if needed and stood back a step.

"I need to get up there to help the people."

"It's not happening. Try it, and you'll regret it." The man slightly raised a large fist with the two men next to him, standing ready. Zack recalled he might have kicked one as he had struggled up to this floor. Zack looked at them for a moment trying to decide whether it would be worth going through them.

As he was thinking, the people in the stairwell began to move slowly. It was not free-flowing, but it was better than the complete standstill it had previously been. In the lobby, moments earlier people had pushed their way into the street and there now was enough room to descend the stairs.

"Call me if you see demons," Zack instructed as he retreated to do a more thorough search of the floor he was on. He did not bother explaining what a demon was and doubted whether this man would listen anyway. The large man spat back some insult which Zack ignored.

Zack decided if there were no more immediate threats, he should probably try to stop bleeding. He had gained a long cut across his right forearm, which needed attention. The rest of his injuries were only minor scratches and bruises. Zack began to pray as he walked away from the crowd at the stairs.

"Thank you, Lord God in heaven for helping me defeat such evil. Thank you for keeping me alive; please guide my actions that I can do your will. Please help me save all the people that I possibly can. Amen."

Zack found an abandoned jersey left on a desk and grabbed it. He then found the stationery cupboard nearby. He sat down and cut the jersey into strips with a newly found pair of scissors. With one of these strips, he wiped his wound as clean as best he could. Then with another, he wrapped it tightly. Returning to the stationery cupboard, he taped up his entire forearm. Zack kept a hold of the scissors and tape; he felt sure they would come in handy again. He stuffed the best of the leftover strips into his pockets.

A faint scream rang out from the direction of the stairwell. Zack ran over but did not find any demons. Or any people for that matter. He peered down the stairs and saw a few flights down people were making their way down. He decided to go up instead and check the remaining floors.

It took Zack the rest of the afternoon to check the remaining floors, and now he was very tired and hungry. He did not find the cause of the scream he had heard earlier. In his travels, he had collected a backpack which he filled with a pair of scissors, tape, cloth and some food he found in one of the kitchens.

Zack noticed it was not as bright as it should be, even with all of the office lighting not functional. He carefully made his way to the edge of the floor he was on and peered up into the sky. His eyes soaked in the Sun that now resembled a bright burning cross in the sky. Zack was a little puzzled that it did not look the one in his vision. He added it to the mental list he was keeping for things he would ask God about when he got to Heaven.

Zack made his way down the floors, checking them for demons or anyone that needed his help, finding neither, he eventually made it to the ground floor lobby. On the last flight of stairs, he heard a loud commotion. He pushed open the door to find it was packed with people. All were scared and confused; some were angry and were shouting their complaints to all nearby. A few were trying to calm the crowd down with no success.

Zack squeezed his way out into the street and found it was teeming with people. His shoes crunched the broken glass that covered the road. He looked around and saw the power was out as far as he could see. All the buildings nearby had been damaged in the earthquake to some extent. Sirens were blaring from every direction but no medical, fire or police services were anywhere to be seen. Zack knew that with an event like this, they would be stretched far too thin. The people around him were demanding help like they were the only ones in need.

Zack thought of his friends and wondered where they were in all this anarchy. Zack decided he would try and head towards Mindy's house. He could remember the address, but he had no map now that his cell phone was out of service. He thought for a moment then decided to check in reception for an old fashioned paper map. He made his way through the crowds and slid over the counter at reception.

"Zack!"

Zack turned to see Stanley and the receptionist who he had met on the way in, Beverly. They were both sitting on the ground. She looked like she was not handling the situation well. Zack was surprised to see Stanley was giving her some food, who now had a black eye. Zack wondered if someone else disagreed with Stanley's food strategy.

"Hi Stanley," he said as he searched the drawers around him for a map.

"Zack, don't leave me again like that. I've been worried sick. You're filthy! Are you OK?"

"Yeah I'm fine."

"What are you looking for?"

"A map, I'm leaving. You should too Stanley."

"Where are you going?"

"To find my friends."

"Where are they?"

"Sundale. Do you know how to get there from here?"

"Um, I've heard of it, you could… no, not exactly."

"I live in the adjacent suburb…" Beverly spoke up. "… take me with you both. I just want to get out of here," she said with desperation.

Zack and Stanley looked at each other.

Stanley nodded and looked at Zack.

"OK, let's go."

Chapter 4:

In my day

Many years ago, somewhere in Eastern Europe, there was a remote village called Ulzbruk. A large mountain range with snow-capped peaks dominated the horizon to the north. Small hills gradually became plains towards the south. The land to the south of the village was used for farming. The residents raised sheep, cattle and goats across the hill country and used the plains for corn, wheat and maize. The closest main highway was a significant distance to the west, which resulted in few visitors. Despite the incessant cold wind from the north, the majority of the small population had lived there for generations. They transported much of their produce to a small city to the west called Huthguart several times a year.

A drunken tourist had climbed into the back of a transport truck in the early hours of the night and had fallen asleep. By mid-morning, a large pothole in the road jolted him enough to wake him.

"Jus' a little long-er," he slurred, holding his aching head in his hands.

Peter was in his early twenties and was seriously regretting drinking as much as he had the night before. He heard the road rumbling past underneath him and decided that he may as well rest until the vehicle came to a stop. He drifted back into an alcohol influenced sleep and awoke a few hours later. The truck was still driving tirelessly on in a direction Peter did not know.

"Derrick? Becca? Camilla! Where are you guys?" he called, rubbing his eyes as he looked around.

He saw the near-empty inside of a large curtain-sider transport. He was in the rear trailer pulled by a large diesel cab. His only companions were a few large wooden crates. Peter was sure that his friends were hiding somewhere closeby.

"Hey! C'mon!"

But as the moments past, he began to realise that he was alone.

"Hey? Hello?"

He strained his hearing for a moment to hear nothing but the rumble of the road.

Peter's mouth was incredibly dry, and he looked around for a drink. A single beer bottle lay rolling to and fro between his feet. It had spilt onto the floor around him and soaked into his jeans.

He searched his pockets only to find his wallet and the keys to their rental car.

"Not again!" He spat.

He pulled himself into a sitting position, resting his back on the rear wall of the trailer. As he did so, he vomited onto the floor next to him. The reek of partially digested fried food filled the air. After wiping his mouth on his sleeve, he drank the last drops of beer left in the bottle at his feet.

"Just great."

He stood and wobbled around the trailer, looking for anything useful.

"Hey! Stop! I'm back here!" He yelled.

The driver was blissfully unaware of the commotion. He had his music playing loud, and the windows wound up. Peter began to open the curtain but decided falling out onto the road was not a good plan. After some more shouting and finding nothing of use, Peter sat down again.

"Surely, we must be nearly due to stop soon?" he wondered.

Unfortunately, the truck did not stop until a few hours later. By then Peter had needed to relieve himself which he did in the corner of the trailer. A loud hiss from the truck's brakes kicked off another round of shouting from Peter. Shortly after that he heard the engine stop and someone approach.

"What the hell are you doing in there?!" he heard an angry voice demand as the curtain opened. The bright day-light flooded in, and Peter had to squint his eyes.

"Thanks, sorry, you know, a good night was all," he explained.

"Hey?! What have you done back here? It stinks."

Peter's eyes saw an older man staring at him, fuming with anger.

"You're going to pay for every bit of damage!"

Peter returned a cheeky smile, which quickly dissolved as he realised the man was carrying a tire iron in his hands.

"Woah. Sorry! I meant no harm," Peter fumbled for his wallet and handed over some foreign currency. He did not calculate in his mind what it would be in his native currency. But the demeanour of the man in front of him changed very quickly.

"It's alright. You can ride up front if you want for the rest of the way," the man said, smiling as he pocketed the significant amount of cash.

"Huh, rest of the way?"

Peter looked around to find himself at a small truck stop in the middle of nowhere. A single diesel pump and a toilet were the only features. Light brown, grassy fields surrounded them in all directions. Tall mountains in the distance rose up to meet the clouds. A chilling wind seemed to go right through him. He did not recognise any landmarks.

"Where the heck are we?"

"Nowhere"

"huh? Where?"

"Nowhere," the man looked at him blankly.

"Take me back to Huthguart."

"Not a chance."

"Please, I'll pay you."

The man paused for a moment as he watched Peter flick through the notes in his wallet. They were all low denominations.

"No, you can wait here, and try and hitch a ride, which won't arrive. Or you can look for transport when we get there."

"Where?"

"Ulzbruk"

"Where?"

"Nowhere" the man replied smugly.

Peter swore beneath his breath.

"Have you got a phone?"

"Nope."

Peter pointed to the toilet.

"Can I make a quick stop?"

"Sure, I'm filling up, you've got a few minutes."

An hour later they had arrived in Ulzbruk. Peter really hoped that the tiny town they were stopping in was just a pit stop on the way to a proper town.

"Get out," the driver pointed as soon as they came to a stop on the side of the road outside a petrol station.

"Yeah, OK, thanks, sorry," Peter mumbled as he climbed down.

The truck roared off as soon as Peter stepped foot on the ground. It was autumn, but it already felt like winter here. Peter quickly decided he did not want to stay any longer than he had too.

Walking into the petrol station, he saw a large lady behind the counter eyeing him closely.

"Welcome you," she said in a very unwelcoming manner.

"Hi, can I use your phone?"

"Custom phone."

Peter quickly discovered English was not her preferred language.

"Yeah, can I use your phone, please? I need to make a call."

"Custom-er phone," she said, pointing to the items on the shelves around her.

"Ah right, yes, I buy."

Peter grabbed a can of drink, chips and some gum and placed them on the counter.

"Twenty."

"Twenty?"

"Twenty it is," Peter felt sure he was paying more than he should have but did not want to fight about it.

"Where is your phone?"

The lady pulled a phone from behind the till and placed it on the counter for him. She also pulled out a small egg timer which she tipped over.

"Short call."

"OK yes,"

Peter dialled the number of the hotel he and his friends were staying at.

"Hi, I want to talk to Derrick in room three."

An angry lady speaking only in a foreign language spoke for a moment then hung up.

Peter dialled again quickly before the lady could take the phone back from him. This time he dialled again with what he hoped was the correct last digit.

A friendly voice answered.

"Hi, I want to talk to Derrick in room three please."

"Yes, Derrick sir, very good."

The line made a few clicks, and then a familiar voice answered.

"Peter, you crazy bastard, we've been worried sick!" Derrick spat.

"Sorry, yeah, can you come get me?"

"Where are you?"

"Some tiny village in the middle of nowhere."

"Huh?"

"I may have fallen asleep, and ended up here. Ulzbrook I think it's called."

"Never heard of it."

"Me either, just come quick. I'm at the petrol station."

"Yeah sure. We lost the key to the rental, so once we've got that sorted, we'll be right out."

"Derrick, you'd lose your head if it wasn't stuck to your body."

"Yeah, you too."

The line went dead, as the lady behind the counter had unplugged it from the wall.

"Time gone, more money, more call."

"You gotta be kidding?"

"You make two calls. More money, more call."

Peter had had quite enough of this lady. He took the items he paid for and stomped towards the door. Just as he was about to leave, he tipped over a display rack onto the floor.

"Bill me!" He spat with an offensive hand gesture to match his sentiment. The lady began screaming at him as he ran off.

Once Peter had made it a short distance down the road, he ate and drank his high-priced convenience items.

"Uh… it'll take them ages to get here," he whined to himself.

Walking down the main street, he did not find much that was of interest to him. Of the few shops that lined the narrow road, many it seemed had already closed for the day. Up ahead, there were cars and a collection of trucks parked on either side of the road. Then Peter saw a sign that made him smile. It translated to 'Tavern' and was one of the few words Peter had learnt on his overseas experience. He walked in to find it empty apart from the bartender and an older man mopping the floors.

Peter approached the bar and sat on a stool and did his best to order a beer. In the end, after pointing and a few hand gestures, his drink arrived. He decided to order more drinks to pass the time. Soon enough, he was very drunk - again.

It seemed like only moments later, and people began to file in after finishing up their day's work. The place was a cacophony of foreign tongues greeting each other and discussing the day. Peter got a few cold stares from the locals, but nothing that a few more beers could not wash from his mind.

A stray elbow knocked Peter as a local sat down next to him.

"Hey, watch it!" Peter yelled back.

The large bearded man muttered something in the local language that Peter did not understand.

"Clumsy oaf," Peter said angrily as he pushed the man's drink into his lap.

Furious, the man stood up and shouted a slew of foreign words at Peter.

"You sure look stupid, babbling like that," Peter scoffed.

"You, ground dirt!" the man threw his best English insult.

Peter threw a right hook which connected with his jaw. He began to topple, and Peter followed up with a few more wild punches. The man landed just a single punch on Peter before he crumpled to the ground. Peter began to draw a victorious breath as he felt a tap on the shoulder. He turned into a punch smashing into his face from the patron that was sitting behind him. Reeling, Peter took a step back and blocked what he could of the incoming blows. A big right hook missed its mark, and Peter stepped in with a swift uppercut. The man was launched backwards, and his head hit on the bar. By this stage, the tavern was in an uproar as a mob rushed over to deal with the violent tourist.

Peter grabbed a bottle from the bar and swung it around into the nearest face. A lady who was shouting at him received a deep gash in her forehead and tumbled back in pain. A pair of large men grabbed an arm each as another local rained punches into Peter's stomach. Peter couldn't break their grip and had the wind knocked out of him. Refusing to yield, he lifted both his legs and kicked his attacker over the table behind him. The two men struggled to keep a hold of Peter as he squirmed. Another local stepped up and landed a few punches into Peter's face and chest. Peter spat out a bloodied tooth and swore at the top of his lungs. He lifted his legs and swung his feet back into the knee of one of the men holding him. He buckled over, holding his knee, releasing his grip in the process.

Peter swung his newly freed arm into the face of the other man. Before another strike could find its mark, he released Peter's other hand and blocked the incoming blow. Peter was knocked back from a kick from another person entering the fray. Peter tumbled over onto the ground. Kicking fallen stools at his pursuers, he gained enough time to regain his footing. As he stood, he lifted a chair above his head.

"I'll take you all on!" He challenged.

The locals called back insults as two of them drew knives.

Peter gulped.

An impact to the back of his head dropped Peter to the floor. He went limp, and his eyes rolled back in his head momentarily.

"It's over," a man called as he placed a large boot onto Peter's chest. Some discussion ensued none of which Peter understood. He remained lying on the ground struggling to stay conscious. His body decided now was a good time to vomit, which he launched on to the floor beside him. It seemed clear that there was no fight left in him and the others in the tavern began to reassemble the place.

"A few more minutes and you'd be dead," a voice from above Peter declared.

Peter just groaned as he looked up at the old man with a broom in his hand.

"You're paying for damages," he said as he bent over and pulled Peter's wallet from his pocket. Extracting all the notes, he handed them over to the bartender in two piles. Who after a brief count, nodded and poured a drink for everyone in the tavern excluding Peter. The old man returned and held the broom up to Peter's face.

"Are you going to cause any more trouble?"

Peter shook his throbbing head.

"That's the first smart move I've seen you make," Peter began to realise that this man knew both English and the local language very well.

"D, drink for the pain?" Peter held his hand up.

"Not a chance."

Eventually, Peter regained enough of his senses to enable him to slowly mop up his vomit and sweep away the broken glass. The old man watched him carefully, and once the place was restored, they sat in a booth in the corner of the tavern. The old man brought him a jug of water and some paper towels to tend to his injuries. Peter was a mess of pain and drunkenness.

"Who are you?

"I'm Father Dominic Anglesto, call me Dom," the thin, grey-bearded bald man said.

"Huh? You're like a priest or something?"

"That's right."

"Shouldn't you be in a church, not a bar?"

"The answer to that question will take some time. First, what's your name?"

"I'm Peter."

"Hello Peter."

"Hang on, did you hit me in the head before?"

"Yes I did. My apologies."

"Priest's can't go hitting people with broom's ya know."

"I agree, but I thought a sore head would be better than several stab wounds."

Peter paused for a moment. As capable as he thought he was in a fight, he admitted he would have come off badly versus two men with knives.

"Yeah. I guess."

"What brings you to this place Peter?"

"A lot of drink and a few bad decisions."

"Ah, I see." Father Dominic pulled a photo from his pocket and placed it on the table.

"Have you seen this girl?"

Peter looked at the photo; it showed an attractive young woman with a party in the background.

"Her name is Angelique Montague, twenty-six years old, brown hair, about your height. You may have seen her in the drinking establishments before this one? She has gone missing."

"Huh?"

"Do you recognise her?" Dom held up the photo.

"No, sorry, I haven't seen her. But, I thought you said you were a priest?"

"I am."

"Priests don't go looking for missing people. That's what policemen do."

"Please take another look, do you know anyone in the background?"

Peter squinted into the Polaroid and tried to make out some faces.

"Maybe that blonde? It's hard to be sure. Let the cops take care of it."

"How about these?" Dom pulled out a few more photos of young women and showed them to Peter. One by one, he shook his head.

"Surely the police will have someone looking into it?"

"They have very few resources in somewhere as remote as this, and they have found nothing so far."

"Why do you care?"

"I'm from a little town to the west of Huthguart. Angelique was a member of my parish there for many years; I know her parents very well. They have been worried sick about her. She's been gone for almost two weeks now. I'm just trying to help if I can."

"So why are you in this tiny dump?"

"In my travels, I discovered that she's not the only one who's gone missing. From what I could tell, no-one has been reported missing from here. So I thought I'd check it out."

"Oh good. So you've got a car? Can you drop me back to Huth-guart?"

"Sorry no, I caught a ride with a truck driver."

"I did too."

"Peter, I was hoping you could help me find them?"

"Why would I do that?"

"I just thought an able young man such as yourself could spend his energies in a more productive fashion. We show this world and the next what's important to us by what we spend our time on." Dom looked to the vomit stain on the ground as he spoke.

"I didn't ask for a lecture old man," Peter stood up and stormed out.

Father Dominic called after him, but Peter ignored him.

Walking out onto the street, Peter looked up and down the main road to see only three streetlights. It was dark and cold, and Peter wished he was in a nightclub drinking with his friends. He waddled his way down the street, trying to remember where he said he would meet Derrick. He eventually made his way back to the petrol station, which was now closed. He sat down on the forecourt and waited.

In the cold, it did not take long for Peter's patience to run out. He stood up and paced the forecourt for a few loops before walking over to the shop window. Peering through the glass, he thought he saw some foreign alcoholic beverage in one of the fridges.

"That'll d-do nicely."

Peter took a step back and kicked in the bottom panel of the glass door in. Broken glass crunched under his boots as he bent down and reached up to the door handle on the inside of the door. A satisfying click declared the lock was now open. Peter opened the door and walked in. He went straight to the back fridge and opened the bottle he had his eyes on from outside. He opened it and took a big swig. A cool fruity liquid flowed into his mouth.

"Not bad, not..." he slurred.

A brief walk around the shop yielded some other drinks to try. He sat down behind the counter and drank until he fell asleep.

A few hours later, the phone on the counter rang next to him. It startled him from his groggy slumber.

"Dammit! Be quiet."

Peter felt the desk was too far away and waited for the person on the other end to give up. The phone kept ringing. Peter held his hands over his ears and tried to get back to sleep. The phone kept on ringing. Peter begrudgingly stood up and picked up the receiver.

"Stupid Petrols 'r us. What the hell do you want?" He began to crack up at his joke.

The voice on the other end began to talk, but Peter wasn't listening.

"Oh hello, hello, I'm stupid calling person petrol, night time!" Peter spat as he went to hang up the phone. He stopped for a moment as he heard the voice on the other end, call his name with a familiar voice. He held it up to his ear again.

"Who'sss this then?"

"Peter! Can you hear me? Peter! It's Derrick!

"Oh Derry my bud, would you like some petrol?" Peter began laughing again.

"Peter snap out of it, you idiot. Camilla, she's…"

"I think I gave her, keys, jus' ask them," Peter said, hanging up.

He then pulled the phone from the wall and after a few more swigs of his drink fell back to sleep.

In the early hours of the morning, a cold draught coming into the petrol station from the broken glass door woke Peter up. He struggled to remember everything that happened the previous night. He vaguely recalled talking to Derrick and picked up the phone on the desk. He tried to plug the cable back into the phone, but it had been ripped out, socket and all.

"Dammit!"

Peter decided he had stayed here long enough. He stood up and made a slow walk out through the glass door onto the forecourt. A dark starry night twinkled above him. He put his arms around himself as the bitter cold bit gripped him. He then realised he had cut his arm on the broken glass and wiped the blood with his sleeve.

Peter trudged slowly down the road, unsure of where he was going. It seemed everyone in the small town was still asleep or elsewhere. He felt alone. He tried to remember what Derrick said on the phone to him yesterday.

"Hurry up, Derrick."

Peter sat down in the front door of a farm supply shop. He was thankful he now was out of the wind. Before he knew it, he had fallen asleep again. What seemed like moments later, he woke. Looking around, he saw the faint shimmer in the distance of the sun. It had not yet risen, but it wouldn't be too far away. Peter stood and walked back onto the street. A dim glow of brake lights caught his attention. A car was parked by the petrol station that was not there earlier. Peter slowly made his way over. As he got closer, he realised that it was his rental car.

He broke into a run and looked around for his friends. As he got closer the driver's door opened, and Derrick climbed out.

"You stupid drunk idiot!" he screamed.

"Woah?!, Hello to you too," Peter replied, seeing the fury on his friends face.

"We've been looking for you for hours! And Camilla is still missing!"

"Huh? What are you on about?"

"Peter! …" Derrick shouted, holding him by the shoulders and shaking him. "…Camilla has been taken!"

Peter could tell Derrick was not joking around and he tried to focus despite the alcohol still in his system.

"Tell me everything."

"We were at a petrol station somewhere between Huthguart and here. Becca and I were in the shop buying supplies, and Camilla left the car to go to the toilet. When we returned to the car, we waited for her. She never came back! We were so stupid! We…"

Peter could see his friend was wracked with worry.

"Derrick, tell me what happened next."

"Yeah, damn. OK, so we eventually go to check the toilets, and Becca found her handbag in the rubbish bin. At that point, she starts screaming. I run in there thinking she's being attacked. It took me a while to get it out of her. That someone took her. What the hell Peter. Who does that? I'll kill them all, I'll…"

"Derrick."

"Yeah, so we asked the other people at the station. There were probably two or three vehicles that left during that time. We don't know which way they went. Maybe one of them was blue? Police said she needs to be missing for twenty-four hours. Stupid!"

"We will find her." Peter declared. He tried to act as sober as he could.

Becca now emerged from the car and began slapping Peter with bitter fury.

"It's all your fault! Drunk fool!" she hollered.

Peter let her blows rain down on him as her words soaked into him.

"We'd never had been there if we weren't looking for your stupid ass!" she spat glaring at Peter.

"I'm very sorry…" Peter began before another slap hit his face.

"OK, Becca, OK." Derrick pulled her off him and tried to calm her down.

She broke into tears and Derrick held her.

"I know where we can start," Peter began as he made his way over to the driver's door of their car.

"Woah, you're not driving anywhere buddy," Derrick pushed him aside and they all hoped in.

"Where?" Becca asked, hopefully.

"I was talking to a guy last night; he said other girls had gone missing. We need to talk to him. Drive to the tavern," Peter said, pointing.

Becca glared at him.

"I won't take another drink until we find her. I promise," Peter said sincerely.

Becca nodded.

They drove the short distance up the road to the tavern, and they piled out.

Peter went up to the closed door and started thumping on it with his fist.

"Open up!"

He continued to bang on the door for a few minutes with no response.

Derrick joined him and they both banged on the door as loud as they could.

"There mustn't be anyone in," Derrick said, giving up.

Peter stopped too and rattled his brain as to how he could find the priest again.

"I guess we have to wait."

Derrick nodded.

Becca stomped her way back to the car and held down the car horn. It blared loudly in a continuous blast through the air.

"SHUT UP!" a voice screamed from a now open window above the tavern.

Peter recognised him as the bartender from last night.

Becca released the horn.

"Hey! We need to find that priest guy, urgently!" Peter shouted up at him.

"Go! away!" he yelled back.

Becca pressed the horn down once again drowning out Peter's attempt at trying to convince him. The window slammed shut, but after a few minutes of the horn assaulting the bartender's ears, it opened again.

"Shut it off!"

Becca immediately obeyed. Peter's ears welcomed the silence; he was just about to tell Becca to be quiet and was glad he managed to resist just long enough.

They all looked up to the window expectantly.

"The blue house, at the end of the road, first on the left past town..." he pointed as he spoke. "...but you didn't hear that from me."

The window slammed shut as they called out their thanks. They jumped back into their rental car, and after a few minutes driving, they found a solitary wooden house. It had a pale blue tin roof and sat at the end of a long gravel driveway. It was surrounded in grassy fields, with a few cows scattered about. They hopped out and made their way to the front door. Derrick started knocking loudly.

"Hello! Anyone home?"

They began to hear movement inside, and a moment later the old man opened the door wrapped in a light green dressing gown.

"What's going on?" he asked, rubbing his eyes.

"Our friend, she's missing. Just like what you said last night."

Dom looked over to Peter then the others.

"Ah yes, Peter, I'm Father Dominic. Please, call me Dom. And who might you two be?"

"I'm Derrick, and this is Becca, our friend Camilla was taken last night. Please can you help us?"

"The police aren't doing anything!" Becca added.

"Taken? Are you sure?"

"Absolutely"

"We stopped at a gas station; she went to the toilet. We found her bag in the rubbish, but she had disappeared," Derrick explained.

"I see. I'm sorry to hear that. I'm not sure what Peter has told you I can do exactly. But you're welcome to come in, and we can try and figure it out together."

"Thanks sir."

They followed him inside and into the dining room. The old wooden house looked like it had remained as it was for years. The wooden floor was worn and tired. Pale floral wallpaper barely held to the walls. The place smelt faintly of spices. They sat down at a large wooden table, and Dom put the kettle on.

"Coffee anyone?"

"Yes please," they all replied at once.

There was a stack of folders on one end of the table. He opened the top folder and took out a photo and slowly showed to each of them.

"Have you seen Angelique? She went missing about two weeks ago."

They each looked at the photo, but much to Dom's disappointment they each shook their heads.

"Sorry, no. Is that the Huthguart West tavern?" Becca added.

"Yes, it is. Do you recognise anything? Anything at all?" Dom pleaded.

"We've only been in the country for a week, I'm afraid. But I recognise the place."

Dom nodded.

"She was walking home one night, but never reached her destination."

Dom opened up the folders and spread them over the table.

"Woah, how many have gone missing?" Derrick said in alarm.

"Five, that I'm sure of, your friend makes six. But I presume many, many more..." Dom began.

"... I've done some interviews with family and friends of the missing and made my notes as best I can. As far as I can tell, all of these women seem to go missing between one place and the next. But, I don't feel like I have made much progress I'm afraid."

Becca began to show that the hope she was holding on to was starting to fade away.

"We'll surely be able to find something amongst all this," Derrick said as he put an arm around Becca.

The kettle squealed and Dom stood up to make the coffee.

"Please, have a look," he offered.

They each grabbed a folder and flicked through notes, photos, missing person's reports and maps. They studied the documents as Dom made them breakfast, then lunch. They reviewed their stop at the gas station again and again. Dom added a new folder and made notes. He looked up as if he had something important to say.

"Did you know that God loves you so very much! He gave up his only son in sacrifice to pay the price of all sin. So that we can all enter heaven to be with him." he explained.

Peter guessed that's what priests do.

"Oh yeah," was the most vocal response he received from anyone.

"Well, I'm sure we can talk more on that later if you'd like."

"Perhaps another time?" Becca said politely.

Dom nodded with a smile.

It was late afternoon when Becca spoke up.

"Hey, this one talks of a blue truck being in the area. Wasn't there one at the gas station we were at?"

"Yeah, so? 'Blue truck' isn't very descriptive. It could be nothing. What else?" Derrick leaned over Becca's shoulder.

"Was that driven by the tall guy with the beard?" Becca replied.

"I'm not sure."

"What other details can you remember of the blue truck?"

"Um, it had some bumper sticker on the back. Oh, what was it? 'If you can read this, you're too close' yeah that was it. What other details are in that report?"

"Just 'blue truck', that's all."

Derrick slumped back into his seat.

"I've seen a blue truck with a bumper sticker around Ulzbruk. Though I can't remember what it says," Dom added.

"Where can we find it?" Peter blurted, delighted that it seemed like they had made a breakthrough. His head was beginning to ache.

"It could be nothing, but surely its worth try?" Derrick said hopefully.

"I'm not sure sorry. Many people here work at the mill. We could try the car park?"

"Great idea." Derrick stood up to head out.

"Would you like to come with us mister priest?" Becca asked.

"Yes, but please allow me a moment to warn you of something."

"Huh?"

"I'd recommend you take a seat for a moment."

Dom retrieved another folder from the kitchen. It read 'Sons of the

Snake' on the cover.

"What's all this?"

"It's a possibility that a cult could be responsible for the missing women. I haven't been able to gather much information on them."

"Oh great, a bunch of crazies?" Derrick added.

"I just want you all to be prepared for the fact that if we do find our missing friends, they may not be alive..." Dom hesitated for a moment, "...or in one piece."

Becca looked horrified.

"Don't worry about all that stuff. We'll find them alive and well. They were probably just taken for ransom. They'll be OK" Derrick said firmly.

Dom nodded and closed the folder.

As they walked out, Dom grabbed his walking stick and shut the front door. They squeezed into the rental car and headed down the narrow rural road towards the mill. Peter watched all the fields and trees whizz past as he tried not to think about what had happened to the missing women.

Dom gave Derrick directions, and several minutes later they arrived at the mill. There was a large car park, and they drove slowly looking for a blue truck. After two loops around they were confident it was not there.

Everyone was feeling deflated and unsure of the next step in their investigation.

"Shall we loop around one more time?" Derrick offered.

"Nah, we would've seen it if it was here," Peter spoke what they were all thinking.

"It's nearly time for most of the workers to finish their day's work. We could wait around and see if you recognise anyone?" Father Dominic was aware of how desperate his plan sounded. However, it was much better than no plan. Derrick pulled into a car park, and they waited. They hoped they could think of a better idea.

What felt like a very long time later the large barn doors opened and several workers made their way to their vehicles. Becca and Derrick tried to get a good look at each one as they passed their car. Derrick could barely remember any details of the people that came in and out of the petrol station the previous day, but he hoped that seeing somebody would jog his memory. One of the men walked out of the barn and lit a cigarette. He stood around for a while, and the car full of observers tried not to stare. A few minutes later, the dull rumbling of a truck could be heard as all eyes watched the entry gate to the mill. Much to everyone's amazement, a dull blue truck pulled in.

"That's it!" Becca yelped with glee.

"Shhh!" Derrick tried to calm her.

Dom and Peter did their best to peer from the backseat.

The blue truck slowly pulled in and picked up the smoking man. It then drove slowly past them and out the exit.

Becca pointed as covertly as she could at the distinctive bumper sticker on the back. Now everyone was certain this was the truck from yesterday. They all hoped it was relevant.

"C'mon Derrick! Follow them!" Becca demanded.

"Yeah, yeah, let's just give them some room."

"That's what their bumper sticker says after all," Peter added with a smile.

Becca did not find it funny.

Gradually, Derrick pulled out onto the road and followed the blue truck at the largest distance where he could and still keep an eye on it.

"What'll we do when they stop?" Peter asked.

No-one was sure. The mood very quickly became very tense as they watched the back of the blue truck trundle along in front of them.

The truck continued through town and out into the northern hill country. After several minutes of driving and a few streets, a large black truck came into view on the opposite side of the road as they rounded a corner. The black truck swerved across the centreline as it approached them.

"What the…" Derrick began.

Derrick swerved. The truck hit the rear quarter of their car flipping it over in a mess of shattering glass and crunching steel. Their rental car rolled a few times before it came to a stop in the ditch on the side of the road. Luckily, it was the right way up. Screams of pain were loosed from Becca's lungs as glass embedded itself into her chest and arms. Derrick had a lot of blood oozing through his hair, and it hurt when he breathed. He wondered what internal injuries he had. Father Dom's leg twisted badly at the knee. It looked like he would never be able to walk on it again. Like the others, Peter was covered in small cuts and bruises.

"Is everyone OK?" Peter said, wiping the blood from his face.

Father Dom was groaning next to him in the back seat holding his knee. He looked to be in serious pain.

"Try and, stop the bleeding," Dom said between pained winces.

Derrick regained his senses enough to help Becca in the passenger seat with the glass shards. She screamed as he pulled a small piece out of her arm.

"Help!" Peter called as he turned around to see what had happened to the other vehicle. The large truck had come to a stop in the middle of the road, and two men hopped out. A moment later another truck arrived, and more men piled out of the back. They were carrying rope and firearms.

"They're coming!" Was all Peter could think to say as he started to panic.

One of the men opened Peter's door and punched him repeatedly in the face. More cries erupted from his friends as they were all dragged from the ruined car. Peter found himself face down in the mud as his arms were tied behind his back.

"What the hell are you…"

Derrick' protests were silenced with more punches.

Peter saw his friends get tied up similarly until a black bag was thrown over his head. The rough material over his face smelled like chicken feed. He began to cry out, but before he could shape any words a kick to his chest knocked the air from his lungs. He was pulled to his feet and marched forward. He looked down past his chin to see as much as he could. He gathered they were walking him back to the road.

Peter was hoisted into the back of the truck. He lay down and twisted his head slightly to get a small view of the road. He saw a tow truck approaching them a short distance down the road. Derrick landed with a thud next to him, and he lost his view. Peter tried to track the tow truck as best he could with his ears. Over the next few minutes, he heard it begin to tow their rental away.

"They planned it," he whispered as quietly as he could to Derrick.

Peter heard only pained moans as the reply.

Becca cried out as she landed onto Derrick' legs. More cries of pain came from the direction of their rental. They were trying to get Father Dom to walk to the truck. But it was evident his knee was not going to allow that.

"Hurry!" Peter heard one of the men yell.

Peter tried to twist his head again to try and see what was going on. He could not see anything despite his best efforts. The groaning of Father Dom was getting closer quickly, and he gathered they must be carrying him. Peter heard Derrick and Dom cry out as Dom landed in the back of the truck with them.

The large diesel engine started up. Some of the men climbed over them, and Peter had a foot planted on his chest. A minute later, he felt the truck turn around and head back the way it came.

"You don't have to do..." Father Dom started to plead, but the dull sound of boots and fists stopped him quickly.

Peter tried to keep track of what direction they were going as he felt the truck slow down to make a left turn. Or was it a right turn? He was not doing well.

"Surely there'll be heat for this..." an unfamiliar voice spoke from above them.

"Shut your filthy face!" another commanded.

Peter lost track of time but gathered they must be miles away from where they were taken by now. He felt like they were slowing to a stop. A large bump loosed more cries from them as they drove onto a rough driveway. Peter had now lost all sense of direction as they followed the winding path. A hiss of engine brakes announced their abrupt arrival at their destination.

"Up!" the voice from earlier demanded.

Peter scrambled to his feet as they were lowered onto the ground. Beneath the bag on his head, Peter saw the blue truck they had been following earlier. He decided they must have seen them following. Now that he thought about it, it was the only rental car in town, and with the low traffic on the roads, it would have been easy to spot them. He did have a glimmer of hope that they would have only made such drastic action if they were indeed the kidnappers. Peter hoped that meant that Camilla would be here too. Wherever 'here' was. More groans of pain escaped Dom's lungs as they tried again to force him to walk on his wrecked knee.

"Nah, just carry him. It's not far."

"You carry him!"

"It was your idea."

"Shut your traps! You can both carry him," the leader of the group walked past Peter, he had dusty black boots and worn blue jeans.

They were moved across dusty dirt, over some brown grass and halted at a large structure. Peter assumed it was a barn by the shadow it cast over his head bag and sound of the door opening.

"In, go!"

There was no retort from the prisoners now; none of them wanted their current injuries worsened by another beating. Walking inside, Peter smelt straw and trampled some beneath his feet. He heard the door shut behind them. He then heard another wooden door being swung open and was pushed forward again.

"Walk down the steps, or I'll throw you down."

Peter walked at the front and gingerly placed his foot out in front of him. He walked down ten very steep steps into almost complete blackness. He missed a step and fell flat on his face into hard dirt.

"Get up worm!" Strong arms hoisted him back to his feet roughly. He was made to face the dirt wall as he awaited the others. From the cries of pain, grunting and swearing, it was clear they had trouble bringing Dom down.

"C'mon then!"

They hobbled their way into the darkness. It was near impossible to see anything through the bag on his head. Peter repeatedly hit the walls of either side of the long tunnel. When his captor had enough laughter, he began to steer him with firm hands on his shoulders. Occasionally, they would pass a dim light attached to the roof above them. In the light, he saw the floor of the tunnel was well trampled. The air smelt stagnant. There was a faint sound of water dripping somewhere nearby.

"Wait."

The leader pushed past him and opened a door in front of them. They walked through, and he stopped them again. The air felt somewhat fresher here, and he felt like they had entered a larger space.

"Here will do."

Peter was shoved forwards and his head pushed downwards. He felt a rope pass between his arms and a moment later it was pulled tight.

"We'll be dealing with you lot proper soon," a sinister voice promised.

Peter heard the men leave, and the door shut behind them.

"Are you guys, OK?" Derrick asked.

Peter swore under his breath.

"We'll be OK. Can you get a hand free?" Dom asked. He was surprisingly calm.

They tried to wriggle free of their bonds with renewed vigour but with no success.

"Ah!" Derrick yelled.

"What?" Peter responded.

"I'm bleeding."

"Yeah, we all are."

"No, I mean, hold on…" Derrick wriggled around for a few moments. "Yes! Oh thank God!" he declared.

A faint sound of rope being cut filled them with hope.

"Derrick?!" Becca demanded

"There was a shard of glass from the car imbedded in my shoe. I think I can use it to cut the rope."

"Good man! Hurry"

A moment later the bag was pulled off Peters' head. Derrick's bloodied face was smiling in front of him. He was loose from the ropes in less time than expected. Peter looked around to see them sitting in a dark cave. A strong looking wooden door blocked the way out in front of them. Behind them, the cave opened up into a large area. There looked to be some sort of altar made from stone and a deep crevasse behind that. Peter strained to hear the sound water flowing below.

Derrick had only cut half of Peter's rope when they heard men approaching again from the tunnel. Peter's heart was racing.

"Hurry!"

"No time!" Derrick quickly threw the bag back over Peter's head and sat down again as if he was still tied up.

A second later, the door swung open and Peter heard several men enter.

"…so many at once, is he not getting greedy?"

"Just think, we'll be able to let so much blood."

"Mmm, I'm looking forward to that."

"We haven't even finished the last one yet."

"Yeah, great isn't it?"

"Oh look, four of them, that's better than I was hoping."

"Quiet you lot!"

"Why? They'll never leave alive; we can talk freely. We…"

"Shhhh. He's coming."

Peter heard the people shuffling into position. He lost count of how many had entered. It would be far too many for him Derrick and Peter to punch their way through.

After a moment, another man walked in.

"Let us begin," he had a gravelly voice and spoke with authority. Others took action without hesitation.

"Yes, Sire."

Peter could hear chains and metal objects being moved about. He saw the last man was wearing a black floor-length cloak as he walked by.

"The altar is ready," one voice declared.

"Shall we finish the last offering?" another voice asked eagerly.

"Silence!" The dark-cloaked man demanded.

He was pacing up and down in front of Peter and his friends. Becca was whimpering quietly from beside him.

"We take the old man first."

"No!" Derrick cried out. Becca began to wail. Peter wrestled with his restraints but couldn't break them.

Peter heard the dull thud of fists interrupting Derrick' outburst.

"Quiet fodder!"

Peter gritted his teeth, if only he could get his hands free! The two of them might stand a chance. Peter had been well versed in street fights since his early youth. He was not afraid of taking on greater numbers. But with the bag on his head, he could not tell if they were carrying weapons. He decided to focus on trying to break his restraints.

A pained groan burst from Dom as they lifted him to his feet. Dark-cloak saw the puddle of blood that was left from where he had been sitting.

"We don't want him expiring early, so we are going to perform the full ritual."

A cheer of support rose from the blood-hungry crowd.

"Peter, are you good?" a hushed whisper came from Derrick amidst the noise. Peter knew just what he was asking.

"Not yet."

Peter managed to find a threadbare patch in his hood and peered through with his left eye as best he could. He could see about a dozen men and women kneeling in a group all facing one direction. They seemed to be delighted that things were going quicker than what they normally would be. He moved his gaze towards the direction they were facing and saw two large men chaining Dom to a large stone altar. Dark-cloak stood nearby next to a small table. Peter could not see what was on it. But he heard the clunk of metal occasionally as the man seemed to be checking the items.

Off to the very side of the chamber, Peter saw a near-naked female body. It was facing away from him tied up to a small stake in the ground. The ground around it was stained with blood. Peter's heart jumped in his chest as he saw it move slightly. Whoever it was, they were still alive, if only just. The crowd seemed to be ignoring them and focused on the altar.

"We begin in blood!" Dark-cloak declared. He held up some sort of tool. An approving moan of desire came from the crowd. At this point, they all stood up. The leader began chanting something Peter could not understand. The crowd recited back a reply of some sort. He then moved toward the altar. A moment later, a shriek of pain filled the cavern followed by applause from the crowd. Becca started screaming. Peter decided he would go for Dark-cloak first. He tore against his restraints with renewed vigour. Blood began to trickle down into his hands from his wrists.

Peter saw the leader approach the altar again, another scream of pain erupted. Peter saw him hold bolt cutters high above his head. The man spoke another language and asked the crowd something. There was a reply from the crowd again in a similar fashion.

"Shall we advance already?" Dark-cloak asked.

The crowd roared their approval.

"Disgusting cult freaks," Peter heard Derrick spit under his breath.

Dark-cloak walked over to the little table and held up a hammer. Peter poured more energy into getting his hands loose but with no success. Dark-cloak held the hammer up for the crowd to see then turned back to the altar. Peter saw him raise the hammer above his head. At that moment he saw Derrick pulled the bag off his head and stood up. Before Peter could smile at the thought of Derrick breaking a few jaws, Derrick sprinted out the unlocked door.

Peter gaped in disbelief. He could not comprehend that his lifelong friend had left him to be tortured to death. Before he could fathom the betrayal fully, his ears filled with the sound of crunching bone and agonising pain. The crowd revelled in the horror as Dark-cloak hammered both of Dom's knees into a bloody paste. It seemed he lost consciousness for a moment or struggled to breathe as his screaming stopped for a moment before another pained groan carried on.

"Sire!"

Dark-cloak turned to see Derrick had fled. He was furious.

"You two, get him. NOW!" he bellowed.

Two large cultists sprinted out the door after Derrick.

"We will continue. It seems this feeble old fool doesn't have much left in him."

"Shall we advance?"

Another roar of approval from the crowd erupted. Dark-cloak approached the little table. Returned the bloodied hammer and held up a long knife. The crowd hollered in delight at the sight of the ceremonial blade. Peter began swearing at the top of his lungs. He called on every vile word and curse he could muster down on them. The closest cultist casually walked over to Peter and kicked him in the face.

"Shut it."

Peter reeled back in pain. He felt helpless.

Dark-cloak spoke some vile words and ran the knife past Dom's face and down towards his stomach. He slipped the knife under his shirt and cut it open up to his chin. As he did so, the two men next to him staggered back a step. Around Dom's neck was a set of rosary beads and a small necklace with a distinctively shaped cross on it. Dark-cloak took a few steps back and screamed at his followers.

"You brought a priest of the living God here? Idiots!"

"Sire, we…" a cultist began.

Dark-cloak stepped towards him and drove the blade into his neck. He held him there for a moment then threw him into the dark chasm just beyond the altar.

"Feed the worms with your stupidity!"

Peter quickly looked back to the altar just in time to see both men near Dom leap into the chasm to their deaths. Panic started to break out into the crowd. Peter heard Becca gasp in disbelief. He turned to see she had pulled the bag off her head. Peter wriggled and did the same.

Father Dominic drew in a deep breath. A serene peace held his face; where but a moment ago it was twisted in pain. He sat upon the altar. Thick chains held back his arms. He extended his arms out to his sides, then eyed Dark-cloak. He brought his hands around into the front of him with a loud clap and the chains shattered. Broken metal links flew in all directions. For a moment, the crowd of cultists was frozen in fear. Father Dom kicked free of the chains around his legs with similar ease.

Dark-cloak aimed the knife towards his foe, and his cultist minions rushed towards him. A great booming voice came out from Father Dom. It was loud and powerful. It seemed to shake the air with holy energy.

"The Lord God Almighty is my strength. Through him, I can do all things. Now you will all be banished back to Hell!"

The cultists snarled and made disturbing inhuman growling sounds.

Dom leapt off the altar and stood before them. Peter could see some of his toes were missing and both knees were in completely ruined. But regardless, he stood.

He kept his eyes forward and took a step, then another.

"Kill him!" Dark-cloak screamed.

The crowd around him rushed forward. As the first pair approached, Father Dom ducked and sprang back with a flat palmed uppercut to the forehead of the closest attacker.

"Be gone!" He commanded

The man who was hit struggled to stay standing; he looked to be fighting with himself while twitching and squealing.

"Get out!" Father Dom called as he hit another.

"In the holy name of Jesus Christ of Nazareth be gone!" He roared. The cultists tumbled over and writhed on the ground in pain. The first two whom were hit, stood up and leapt into the chasm to their deaths.

"These are mine!" Dark-cloak declared as he spat back unholy curses and commands to his kin.

He slashed wildly at those around him.

"Kill him!"

Those close to him dashed towards Dom with renewed ferocity. They started punching Dom with all their strength. Dom was knocked back a few steps by a savage right hook. He struggled to block the incoming blows as more surrounded him. Amidst the screaming, Peter heard two dulled gunshots in quick succession.

Despite the damage he was receiving somehow Dom stayed standing.

"Flay him!" Dark-cloak shouted as he tossed weapons from the table to his followers.

Two of the larger men held one of Dom's arms. A third approached with a serrated knife.

"Die!"

An ear busting crack reverberated throughout the underground chamber. The knife-wielding cultist was thrown backwards. Derrick stood in the doorway, but he now held a rifle in his hands. He racked the bolt and fired again. The closest large cultist holding Dom had his chest punctured and fell backwards.

"Kill him! Kill him!" Dark-cloak screamed. The crowd left Father Dom for a moment and surged towards Derrick. Another few shots dropped two more. Peter jumped to his feet, and shoulder charged one before he could reach Derrick. Derrick turned his rifle towards Dark-cloak and racked the bolt.

"Enough!" A deep voice burst out from somewhere inside Dark-cloak as he made a violent backhand motion in Derrick' direction. Some unseen force threw Derrick back against the wall behind him, and he crumpled into a bleeding wreck on the floor. Dark-cloak looked to Peter and Becca next and cast another demonic slap. Peter began to brace for certain death.

A huge burst of air pressure from in front of him staggered Peter back a step. Otherwise, he was unharmed.

"I will cast you out Demon!" Father Dom was holding up his hands as if he was pressing on an immense invisible weight. He took a step forward, and a mob of cultist was thrown backwards to the ground. Father Dom stumbled, due to exerting so much energy. Peter could still not comprehend that he was still moving around. He then turned to Peter and spoke.

"Solutam vincula!"

Peter felt his arms pulled outward and the rope around his wrists snapping.

Father Dom now looked drained, and he was leaning over as if he was supported by an invisible angelic ally next to him.

The two remaining cultists were loosed of their spiritual torture and set upon Dom with vicious blows. Peter ran forward and punched his way through one before he was cast aside. Dark-cloak strode past Peter and plunged his knife deep into Dom's chest. Dom spluttered forth a mess of blood and held Dark-cloak's hand as he tried to stop him twisting the blade.

Peter threw all the strength he could muster into a punch to the side of Dark-cloak's head. His head jerked violently with the impact, but it did not throw him to the floor as Peter expected. Peter rained down blow after blow until Dark-cloak had to divert his attention away from Dom. At that moment, Dom withdrew his hands from around the blade and placed them on the forehead of the two remaining cultists.

"Be gone!"

They both ran screaming towards the chasm and jumped off the edge. Peter picked up the bloodied pair of bolt cutters and swung it into Dark-cloak's head. What should have been a fatal blow only staggered him back a step. Dark-cloak extended his hand towards Peter and flicked his wrist. Peter was thrown back by some invisible force and was splayed out onto the ground.

"Release this man in the name of Jesus the Christ!" Dom commanded as he reached both hands and gasped Dark-cloak's head as he turned to face him. He struggled and squirmed. But the prayerful chant from Dom was too much. He fell to the ground for a brief moment before leaping off the cliff.

Upon realising no threats remained, Dom closed his eyes and held out his hands. His gaze began with Peter, then passed to Derrick, Becca and finally rested on the near-dead body at the back of the cave.

"Sana vulnera," he spoke the healing words reverently with the last of his spiritual power.

Dom collapsed to the ground. Peter felt energy flow into him as he rushed over. The knife wound in Dom's chest looked much more serious up close.

"I, don't know what to do," Peter stammered

Dom slowly shook his head. His breathing became fast-paced and shallow.

"Peter!" Dom cried as if his vision was failing him.

"I'm here," he replied.

Dom spoke holy scripture:

Isaiah 26
⁴ Trust in the LORD forever,
for the LORD, the LORD himself, is the Rock eternal.

Peter nodded.

"…carry on…" Dom managed to say between gasps as he took an ornate gold ring from a finger on his left hand and set it in his.

"I will," he promised.

Peter looked at the ring; it was strangely bulky and had an emblem on the front which Peter did not recognise. A spluttered cough returned his gaze to Dom who had breathed his last. Dom's vacant eyes looked past Peter.

"We need to get outta here!" Derrick called as he got back to his feet.

"Camilla!" Becca cried as she ran over to the body on the far side of the cave. Peter saw her help her to a seated position.

"She's chained!" Becca screamed, unable to pull her friend free.

Peter pocketed the ring and ran over with the bolt cutters. As he got closer, he began to recognise Camilla under the mud and blood caked on her. She looked delirious and only barely conscious. Peter cut her free of the metal manacles around her hands and feet. He saw she was covered in countless small cuts. There were a couple of large wounds in her thighs that had crude bandages taped to them. Peter shuddered at the thought of how long the cultists were planning on keeping her alive only to bleed her.

Derrick rushed over, and he and Peter picked Camilla up. Becca led the way holding the rifle as they left the sacrificial chamber. They stepped through the open door and moved through the tunnel back towards the barn. At the base of the steps, Derrick climbed up and between the three of them they managed to get Camilla up and out. She occasionally groaned in pain but did not speak. The four opened the barn doors, and daylight washed over them. The fresh air had never smelled so sweet.

Many years later, Peter changed his name to Kephas. He explained it represented how much he had turned his life around. Indeed he had. He gave up his alcoholic ways and was ordained a priest. He later went on to enlist in the Holy Order of Salt and Light.

CHAPTER 5:

TURMOIL

The elevator made a faint tone to announce its arrival at Jenson's floor. He walked in and double-checked he had everything he needed. Everything had gone to plan. He wondered what Sandra was doing right now. He checked his phone, but there was still no signal.

"Probably another few hours before that's up and running again," he thought to himself calmly.

He knew that other cells would be executing their plans today. He was not aware of any details. But he knew it was in capable hands. He wondered what project they would move him onto next. The elevator rumbled as it moved up to the surface.

The elevator doors opened and let in screams from the ground floor. It looked like a bomb had gone off. Large chunks of the walls had blown out; small fires were burning all over. Ash lingered in the air, smelling of burnt plastic. Jenson stood motionless for a moment. His mind could not comprehend what was going on.

"This can't be happening!" he stated quietly.

A very calm and collected Jenson melted into a panic. He rushed through the office, ignoring his injured colleagues. He stomped his way through the shattered glass door and onto the street. The tall office buildings surrounding him were shattered wrecks. Glass, debris and blood covered the ground. He knew things would get bad. But he expected nothing of this scale. Smoke was rising from a multitude of locations around him. The closest plume was a short distance away, with many more scattered across the horizon.

"No, no, no!" He ran down the road weaving through the panicked people running in all directions. Stumbling over the uneven ground, he eventually made his way around the corner. He felt a wave of heat sting his face as he saw the flames ahead of him. The South Central Community Centre was well ablaze. The roof had been largely ripped off in an explosion only moments before. Ash and dust were falling like snow. He ran closer to see a deep crater in the scorched ground where the atrium should have been. He gagged as he saw human remains tangled in the rubble. A small group of people were trying to move the smaller chunks of concrete in an attempt to dig out survivors.

"Hey you, help us!" One called as they saw him standing there.

"Impossible," he replied, barely audible.

After a moment, the man gave up with a dismissive wave of his hand and went back to digging. Jenson was shaken to his very core with what was occurring around him. He bit the inside of his cheek, hard enough to draw blood.

"Wake up, dammit!" he commanded himself.

This exact location was a green light on his screen. He vividly remembered checking it. The closest location to the workplace was often used as an example by his three subordinates. He was absolutely sure it was green.

"How?" He asked himself. A moment of thought yielded another explanation.

"It's just a glitch he decided, an infinitesimally small chance; he had to admit. But it was possible. He decided to run to the next site. Clustor street was three blocks away. He turned and ran in that direction. The devastation around him seemed to soak into him. He quickly discovered his lack of fitness and was soon panting hard as he ran. People were crying out for help as he ran past. He did not even look at them. He could not. This was too much. As he ran, he nearly slipped over. When he looked down, he saw he had stood on a large red worm. It was alarmingly large; its broken body leaked blood over the concrete. He tried not to think about it as he continued.

Exhausted and puffing, Jenson made it around another tall office building with all of its glass spilt across the ground around it. He saw another dark plume of smoke rising close by. His stomach dropped. He continued running anyway. Soon afterwards, he made it to the Church of the Cross. It was a burnt-out shell with many of its large bricks embedded into the surrounding buildings. A small fire was still burning in what remained of the rear of the church. This site was another green light on his dashboard. Jenson dropped to his knees and vomited himself empty. He began to cry and sob.

"No. I refuse to believe it," he stood and thought for a moment what the next location was.

He turned and headed in that direction at the fastest jog he could manage. Another plume of sickly smelling smoke ahead of him confirmed his fears. He slowed his pace, reluctant to reach the truth with speed. His mind was already spinning. He thought about returning to the office to double-check his results. But his memory protested. He was sure this was a green light.

"It was green! Green, I tell you!" He shouted aloud in defiance.

Moments later, he came into view of the Central Christian Fellowship. It was in the second story of a large office tower. It was also the only floor of the building on fire. The full terror of what was happening began to sink into his mind. He did this. He caused it all. He was not saving the hundreds of lives like he was told he was. He was responsible for killing hundreds if not thousands. He began to wonder about all the other things they told him. He suddenly remembered what he was told about the sleeping gas.

"No, no, no, no..."

Jenson broke down, lay on the ground and wept bitterly.

. . .

In Brakenside, Bishop Kephas tried to recall all he could of Zack's vision. He could already see smoke rising throughout Brakenside. His fears that the Sons of the Snake had already carried out their plan were confirmed as they got closer. Ahead, traffic lights were out, and cars were abandoned in the street. Many showed damage from recent impacts. Much of the ground was split and broken. Some parts of the road had risen half as tall as a person, with a broken edge to below ground level. Many pipes beneath ground level had broken and murky brown water was gushing over much of the road.

"Goodness me!" Lucy said as she stopped the car abruptly.

They had only just entered the suburbs, but it was clear they could not drive any further.

Mike pulled to a stop behind them.

"Hurry up old lady," he called impatiently.

Deon craned his neck to try and see what was happening ahead of them.

They saw everyone get out of the vehicle and Bishop Kephas beckoned them to do the same.

"Oh c'mon, it ages from here," Mike whined.

Deon climbed out of the car and looked further down the road.

"Mike, everything is wrecked."

The car lurched backwards as Deon jumped back in alarm.

"Watch it!"

He could see Mike laugh as he reversed his car down the road a short distance before parking it carefully on the side of the road.

Mike hopped out then walked over to the group who were all looking the other way.

"Bishop, how can I help?" Deon asked as he approached.

Kephas nodded gratefully in reply.

"Ideally, we'd like to get back to the Cathedral and set up…"

He was cut short by the sound of a frantic scream on the far side of the road.

Bishop Kephas and Father Andrews looked at each other and then sprinted towards the scream.

"Wait here," Father Andrews called back.

Deon, Donny and Lucy stood there for a moment as Mike arrived.

"Where are they running off to? Half price at the priest shop?" Mike jibed.

Deon ignored him as he watched them both run out of view behind a tall wooden fence.

Another faint scream from a different direction could be heard on the faint breeze. The four now felt quite vulnerable in what used to be a very safe neighbourhood.

"This way!" Douglas called to Kephas.

Ahead of them was a small house with its door open and a small splatter of blood on the front porch. They ran up the few steps and went inside.

"We're here to help!"

A short cry from upstairs abruptly stopped. They both bolted up the stairs to find a man and a woman laying in pools of blood that still were growing in size.

"I'll check these rooms," Douglas said, pointing as he stepped past the pair of dead people.

Kephas nodded and went in the opposite direction.

"Anyone here?" He called.

After a brief search, they found neither the survivors nor perpetrators. They re-grouped back at the bodies and bent down to assess their injuries.

"Anything?"

"Nothing."

The middle-aged man had a huge gaping wound across his chest as if a bull had gored him. The woman was similarly killed by multiple large wounds.

"Do you think this…"

More screaming from outside came from the direction of their group. The pair leapt down the stairs and ran back towards them. Between them and their group stood a large Mortkin demon. Lucy was frozen in place, yelling at the top of her lungs as Deon was trying to pull her away. Donny was running back to the car, and Mike was not in view. The demon was just about in striking distance of Lucy as Father Andrews called out

"Demon filth, go back to Hell!"

The creature turned to see Father Andrews jump on the bonnet of a parked car then leap across towards the beast. The Demon charged forward to engage his enemy, confidently holding up its claws, eager to collect another victim. Father Andrews had drawn a small metal cross which he held in his right hand. As the two collided Father Andrews pierced the cross through the demon's arms and into its face. Its pained cry was cut short as it crumpled backwards into the road. Father Andrews made an additional few stabs to confirm the kill.

"Deon, were there any others?" Kephas asked.

Deon found himself shaking his head in shock as he struggled process what he had just seen. Mike emerged from behind a nearby car.

"Mate, what the hell is going on? What was that?"

"You got the Hell part right," Father Andrews replied.

"We need to move," Kephas directed.

"Things have already deteriorated quicker than I thought possible," Father Andrews commented.

"Yo, do you lot know what's goin' on or what?" Mike demanded.

"Not here. Let's explain once we're somewhere safe," Kephas replied.

Mikes additional insisting comments were ignored by everyone.

They hurried off down the street, heading towards the closest plume of smoke. When they arrived, they saw the whole Eastside hall had been demolished. Only a single defiant pillar near the entrance remained standing. Several small fires continued to burn in parts of the shattered remains. There were several people trying to dig through the debris for survivors.

"Let's go!" Bishop Kephas called as he ran forward. Mike looked down in horror as he carefully stepped over what he could only describe as tiny chunks of people. Splinters of wood and fragments of brick had been strewn all over the road and car park. Acrid smoke hung in the air.

"Over here!" A man called waving out from inside the broken hall.

The group rushed over as Mike lingered in the car park. Lucy bent down to pray over someone who had died from their injuries.

"I need help to lift this," a panicked man pleaded.

A large wooden beam and some splintered wood had fallen from the roof. They gathered around it for a moment, and each found somewhere to hold on. As Deon approached, he saw a hand underneath it.

"Three, two, one, heave!" He directed.

As the others were helping, Mike walked off by himself.

They strained and successfully lifted it, then slowly walked it to one side and lay it down amidst the rubble. The man returned to the body under the wood. A middle-aged lady lay there, motionless with a blank look on her face. The man sighed heavily and closed her eyes.

"I'm sorry for your loss," Bishop Kephas said.

"She frustrated me every day, silly woman… but she didn't deserve this."

He stood back up and pointed.

I think there could be more through here. He led them through what was once an office into the remains of pair of toilets. After a brief search, they determined no-one else was left alive in the building. A couple of the fires were still too large to search some areas. But if there were anyone left there, they would have perished long ago.

"I'm John, thanks for your help."

"Hi," Father Andrews introduced each of them.

"I thought more would have been inside?" Donny asked.

"Oh there was, most of the bodies we lay on the grass over there. And some of us somehow made it," he turned and revealed a scorch mark across his back.

"Do you need help with that?"

"Oh no, it's OK. I'm one of the lucky ones."

The group spent an hour trying to bandage up the wounded as best they could.

"We need to move," Father Andrews suggested.

"Agreed," Kephas replied.

"John, we're going to the Cathedral on the far side of town, would you like to come with us?"

"No, my place is here."

"We can offer you protection against the demons."

"The what?"

"You haven't seen the monstrous creatures killing people?"

John looked at them, unsure of whether they were making a strange joke or they were insane.

"I don't quite know what you're trying to get at. Regardless, I have people I need to care for here."

"A worthy pursuit, if things get too dangerous, head to the Cathedral."

"OK. Anyway, thanks for your help today. I hope your destination is in better shape than here."

"Thank you."

"The people here are in good hands."

John waved and returned to the wounded.

Douglas, Kephas, Donny, Lucy, and Deon walked down the road towards the Cathedral. Mike was nowhere to be seen, and after calling for him the group assumed he went off on his own. They had not been travelling long before a few people joined them. The pair of priests in the end times had a calming effect on the panicked people. As they walked around the end of the street, Kephas spotting something.

"What is that?" he pointed towards a house ahead of them with a strange small dark cloud.

"I don't like the look of it, let's go," Father Andrews replied.

The pair ran ahead gesturing the group to keep a safe distance behind them. As they approached, they saw a pair of talons extend out from the shifting dark energy. A moment later, a Mortkin demon had fought its way through into the physical world. The creature saw the priests approaching and howled a loud roar. It began to charge towards them. Douglas and Kephas picked up their pace and drew their holy weapons.

The distance closed between them, but as they drew nearer, another ball of darkness appeared near the demon. It fell to the ground and immediately began a desperate struggle to avoid being sucked back into the darkness. Douglas and Kephas looked on in wonder. By the time they got to where the demon was only a small splash of demonic goo remained. It had been drawn back to Hell despite its roaring protests.

"What did we just witness?" Douglas asked.

"I'm not exactly sure, but it seems the demon is no longer here. That is fine with me."

"Let's dwell on this once these people are somewhere safe."

"Agreed."

"We are not certain how, but the demon is gone. Let's hurry before more appear," Father Andrews addressed them all.

A short time later they had crossed town and had nearly reached the Cathedral. They numbered twenty-three people now as more joined them on the way. Kephas and Douglas picked up their pace as they approached the Cathedral, hoping they were not too late. A column of smoke came into view ahead of them as they rounded a large warehouse.

"No!"

"Hurry!"

They began sprinting as the group behind them struggled to keep up. Douglas made it into view of the Cathedral first, and he slowed his pace. Kephas knew what that must mean. Moments later he saw the once-proud Cathedral lying in ruins. The front entranceway looked relatively intact, but the roof behind had collapsed in. The far side showed scorch marks and bricks had been thrown in all directions. Fragments of glass from the ornate stained glass windows was sprinkled through the rubble like gleaming jewels.

"We must get to St Thomas' immediately," Douglas suggested.

"And leave the scrolls?"

"The rubble will keep them for now; we can return later."

"Yes, let's hope St Thomas' is in better shape."

They turned and jogged back to the group who had nearly caught up.

"Follow us; it's not far now."

They approached at St Thomas' church. A thin trail of smoke wafted skyward from a large crater in the road outside the church. All the windows had been blown out, and the fence on the front side was badly damaged. Debris and broken ground made the last part of their journey slow, but everyone was relieved that the church was still standing.

"OK everyone, one more road to cross then we can rest for a time," Father Andrews encouraged the group behind him. As he walked across the road, a dark rift in reality opened just behind him. A pair of large claws burst through and drove deep into his neck.

"No!" Kephas cried, sprinting forward.

The rift stretched open, and a Mortkin began to climb through. Father Andrews had fallen on to the ground and was gurgling in pain. Kephas rushed to his side and began chanting the prayer of healing. Douglas looked him in the eyes and slowly blinked. Before the demon could fully emerge, the rift began to close again. The demon screamed frantically as it was caught between the two realms. A moment later it was split in two. Demonic goo coated those nearby as the few limbs that made it through to the physical world began to dissolve away.

As soon as the rift closed, Kephas felt his prayers lose some of their power. Douglas made one last cough then died. Kephas reverently removed a ring from his finger then put it on his own.

"You have fought the fight, you have finished the race. Go into the peace of God, my friend."

He stood, all eyes looked to him. Lucy knelt and started to pray. Kephas drew in a deep breath. He could not mourn yet. There was so much to do.

. . .

Elsewhere, Sister Lee stood outside her small school and surveyed her surroundings. A blend of sirens could be heard in the distance, and several fires were sending smoke up into the sky. She continued to pray as she watched. Before her eyes, she saw a rift appear. At first, it was so small she did not notice it. In a flash, it grew in size, and several creatures rushed out from it. She felt cold inside. A moment later she heard screaming from the town below. She prayed all the harder. The rift shrank, and a second later it was gone. She turned her head as something caught her eye. Another rift opened for a moment then disappeared. She stood up and began to make her way back inside.

"Sister Lee!" A familiar voice called.

"Yes Tessa?"

"Please, come back inside. It's not safe."

"You're right. It is not. Assemble the students. We need to pray."

A few moments later, the thirty-one students of the small school were assembled in the classroom and were sitting on the mat. Their ages varied from five to fourteen. All looked scared; they looked to their teachers Tessa and Sister Lee expectantly.

"Listen everyone. We need to pray for protection for our families, friends and ourselves."

Sister Lee paused for a moment, thinking about how she should put things. A faint scream was heard from the distance. It seemed to make the point for her. For the first time since she had arrived at the mission, she had the complete attention of everyone in the room. Sister Lee knelt down.

"Let us begin in the name of the Father, the Son and the Holy Spirit…"

...

Meanwhile, in Brakenside, people were gathering around Bishop Kephas. The plans they had made with the aid of Zack's vision flooded through his mind. The fact that Father Andrews died a short distance away from where Zack described his death was not lost on him. The Bishop stood and gazed across each of those gathered around him.

"Bishop!" A voice called.

"Ah Brother Christopher, there you are."

"I'm so sorry about Father Andrews."

"Yes…" Kephas drifted off for a moment and drew his resolve "…We will see him again in Heaven."

Brother Christopher nodded solemnly.

"Lucy, would you mind staying with him for a time please?"

"Of course,"

"Thank you Lucy,"

Father Douglas Andrews' body was later buried at the rear of the church grounds.

Kephas took Brother Christopher aside.

"Brother, are the supplies intact?"

"Most of them, yes. But we did have some stored in one of the sheds…" he pointed towards a nearby crater.

"Good, then we are better off than we would have been otherwise. Let's start by securing this place."

"Yes Bishop."

"Everyone, your attention please. Gather in the church for your own safety. Explanations will follow."

Brother Christopher ushered the small group into the church then returned to the Bishop who was now digging a hole near the back garden.

"I'm glad we decided to keep these in more than one place."

"It's a blessing indeed."

Brother Christopher helped him, and after a few minutes they pulled out a small metal box. Brother Christopher opened it and checked its contents.

"They are all here."

"Good, let's use the Blessing on the Church and the border of the grounds. That should buy us some time."

"Agreed."

The two men walked around the Church praying in unison. Once they had completed, they began walking what was left of the fence line. As they did so, Kephas felt a surge of spiritual force within him. In the same moment, movement caught his eye.

"Weapons ready!" he called.

The two men drew their metal crucifixes and charged over the road towards an opening rift. Three small demons burst out from it before it the rift flickered into nothingness.

"Be gone!" The Bishop commanded as he began to chant the Rite of battle.

He felt strength surge through his body, and they quickly cut down their foes. Brother Christopher gained a large cut on his arm in the exchange. The Bishop immediately began to recant the prayer of healing. The blood stopped oozing before their eyes, and the wound began to close.

"Amazing!" Brother Christopher exclaimed.

After another few moments of sincere prayer, the wound was only half-closed. The Bishop continued for a few more minutes before stopping.

"I think we are not able to tap into the spiritual realm fully yet. It seems to be only unleashed in short bursts."

"Is that why the demons seem to disappear?"

"Yes, I believe so. Hmm…"

"What is it?

"It seems we'll only have a very short window to heal any injuries via spiritual means. Then it's back to bandages."

"We have some stored as you requested."

"Great, thank you Christopher."

They finished the Blessing around the property then returned to the church. The people assembled within were getting restless, a few of them were arguing about whether they should stay inside the church or venture out.

"Your attention please everyone…" Bishop Kephas began. "…I know many of you are scared, and that's just how you should be feeling in these troubled times. But do not lose hope. The Lord God Almighty is far greater than any of our earthly troubles. Turn to him, and we will be able to get through any adversity."

There were some murmured responses.

"I'm going to find some supplies and return here. Anyone wishing to come with me may do so. Anyone who would prefer to stay here is also welcome to stay. Brother Christopher will remain here to look out for you all."

One of the crowd who had not seen a demon close up looked over at the very slightly built man.

"I doubt you'd be able to protect anybody from much at all," he scoffed.

"If our enemies were physical in nature, you might be right," Brother Christopher replied humbly.

"I'm David Jones, I'll protect all these people," his large moustache twitched as he spoke.

The people around him wondered if they were somehow supposed to know or care who he was. After an awkward moment, he sat down again.

"Thank you. We will need everyone's help," Kephas added.

"I'd like to come with you," Kephas' mechanic Adam offered. His house was on the same block as the church and he had been one of the first ones to arrive. He stood next to Will, who also offered his assistance.

"Good to meet you," Kephas said, shaking his hand. "Thank you gentlemen."

After a brief chat with Brother Christopher, the Bishop, Adam and Will walked out the front gate of the church. Deon joined them as they left.

"Do you have somewhere in mind?" Adam asked.

"Yes, it's not too far from here. I'm hoping it'll be a quick trip."

They walked cautiously down a few roads without incident. Kephas pointed as they turned the corner. The 'EzyStore' self-storage complex was halfway down the road ahead of them.

"You're all prepared for the end of the world huh?" Will asked.

"Thankfully, a lot more prepared than we would've been."

"Huh?"

A gunshot burst the air around them. The four men froze in place for a moment. Then Kephas motioned them forward towards a parked car where they crouched down.

"Where'd that come from?" Kephas asked.

"Maybe a block over? It sounded close," Deon suggested.

They spent a few minutes peering around as best they could, but could not determine anything else. As they waited, Kephas spotted a bloodworm crawling its way up through a grate in the gutter. He stood up and stomped it under his boot.

"What was that?" Deon asked.

"Something most foul, I'll explain details later, but if you see any, crush them."

"Will do."

"Let's continue," Kephas suggested, and they set off at a quicker pace.

"We're nearly there," Will encouraged.

They trotted in the front gates of the storage facility as Kephas lead them down the third row of small locked units. They stopped outside unit thirty-five. Kephas rummaged in his pocket for a moment before he pulled out a large key ring. He opened up the lock and rolled the door upwards to reveal a full storage unit. It was immediately clear that they would not be able to carry everything in back to the church in one trip.

"Woah," Will said.

Steel racks lined the entire space; each shelf was filled with all sorts of food and medical supplies. To the rear of the unit there lay a large pile of improvised weapons. They were mostly tools that had been converted in some way to be more deadly.

"What's all this?" Adam asked as he picked up a crude spear. A long wooden shaft had a kitchen knife bound to the end. Adam ran his fingers over etching in the blade.

"The rite of sanctification involves those holy writings and a blessing. They make these mundane tools into demon-fighting weapons," Kephas explained.

He emerged from behind the shelving pulling two hand-trucks.

"We should be able to take two full sets of shelves with these," Kephas said.

The four men spent some time readying the supplies to be moved. They carefully pulled them out of the unit and locked it behind them.

"Let's head back quickly; I'm sure there will be people in need."

Deon held one set of shelving that Adam steered. Kephas held the other as Will wheeled out the supplies. They were making slow but steady progress out of the storage facility when they heard voices holler at them from across the road.

"Nice haul you gots!"

A large rough-looking man called as he made his way out of a parked van. He was followed by several others. All were wearing a coloured scarf around their necks, which indicated their membership in one of the local gangs, the Street Snakes. Soon a large group had emerged and were closing in on the four men. Will saw a few of them were holding baseball bats, and he correctly assumed many were carrying knives.

"Greetings, come with us to St. Thomas' Church, where you'll be safe. We..." Kephas was cut off by the loud laughter of the gang leader.

"Fool! Nothin' is safe no more," a few chuckles from his minions were accompanied by sinister looks.

"I'm Kephas; this is Will, Aaron and Deon. What's your name?"

Adam did not bother correcting him.

"Spug, my crew, my turf. You're standin' on my street."

"There is danger from all sides, but one..."

Spug interrupted again as he got close enough to see what they were towing.

"My, my, you've got some next-level loot here Padre."

He grabbed a small box off one of the shelves and rifled through it. Deon began to tense up; he felt like things were going to get a lot worse. Adam and Will looked at each other and subtly reached for their weapons stashed amid the supplies.

"Just..."

The gang leader threw the small box at Kephas' face and followed up with a right hook. As he did so, his crew set upon the men with fists and shoved them to the ground. Kephas nimbly side-stepped Spug's punch and dropped into a fighting stance. Infuriated Spug followed up with a flurry of blows. For a large man, he moved quicker than Kephas expected, but he was still able to block and dodge his incoming attacks. Kephas did not throw any punches in return. He continued to hold his hands up in a pacifying attempt.

"Let's talk this through."

Spug had enough and stepped back, drawing a pistol from his belt.

"Try and out-ninja lead!" he yelled, brandishing his weapon in Kephas' face.

Kephas closed his mouth and slowly raised his hands. Spug began to turn away before spinning around with a backhanded pistol whip. Kephas fell to the ground.

"Bishop!" Adam shouted.

"Yeah! That's right, kiss my street yo'. You're in m' house now."

The surrounding gang members landed several kicks into the men laying on the ground amidst spewing insults on them. Spug raised his hand, his crew stopped and waited.

"No safety at all. You knew it. You think you can tax what's mine, payin' me no dues? Not today, not any day now friend. I'm-a givin' you this lesson for free. It's on special like extra man…"

Kephas began to raise a hand but was met with another boot.

"… don't be rude. I'm-a talkin' here. I'm educatin' you on how things are going to be. Anythin' and everythin' around this place is mine. Just some don't know it yet. But oh they will."

Spug swung his handgun around him as he spoke, pointing it in turn to each of the men on the ground.

"Now, I know what cha' thinkin' this fella right here be crazy as one thing. And yeah, you'd be right on that…"

"Damn truth that!" one gang member called out.

A holler from his crew erupted at the private joke.

"…and I bet you thinkin' I be one old those stupid wasters. But not me, I've got plans fool. Solid, rock plans for empowering a crew like this. And first, it's about commodities. I got that schooled into me nice and young. I gotta have 'em then, then others fall in line. And you friends are on that line. Give it up."

He held out a hand expectantly to Will, then Adam, then Deon and Kephas.

"Give it up."

Each of them only gave him a pained and confused expression in return.

"Oh, I know you got 'em. And fools that drag this sweet loot in situations like these certainly have more than what my eyes are seeing this fine day. Punk. You best be sure of that."

"Please, just take it and leave us," Will pleaded.

"Oh, yo' best be hoping that my ears didn't hear some fool spittin' orders to Spug right here. Oh no. That would be proper un-civilian of you."

He bent down and pressed the pistol up against Will's face.

"Have you gotta death wish, boy?" He asked.

Will ground his teeth and shook his head slowly.

"Oh, that's smarts right there. You know what's up, you know it. Anyhow, as I was sayin' give over those keys. Every fool has 'em entering my pantry 'EzyStore', and you're goin' to give me them right damn now."

His jovial expression, as he enjoyed his power trip turned into one of restrained anger.

"We don't..."

Adam was swiftly kicked in the jaw.

Spug racked his pistol and pressed it into his head.

"Speak again, fool."

Kephas tossed the keys from his pocket on to the ground in front of him. Hearing the distinctive sound Spug turned around.

"Ah, now you see, Mr-fancy-moves understands. Just for your cordiality I'm gonna leave you with your lives. Consider them a gift."

Spug motioned to his crew, and they collected up the supplies and made their way back to their waiting van. Kephas, Deon, Will and Adam remained laying on the ground until they were a safe distance away. A moment later the van started up and drove across the road followed by another of their vehicles.

"Gutter filth!" Adam cursed.

"We have to do something; they will clean us out!" Will declared, clenching his fist.

"I agree, they will take it all. But they are not ready to listen to anyone right now. Let's pray they have a change of heart."

"Change of heart? You really haven't a clue priest. These punks have been causing all sorts of trouble for as long as I can remember. This anarchy is probably heaven for them. We have to fight for what is ours."

Kephas replied with scripture:

Proverbs 24
[19] Do not fret because of evildoers
or be envious of the wicked,
[20] for the evildoer has no future hope,
and the lamp of the wicked will be snuffed out.

Will did not appreciate the impromptu sermon.

"Your words are nice and all, but I think bullets would be more suitable."

"Before we escalate further, let me say, I agree with you…"

"What?"

"In that, we do need to fight. But perhaps let's fight the demon hordes before we start fighting other people."

"But how can we do that without all that gear?"

"Faith. It's all any of us really need."

Will stomped off sore and angry; the others began to follow him.

"At least we didn't come off completely empty-handed," Kephas drew out a small scroll from his pocket.

"Huh?"

"It's a blessing of personal protection. I think this will really help us in the times ahead."

They walked slowly back to the church; their new injuries stung all the way.

"Bishop! Are, are you OK? What happened? Are you alright?" Brother Christopher exclaimed as he saw the Bishop approach.

"We had some trouble," Kephas replied.

Brother Christopher opened the church gate and ran across the road to meet them. He went to assist Deon who was struggling the most with his injuries.

"We got attacked by gang scum," Will explained.

Brother Christopher did not need to ask about the supplies they were all waiting on. As the four returned, they could see already many more had come to the church. It was clear that people were aware of the purpose of their journey and watched them with hungry bellies.

"We're going to need to go out again..." Kephas began.

"But first let's gather everyone here together. I do have one thing for you all at least."

Expectant people gathered around. There were hushed voices in the crowd puzzling over the Bishop's new injuries. As soon as Kephas had gathered everyone, he continued.

"Let's pray. In the name of the Father, the Son and the Holy Spirit, Amen. Lord God Almighty, please bless these people gathered here today. Grant them protection from the evil that roams our world and the strength to care for others. May we live to do your will and lead others to you..."

He opened the small scroll and reverently pronounced the holy words

"Benficium protectionis a malo"

A warm feeling washed over all that was assembled. Deon felt his skin tingle, and it seemed for a moment to harden. He felt a surge of confidence, and that despite all the anarchy around him; he felt he could get through it all. The crowd released surprised gasps and chatter as people felt the holy power affect them.

"There are many people out there that need help..." Kephas continued. "Many lack the basics of survival; if we all pitch in, we can save so many! I believe that we can make a community here, of survivors. Who can help me?"

The majority of the crowd, invigorated by their new blessing put their hands up.

"But what about the people out there that don't want help?" A man shouted from the crowd, he indicated to the Bishop's injuries as he spoke.

"It's true. Many don't understand and will refuse our offer. Some will attack us. But lets at least give them a choice for a better way. Some know of no other."

The man merely began to walk away with no reply. Several hands slowly shrunk back at the thought that they would get injured or killed.

After a few minutes of organisation, Kephas set out again, this time with a large group of volunteers.

. . .

Graham and Beth hurriedly made their way through the panicked city towards Mindy's house. The city itself seemed to be crying out in pain, as alarms of all kinds blared their distress. The air had filled with dust and visibility was poor. Graham smelt burning plastic, and his eyes were irritated. They had been travelling for some time through the streets, with many others like them, desperate to be somewhere else and rushing in all directions.

"Graham, look!" Beth pointed up ahead there was a large truck forcing its way through the road clogged with vacant cars.

The sound of the engine roaring and crunching metal filled their ears as they approached. The truck was making good progress and seemed to have enough power to push away anything in its path.

Graham decided that would be a much faster way to travel and he motioned Beth to follow him towards the truck. Many other people in the area seemed to have the same idea, and soon a small crowd was running after the truck. The fastest threw themselves in front of the truck yelling some indiscernible plea. The truck only just managed to stop in time. Shouting erupted followed by honking of its loud horn. With the truck stationary for a moment, a woman clambered up on to it. She began helping people up into the back tray. The furious driver began shouting all the louder, despite the urging of the crowd for him to take them along. Graham and Beth made it close enough to hear.

"Get the hell off my truck. All of you right damn now!" The driver blared the truck horn again.

"C'mon, you can take us with you!" The woman called back.

"I ain't moving until you all get off!"

"Please sir!"

"GET OFF!"

A man ran up to the driver's door and tried to open it.

"Get back fool, before you get run down!"

The desperate man tugged on the locked door, but it wouldn't budge. He pulled himself up to the open window, and the driver punched him square in the face, sending him reeling back to the pavement.

A series of gunshots punctured the air. Glass smashed, and the cabin of the truck was splattered with blood. A moment later, the truck horn began to blare again, and this time it remained on. The crowd began to scatter as screaming rung out. Graham pulled Beth down behind a car.

"Gunfire?!" She cried in alarm.

They slowly peeked up and saw the driver's door open, and the dead driver was pushed out onto the road. The door slammed shut, and the new driver began to set off again. A desperate man ran out from behind a car and stood bravely in front of the approaching truck.

"Just let me on! Please!"

The truck did not slow down and ploughed straight into him. The man was thrown backwards onto the road. The truck crunched into a car parked next to him. It took a moment to push it out of the way. The man on the road painfully rolled just in time to avoid being squashed flat as the truck roared onwards. No-one else tried to approach the truck. As the truck began to move away, a few members of the crowd shouted hollow threats.

"I saw your face! You're gonna pay!"

"Lunatic!"

"Surely the police will be here at any moment?" Beth asked.

Graham thought about that but did not reply. Doverton had a respectable police force, but he doubted they would be anything less than overwhelmed in all the chaos. They crept ahead so that they could watch the large truck smash its way through the street ahead. After a city block, it rammed its way through an off-ramp and onto the motorway. As it disappeared from view, they could hear the engine grow louder as it accelerated to full speed.

Graham and Beth made their way over to the man who had been hit by the truck. He was still lying on the ground but was moving.

"Are you OK there?" Graham asked as he bent down next to him.

"Huh? Yeah I guess. I just can't believe it. He wasn't going to stop!"

"Yeah. Crazy."

The man in a torn business suit sat up as he did so he let a cry of pain escape.

"Ooo that's sore."

"Can we help somehow?" Beth asked

"Thanks, I'm OK. Just need a minute. I'm Steve by the way."

"Hi, I'm Beth and this is Graham."

"Where are you headed?"

"Trenton road."

"Oh, you've got some way to go then."

"Yeah, how about you?"

"Home, not too far from Trenton actually."

"Oh good, want to travel with us?"

"Thanks, but I'm sure you don't want a cripple slowing you down," he said as he gingerly put his weight on his right foot.

"Complete maniac!" An unfamiliar voice called.

The woman who had been helping people on the truck was walking over, her phone in hand.

"How damaged are you?" she demanded, looking at Steve.

"Oh, I'll recover, its…"

"Not a chance. I'm filing a suit right now. I have a photo of him. He's going down. Your injuries, tell me. Name and contact information too. I'm calling my lawyer right… Oh! No signal again? You gotta be kidding me."

She stared at Steve again as she readied her phone to take some notes.

"Look lady, I don't think it's worth your…" he began.

"It's obvious to all of us that you're in shock, I'm going to have to do this at another time then." She walked up to Steve and snapped a full face shot then up-close photos of each of his grazes and cuts.

"Yeah, ten thousand easy for a twisted ankle. You'll do well out of this," she muttered almost to herself as she worked.

"It's Steve."

"Steve, is it, last name?"

"Penkerson"

"Good, good. I'm Kim Snell; we're going to make a lot of money out of this. I'll be taking him for emotional trauma and degradation and hate crimes. But with these injuries, we'll clean up. Anyway, I heard you lot mention you're travelling out of the city? I'm coming too. I've had enough of this stink. Who are you anyway?"

"I'm Graham, and this is Beth. We..."

"Good good, I'm ready as I'll ever be, let's get going."

Beth, Graham and Steve traded looks.

The four of them began a slow walk up the street.

"I'll keep up," Steve insisted.

Graham walked over and helped him walk, regardless.

"Thanks much."

"No problem."

Kim looked like she was just about to speak, but with Graham helping Steve, they managed a quicker pace. She turned her attention to Beth.

"So where are we off to?"

"We're going to Trenton road, in Sundale. Our friend lives there."

Kim couldn't restrain her look of disgust on her face when Beth mentioned where they were going. Beth could guess it was considered 'low class' according to Kim.

"Well, out of the city is a good start. This friend of yours has a house?"

"Yes."

"Good, we could stay there for a bit, and I can write this up properly. You do know where you're going?"

"Not precisely," Beth admitted.

"Fastest route is back this way," Kim said, pointing.

"Thanks, lead the way."

Their small group passed the former truck driver lying dead in the street. The man was in his mid-forties and wore blue jeans and a worn yellow high visibility vest; both were stained in his blood. He had a surprisingly peaceful expression on his face.

"Who was this guy?" Beth asked.

"I don't know. He should have just let us on,"

Kim insisted as she tucked one of her business cards into his pocket, trying to avoid touching him.

Beth shook her head.

"I'm not sure you should hold your breath on this whole lawsuit thing. Everything is in chaos."

"It is today sure, but it will settle down. It always does," she replied confidently.

Beth hoped she was right.

They continued their long walk across town. Beth saw many people running this way and that, some screaming incoherently. They almost constantly heard sirens in the distance, but never encountered emergency service vehicles. They made it up onto a walkway above the motorway and looked down to their destination on the far side.

Sundale was a small suburb just past the central business district. It backed onto where the university had its city campus. The land itself was in a slight recession, with small hills on three sides. This made it cold and damp compared to the surrounding areas. Apparently ideal for student and low-cost accommodation. Mindy lived in a large townhouse on the far side. She stayed there with four others. Each of which were undertaking study of some sort.

"There it is," Kim declared as she pointed.

Beth, Graham and Steve made it up the last of the steps and stood next to Kim on the walkway.

They took a moment to gaze at their surroundings. Smoke was rising into the sky from numerous fires in the city. None of which seemed to have the fire department in attendance. Some roads were clogged with traffic. Many motorists sat in their vehicles furiously honking their horns. Occasionally, a car would speed up the wrong side of the road. Some roads still bore the crashed remains of vehicles that did not manage to successfully complete the manoeuvre.

As they made their way towards the suburb, the height of the surrounding buildings decreased, and more of the sky was visible. Beth looked up at the dimmed sun squinting her eyes. The cross shape on its surface was clearly visible but she could not hold her gaze for long. Kim noticed where she was looking and could not help but look up. A moment later, and they were all looking.

"I've never seen anything like that!" Steve began.

"Amazing!" Graham added.

"C'mon, we can read about the solar flare or whatever later," Kim said.

As she finished speaking, they heard screaming coming from somewhere close by. They all traded alarmed looks. A short distance ahead there was a petrol station. The scream sounded like it was coming from there.

"Let's check it out?" Graham asked.

"No way! My calendar is already in tatters, I don't need a new crisis," Kim stated.

"They might need our help," Beth replied.

"Go, I'll catch up," Steve added as they all ignored Kim.

Graham and Beth ran across the road towards the petrol station.

As they approached, it looked empty. A few cars sat vacant next to the pumps which were not working.

"There!"

Graham pointed inside at the movement between the isles of convenience food. Some of the boxes of the top shelf fell to the ground, but they could not see what caused it. The screaming stopped abruptly. They were just about to open the doors when a man stepped into view, holding a bloodied knife. He stopped when he saw them and stared at them with cold eyes. Graham slowly took his hand off the door handle.

"Let's go," he said quietly.

"Yeah," Beth replied.

They both cautiously backed away. The man just stood and watched them from inside the store. Just as Graham turned to leave, he saw him hold his knife up and point it in their direction, but he made no attempt to follow them.

"Well?" Kim asked as they returned to the far side of the street.

"Some guy stabbed someone in there. We should get going," Graham replied as he helped Steve again to move on at a quicker pace. Graham felt a little guilty, but he reasoned the person screaming sounded dead already, and he doubted his ability to disarm the knife-wielding man. Kim snapped a photo of the petrol station as they left. Beth heard her mutter some comment about low-class people to herself as she did so.

After a long stretch of walking, they had finally cleared the business district and residential housing now surrounded them. Steve explained that they were a few streets away from Trenton road.

"I hope your friend has facilities for some decent refreshments," Kim badly concealed her desire for a rest.

"Yeah," Graham added, Steve seemed to be getting heavier with each new street, and he did not feel like talking with Kim anymore than he had to.

Finally, they made it to the start of Trenton road. Beth made it to the corner of the street and looked down the road. The road was very long and halfway it weaved off to the right concealing the rest from view. It was lined both sides with large houses jammed into small plots of land. There was the occasional large flowering tree flanking the road scattered all the way down. The small red flowers looked very festive.

"Its number three hundred, and ninety-nine," Beth explained.

"That's got to be on the far-end I expect," Steve said, pointing.

They started to make their way down the road when they all heard a loud, clattering sound. They all looked to their right and saw something scuttle down from a nearby roof.

"RUN!" Graham commanded.

A second later, a Scarkin Demon jumped up onto the fence and began to scamper towards them howling as it did so. Kim started screaming as she ran off. Beth ran after her as fast as she could. Graham and Steve tried their best to pick up the pace, but it was clear they had no chance of outrunning the demon.

"Get going!" Steve demanded, pushing Graham off him.

"You won't make it alone," Graham pleaded.

"You can. Go!" He insisted.

Graham hesitated for a moment his eyes locked on the approaching demon. Zack's sketches and explanations made for a good likeness. Graham remembered how deadly Zack said they were.

"Graham! I need you!" Beth cried back to him.

He turned and ran after Beth. Upon seeing him follow, she resumed her run up the street.

Steve limped into the driveway of the closest house. He only made it halfway to the house before the demon set upon him. Screams of pain rung out down the road as it ripped deep wounds in his flesh. Graham stopped for a moment wishing he could do something to help.

"C'mon!" Beth yelled.

The remaining three ran down the road further from the screams. Steve fended off the demon in vain as it toyed with him. The screams broke into fits of gasping and then a quiet death rattle as Steve died. The Scarkin made its way back to the road and spotted another group of travellers emerging from a side street and sped off in pursuit.

Graham, Beth and Kim heard a peppering of gunshots, then more screaming. They kept running, too scared to look back. Graham kept running through what he could have done in his head.

"Three seventy, we're nearly there," Beth called back to Graham and Kim.

They continued around another bend in the road and frantically searched for Mindy's house.

"Here!" Beth yelled as she ran up to the door of a nearby house.

"Mindy! Open up!" Beth called as she repeatedly knocked on the door. Beth tried to look in the windows but could not see if anyone was home. A moment later, she heard a series of locks open from the inside. The door swung open to reveal Mindy's smiling face.

"Beth! Graham!" Mindy cried as she hurried them all inside.

"Where's Zack?"

"He must be still on the way here," Graham replied.

They locked the front door behind them. They stood panting in the entrance way for a moment, and Mindy pounced on them with a big hug.

"I'm so happy to see you!" she cried.

"Mindy!" Beth hugged her back with equal vigour.

"Great to see ya. This here is Kim," Graham added.

Kim waved a greeting as she struggled to catch her breath.

"Get away from the windows!" A voice called from elsewhere in the house.

"That's Lisa my flatmate," Mindy explained.

Lisa walked in from the kitchen and shooed them into the lounge.

"In here, in here."

She returned to the window and cautiously peered out before returning to the lounge.

"I'm not sure what's going on, but whatever is making all those people scream, I don't want none of that in here," Lisa said.

"Agreed," Graham nodded.

"So where's Zack?" Mindy asked again.

"We were hoping he'd beat us here. Before all this chaos, we dropped him off at the Gold Star offices. Don't worry, I'm sure he's OK. He'll probably turn up here any minute."

"I hope so."

"He'll be fine..." Beth reassured her. "...If anyone will be able to survive in this mess, its Zack."

Mindy nodded.

After introductions and a brief chat, Mindy brought out sandwiches and bottled water.

"Thank you," Kim said sincerely as she quenched her thirst.

The five of them talked into the evening as they waited for Zack to arrive and Mindy's other flatmates to return home.

. . .

Zack, Stanley and Beverly made their way out onto the street. It was packed with people who had evacuated the surrounding buildings.

"Stay close," Zack called as they weaved their way through the crowd. Screaming erupted from a short distance away and a surge of people pressed against them. Zack could not see what was causing the panic, but it was enough for people to flee for their lives. He tried to push his way against the tide of people but was pushed back despite his efforts.

"Whaddya doing?" Stanley hollered, trying to be heard above the panicked cries.

Zack ignored him and continued to try to push into the fleeing people. He was nearly knocked to the ground as a large man in the crowd slammed into him as he pushed others out of his way. Zack was lucky enough to get knocked into the person behind him and did not get laid out on the ground.

Another few cries burst out around them as people who were not so lucky got trampled. One sounded very close, but Zack could not do anything to get closer. He decided to follow the flow of the crowd for a moment then managed to scramble up onto the bonnet of a parked car. He stood up and tried to see what was going on. He was surrounded in a sea of panicked faces. Zack's eyes darted back over the crowd to see a bloody limb been thrown up into the air. He felt a tug on his leg and toppled over into the crowd.

"Idiot! We gotta go now!" Stanley cried, releasing his grip on Zack.

"I can help damn it!" Zack shouted back.

A short distance away, a man in a business suit stood amidst the crowd. He was shoved into the shop front he was standing next to, as others scrambled to get past him. Eugene was no coward, and he was sure whatever people were fleeing from could be overcome. He waited as people surged around him. As the majority of people had now passed him, the crowd began to thin out as the stragglers desperately tried to catch up.

Eugene looked back up the road to see several dead bodies and blood splashed over the ground. His mind took a moment to try and understand what was happening. He unconsciously took a step or two forward so he could see past the people fleeing in front of him blocking his view.

A blood-chilling scream stung his ears as he witnessed a lady running be picked up off the ground by some unseen force. She seemed to be held up by something holding her waist. She struggled as best she could but could not get free. A moment later she rose in the air before smashing back down repeatedly into the concrete. Her screaming abruptly stopped with the first impact. Eugene could not help but stumble back a few steps. The lifeless body of the woman was then flung across the road through a shop window, sending shards of glass flying.

The next closest member of the crowd crumpled before Eugene's eyes as if he was crushed by something invisible but enormously large and heavy. He was squashed into a broken pile of blood and bone with not even a chance to cry out.

Eugene desperately looked around for what could be killing everyone, but he could not see anything. Several people were knocked to the ground all at once with many of them bleeding from fresh wounds that seemed to have come out of nowhere. Eugene turned and fled with the others, but it was too late. A surge of pain signals soaked his brain for a fraction of time. Eugene died before both halves of him fell to the ground.

Further up the road Zack, Stanley and Beverly ducked into an alleyway to escape the crowds.

"What on earth is going on?!" Beverly cried, barely holding it together.

"Whatever it is, we need to get far away from it, and fast," Stanley began to trot away. A few people from the crowd behind them sprinted past. Beverly hurried after Stanley as fast as she could. Zack was unsure of what to do for a moment. He braved a peek around the corner. As he did so, he was nearly bowled over by someone running into the alley.

"Run fool!" they cried.

Ignoring them, Zack returned his gaze down the road. By now hundreds lay dead, strewn into a bloody mess all over the road and the surrounding buildings. Zack even saw a body that was hanging out of a second-story window. Ahead of him, he saw people running in all directions, but no trace of what was causing the slaughter. He turned and ran to catch up with Stanley and Beverly.

The narrow alley was lined with graffiti-plastered walls and the occasional large rubbish bin. On the far end, it opened out onto another street. But there was little visibility beyond that. The people running ahead of them did not come back screaming from the other direction, so it must be safer than what they were leaving behind.

Zack watched Beverly turn left as she exited the alleyway and he went after her. Ahead of them on the busy city street, he thought he saw a glimpse of Stanley amidst the others fleeing. They ran a little further down the road. As they did so, the crowd began to slow and then halted. Some were crying; others looked to be in shock. No one was close enough to see what had occurred. Several had minor cuts and bruises. Recently, that was nothing unusual.

"Up here!" Stanley called back.

They followed him over the road and across one more city block. He stopped outside a small bakery which had the entire glass frontage smashed in.

"C'mon!"

Beverly and Zack arrived a moment later panting.

He led them inside and heard broken glass crunching beneath their feet. They sat down behind the counter for a moment and caught their breath. Then they began to hear a struggle in the kitchen behind them.

"Help!"

They all rushed into the kitchen to find a man and a woman struggling up against the counter. The woman's clothes were torn, and the man held a knife to her face.

"Get out! This doesn't concern you," the man yelled back at them. He pointed the knife in their direction for a moment.

Beverly backed up as Stanley and Zack stepped forward.

"Let her go," Stanley commanded.

Zack eyes immediately searched the room for a weapon. Only large pots, pans, plates and ingredients were in reach.

"She's mine," he said, turning to face them as he began to buckle up his trousers.

Zack charged forward with Stanley close behind him.

"Back…" the man began.

The woman kicked him and struggled free. He turned and slashed her with the large knife. She fell to the ground screaming as blood spurted over them. Zack grabbed a small metal pot as he darted across the kitchen. The man swung back towards them with another wild slash flicking blood across the room. Zack raised an arm which the knife slashed across. He howled in pain, channelling it into a strike with the pot. The man fended in time but was knocked back as Stanley charged into him.

A quick few punches pushed him back further as Stanley laid into him. Zack was surprised at how quickly Stanley moved. Zack brought the pot down upon the man's head with a satisfying thud.

"Blau-agh…b…" the man garbled words came out incoherently.

He dropped the knife, and his eyes began to flutter. As he began to topple backwards, Stanley launched a right hook into his face. His head snapped back violently and hit the edge of the oven. He slumped to the ground. The woman's cries turned into sobs as she saw her attacker drop.

"He, he, he…" she wept.

"It's OK, you're OK," Stanley assured her as he checked her injuries. A long cut across her shoulder went down into the top of her right arm. She had a black eye and a few bruises.

"It's alright; you're safe now."

"There's more of them," she wailed.

"Where?" Zack asked.

"I don't know, he, they… just…"

"You're alright dear," Beverly eased Stanley aside and tended to her wounds with a dishtowel. After checking them, she pulled off her cardigan and put it over her shoulders.

Zack released his grip on his injury for a moment, and blood immediately oozed from the new cut. He grabbed an apron and wrapped it tightly around his arm.

"Let's check," Zack motioned to Stanley.

They quickly checked for others nearby.

"I'm Beverly, what's your name?"

"Kirsty, its Kirsty."

"OK, look Kirsty, you're going to be fine. It looks like lots of blood, but it's shallow. You'll heal. You'll be OK."

As they left the kitchen, another man strolled up to the bakery doors with a grin on his face.

"Hey, is it my turn yet?"

He looked at the pair of them then turned and fled. Zack and Stanley made chase. By the time they got to the door, he was weaving through the crowd outside. He looked to be heading towards a large group of men on the other side of the road.

They returned to the kitchen.

"We need to move," Zack declared.

"Yeah, let's get going. C'mon," Stanley helped Beverly and Kirsty stand up.

"There's a side door here," Zack called, and they made their way over to him. Stanley grabbed a bag of dinner rolls from the bench as he passed. Zack heard the crunching of glass under many boots as he shut the door behind them.

"Quick! Now!" He rasped.

They fled down a service alley that backed onto the many small shops lining the road. Once they reached the end, they crossed the road.

"Here!" Zack called as he made his way into a travel agency with broken glass doors.

They filed in behind him and made their way into the back office. They opened a door with a 'staff only' sign and found a small room. It contained a large couch and a small table, chairs and kitchenette.

"This will do fine," Zack said nodding as he closed the door behind them.

He then grabbed a chair and wedged it under the handle of the door.

"How are the injuries looking?" Stanley asked Beverly.

"She'll be OK, a very large cut, but thankfully it's not too deep..."

Beverly sat Kirsty down on the couch and sat next to her.

"You'll be OK dear."

Kirsty turned and nodded her appreciation. A creaking sound at the far side of the room caught everyone's attention.

"Stanley," Zack pointed to the toilet door.

They both approached slowly, ready to attack.

"Take everything! Just leave me," a new voice called out, trying to be brave.

Stanley and Zack relaxed a little.

"Who's in there?" Stanley asked, knocking on the door.

"Nobody, I'm no one, just leave me and go!"

"We're not going to hurt you," Zack assured.

"I'm not coming out," she said defiantly.

"Sorry, but we're not leaving, it's not safe out there," Stanley stated.

There was no further reply.

Stanley and Zack spent a few more minutes trying to convince them it was safe to come out with no luck.

"Just leave her be," Beverly suggested.

At that, they both sat down at the table.

'Anyone else starving?" Stanley asked.

They all nodded.

"We've got some food out here?…" Stanley offered to the mystery person locked in the toilet, but he got no reply.

"…very well then, suit yourself."

He opened up the large bag of dinner rolls and handed one out to each person. They sat and ate and slowly their levels of adrenaline started to drop. Zack found an urn on the wall for boiling water. With it, they were able to fill some teacups, and each have a drink of clean water.

"Thank you, everybody…" Kirsty said as she finished her drink. "…I don't want to think about what would have happened if you had been much later…" she drifted off for a moment.

"Let's stick together. We'll all be OK," Zack suggested.

"It's sad, isn't it?" Beverly began "Our world seems to be on the precipice of such greatness. We've been enabled by so much technological advancement, yet it seems to be saturated in cruelty."

Zack and Stanley nodded.

They heard a faint scream from somewhere outside. It was enough to remind them of the dangers on the street. Stanley got up and checked that the chair was wedged securely against the door. They chatted for the next few hours unsure of their next move.

Beverly stood up and approached the toilet door.

"Sorry, but please can I use the loo? I really need to go," Beverly pleaded.

"I just can't; I'm too scared."

"You can't stay in there forever. Stick with us, and you're stronger than you realise. You don't know what you can do until you really need to do something."

"Yeah, it's OK, just don't let the fear paralyse you."

Zack quoted scripture

Joshua 1
[9] Have I not commanded you? Be strong and courageous. Do not be afraid; do not be discouraged, for the LORD your God will be with you wherever you go."

No reply came.

"Look I'm really sorry everyone, but would you mind looking the other way, I can't hold anymore. I'm sorry. I'll try not to make too much of a mess," Beverly placed a cup on the ground outside the toilet and began to undo her trousers. Everyone else in the room turned away to give her what privacy they could.

"Hold on. I'll go straight back in here once you're done OK? No tricks," a small voice said.

"Yes fine, please, quickly," Beverly said desperately.

The toilet lock snapped open and a middle-aged lady stepped out.

Beverly quickly ducked past her went into the toilet.

"Thanks so much," she said as she shut the door.

"I'm Zack; this is Stanley and Kirsty. Beverly is in there," they each offered friendly smiles.

"They are good people," Kirsty assured.

"I'm Sarah," she replied but didn't move from where she stood.

Beverly finished and opened the door.

"Thanks again,"

True to her word, Sarah slipped back into the toilet and locked the door.

They decided to stay where they were for the night and think of a plan tomorrow. Beverly and Kirsty slept on the couch and Stanley and Zack on the floor. Despite more offers, Sarah remained in the toilet all night.

In the morning, they all awoke, stiff but grateful for the rest in relative safety. Zack only now thought that perhaps they should have slept in shifts to maintain watch. Thankfully it was not needed.

"I need to go and find my friends," Zack explained.

"And we can't stay here forever," Stanley added as he rustled through the cupboards.

"I'm happy to go. What would you like to do Kirsty?" Beverly asked.

"You said you're heading out of the city, right?"

"That's right."

"I'll stick with you all if that's OK?"

"Certainly! We're happy to have you with us."

"Good, good. OK, this is everything." Stanley made a small pile of food on the table from what he found.

It was enough for breakfast for everyone, but no more.

"Sarah, we're going to be leaving soon. Would you like to come with us?" Zack offered.

No reply came from the toilet.

Zack approached and knocked on the door.

"Hello? C'mon. You can't stay in there for the rest of your life."

There was no reply.

They all sat at the small table and ate a breakfast of stale sandwiches, apples and a jar of jam. They left a portion on the table for Sarah.

"We've left you some food, but you'll need to find more," Beverly explained.

"OK, let's go."

Zack pulled the chair out away from the door and opened it. As he did so, the toilet door opened once more. Sarah immediately went to the table and scoffed down the last remains of the sandwich.

"I'll come too," she finally admitted.

"Great! here," Beverly offered her a cup of water.

Zack, Stanley, Beverly, Kirsty and Sarah left the travel centre and ventured out onto the street. A chaotic world greeted them with an unknown foul stench and dust drifting through the air. Many of the people in the street had dispersed, and there was no sign of emergency services or help anywhere.

"Let's get going," Stanley said, pointing further up the street.

They walked for hours through the battered city. Smoke rose from various fires still burning despite the wail of sirens and alarms from seemingly all directions. Zack was constantly treading on broken glass and debris as they headed toward Sundale.

. . .

Back in Mindy's house, Graham, Beth, Kim, Lisa and Mindy had spent the night waiting for people to return. Nobody had done so. They stayed in the house, eating what was left in the cupboard and keeping quiet.

"Perhaps he's headed back to Brakenside," Graham suggested.

"Why would he do that?" Beth asked.

"You know, all his gear is there. All those preparations he made, supplies, weapons etc. He was right all along, and he'll finally be able to use all that stuff."

"Wouldn't he have come for us first, though?" Mindy asked.

"Yeah, I thought so, but it doesn't take a day to get across town. Maybe he's going to bring those supplies to us here?"

"Hmm, I don't know about that," Beth replied.

"OK then, let's give him until four this afternoon. He'll show up before then anyway, and all this won't matter. But if he doesn't show, shall we make a move to Brakenside?"

That suggestion got a few nods, four was still several hours away, and they were all confident Zack would show up by then.

"Why would I want to go to Brakenside?" Kim protested.

"Trust me; we want to be where Zack and his Priest friends are," Graham explained.

"Nonsense, Doverton has everything Brakenside does and much, much more."

"You're welcome to stay then," Graham had had just about enough of Kim.

"Good, I will."

"That's fine with me."

"Fine."

Contrary to everyone's predictions, four o'clock came, and neither Zack nor any of Mindy's flatmates had arrived.

"He must have thought we were going to head to Brakenside and went there," Mindy suggested, hopefully.

No-one wanted to verbalise that everyone who had not returned could easily have been killed.

"That's probably it. We know he has stuff prepared there, right? Yeah. I bet he's expecting us to meet him at his storage place. It makes sense now that I think about it," Beth thought aloud.

Graham nodded.

"Are you sure this Zack guy you mentioned is worth leaving Doverton for?" Lisa asked.

"Yeah. You should see all his stuff. It's been like his whole life's focus for ages. Put yourself in his shoes. He was convinced that the world was going to end. So he did all he could think of to prepare and help others…" Graham paused for a moment. "…admittedly I didn't believe him. Not really. But obviously, I'm sold now."

"I guess we did kinda make it hard for him sometimes," Beth added.

"He could have tried harder too," Mindy said.

Graham nodded. "Yeah, anyway. Let's go."

"Well if you're so sure, then I'll come too," Lisa decided.

They spent some time readying anything they thought they could use then loaded up Mindy's car. Kim just stood around, watching them silently. As they hoped in the car, she spoke up.

"Well, I'm not going to be left alone here. I'll travel alongside you just for now," she said hopping in the passenger seat.

Graham looked at Beth. She shook her head.

"It'll be OK," she assured him quietly.

Graham let out a sigh as they set off.

Mindy drove slowly down the road in her old car. It didn't take them long to find the road blocked up ahead with vacant cars left in the way.

"Hold on!" she called as she mounted the curb and bounced her way over driveways and footpaths.

"Steady on!" Kim protested.

After they had cleared the roadblock and smashed a few letterboxes, they returned to the road.

. . .

A few blocks away, Zack, Stanley, Beverly, Kirsty and Sarah began walking down Trenton road.

"We're nearly there," Zack promised.

A short time later they made it to Mindy's house.

Zack ran up the path to the front door.

"Mindy! Graham! Beth! We made it!"

The front door did not open for him as he expected and so he began to knock furiously.

"Hey, let us in."

Stanley followed him up the path.

"Let's not attract attention huh?"

Zack tried to open the door, but it was locked.

"I'm gonna try around back."

Beverly, Kirsty and Sarah walked up and waited by the front door.

"Where are they? Weren't we meeting his friends here?" Beverly asked.

Stanley shrugged.

A moment later Zack opened the front door from the inside.

"The toilet window was left open," he explained.

"So they aren't here?" Stanley asked.

"No, not sure why not. Anyway, come in."

They filed inside and sat in the lounge, thankful to take the weight off their feet for a moment.

"I don't get it. I thought they'd be here before us. Maybe they got held up as we did?" Zack puzzled.

"Yeah, probably," Stanley replied as he looked through the kitchen for food.

Zack peered out the lounge window expecting to see his friends arrive.

"They can't be far away…"

"I might lay down for a bit if that's OK?" Kirsty asked.

"Yeah sure, sure. Grab a bed wherever. Let's wait an hour or so. I'm sure they'll turn up then we'll make a plan."

They waited.

. . .

Sister Lee looked up at the dreary sky above her. It had been three days since the sun had darkened. It was the middle of the afternoon, and she was praying in the garden of her school.

"Dear Almighty God in Heaven, please have mercy on us. Guide us all to a new, better way. Help us see your likeness in each other and love, not to hate each other. Bless..." She was distracted for a moment as a light shone against her closed eyes.

"...Bless us in our time of need..."

This time she couldn't ignore the light, and she opened her eyes. Upon doing so, she immediately averted her gaze. She had been facing upwards into the dim sky. As she looked on, she witnessed the brightness of a normal sunny afternoon return. She squinted up towards the bright sun blazing in the sky. The four charred sections of the sun looked to be slowly coming away, like a scab after due healing time. They slowly floated away from the sun and made way for its light to reach Earth unhindered again. Sister Lee began to feel her face warm once more. She could not help but smile.

"Praise the Lord God! Alleluia, Alleluia!"

Sister Lee stood up and ran back into the classroom.

"Everyone look! The sun is bright once more!"

A room full of smiles looked to the windows as everyone hurriedly made their way outside. As they were just about to squeeze past her, a series of clicks were heard throughout the building. All electrical power had ceased. Sister Lee felt different somehow. She knew what had happened but could not explain how she knew. She felt the spiritual assault had been held back. The spiritual and physical realms had been separated once more. As the days followed, she proved to be correct. No more demons tore their way into the physical world.

CHAPTER 6:

DISTRIBUTION

Three five-man teams in black military SUVs were making good progress up the wrong side of the motorway heading towards the central business district. Inside the first vehicle, their commander made some last-minute checks. Henry Jones was leading the third mission in as many days. He did not want to slip up now.

"Are you certain that this layout is current?" he pointed to a paper floor plan on his lap.

His second-in-charge, Logan Perkerson sat next to him. They were both clad in black battle attire, including armoured chest plates, ammunition belts and tactical pouches.

"Yes sir, they made some small changes to the fifty-first level a few years back, but nothing on file since."

The three vehicles came to a stop, and the fifteen men got out and formed up on the lead vehicle. As they moved, they trained their assault rifles in every direction, smoothly transitioning past each other as needed. Four men broke off from the group and set up position a short distance from their vehicles. Anyone foolish enough to attack them would have to deal with a well-trained force.

"Go!"

A few hand signals later, and they had secured their location in the middle of the motorway.

Captain Henry Jones stepped out of the vehicle and surveyed the scene.

"It looks clear sir," Logan added.

A nod was the only reply. They were not expecting anything different.

They gathered around the lead vehicle as their captain addressed them.

"We proceed as planned to the extraction point. We go on foot from here and take the shortest route. Spotters setup positions here and here..." he pointed to the paper map rolled out onto the bonnet as he spoke.

"Once we extract, we stop for nothing as we head back here. Giddy and Sanchez will have our rides ready for us. We got this."

"Yes Sir!" they all replied in unison.

"Move out!" Logan commanded.

As directed, Giddy and Sanchez remained with their vehicles while the others quickly departed. Logan led them to the edge of the motorway where they dropped a short distance down to an onramp below. They followed it to the street and around the block. Upon reaching the corner, two men broke off the main group and began climbing fire escape ladders on the side of the road. Moments later, they had a rooftop position with a line of sight to the target building.

The main group split into two and moved across the road towards the large financial building. Logan saw a pile of bloodworms wriggling out through a broken pipe in the road. But he turned his attention back to his objective. The glass doors on the ground floor crunched under their boots as they made their way into the foyer.

"Stop right there!" yelled a security guard from the elevators.

He had his pistol drawn and was trying to get his radio working with his other hand. Another guard who was reading a book snapped to attention and drew his pistol. Logan held up his fist, and his team stopped. He signalled with his fingers, and they dropped from a high ready stance with their sights on the two guards to watching the entrance behind them.

"I'm Sargeant Logan Perkerson of the seventy-fifth regiment. We're here to help. What's the situation here?"

The guard hesitated for a moment, unsure of the newcomers.

"Stay right there…"

"Oh forgive me, you probably haven't got the comms yet. It's OK I've got a paper copy if that's alright?"

Very slowly, Logan took out a document pack from one of his pouches. He held it up for the guard to see. A distinctive crest was on the top of a letter; it matched the logo on the marble floor which they stood upon.

"Oh thank goodness," the lead guard said with much relief in his voice.

He waved to another guard who only now just came into view. They all lowered their weapons.

"The place is a complete mess with no power. I'm sure head office has told you as much. Did you OK it all with Derrick?"

"Yes, Derrick Lyme approved it this morning. You know how he is, happy to get stuff done."

"Oh yeah, he's good people. He's strict for the most part, but yeah. Anyway come in…" he waved the team over as he spoke. "…I'm Gus, this is Steven and Brynn."

They each waved in turn.

"Hiya, call me Logan, and this is my team," he rattled off their names.

Each man nodded quietly in turn.

"The boss still on fifty-three?"

"Yeah, sorry but the express elevator is out, with the power and all. You'll have to take the stairs.

"Let's get some juice in this building to start then shall we?"

"Huh? That's not possible?"

"Humour me, Gus. Where's the alarm control panel?"

"Over here. But I can only reset it if the power comes on again. And that ain't going to happen…"

They walked behind the security station into a small office. A large panel with a keypad and screen was in the wall next to Gus.

Logan just smiled as he tapped his ear.

"Command? We are established. Light her up."

Gus wore a confused look on his face.

"How'd did you…"

All at once, the remaining lights in the foyer came on and with it the building alarm. It was mind-numbingly loud.

"Can you?"

"I gotta…"

The two men shouted at each other for a moment, then Gus punched the twelve digit code into the keypad. The alarm siren shut off and Logan sighed with relief.

"Thanks Gus. You really helped us out."

"Happy to …"

Gus' voice trailed off as they walked back out to the foyer. Steven and Brynn's bodies were being dragged across the floor by their heels. A puddle of blood smeared over the floor.

As Gus went for his weapon, Logan plunged his knife into the back of his neck. Gus' body immediately slumped to the floor. He bent over and plucked his security card from around his belt.

"We've got the green light," Logan directed his team with another hand signal.

They split into two teams and took separate elevators to the fifty-third floor. The elevators opened into a large corridor. Two guards were standing with assault rifles aimed at them.

"Don't move!" one yelled.

Logan walked forward casually.

"Stand down. Gus sent us up first, he'll be along shortly…" he held up the document again. "…take me to the big man."

"See I told you! Reinforcements, finally!" One guard said thankfully.

"Yeah, yeah."

"He's in his office, like always. I'll take you. *Just* you, mister…?"

"I'm Logan Perkerson of the seventy-fifth. Look, my team can come with me, that's our orders. It's fine."

"We have our orders too. Just you, sir."

Logan swore in his mind. Damn this fool for sticking to protocol.

"Sure, sure, we're all just grunts, right?"

"Yeah, sure."

"OK boys, you heard him. I'll be back soon. Help Gus with the gear when he comes up, will you?"

"Yes sir."

Logan stepped forward; the head guard stopped him again.

"No firearms," he stated sternly.

"Your house, your rules,"

Logan reluctantly unstrapped his assault rifle and handed it to the closest guard.

The head guard was now satisfied and walked down the long corridor behind them. Logan followed. He knew things were going to get a lot messier than he preferred.

"Through here sir," the head guard opened the thick office door after unlocking it with his swipe card and key code.

Logan walked into a large room with a large desk at the far end. Behind it sat a large man with a furrowed brow. He was halfway through a large bottle of brandy.

"Finally someone's here to take me outta this hell hole!"

"Yes sir, but first we have a priority to attend to," Logan removed the document from its plastic sleeve and laid it on the desk. He placed a tablet next to it followed by a pen.

"Huh? What is it?"

"I'm not a lawyer sir," Logan said with a smile.

The man fanned through the forty-page document and turned on the tablet. He returned to the document and began reading.

"Respectfully sir, these need your approval immediately."

"Quiet!"

By the elevator, the remainder of Logan's team waited trying to look as relaxed as they could. The head guard beckoned one of his men to stand by the office door and walked over to the elevator. Pancho stood closest to him, and despite trying to avoid eye contact, he began a conversation with him.

"So Gus will be up soon?"

"That's right; he's helping the rest of our team."

"Big team then."

"Yeah, you know they like everything top-notch around here."

The head guard nodded.

"They sure do."

Logan knew he didn't have long. He tried his luck a little further.

"Please sir, we need to hurry. Lives are on the line …"

"I don't pay you to talk!"

Despite his reply, he pulled the tablet closer to him.

"Hobson has signed already… hmmm…" he said to himself.

Logan looked around the room. The two guards standing behind him looked ready for action at any moment. That was going to make things difficult. Finally, the executive pulled the tablet over next to him and entered his key-code. The company logo flashed up, and the screen lit up with a series of menus. He scrolled through a few of them and then returned his gaze to the document. He now had one in each hand and was double-checking the physical and digital copies.

Out in the corridor, the head guard continued his chat.

"I bet Gus went on and on about his new kid, huh?"

"He didn't say anything to me sir."

"Oh that's funny, normally he can't wait to show off a picture or two."

Pancho shrugged.

The head guard waited by the elevator tapping his foot.

"So Gus and Brynn will be up soon?"

"That's right. Don't worry."

"Yeah, let's just relax huh?" The head guard eyed each of Logan's men in turn. He noticed a couple of specks of blood on Pancho's leg. It was the last straw.

"OK, hand in your weapons; I'll get some coffee brewing," he offered casually.

Logan's men did not move.

"Thanks, but we'll keep hold of them," Pancho replied politely.

"What happened to my house my rules?" He said, slowly moving behind the desk.

The other guards snapped into a ready state.

"Don't sir. Just don't," Pancho pleaded.

"Threat!" He yelled as he punched the alarm button on the side of the desk.

Back in the office, Logan began sprinting towards the executive as automatic gunfire exploded from the hallway. The two guards behind him immediately aimed their pistols. The first had lined up his shot on Logan, but before he could pull the trigger, a large calibre rifle round punched into his face. He was thrown back by the impact. The window next to them shattered as more rounds tore through the thick glass.

The second guard wildly let off half a clip before the many bullets entering his body sprawled him across the ground. Logan caught two rounds in the exchange. One in the centre of his back armour plate, the other grazed his left forearm. Logan fell to the ground as pain shot through his system. The exec clamped both his hands over his ears and fell off his seat onto the floor. After taking a minute to choke down the pain, Logan picked up the guard's pistol and grabbed the tablet from the desk before it timed out and locked itself. He scrolled down to the new contract and accepted it.

"What the hell are you doing?" The terrified man in the business suit yelled.

"Just business," Logan stated coldly.

Gunfire in the hallway became bursts of shots, then a moment of silence. Logan listened as he tried to picture what was occuring. He had absolute confidence in his team, but with even with all the training in the world, automatic gunfire at close range would be no less deadly.

Two more shots one after the other rang out.

"Extraction clear!" Logan heard one of his men shout.

Logan walked over to the executive who held out his hand, expecting to be helped to his feet. Instead, he received two bullets to his head. The tablet demanded fingerprint identification to continue. Logan grabbed the dead man's right hand and pushed his thumb onto the screen. A green complete message lit up the screen, and Logan smiled.

"Thank you for your co-operation."

He grabbed the pen from the desk and forged a signature on the last page of the document. It was not a great representation, but it would have to do. Logan doubted anyone would ever get the chance to check the paper copies. He took a moment to stand by the shattered window and waved out to his sniper on a distant rooftop. He clicked his radio.

"Thanks Badger, I would've been a goner without you."

"I'm always watching over you," was the reply.

Logan waved then turned back inside.

"Let's move!" He called.

Logan returned to the hallway to find bullet holes everywhere and blood covering the floor. All of the building guards lay dead. To his surprise, Pancho had taken a couple of rounds to his armoured chest plate. He looked to be holding back his pain.

"Are you good?"

"Yes. I'm ready."

It was clear that the head guard knew his craft. All the other locations had been a complete walkover. Logan bent down and closed the dead man's eyes as he walked past. He thought about what a waste it was to lose such a competent man. He turned back to his men.

"Do it."

"Sir."

Pancho unpacked an explosive charge and set it on the wall next to them. He set the timer then returned to the elevator.

Logan pressed the transmit button on his radio.

"The deal is done."

Elsewhere, contracts were signed, deals were made, favours called in and murders committed. Birthed in chaos, the World Governmental Organization was formed. It was comprised of multinational corporations, governments, private military and key industry stakeholders. A global crisis was all that was needed to override the many checks and balances that would have ordinarily never allowed such an entity to be created. The WGO now had the ultimate power and authority across the entire globe. As soon as they were able to, they exercised all the power they could.

...

A small boy in Doverton was one of the first to witness the WGO's actions. Simon Cho sat atop the tile roof of his dead parent's house as he watched the various fires in his neighbourhood burn. He was hungry and had just about given up all hope. Movement in the sky caught his eye. He peered off into the distance. His house overlooked a large industrial district, and he thought he saw something small leave one of the huge warehouses. The air was hazy, and it was difficult to be sure.

A moment passed, then a flood of movement filled his vision. He stood up and shouted in delight. A countless swarm of delivery drones flew up into the sky. Each small craft had four electrically driven rotors and carried a small cargo box beneath them.

"Over here!" He yelled, waving furiously.

Simon did not think he would live to see any resemblance of human civilisation again. He watched in anticipation as he saw the swarm begin to disperse in all directions. The drones had been a common sight before the end times, but he had never seen the full fleet depart at once before. He was sure this was a good sign. The drones methodically separated into eight distinct directions. As they began to come closer to him, he expected to hear their high pitched noise. Instead, it was almost a roar.

A huge number of drones flew overhead just a few blocks away. Simon kept waving but gradually began to lose hope again. More movement caught his eye, and he spun around to see another warehouse across town let loose another gigantic swarm of drones. These immediately flew to the first warehouse and disappeared inside. As he continued to watch, the drones began to emerge once more, this time laden with cargo. They departed and began to spread out. There was a mathematically perfect spread of drones.

218

In unison, each drone then began to descend to ground level. Simon could see the closest one come to a landing in the gym car park in the street opposite his house. The drone landed for a brief moment, then shot back up into the sky again at a great pace. Simon saw that it left its cargo behind. He watched as more and more drones made their way back into the sky then return to the warehouse they had originally come from. Simon clambered down from the roof and sprinted towards the gym. As he did so, he saw many of his neighbours do the same.

"Jackson! Did you see them?"

"Of course Simon. Everyone did."

Simon remembered why he did not like to spend time with Jackson. Regardless, they ran together to the gym. As they came to the end of the street, they saw a small group had already made it there before them. Simon watched them run away with something small in their hands from the cargo site. His pace slowed as he saw people ahead of him leave empty-handed.

"It's my lucky day!" A man yelled as he scampered off with his prize.

Simon and Jackson made it to the car park as others had all left. They approached to see a large cardboard box. It had paper attached to all sides printed with writing of all sorts of different languages. Simon read it aloud

"Emergency Supplies. Please distribute equally. More help is coming."

"Hey look!" Jackson picked up some cardboard scraps from a bush nearby and brought them over to show Simon.

"Huh?"

They both looked it over. It was the packaging of one of the latest model smartwatches.

"A fancy watch? Not food or medicine?" Jackson said puzzled.

"It must be a mistake?"

"I don't get it?"

Simon looked around and back on the road he saw two men bickering over one such box. One of the men already wore the watch on his wrist.

Simon's hope began to fade again.

"Another government stuff up."

He waved goodbye to Jackson and began to head home. The two men fighting over the watch ahead of him started to shout louder.

"Take it off now, or I'll take it off your dead body!"

"Just you try it punk!"

The first shoved the other, and a moment later punches were being thrown. Simon just walked around them at a safe distance. His recent fears of humanity disintegrating were confirmed.

"Stand by!" A loud female voice commanded.

The two men fighting de-escalated to scuffle for a moment, they both stared at the watch which now had a blinking green light on it.

"Stand by!" the voice repeated.

Simon heard the same message off in the distance.

"Boot sequence complete. Default language selected. Survivors detected. Please gather more before instructions continue..."

A countdown timer shone out from the screen. It was mesmerising to see after they had been without all power for so long. He looked around to see others, staring at the new watches in wonder.

"Hey kid, come here!" The man wearing the watch called.

The other called to Jackson and another lady on the far side of the street. Soon a small group assembled around the watch.

"Maybe they are going to airlift us out of this dump?" the woman offered.

"Shh! Its nearly time!" Jackson stated as they watched the timer tick down to zero.

"Loading..." the screen blinked a few times.

Simon looked up and down the road to see a few other groups huddled together.

A young woman's face was projected up from the watch and smiled at them all. She looked almost life-like. The same voice continued as she spoke.

"Greetings survivors. I am 'B-three-five-five' an artificial intelligence assistant. You can call me Bess. Do not fear. The World Governmental Organization will be assisting you back to a safe, productive life. The threat has been dealt with. Essential services will be coming back online soon. More instructions will follow."

Those around the watch traded looks with each other. They discussed for a moment as they waited for the next message. They did not reach a consensus on anything.

"Stand by…"

They stopped talking and listened patiently.

"Forty. Nine. Stafford lane. Large green building. Distance, three hundred nineteen metres from present location…"

There was a moment of silence again. Bess' face was devoid of all emotion as it spoke.

"…You must all travel there now. Supplies are limited. Those who are late will receive none. Stand by. Prosperity through the unification of all peoples."

The projection of her face remained for a moment before fading away. The screen on the watch now displayed another countdown timer. The two men who were fighting a moment earlier both seemed to know the location that was spoken of and without a word they set off at a running pace.

"Hey wait for us!" Jackson called in vain after them.

Simon looked around to see others begin to head in the same

direction. Some sprinted at their top speed others walking slowly.

After it was clear no-one would wait Jackson ran off. Simon thought about what he should do. He was not allowed to go past the end of the block without permission. But now that his parents were dead did that still apply? He decided he would go and have a look; he could always make his way back home afterwards. He ran off behind Jackson.

"Jackson!"

He did not wait, either.

After several blocks of running, Simon had passed several groups of people who had now resorted to walking, panting and out of breath. He had finally caught up to Jackson, and the two of them ran together in the middle of the road. They were now on Stafford Lane, and they kept their eyes out for a green building. The road was the border of the commercial part of town and had several small offices, a school and many houses.

As the two of them ran, they saw a crowd gathering around a large, dark green warehouse. It was surrounded by a tall steel fence with barbed wire around the top. The two boys squeezed their way through the crowd and managed to make it up to the fence. Looking through the chain-linked gate, three armed men patrolled around the inner courtyard with automatic weapons.

"Stay off the fence!" One guard shouted, raising his weapon.

A man who had thrown a jacket up onto the barbed wire was looking for a way to climb up.

Another man in a white coat stood on the inside of the fence.

"Calm please everyone! Calm now. We don't have long to wait. Just a few more minutes."

"We're starving out here!"

"Just give us the food!"

"C'mon open up!"

The crowd shouted back at him.

"Hey Benjamin!" A woman opened a small side door of the warehouse and rushed towards the man at the gate.

"Benjamin! We did it; we're ready, shall I open up?" She asked.

He turned and tried to keep his voice from being heard from the crowd.

"No, we wait for Bess."

It was clear from the fury erupting from the first few lines of the crowd that he was not quiet enough. They started shaking the fence.

"…we haven't had the all-clear yet. Please everyone be patient. We'll be ready soon…"

"She just said you were ready! Open up!" One person shouted from the crowd.

Benjamin stood back and folded his arms.

"We wait," he stated.

A short time passed as those in the crowd who had AI watched the countdown timer. The crowd calmed down as they realised it was less than a minute to go. Voices dropped to an expectant hush as the countdown timer reached zero. All faces looked up to Benjamin. He looked down at his watch too. He returned to his arms folded position. The watch face now displayed

"Stand by…"

"Open up! We waited for your stupid timer, we're starving out here!" Another yelled.

Simon peeked over at the nearest watch; the standby message kept on flashing.

"Ridiculous!" a man shouted as he began climbing up on a bin towards the jacket, he had thrown over the barbed wire earlier. As he neared the top, he turned back to the crowd.

"I'll bring some back for you all!"

A great cheer rose from the crowd, and the fence shaking resumed.

Meanwhile, Benjamin had walked over to the closest guard and came back with his assault rifle.

"Get down!" He yelled, barely audible over the crowd. The metallic clack of the rifle indicated it was ready to fire. The climbing man ignored him and wriggled his way over the barbed wire, unavoidably cutting himself in the process. He dropped down to the concrete on the far side with a thump. Another cheer rose from the crowd. Benjamin walked a little closer with his rifle aimed at him. The man began to stand up and dust himself off.

"Ya see, all we people want is…"

Ear piercing gunfire burst out as Benjamin fired a shot into him. As soon as Benjamin steadied himself against the recoil he fired twice more. The bullets slammed the man back onto the ground and splattered the crowd behind him with blood. A single drop splashed onto Simon's hand. Screams erupted everywhere. Benjamin aimed the rifle at the crowd. Simon was pushed over as the crowd surged in all directions.

"Stand by," a loud female voice commanded. The crowd dispersed as quickly as humanly possible, screaming as it did so. Benjamin paused and looked at his watch. He spent a moment reading from the screen.

"Open the gates!" He called back to his man.

The large gate rattled as the motor winched it open. The warehouse doors also opened at the same time. The internal lights now lit up the inner courtyard. Some members of the crowd could not help but turn around. Simon pushed himself up off the ground and sat there dazed. He had been kicked in the head, and blood trickled down his face. Jackson was nowhere to be seen. Benjamin walked forward and bent down next to Simon.

"Come with me."

He took him by the hand and helped him to his feet. He led him across the courtyard.

Simon held his head with his free hand. There were many crates of food being opened by the many warehouse staff before him.

"This way," Benjamin said, leading him to the first crate.

He reached in and pulled out an AI watch and strapped it to Simon's wrist. He then walked to the next crate where a member of staff scanned his watch then pulled out a small bag of rations and handed it to him.

"There you go. Come back tomorrow for more," Benjamin said, turning him around and ushering him to walk out the gates again.

Simon grasped the bag in his hand and walked bewilderedly out the gate again. As soon as he had made it a few steps outside, he sat down in the street and ripped open the small bag.

The crowd, which moments ago were running for their lives had cautiously halted to watch the fate of the young boy.

Simon opened a small plastic bag to find a muesli bar with a picture of an apricot on it. He bit into it vigorously as he rifled through the bag for other items. He drew out a small drink bottle next, which looked to contain juice. He opened the lid and took a big swig. It was sweet, but it tasted a little like medicine.

Simon let out a big sigh of satisfaction and continued chomping his muesli bar. Around him, the crowd slowly began to make its way forward again. One man with a watch cautiously made his way forward holding his arm up as he did so.

"I have one!" He declared.

"All are welcome..." Benjamin began. "...who obey the rules. Those who do not, will not live," he said coldly. No-one doubted him.

The man got his watch scanned and was handed a bag of food. He took it and ran out the gate, across the road then out of sight as he ducked behind some trees. Upon seeing his success, the hungry crowd pushed forward to the gate again.

"Make an orderly line!" Benjamin called.

Everyone obeyed without question or murmur of complaint.

Simon sat in the street, eating his fill with his back to the crowd. As he raised his hand to his mouth, he saw the single drop of blood on his hand. He paused, then wiped it off onto his jeans.

. . .

Zack, Stanley, Beverly, Kirsty and Sarah were at Mindy's house when the sun brightened.

"Hey look at this!" Stanley called as he looked out the kitchen window.

"The sun is back!" He pointed happily.

"Huh?" Zack didn't understand what he could mean.

Stanley pushed aside the furniture they had used to block the front door and made his way outside.

"Idiot! What are you doing?" Kirsty cried.

Ignoring her, he walked down the path and stood in the sunlight. He raised his arms and twirled around. He drew in a deep breath.

"Ah, feels good."

"The demons! They'll get you!" Kirsty called from the doorway.

Zack peered out the window up towards the sun. He was shocked at how bright it was.

"That can't be right..." he muttered as he walked outside.

"Wonderful isn't it?" Stanley said, slapping him on the back.

Zack was lost in thought. The others made their way outside too. Zack walked out to the road and looked up and down the street. He saw other people slowly make their way out of their houses and look up into the sky. Zack slapped himself on the cheek, trying to wake himself up. This was not like his vision at all. He wondered if he had forgotten something. He wondered what this could mean.

"Cheer up Zack!" Beverly said, walking up to him "Everything will go back to normal soon. I'm sure of it."

Zack smiled weakly.

For the rest of the afternoon, he patrolled the house looking for demons. He saw none; he heard none. Regardless, he did not drop his guard. Stanley walked out of the house and made his way over to him at the end of the driveway.

"Hey Zack, we've got to get going. Surely your friends have found somewhere else to be."

"They should have been here by now..." Zack replied.

"We better find somewhere that has more food. We've got enough left in the cupboards to last a little longer, but surely we should take some with us just in case, right?"

Zack let out a big sigh. He had been putting off this decision long enough. With each hour that passed, he had hoped to see his friends come down the street. He had convinced their small group once the sun brightened to give him a bit more time to wait for them. It seemed that Stanley was declaring that time was up.

"They'll be safe I'm sure," Stanley added.

"Yeah. Well, I'm going to head back to Brakenside. All my kit is there. I'm not convinced this is over."

"I hope you're wrong," Sarah added as they left the house.

"Me too," he replied.

"OK, you're up first Beverly. Point us the way."

They had decided to continue as a group as they returned to their homes. Beverly's house was closest. Then Kirsty's was only a few suburbs beyond that. Sarah lived a further still. Both Zack and Stanley had decided to head back to Brakenside. Stanley said he wanted to return to check on his elderly mother.

They walked the few blocks to Beverly's house without incident. Beverly took the mail from her letterbox then walked up to her front door. She unlocked it and beckoned them in.
"Come on in!"
"We really better get going," Zack replied.
Beverly looked to Stanley.
"At least grab a snack before you head out," she said, smiling.

Stanley thankfully made his way inside, shortly followed by everyone else. Beverly's home was very tidy and smelt faintly of the lavender plants in the front garden. They walked into the kitchen, and she sat them down and prepared what food she could that had not spoiled.
"I'm truly grateful to you all. I honestly think I would've never made it home by myself."
Chewing mouths smiled back at her.
"You have a lovely house Beverly; I think my mother has the same curtains," Stanley mentioned.

They continued to chat for a while. Zack receded into his mind. He recalled scripture.

Isaiah 13
⁹ *See, the day of the* LORD *is coming*
—a cruel day, with wrath and fierce anger—
to make the land desolate
and destroy the sinners within it.
¹⁰ *The stars of heaven and their constellations*
will not show their light.
The rising sun will be darkened
and the moon will not give its light.
¹¹ *I will punish the world for its evil,*
the wicked for their sins.
I will put an end to the arrogance of the haughty
and will humble the pride of the ruthless.

Zack knew the end was coming. He knew it in the very core of himself. He could not tolerate talk about such mundane things any longer. He felt like the world was ending for him, but everyone else had already moved on. Zack stood up.

"Going already?" Beverly said in alarm.

"Yeah, we don't want to be travelling at night if we can help it," Zack explained.

"Alright, well stay in touch everyone, we should all catch up for coffee one day."

"Good idea."

She hugged each of them as they left and stood waving in the doorway.

They kept walking towards Kirsty's house when Zack heard an unusual noise. The group turned to see a drone flying low across the street. It had a strip of lights attached to it with a blinking green arrow pointing ahead.

"Stay calm, help is coming," a female voice broadcasted out from the drone as it sped along.

"What the?" Stanley pointed.

Stanley broke into a jog and headed after it. He rounded a corner and pointed ahead of them with a look of shock on his face. Zack knew what it must be and he sprinted forwards ready to carve death into his demonic foe.

"Where?" Zack called as he looked all around him. But he saw no enemy. Zack's gaze returned to Stanley, who just continued to point.

"The traffic lights, that sign! Look! The power is back."

Up the road ahead of them a set of traffic lights flashed orange. Zack was alarmed with how quickly normality was returning. Part of him was delighted, but he could not shake off the feeling that danger still lurked around every turn.

"This way!" Kirsty called as she jogged up her street.

"But the drone?" Stanley asked

"Later," she replied

They walked into Kirsty's flat. She loosed a tiny squeal of delight when she flicked the light switch, and it turned on.

"I'll make you all dinner, and that's final."

Zack and Stanley were ushered into the lounge as Sarah and Kirsty began to cook dinner.

Stanley dropped into the comfy sofa next to Zack and turned the television on.

"...and that's it really..."

There was an interview with someone in a white lab coat on the screen. Stanley flicked through a few more channels.

"Huh?"

"Give it here," Zack nabbed the remote and flicked through even more channels.

The same footage was on every channel.

"I guess it must be one of those emergency things then."

The interviewer on TV continued.

"Neron, Could you put that into some more basic words for our viewers?"

"OK sure…" the man in the lab coat said as he thought for a moment.

"The Transcendental spectrum or 'T-spec' has always been there. We've just never been able to interact with it before. Imagine it like radio waves, but until now we've never had a radio."

"Why now?"

"Well, the solar event let loose radiation across Earth that we're not used to. We're still investigating the details."

"Will it happen again?"

"Probably in another 100,000 years or so I'd expect."

The reporter smiled with relief as she turned back towards the camera.

"There you have it. For those of you just joining us, you can relax now. The danger has passed. I'll repeat that. If you're watching this, it's all going to be alright. We're going to play the message again. Then afterwards we'll continue…"

The footage cut to text on the screen in many different languages. It read:

"The danger has passed. Report to your local aid centre. Follow the signs."

"Signs? What signs?" Kirsty asked.

Zack turned to see Sarah and Kirsty watching from the kitchen.

"Maybe those drones?" Stanley suggested.

"Shall we go after it again?" Sarah asked

"After dinner," Kirsty said.

"Good idea," Stanley added.

The television displayed various safety messages for the next hour.

They ranged through all topics. One message reminded people not to drink stagnant water. Another gave brief instructions on C.P.R. Another scientist explained that a coronal mass ejection is a significant release of plasma and magnetic field from the sun. And they have discovered a new type of this phenomenon.

"Beans and rice Ok?" Kirsty asked as she emerged from the kitchen.

"Perfect!" Stanley said gratefully as he watched the steam rise from the plate. Hot food seemed like such a treat after going without for what felt like so long. The four of them sat and watched television as they ate.

The interview came back on, and they all watched intently. It looked like the start of what they had watched the end of earlier.

"I'm here with Dr Neron Tetrarch, lead scientist here at the University. Perhaps start with how it's possible that people can watch this broadcast."

"Certainly, my colleagues and I have been working hard to combat a new type of solar radiation, during this work; we've discovered a new way to generate electricity. It's completely remarkable. It's possible to generate without huge power plants, without huge damaging effects to the environment, and best of all recently we've managed to distribute it through the existing power grid. Well, most major centres so far, more rural networks are underway..."

"Hang on; they are pretty much saying, that all this madness is over and now they have free power?" Stanley asked aloud.

"I knew somebody smart would figure all this out," Sarah said with relief.

Zack remained silent. He began to wonder how much of his mind he could trust after suffering what he did.

They chatted for a while before Kirsty spoke up.

"I guess you'll all have to stay the night here then; it's getting dark outside."

At that comment, Zack bolted to the window and peered up into the sky. To his surprise, it just looked like a normal evening sky.

"Are you OK with that Sarah?" Stanley asked.

"Yeah sure, it seems things will be back to normal sooner than I thought anyway."

"Yeah. Thank goodness."

The next morning after breakfast, they decided to investigate the drone as a group before heading off to Sarah's house. Upon walking outside, they did not see any drones.

"Surely there will be some around here somewhere," Stanley said.

"Yeah, let's check where we last saw that other one," Sarah suggested.

"Good idea."

The four walked off down the street a short distance. Zack noticed a young man running towards them. Zack took a breath and readied himself should he need to fight.

"What do you want?" He called

"It's your lucky day! ..." He replied, "...here let me show you."

He pulled his sleeve back to reveal an AI watch.

"Well good for you," Stanley jibed.

A female voice began speaking as a projection of a young woman shone out from it.

"Do not fear. The World Governmental Organization will be assisting you back to a safe, productive life. The threat has been dealt with. Essential services will be coming back online soon. Report to your closest aid station."

"Huh?"

The young man walked passed each of them and stamped their left hands with his watch.

"There you go, now you'll get extra rations. And so will I. Help as many other people as you can get to an aid station. You'll be helping yourself by doing so too."

"Yeah, well we don't all have the latest tech kid."

"Oh, they are giving these out for free! Part of that WGO thing, I guess. Head over to Burkenham street warehouse, that's the closest one. They'll explain it to you all."

Before they could ask any more questions, he ran off up the street with a wave. Zack watched him approach another group of people and repeat the process.

"Well, we gotta check out this aid station. At least we have an address now. Is it far from here?"

"Not too far, follow me," Kirsty offered.

They had been walking a block or two when Zack saw more and more people walking in the same direction. Above them, they saw the occasional drone whizz past.

"See I told ya," Stanley said with a smile.

Around the next corner, they were met with a long queue of people. They took their place at the end of the queue and slowly moved forward a step after a minute or so.

"Do you know what this is all about?" Zack asked the man in front of him.

He turned and replied.

"Watch this guy coming up on the far side of the road. That's enough for me."

Zack peered past him to see a middle-aged man walking out of the warehouse complex ahead of him with a bag in one hand and a new watch on his wrist. Zack watched him fiddle with the strap then fish out some food from his bag.

"They are just giving it out for free?" Zack asked.

"Yeah looks like it," the man replied.

"I just hope they don't run out before it's our turn."

"Yeah, me too."

After a couple of hours patiently waiting in line, Zack's group had made its way up to the gate. He observed the man in front of him walk up to a desk in the courtyard where three people sat surrounded in boxes. Either side of them, two men stood watch with assault rifles. They routinely walked up and down the fence line where everyone in the queue could see them.

"Next!" the woman at the desk called.

Zack stepped forward.

"Hi, I was wondering if ..."

She ignored that he was talking to him and slapped an AI watch on his wrist. It automatically tightened until it was secure as a loading screen was displayed.

"Food's that way," she said pointed to the next booth.

"It's just..."

"Next!" she yelled passed him.

Zack felt Stanley push him along as he stepped forward to get his watch. Zack walked forward a few steps to the next booth where a young man was handing out sealed plastic bags. The bags were semi-transparent, and Zack could see the food of different types inside.

"Scan!" He called as Zack stepped up.

"Excuse me, I..."

The young man held up his watch towards Zack's, and there was an audible 'beep' he checked the screen then picked up a food bag and put it in Zack's hands.

"Scan!" He called again ignoring Zack's attempt at conversation.

Zack walked to the man in front of him, handing out water bottles. Zack raised his wrist as the man scanned it. Another beep later and Zack had a water bottle in his hands. He wandered out of the complex pausing just beyond the gate. Zack turned as he heard Stanley approach. Kirsty and Sarah followed shortly after him.

"Free food!" Stanley said with a big smile. "Things are sure looking up."

Zack smiled in reply.

"Back to my house for lunch?" Kirsty offered.

"Sure," Sarah responded.

As they walked, their watches booted up and played another recorded message.

"Greetings, I am Bess. An Artificial Intelligence built to help you. Your current balance is two Creds. This is enough for two more rations of food and water. After this, you will need to work to earn more Creds. This can be done in several ways explained shortly. Tap here to watch a video."

Zack tapped where it was indicated. He watched a clip of someone bringing other people into the aid stations. When they got their watch, his Cred balance was increased.

Bess continued.

"Previous wealth and currencies are no longer accepted. We have numerous vacancies in food and medical distribution that needs no previous experience. More specialised roles exist and can pay higher rates. Note all non-essential roles are no longer required. If your previous occupation was in one of the following industries, please select a change in vocation."

A list of industries with various jobs was displayed on the screen.

"It looks like entertainment of all types doesn't exist in the future huh?" Stanley added as he watched the same messages.

The following screen had a list of industries that were deemed still important. Zack scrolled down to see 'Security' he tapped on it and saw a map of Doverton with various locations that were offering Security jobs.

"Amazing!" Kirsty spoke aloud as she worked her way throughout all the features of her new watch.

Bess continued.

"Please note, due to the worldwide circumstances of the 'Unification Event'. Article 3 of the Universal Declaration of human rights has been temporarily amended. More details will follow at a later time."

"Well, I guess they'll be no lazy people in this new future. It seems like you work, you eat. You don't, and you don't," Sarah summarised.

"Yeah, I guess."

Zack tapped on the 'about' icon for Bess.

"B355-Tspec or Bess is a prototype artificial intelligence whose sole responsibility is to manage the continuation of the human race worldwide. Due to the collapse of societal norms, Bess has been given complete autonomy to restructure and recover a 'normal' way of life. In two to four years depending upon local circumstances, the goal is to reinstate a human-based governmental body. In the meantime, the World Governmental Organization will govern through Bess directly."

Zack tapped on 'WGO' and listened to Bess explain.

"The World Governmental Organization or WGO is a worldwide entity designed to unify and govern the human race. Prior to the unification event, multiple countries signed an acceptance submitting to this authority on the condition that they were completely unable to govern in an emergency. As the entire globe suffered at the same time, the WGO is now the sole ruling entity. Unification of law, commerce, health, services and all data is just one of the many benefits this brings."

Zack tapped the clock icon.

"The day is Wednesday. The month is Unity, day three. The year is zero, zero, zero, one."

He closed his eyes and drew in a deep breath.

. . .

Logan sat in his vehicle with his assault rifle at his side, watching out the windows for any sign of movement. His radio clicked.

"Team 1 in position."

A moment later, it clicked again.

"Team 2 in position."

He pressed the transmit button on his lapel.

"Move in... and don't get complacent."

"Moving in. Yes boss."

"Moving."

He looked out his window towards the cemetery. He started to wonder about the people he was working for. He had led his team on missions with all sorts of high priority targets and now this? He did not understand why they had ordered his team to extract something from a graveyard in the middle of nowhere. His men felt the same way. Their looks of confusion were still fresh in his mind when he explained it to them.

The cemetery was nestled in an insignificantly small town. He doubted there would be much of value here. When their vehicles pulled up they felt more and more like this mission was a waste of time. In the back of his mind, he wondered if they were planning on bombing the whole place to get rid of him and his team. He surveyed the empty street ahead of him. No-one was around this early in the morning.

Regardless, Logan tried to operate professionally. Since suffering injuries in their previous missions he had elected for two vehicles, two three man teams, with himself and Badger on overwatch. He had decided to stay in the lead vehicle in case they needed a quick extraction. Badger lay on the roof of a nearby two-storey building watching the area with his rifle. Giddy led team one and Sanchez led team two.

"One Tango on the east side… looks like he's tending the flowers," Giddy reported.

"Has he seen you?" Logan recalled their directive of no witnesses but did not feel like the local gardener would be a threat to his team.

"No, he's facing the other way. Orders?"

"Hold one."

"Holding…"

"Team two is at the crypt."

"Breach."

At that moment Pancho swung a sledgehammer into the wooden door of an ancient-looking crypt. It had metal reinforcing and looked like it stood the test of time well. As the hammer crashed into the door, the gardener stood up. Giddy's assault rifle spat a two-round burst through his suppressor. The gardener crumpled backwards to the ground, dead.

"Target down."

"Damn it I said hold!" Logan spat.

"He would've seen us," was the cold reply.

Logan ground his teeth.

"Acknowledged, Cover team one, don't engage any more targets without my go."

"Sir."

Logan got out of his vehicle and looked up and down the street. No movement, the early morning chatter of the birds carried on as if nothing had happened. He returned to his vehicle. Their intelligence team advised it was possible but unlikely that they would encounter heavy resistance. He wondered what they had neglected to tell him.

"Badger?"
"All clear."
"Team one?"
"Ready to move in."
Pancho pulled his sledge free from the broken door. It still stood in its frame, but he had broken enough panels of wood that they could squeeze through.
"Proceed with extraction. Let's make this quick."
"Entering now," Giddy replied as he signalled Pancho through the door.
He bent down and tried to force his way through the door, with some difficulty, he forced his way through. Some more thumping sounds were coming from inside, and a few moments later, the busted door swung open.
"Let's move," Giddy directed.

The three men entered into a small chamber; the air was cold and stale. They flicked on their lights attached to their weapons and saw a simple stone coffin in front of them. All the surfaces inside were bare except for layers of dust. It struck Giddy as odd that nowhere in the crypt did it say who was in the coffin. There were no names, no dates and no poems.

"OK, crack it open."

Pancho drew his sledge again and began laying into the coffin with his considerable strength. After the first few hits, it split and cracked. Subsequent hits broke holes into the top until the whole coffin lay open.
"Well, I'll be damned!" Pancho admitted between breaths.

They peered into the coffin to see a ladder leading downwards into the darkness. Giddy dropped a glow-light into the hole and watched it fall to the bottom and lie amidst the broken chunks of the coffin lid.

"I tell you what; these guy's intel is always spot on," Giddy declared.

The others nodded.

Pancho climbed in first, and moments later they walked down a small passageway. Stone bricks lined the walls, ceiling and floor. It looked to have been built very sturdy with no dirt or water seeping through anywhere, despite its obvious old age. As they walked along, they noticed wall-mounted torches were evenly spaced down the hallway. The ceiling height increased as they entered into a small room.

There were two simple bunk beds on the far wall and four wooden chairs in the middle of the room. There looked to be an area for cooking, albeit it simple and very old. What puzzled Giddy most was the weapon racks on the wall. They were empty, but Giddy recognised them regardless. The place looked like it had been undisturbed for a generation.

"Some sort of guard room?" Pancho asked what they were all thinking.

"We're not here to sight-see, let's get going," Giddy directed them to the hallway on the far side.

Giddy's radio crackled and a poor quality signal came through.

"Team one report."

The hallway in front of them abruptly ended with a large reinforced iron door. It looked very durable. Pancho dropped his sledgehammer and rummaged through his bag.

"We're in the catacombs. But we'll need to use charges to proceed."

"Do it."

By this time Pancho had pulled out a small door charge from his bag and looked to Giddy expectantly.

He nodded.

Pancho prepared the explosive then all three men retreated to the guard room. A burst of smoke and dust billowed from the hallway as he detonated it.

Logan heard the dulled but distinct thud from the car. Birds in the trees above the cemetery broke from the trees squawking in alarm. He pulled his rifle into his shoulder and scanned up and down the road. He hoped the locals would sleep through it. The moment passed, and Logan was about to relax when his radio clicked.

"One target moving quickly from the East, shall I engage?" Badger's voice spoke calmly.

"Team two, get into defensive positions. Badger, hold fire until we see the rest of them."

"Ready."

"Holding on you."

The man ran across the path leading into the cemetery towards the sound of the previous explosion. Badger tracked him in through his telescopic sight. He had trained on vastly longer ranges than this with ease.

Another tense moment passed.

"Badger, where are they coming from?" Logan peered from the car as best he could but could not see the others yet.

"No more targets at this time. Sir, it's an old man."

"Say again?"

"This is not a response force. He looks like a priest or maybe its pyjamas. He's about to reach team two's position. Shall I engage?"

"Hold one. Break, team one are you nearly done in there?" Logan wanted to avoid killing any more unarmed civilians if possible.

"Not even close. They have another door down here sir."

"My window is closing sir," Badger insisted.

"Send it."

Badger flicked off the safety and tracked the man as he ran behind a large crypt. He followed through and waited on the far side. The second or so it would have taken the man to cross to the other side passed. He did not appear. Badger scanned back to the other side and saw no movement.

"Badger?"

The muffled crack of his rifle dropped the old man on the far side of the crypt. His scope hung on his target for a moment. Badger was reminded of his grandfather. He loaded another round and continued to scan the area.

"Target down."

"Understood, watch for more. Break. Team one, will you need to hard punch another door?"

"Negative, sledge should work for us. We'll just need some time."

"You've got a few minutes after that…"

A burst of suppressed gunfire peppered across the cemetery, dropping a man at the rear of the cemetery as Sanchez watched his sector.

"Target to the North down," he reported.

"Copy. Badger, watch North!" Logan commanded.

"Already on it. No other targets."

"God damn it! Sir, there's another door behind the last one. What the hell did they keep down here?"

"Team one. Hard punch it. Expect resistance shortly," Logan knew that any moment they would be outnumbered.

"Yes sir."

Another bullet cut through the morning air. Badger loaded another round.

"Target down, Southeast… Sir… this can't be right?"

"Movement!" Sanchez called as he saw a figure weave between the gravestones.

"Man down! Glacier is down," Herc called in alarm.

Logan started the engine and drove the vehicle up over the footpath into the cemetery.

"Where?"

"Watch your sectors!" Logan spat.

Herc arrived at Glacier's body. He lay face down in the grass behind a large blood smudged gravestone. Herc rolled him over and checked for vital signs.

"Glacier is alive."

"Sir this is all messed up!" Badger sounded confused and alarmed. Not something Logan was used to hearing.

"Report."

"Sir, he's the same grandfather?!"

"Badger, say again. Spit it out man."

"He looks just like the first target. Sir, I mean it, exactly identical."

Badger's scope rested on his latest kill. He then tracked over to his first kill. Both were old men in unusual garb. Both had a stubbled beard, both wispy grey hair, balding on the top. The exact same face."

"You missed?"

Badger was slightly insulted at the suggestion.

"No sir, bodies are laying put."

"Well, just keep dropping them."

Logan had heard of some high-grade face masks in the industry, but nothing that would fool Badger at this range. He decided to worry about it later.

"Team one, what's taking so long?"

"Hold one."

Another dulled explosion shook the cemetery.

"Door three down, sir."

Logan drove further into the cemetery his weapon ready at his side. He saw no targets as he bowled through some flowerbeds on the way to the target crypt.

"Keep 'em back lads we're extracting hot."

Herc checked on Glacier's injuries. He did not find anything other than a large bruise on his forehead where he looked to have hit the stone on the way down.

"Drop your weapon!" an unfamiliar voice said from behind him. Herc could not help but smile. He knew only fools gave their enemy a chance in combat. He would end him quickly.

Herc spun around, drawing his pistol as he did so. The man before him knocked his pistol from his hand with a flurry of quick strikes to his arms and hands. Herc charged forward but immediately was thrown over the man's shoulder into the dirt. Herc reeled in disorientation and pain as he found himself looking up into a boot stomping down on to his head.

The attacker was thrown sideways into a nearby gravestone as a burst of bullets from Sanchez' weapon made impact. A second later, Sanchez felt a surge of pain for a brief moment before he blacked out. Logan made it to his position a moment later and fired his sidearm from the window as he crunched to a halt. Two of the shots hit the old man standing over Sanchez, and he stumbled back a step before dropping to the ground.

Logan could hear Badger firing round after round.

"Team one, move it!"

Giddy waved the dust cloud from in front of his face. His ears were still ringing from the blast.

"We'll get it done," he assured his team leader.

He turned to direct his men.

"Cobolt go back to the guard room and watch the stairs. Pancho you're with me."

"On it!"

Giddy waded through the dust, smoke and fragments of the broken door. He took another few steps forward to reveal yet another door stood in his way. This door had no handle on the outside as if it was only to be opened from the inside.

"Pass me another door charge."

"We have none left."

Giddy looked back through the three busted doors to see Pancho holding up his sledgehammer.

"OK, watch my six, I'll use the sledge."

Pancho tossed it to him and dropped to a knee with his assault rifle trained back down the hallway.

Giddy turned towards what he hoped was the last door. He took a step forward and swung the hammer with all his might into the bottom hinge. The iron hinge buckled slightly as dust erupted from the door. It felt remarkably solid. Giddy realised just how hard Pancho must have been working already. He took several more swings without stopping to assess between each strike. He stopped to catch his breath and bent down to see the wood had been smashed away from the hinge, but behind it, he could see a layer of stone bricks.

He swore aloud. This was going to take a lot more time than they had.

Cobolt's weapon spat bullets in controlled bursts further up the tunnel.

"Targets incoming!" Pancho heard him yell.

He heard another few more bursts, then a telling silence.

"Giddy! Hurry up!" Pancho yelled with his assault rifle trained on the doorway.

Giddy smashed the hammer into the middle centre of the door, more out of frustration than strategy. To his surprise, the aged wood splintered and broke. Two panels fell backwards into the darkness behind.

"Hold 'em off Pancho!"

Another series of hits cleared the majority of the top half of the doorway. As he leaned forward, he saw the stone bricks only made it halfway up the door. A pile of stone bricks and tools lay not far from the door. Giddy turned in alarm as he saw Pancho hurry down the hallway towards him.

"I've set up some claymores. That will give us some time."

"Good man," Giddy replied as he clambered through.

Pancho followed him into the darkness beyond.

"Bloody hell. Look at this poor sod…" Pancho shined his torch at the ancient remains of a human body sprawled out behind the pile of bricks. "…these guys were barricading themselves in here? They sure took things seriously back then."

"Yeah. Hey look…"

Pancho pointed to where his hand had smudged off the dust from the wall. Underneath were some ancient writings. He wiped more dust away to reveal the whole wall was covered. Neither could read it but recognised a few skulls.

"…Maybe it's a warning?"

"We've got no time, c'mon!"

They followed the short hallway to an opeining into a very large chamber. Giddy cracked a few glow-lights and tossed them throughout the chamber, filling it with a yellow-green light. It was circular, and the roof rose in height towards the centre.

"Get me out," an unfamiliar voice rasped through the darkness.

Giddy and Pancho immediately raised their weapons towards the sound. Sitting in the centre of the room was a cloaked figure. Giddy blinked his eyes consciously to confirm what he was seeing. A little old man sat cross-legged on a small dais. He looked like he had been sitting there for a century. His eyes were disturbingly piercing. He looked to be caked in dust. The dais was surrounded in a murky liquid.

A skeletal body lay on the ground in front of him. It was alarming to see one of its legs was on the other side of the room. There looked to be scratching in the bloodstains around it. Giddy thought he could read the word 'LIAR'.

Giddy's eyes locked on to the man sitting in the darkness.

"Now!" It commanded. The voice rattled as if it was forced up through a decaying throat.

"What the hell is this?" Pancho asked, looking to Giddy, desperate for some explanation.

"This is it," Giddy replied.

"You gotta be kidding?! I ain't ...."

An explosion behind them sent a wave of pressure and dust crashing into them. Pancho's mines signalled that they were out of time.

"C'mon then let's go," Giddy commanded the old man.

He held up his hands to show the large iron manacles around his wrists. As he began to stand, both men fought some feeling deep inside that tempted them to open fire. The old man stood and lifted his legs to show the large chains holding him in place. His arms and legs were skeletally thin; his skin was stretched and pale over sinewy muscles. The hair on his head and beard were so long it looked to cover him like a cloak.

"I am Tolech. Who are you?" He asked.

Giddy motioned for Pancho to free him. Despite a protesting expression, he obeyed.

"Introductions later, I'll watch the door."

Giddy made his way back to the hallway. As soon as he did so, he saw a figure clamber through the broken doors and run towards him. He opened fire and landed three hits centre mass. The man dropped into the dusty floor.

"Targets incoming!" He called.

Pancho stepped forward towards Tolech and began to assess his bonds. Confusion spread across his face as he saw Tolech's wrists and legs had withered to such an extent it was clear he could remove them at any time. Tolech shook his arms free and grabbed Pancho by the face.

Giddy watched in shock as a flood of men rushed down the hallway towards him. They all looked to be old and wore some type of priestly robe. Giddy pulled the trigger and felled them with murderous ease. To his horror, even more, men scrambled down the hallway towards him at a frantic pace. The bodies were stacking up all over the floor, but they kept coming. Giddy took a step back as he saw the faces light up in the torchlight attached to his gun barrel. They were all identical.

His assault rifle made a distinctive click as his magazine ran dry. He fluidly snapped in another. With the pause in fire the army of old men rushed closer. With a full magazine, he flicked to automatic fire and blasted his attackers backwards. Logan was shouting something over the radio, but Giddy did not hear it. Another click, and another magazine later his attackers did not relent. Finally, he swapped to his sidearm and dropped his foes that were getting alarmingly close.

"Pancho!!!"

"He can't hear you," Tolech replied from behind him. Giddy spun to see Tolech standing behind him, his beard and ragged clothes now covered in blood. Pancho's headless body lay in the centre of the room behind him. Tolech lunged with alarming speed towards Giddy.

"No!" Giddy yelled as he pulled the pin on the grenade he had strapped to his belt.

Another explosion underground rocked the cemetery. Logan stood over Sanchez' unconscious body; he looked towards the entrance to the crypt. He hoped to see his team emerge.

"Team one? Team one!?"

There was no reply.

Logan turned just in time to see an old man face to face for a brief moment before a killing shot from Badger threw him to the ground.

"That was my last rifle round. I'm moving in" Badger reported.

"Stay sharp; these guys are more than they seem."

"Sir!"

Logan turned on the spot trying to see where the next attacker would come from.

"Lower your weapon," a voice gently spoke from behind a nearby gravestone.

Logan raised his rifle and sidestepped to reveal an old man standing there with his hands up.

"Get on the ground, or you're dead!" Logan roared.

"Whatever they told you, it was a lie," he replied calmly.

Logan knew he should have dropped this target by now, but he hesitated. Looking at the man before him, it was clear he was a priest. He carried no weapons but had somehow managed to drop nearly his entire team.

"Call your men; tell them not to open the crypt. You don't understand what's down there."

"What are you?"

"I'm just a man. But what you're looking to free is not."

"Why did you attack my men?"

"It's my duty to keep…"

A gunshot rung out from nearby, the old man collapsed to the ground. Badger emerged from behind a large crypt with his pistol in hand.

"Why didn't you drop him?" Badger spat.

Logan could tell Badger had lost some respect for him. The protocol was clear, and Logan did not follow it.

"I… he…"

Badger looked away shaking his head. Logan and Badger patrolled the area for a few moments but found no other targets. Badger bent over his last kill and beckoned Logan over. It was the elderly man; blood was flowing from a wound in his head. Logan ran over as he saw Badger rifle through his pockets. A moment later he drew out a wallet and some keys and a pen. He opened the wallet and pulled a drivers licence out.

"Emil Linnlock. That name mean anything to you?"

"No, that hasn't come up in any of the intel. What tech has he got?" Logan asked.

"No tech so far. He's got a fancy cross thing. Oh, something in this pocket… a book. Yeah, a Bible."

"Check the face mask," Logan instructed as he bent over the body. He ran his hands along the chin and around the scalp. He found no trace of any type of mask.

"What was he doing before you down'd him?"

"This one was stationary, kneeling, looked to be praying, I guess."

"Let's check the…" Logan turned towards the other bodies. They had vanished.

"Huh?"

"They were right here!" Logan jogged back to where he was standing earlier. The grass was flattened where moments ago a body was laying. Now there was just grass. Badger made his way over to where he remembered dropping a few targets. He found nothing.

"Team one report?!"

Sanchez awoke and stumbled to his feet, before dropping back to a knee.

"Sanchez, are you good?"

"No sir. I feel like I was hit by a bus. Did we get them all?"

"I don't know. But the area seems secure."

Sanchez hobbled over to Glacier and Herc and tried to rouse them.

"Ah, fresh air at last," Tolech said as he strolled out of the crypt behind them.

He wondered how his thrall in Eastern Europe was doing.

CHAPTER 7:

DOMINATION

With more luck than Graham had expected, Mindy had managed to drive them safely to the city limits. Her car was pretty beaten up by this point, having on multiple occasions been driven through fences, hedges and the like. But the engine was still sound, and they had enough fuel for a return trip to Brakenside.

Kim had been quite vocal at her every discomfort of the trip. Graham had on more than one occasion contemplated ejecting her from the car and driving away. Beth had done a good job of defusing the situation but now, even she was getting tired of her complaining.

"Nearly through," Mindy said cheerfully.

Since Mindy had regularly travelled between Doverton and Brakenside, she knew several side routes. These were proving invaluable as the main highway was clogged in both directions. They were travelling cautiously up a long country road parallel to the main highway. A thick native forest bordered both sides of the road with some trees extending their branches above them as they drove past. They had been travelling for some time when the road came to a junction. Mindy slowed to a stop.

"Which way team?" she asked.

"Don't you even know where you're going?" Kim spat.

After a breath to calm herself, Mindy replied.

"I do know where we're going. Both roads will take us to Brakenside. One goes closer to the coast; the other is more inland."

"Seeing the ocean would be nice after all these trees," Lisa suggested.

"We should be taking the most direct route. The scenery is irrelevant," Kim insisted.

"They are both about the same actually. Last year I took the left road when they…"

"Left it is then," Kim decided.

"Mindy, some of us are grateful that you're driving us in your car to safety. I'm happy for you to decide," Graham remarked, looking at the back of Kim's head.

"She asked for our opinion, now she has it," Kim concluded.

Mindy turned the car left and set off again, realising that they could be arguing over it for hours.

They travelled along the narrow country road as it wound its way over a series of small hills. The forest had been hewn down into farmland with the occasional pocket of defiant old trees. In the distance ahead of them as the road veered to the right were two cars. They were stationary in the middle of the road. It was clear there had been an accident. Mindy slowed down as they approached. They could not see any of the occupants. As they got closer, they heard glass crunch beneath their tires as they came to a stop.

"Let's check it out" Graham suggested.

"Yeah,"

"Can we make it past?" Kim interjected

Mindy looked on the left side of the road; a metal railing was on the outside of the turn with a large 'slow' sign just beyond it. Trees peppered farmland behind that. On the right-hand side was a very muddy verge that went down to a section of forest. Mindy could hear a stream flowing somewhere nearby.

"Hmm, I don't want to get stuck in that," she said, pointing.

"Just squeeze us through on this side," Kim commanded.

"Look, Kim. Just close your mouth!" Graham burst out, unable to contain himself any longer.

"I beg your pardon?! Nobody talks to me that way. I was merely suggesting we manoeuvre through on the left. Such rudeness, when all I've done is help you uneducated lot."

"What did you…"

A gunshot ripped through the air from the tree line on the left and ended the conversation.

"Get out of the car!" A loud voice boomed as two young men emerged from their hiding places. They both were holding rifles on their hips. One ejected a spent round and locked in another.

Graham instinctively lowered his head and reached an arm over Beth.

"OK, let's take it …" Graham began. He did not like the look of the situation. To everyone's surprise, Kim swung open her door and stomped towards the two men.

"You inconsiderate, reckless fools! Have you any idea how dangerous what you just did is?" Spittle flew from her mouth in her rage. The four remained in the car their eyes watching the two gun-toting men. One broke into a smile.

"What've we got here Ollie? A real firecracker!" they began to chuckle.

Graham leaned over to Mindy and spoke in a hushed voice.

"Get ready to get outta here in a hurry."

Mindy gripped the steering wheel harder as they aimed their rifles in their direction.

"Turn off the engine, the rest of you get…"

"Unbelievable! You ignorant, stupid lout! How dare you point that thing at me!" Kim stropped forward and slapped the rifle towards the ground.

"Hooo-wee! Look at her go! She's firing on all cylinders," one of the men chuckled.

Graham reached forward to stop Mindy turning off the engine.

"Put it in reverse," he said quietly.

"You can close your unsightly mouth! Have you ever been to a dentist? Or used a toothbrush? Can't you see…"

Kim turned to point towards the cars in the road.

"…that we've got a situation here that we need…"

The butt of the rifle smashed into the back of her head, and she staggered forward.

"Floor it Mindy! Let's go! Let's go!" Graham cried.

"Ooh, Right in the noggin' that sure shut her flapping mouth!" Ollie jeered.

Kim stumbled back to her feet with blood dripping through her hair.

Ollie raised his rifle at her and fired. The bullet tore through Kim's midsection.

Mindy's car lurched into reverse as she slammed her foot on the accelerator. Ollie raised his rifle and fired at their vehicle.

"Stop em!" He shouted.

Kim held her stomach; her face quickly turned pale. She stumbled a few steps before collapsing to the ground. Metal crunched as bullets slammed into their vehicle. The windscreen shattered as a round punched through it. Glass raked across Mindy's face and chest as she cried out in pain. At that moment the car dropped off the road into the muddy verge.

Beth scuttled forward into the passenger seat and held the wheel.

"Forward! Go! I'll turn us" Beth yelled.

Mindy shifted into drive and blindly accelerated again as she held her bloodied face in her hands. The car jolted forward, and small stones flicked out from the wheels as they spun around.

"They're aiming at…" Lisa began as a bullet punched through the rear window. It ripped a hole in her shoulder.

"Down!" Graham cried as he pulled Lisa's head out of view. Another round cut through the air and grazed Graham's forearm. The car was filled with screaming as Beth steered them back to the direction they came from. The occupants bounced as the car bumped back onto the road.

"Faster Mindy! Go, go!"

More rounds whizzed around them as Mindy accelerated them away. As they made their way further from the gunmen, fewer rounds came close.

"Turn!" Beth cried as they swung through a left turn at pace. They were thrown against the side of the car and Beth was sure at any moment she would lose control. They veered across onto the wrong side of the road and into the ditch on the opposite side.

"Slow!"

Mindy jumped on the brakes, and the car skidded to a halt. It came to a halt dangerously close to a very large tree.

"Is everyone OK?" Beth asked in a panic.

Blood had smeared and splattered throughout the car. It was difficult to tell whose it was.

"We gotta keep going!" Graham declared through gritted teeth as he held his bleeding arm.

"I can't, I can't see," Mindy sobbed.

"I'll drive…" Beth decided. "…Graham get Mindy in the back."

"OK."

Mindy unbuckled her seatbelt, and Graham pulled her through the two front seats into the back. He could not help a cry of pain escape as he used his injured arm. Mindy shrieked as glass embedded further into her chest in the process. Beth scrambled over to the driver's seat and skidded the car back onto the road. Graham looked out the broken rear window and saw a vehicle approaching.

"They're coming!" he cried.

Beth put her foot to the floor, demanding all she could from the poor vehicle. It responded well, and they sped away down the road.

"Is Lisa OK?" Mindy asked

Graham looked over at her; she was breathing erratically and had a vacant look on her face.

"She's hurt bad."

Beth careened through the intersection and took the road heading towards the ocean. They rounded a corner, and Graham lost sight of the trailing vehicle.

"I can't see them."

"I'll make sure they don't catch up," Beth declared.

"Let me see," Graham gently pulled Mindy's hand away from her face.

"You're cut up pretty bad, but the glass isn't in your eyes, but your eyebrows, forehead and cheeks are all messed up."

Mindy managed to slow her breathing a little and wiped her eyes on her sleeve. Ridding some of the blood from her face, she blinked repeatedly realising she could still see. The car lurched side to side as Beth sped them down the narrow country road.

"Graham are you OK?" Beth asked, keeping her eyes on the road.

"Yeah, I will be," he said, wrapping his arm in his jumper.

"Lisa! Lisa? Are you alright?" Mindy tried to get her attention.

She turned her head a little but did not reply.

"We gotta stop the bleeding," Graham said as he put his good hand on her shoulder, pressing her against the seat. Blood oozed from the wound through his fingers. He looked at Mindy without speaking. Mindy tried to control herself and calm Lisa.

"We're nearly at the sea Lisa. Brakenside is just beyond that. You'll see it any moment now."

Lisa's eyes began to look heavy, and she spluttered blood out from her mouth. They rounded a bend in the road and in the distance they could see the ocean.

"Look over there Lisa. Lisa! Look," Mindy turned her head.

For a moment, a smile spread across Lisa's face. They continued their drive to Brakenside in pained silence.

. . .

Kephas, Brother Christopher and Deon had set out with a large group of volunteers into the suburbs surrounding the church. It did not take them very long to find people in need of help.

"Over here!" Kephas called.

Brother Christopher came running over with a large first aid kit. A young man lay on the ground in front of them. Moments earlier, they had pulled him out of a crumpled car. It looked like he had been trapped there for some time. He rasped something incomprehensible.

"You'll be alright, save your strength," Kephas assured him.

Brother Christopher pulled a bottle of water out from the bag and offered some. He gratefully quenched his dry throat. They checked his injuries over while he drank.

"First aid!" Another survivor from their group called.

"Coming!"

Brother Christopher pulled out some bandages and left them with Kephas. He tended to his wounds as best he could. After a few minutes, Kephas helped him to this feet, and he supported him walking back to the church.

Brother Christopher jogged over once more.

"We're nearly out of first aid."

"All of it?"

"The only remaining is the supplies stored at the school."

"I did not think we'd need to use those so soon."

"Bishop, it seems like events are not identical to Zack's vision. Why?"

"I do not know. But I'm glad that we prepared what we did because of it. Otherwise, we'd be in a much worse state."

"Agreed."

After just a few hours they had managed to bring back two dozen grateful survivors. Upon their return, they found more people had flocked to the church.

"Bishop!"

Kephas turned to see some familiar faces.

"It's good to see you Sandy," he said with a smile. "...and you too Sister!"

Sister Paula looked battered but in good spirits.

"You've sure let this place go a bit haven't you," she said with a smile.

"Yeah, the landscaper got a bit carried away,"

"Bishop, I've directed newcomers to the primary school across the road. We've set up the hall as a first-aid centre."

"Thank you Sandy; I'm sure you'll have the place running smoothly in no time."

"I'll certainly try," she replied.

Kephas and Brother Christopher were distributing supplies when Deon walked up with a new survivor.

"Excuse me, Bishop, we have some news. I think you should hear."

"Oh?"

"This is Rose. This is Bishop Kephas and Brother Christopher."

"Hi"

"Hello there."

"Just tell them what you told me."

The young girl stepped forward and held out her arm. She wore a very new looking AI watch.

"I went to the community centre on Larkin road, and they just gave me this. They have food and stuff too. They said I should tell everybody. So uh, yeah. Go get some free stuff."

"Wonderful! Tell me Rose, do you think there would still be some left?"

"Yeah, they had a whole heap of it. Boxes and boxes of watches. Big crate things of food. I've eaten mine already, but they said I could go back and get more tomorrow."

"Thank you Rose; you've been a great help. Many people will be better off because of you."

"You're welcome," she said as she looked back to Deon. He nodded, and she returned to her friends waiting nearby.

"Do you think there will be as much as she said?"

"Let's not get people's hopes up just yet. I'll go take a look, but if so, that'll be a huge step forward."

"Agreed."

"Deon, would you like to join me?"

"Sure. When?"

"Let's go right now. Brother Christopher, are you OK to manage things while we're out?"

"Yes, I've got plenty of helping hands here."

"Thanks. We'll be back as soon as we can."

Kephas put down the box he was holding and left the hall with Deon.

"Right, let's be off," he declared as he set off at a jog.

Deon did not expect the old man to set such a pace. He began to wonder what he had volunteered for.

After they had travelled several suburban blocks, they arrived at Larkin road. As they approached Deon stopped for a moment to catch his breath. As he did so, he pointed skywards. Kephas stopped and looked up. They saw a drone hovering in the sky with blinking green lights. From their best guess, it was above the community centre.

"Its one of those buzzing things."

"A drone Bishop."

"Yes. It seems they are in quite good shape then."

"I guess they have power back on then."

"Good, good. Let's go and see."

After a few more minutes of jogging they made it up to the community centre. As they walked into the car park, Kephas could see a man in a white lab coat waving them forward. Behind him patrolled a few guards. They were more heavily armed than expected, but Kephas reasoned food and supplies were the most valuable items right now.

"Come along! We can help!" The man waved cheerfully.

As they walked up Deon read the label on his lapel, it read 'Bill'.

"Grab a watch, get some food!"

"Hello, we're hoping you're able to share some supplies? We've got quite a number of survivors in our church and the primary school."

"Yeah sure, just send them here. You can get Creds for doing so too," he said as he slapped an AI watch on Kephas' wrist.

"Oh, I'm not a technical person…" he began.

"No watch, no food. One rule for all, and through all, Unity."

"I'm sorry I don't think you understand."

"Next."

Kephas didn't move.

Bill stepped slightly to the side and gave Deon a watch.

"We have a large number of people. Over one hundred by now, I expect. Can we send them here?"

"Yes, that's fine. We've still got plenty…"

Bill waved towards a couple of steel containers placed at the rear of the property. A particularly fierce guard stood in front of it eyeing them.

"Can we take some supplies back to our people?"

"Not a chance. They have to come here, like everybody else. One rule for all you see. Here, take your bags, listen to the video, Bess explains it all."

"Bess?"

"The watch, press the button. You'll see. Bye."

He dismissed them as he began to attend to newcomers that had walked up behind them.

"It's OK Bishop, I can work these things," Deon said confidently.

"Great, thank you Deon."

They walked back towards the road, checking their supplies as they did so. Deon showed Kephas the basics of his new watch, and they listened to Bess explain the WGO Creds, rations and more. Deon noticed a concerned look on Kephas' face during a couple of points.

"Amazing…" Kephas said when the tutorial had finished. "…and this is all in this little device?"

"Yes Bishop."

Kephas took a bite out of one of the ration bars. His face indicated it did not taste all that great, but it was edible and according to the package very nutritious.

"I'm not sure on a few things that computer lady said. But the food is good. We should get everyone here before they run out."

Deon nodded.

The pair returned to the church at a quick pace. Kephas stood up on a car parked outside the school.

"Everyone! Your attention please!"

People slowly started to gather around him, and soon he stood before a crowd of hungry people. Almost all of them eyed the food bag in his hand. Just before he began to address them, Deon stood up by his side and tapped a few buttons on his watch and then pointed it across the crowd.

"What's all this?" Kephas asked.

"I've registered these people as associates to your device, so you can earn some Creds."

"Thank you," Kephas replied with a 'you'll need to explain that to me later' look on his face.

Kephas returned to face the crowd and held up his bag.

"Not far from here is food and water. We can't bring it back here, but we can go and collect it. I propose that we all travel as a group. I know many won't make it alone. Please let us help one another as we would like to be helped."

"How far?" One called from the crowd.

"Several city blocks, and yes it will have to be on foot. The roads are clogged with crashed vehicles. Please if you'd like to volunteer to help, please make your way over here to me. If you'll need help or know someone who does, make your way over to Brother Christopher. We'll leave as soon as we can."

A short time later, every survivor started the trek to the Larkin road aid centre. Deon was surprised at how many injured they now had. Roughly half from his count had injuries of some type or other. The pace was slow, but they were making steady progress. The strong were carrying the weak in every different manner possible. Some carried them on their back, others in pairs, others in makeshift stretchers. Kephas smiled as he saw everyone come together to help out. He saw even some of the injured carrying children or leaning on each other for support.

"We're going to be OK Bishop," Brother Christopher said, walking alongside him.

"We will."

"This food is such a blessing."

After a slow journey, their large group amassed in front of the aid centre. At first, upon seeing such a large group approach, the guards burst into action and readied their weapons. Before things got too tense, the Bishop turned and raised his hands to call everyone to a stop. He, Brother Christopher and Deon began to sort people down to single file. The guards relaxed that this was not some sort of attack, and the survivors were beckoned forward.

One at a time, each received their watch and supplies. Upon leaving the facility, Deon directed them to the small park across the road. The survivors then sat upon the grass. The first to arrive ripped open their bags and started eating. People waiting in the queue grew restless. Kephas was on the far side of the crowd but could tell things were becoming tense. Brother Christopher felt like at any moment he would have a riot on his hands to deal with. There were far too many for him to handle.

Then something happened that Brother Christopher did not expect. People stopped chewing, and they closed their bags. They waited for the others in their survival family to join them. First just a few, then more and more until everyone sat on the grass patiently waiting. The mood changed, and smiles grew across people's tired faces. After everyone had been processed, they sat in the sunlight like a real community. Bishop Kephas again stood before them.

"May the Lord God bless this food that we are about to eat. May it be the fuel we need to heal, help others and do your will. Thank you for all your blessings upon us. Amen."

The crowd echoed back 'Amen'. They all ate their fill, and their hearts felt lighter.

An hour later, they began the slow trip back to give themselves plenty of time to get back before dusk. That night they set up many of the classrooms in the school to house the injured. A few more seriously injured people needed extra care after the journey. Otherwise, everyone was feeling much better. The hopelessness of a collapsed civilisation began to wane. Chatter amidst the people talked of how things would continue to improve. Kephas and Brother Christopher were talking in the church office when there was a knock on the door.

"Come in."

Sandy walked in the door, wearing a big smile.

"Hello Sandy, it's good to see you."

"Thank you, and you too Bishop. I have an idea I was hoping to run past you."

"Sure, what is it?"

"I was thinking; we can return to the aid centre once a day for more supplies. But a daily trip carrying stretchers is going to get very hard for the people…"

Kephas nodded thoughtfully.

"…What we need are supermarket trolleys. That way we can wheel all the injured down and back. Even carry those bags of food in one. It'll be much easier."

"Great idea, though I expect the supermarket may not be very safe. Let me take a team to find out. Thank you Sandy."

She smiled and left the room.

"Why do you think the supermarket will be dangerous?"

"It has the most important resources for survival right now. People are prone to fight over such things."

Brother Christopher nodded. "I'll come with you. I have every confidence Sandy can keep this place ticking along smoothly."

"OK, let's keep the team small, I don't want to unduly put others at risk."

"Meet me at the gate in a few minutes, and we'll set out."

"Agreed."

Both men stood up and left to get ready.

Shortly after that, Brother Christopher arrived at the gate to see Kephas and Deon waiting there for him. He gave them a thumbs-up signal as he approached.

"Sandy's happy to run things while we're out."

"Good, good, let's be off."

The three men slipped through the church gate and out onto the street. During the past few hours, volunteers had cleared the cars from most of the road between the church and the school. Things were slowly looking like they were returning to normal. Deon paused for a moment and listened. For a change, he did not hear any alarms wailing in the distance. It was an overcast day in Brakenside, but occasionally the sun peeked through the clouds and shone warm light down on them.

They headed for the supermarket at a quick walking pace. Slower than Deon had thought, but he did not doubt that he would get enough exercise before he was back at the church. There were fewer people out on the streets now, since the power had come back on, many people stayed in their homes. They made good progress through the suburbs. Soon they had reached the far end of the road with their destination on it. As they walked, they began to hear sounds of shouting and glass breaking.

When they cleared a bend in the road, they saw the supermarket was a mad free-for-all. There were swarms of people running in and out with armfuls of goods. Some fought in the doorway; others lay in pain on the ground; some looked dead.

"Quickly!" The Bishop directed.

They ran towards the supermarket; no one paid them any attention as they approached, each busy with their own intentions.

"Stop all of you!" The bishop called.

The authority of his voice caused the people fighting in the doorway to pause for a brief moment before throwing more punches at each other.

"We'll check the wounded," Brother Christopher offered, nudging Deon with him.

"Stop!" Kephas commanded again as he approached two men wrestling over a laden trolley in the doorway. They threw several punches as he approached, ignoring him entirely. As Kephas got close, he saw one of the men pick up a shard of glass from the floor and slash at his opponent. Blood splashed around them as Kephas interceded.

"Cease!"

Kephas barged between them and disarmed the man with the weapon with expert level martial skills. A moment later, he was holding one in place with a twist of his arm. The other he tried to slow the bleeding with pressure to his wound.

"I say again, stop this, now!" The man struggling beneath him relented and started to catch his breath.

Kephas released him, and he bolted away grabbing a bag from the trolley in the process.

"Thief scum!" The wounded man called after him.

"Will you be alright?" Kephas asked as he quickly wrapped the deep cut in his arm.

"Yeah," he replied, gritting his teeth through the pain.

"I'll be back, wait here," Kephas stood and bolted across to the next brawl.

Meanwhile, Brother Christopher and Deon had found their first injured person. She lay on the ground holding her face, which was covered in blood.

"We're here to help."

They rolled her over gently to see even more injuries to her chest and arms.

She groaned in pain.

Brother Christopher un-slung his bag and pulled out some bandages. "You'll be alright. Deon, check the next one."

"OK," he took a few bandages and ran to the person on the ground nearby.

She cried out as Brother Christopher extracted a small piece of glass.

"Sorry, sorry, you've got glass all through this," he wrapped a bandage around her forearm.

"Thank you," she said between sobs.

Gunfire close by pierced the air. Deon looked for Kephas and saw him sprint inside towards the source of the sound. A surge of people fled the supermarket running as if their lives depended on it, which they did. Deon's focus returned to the injured man in front of him. It looked like he had been stabbed some time ago and a large amount of blood oozed from his abdomen. The man looked to be struggling to remain conscious. Deon began to bandage the wound as he jerked suddenly then became very still. He tried to remember his first aid training.

"Danger, Response, Send for help, Airways, Breathing, Circulation..." he reminded himself.

He shook the man by the shoulder.

'C'mon, wake up."

The man's hand dropped away from where he was holding his stomach, and with it, a large amount of blood spilt out. His injuries looked fatal. Deon hesitated for a moment then slowly stood. Another gunshot cracked loudly, followed by another. Deon ducked instinctively and hurried over to the next person on the ground. An old man lay before him shaking in fear.

"Where are you hurt?"

He did not reply and seemed to be looking off into the distance.

Deon checked him over and couldn't find any serious injuries.

"C'mon lets go!"

Deon pulled the man to his feet and helped him away from the supermarket doors.

"We gotta get people away from here!" Brother Christopher hollered over to Deon.

He nodded in reply as he made his way over with the old man. Brother Christopher had moved a few injured people to behind a blue van parked on the curb. After helping the old man over, Deon and Brother Christopher ran back to get more injured people. At that moment, another wave of people escaped from the supermarket fleeing desperately. One rushed over towards them, yelling.

"Beth?! Mindy?!" He called frantically.

The roar from a swarm of motorcycles filled the air. A moment later they were zooming through the supermarket car park. The lead biker raised a submachine gun in one hand and fired into those around him. The high rate of fire emptied the magazine in a brief moment. Many who were fleeing with food fell to the ground. Some were dead; others stumbled to find cover. As he began to reload another biker behind him pulled in and did the same.

Screams filled the already chaotic air. People were running in all directions. Deon dashed back to the vehicle with the injured. Brother Christopher appeared a moment later. For the moment they were out of the line of sight of the two bikers.

"Where's Kephas?"

Deon shrugged.

"I don't know. What do we do now?"

The two gunmen dismounted and stood by their bikes, weapons in hand. Deon recognised the patches of the local gang but not their firepower. They just stood guard as more and more bikes filed in. Lastly, a single bike rolled in. It had every accessory imaginable. Gold wheels, gold trim, gold everything. The rider was equally clad in a gold chain; he even wore a helmet with a gold crown painted on it. He dismounted as the other bikers made way for him to walk forward through them.

"Oh boys, you gone and chewed 'em up real good," he said, walking past a body peppered with holes.

At that moment, Kephas walked out of the supermarket doors.

"Spudge wasn't it? This is…"

"Oooooh! There he is boys. My absolute favourite ninja-priest-man. Now I know that you weren't gonna start talkin' to me without permission," Spug spat back.

Kephas continued to walk forward despite the pair of submachine gun-toting gang members staring at him.

"You don't need to do this. There is another way. Just let…"

"Now, I gotta stop you right there fool, coz one more step and you're gonna get dropped. Real quick-like. And I ain't finished talkin' to you yets."

Kephas kept walking towards him. Spug raised his hand, and his two gunners raised their weapons. Regardless Kephas kept walking until he was at point-blank range. The two men looked to Spug for permission to fire, but he kept his hand up.

"No point in shouting is there?" Kephas said coolly.

A smile spread across Spug's face.

"You've sure got a set of rock-solid stones on you now don't cha?…"

Spug dismissed his men, and they aimed their weapons back at the cowering locals.

"…Too bad you're wrapped in them linens boy, you'd be a straight-up gang banger," he looked back to his crew who started to chuckle. Kephas saw a couple of them had pistols the rest were carrying knives and clubs.

All had now dismounted and stood around Spug.

"Put your weapons away, there has been enough death today already," Kephas declared.

Spug snarled and raised a pistol of his own and aimed at Kephas' head.

"No-one. Not no single one at all, tells my own self what to do up in here – my own hood. You're just a peasant in m' kingdom. Keep your trap shut, zipped shut see?"

Kephas surveyed those around him. He did a mental count of the able, the injured and the dead. He looked at lines of fire, cover and escape routes. All came up poorly. He drew a deep breath. He closed his eyes and started to pray in his mind.

"Hey! Am I boring you grandad? Are ya missin' ya afternoon nap? You gotta get back to dat rest home for a sponge bath?"

His crew cackled with laugher and spat forth similar insults.

Kephas opened his eyes.

"Let's make a trade," he offered.

"Well OK, yeah, that's great. Oh no wait! you're piss out of luck boy'o. You ain't got a damn thing, that I don't got. All this is all mine," he motioned to the supermarket with his pistol.

"That's the problem though, you've got something you don't want."

"What cryptic mess you be spinnin' now?"

"The injured and the dead."

"Huh?"

"Let me take the injured and the dead from here. They'll only get in your way and foul up the place."

"Oh damn. This genius is top notch now ain't he? Well now I gotta admit, you've got a point. I know my boys don't like cleanin'. So Padre, spit it. What do you want for doing me this solid?"

"Nothing, but we'll need a number of trolleys to cart the dead away."

"Well that ain't nothin' now ain't it?" He rocked back and forth on his feet thinking for a moment.

"What's stopping me from icing you all right here?" He threw his pistol up into Kephas' face once more.

Kephas looked back at him calmly this only infuriated him more.

"I'm not stopping you from doing that. But you'll have fewer bullets and more bodies to deal with. Let us clean out the bodies and the wounded from the supermarket, and we'll be on our way. You can have all the food and supplies in there."

"OK, so clean up like yo' said, but you don't need no trolleys."

"If you prefer, but that will take a lot longer."

"Nah, I don't wanna even wait. OK, you get that stack of trolleys and no more," he pointed to the trolley bay with his pistol.

"Agreed."

"Alright get to it cleaner boy. You better be a fast mover, my crew is hungry."

"The fastest way would be if we all helped to…"

"Oh nah, nah. That's peasant work. You get to it. We're gonna wait just here."

"We'll get started then."

Kephas turned and walked back towards the supermarket. He gestured with his hands for people to come out of cover. Initially, no-one moved. Kephas walked towards the closest injured person and began to dress their wounds. Brother Christopher slowly stood and walked over to help. Deon followed, and soon many others were helping tend to the wounded.

"You're Zack's friend, aren't you?" Bishop Kephas asked one of them.

"Yes, I'm Graham. Where is he? Have you seen Beth and Mindy? They were just here a few minutes ago," Kephas could hear the panic in his voice.

"I haven't seen any of you since all this began. He's not with you?" Kephas looked around at the dead around him, fearing who he would recognise.

"No, we were separated before all this…"

Kephas helped a middle-aged lady to her feet.

"Can you walk?…" Kephas watched as she bravely nodded. "…Good, good, make your way over to that van," he said, pointing.

Graham rushed over to the van.

"Mindy! Thank God! Where's Beth?"

"She went in after you. I don't know," Mindy replied weakly

"I'll be right back," Graham darted off towards the supermarket. He checked each of the bodies laying limp in the entryway. A few paces into the supermarket he recognised Beth's shoes. Her body was underneath a man who looked to have been shot moments earlier. Graham rolled his body off her. Beth lay with her eyes closed, but she was breathing.

"Beth? Beth! I'm here; It's OK, you're OK."

He desperately checked for injuries, finding none he lifted her head onto his lap. In doing so, his hand became red with blood from a large cut on the back of her head. He saw her face twist in pain and Beth started to groan.

"Over here! Help help!" Graham yelled desperately.

Brother Christopher came running over.

"Uuuh, my head," Beth slurred.

"Let me see," Brother Christopher said as he knelt next to her.

He turned her head very gently and applied the last of the bandages he was carrying.

"Look here," he said, holding up a finger moving it side to side.

Beth followed with her eyes but kept groaning.

"Brother!" Deon called from a short distance away.

"She'll be OK. Just watch that blood loss," Brother Christopher stood and hurried over to Deon.

A short time passed, and all the injured were now stabilised or had since died. Kephas, Brother Christopher, Deon, Graham and three others now began retrieving the bodies. Spug walked back and forth amidst his crew, who were chatting and smoking. The survivors loaded up fourteen bodies into supermarket trolleys and with the injured helping they began to leave.

"Oh you missed a spot, cleaner boy," Spug said, pointing with his pistol to blood splatter on the ground.

"The rain will wash that away. Please let us leave now," Kephas replied.

"Well ninja-man, yo' did as yo' said. I like that. You're lucky I'm in such a generosity like mood. Alright, yo' and yours can get gone."

Spug motioned to his men, and they made way for the procession of injured and dead to make their way past.

Kephas began to push his trolley of bodies when Spug stopped him.

"Just stay back for a bit so we can chat."

Kephas waved the survivors forward. They slowly pushed their trolleys along. Upon reaching the curb, Deon and Graham stopped to help others lift their trolleys past. Finally, just Kephas and his trolley remained. After a short distance up the footpath, they stopped to wait for the Bishop.

Spug turned to Kephas with another smile on his face.

"Damn son! You've got a loyal crew right there. Whatever you've been spouting, they sure are buyin' it."

"You said you wanted to talk?"

"Oh yeah, straight to the business at hand. OK man. Here's what I've been thinking. While yo' peasants been pushin' my crew let me know that I've let yo' off too lightly yo' see. And I ain't sayin' that it's no democracy up in here. 'coz it ain't. I tell you that straight. They just got me thinkin' is all. I've got a smart crew yo' see."

Kephas looked back expectantly.

"So I'm gonna sweeten our deal for ya'. That way, we can be square. Hold out your hand."

"What?"

"Hold out your damn hand!" Spug raised his pistol, and his crew raised their weapons.

Kephas prayed silently in his mind and raised his left hand.

"Now that's it boy. Spug walked forward, pressed his pistol on Kephas' palm and pulled the trigger. It blasted a hole through his palm, and he cried out in pain. The gunshot made everyone but Spug's crew jump. Kephas instinctively dropped into a fighting stance and drew a deep breath.

"Oh sizzle! Look at yo'. Straight up, you're pure gangster on the inside of those robes boy. Check yo' out sizzling!"

Spug lowered his pistol and began laughing maniacally. He waved to his crew who lowered their weapons and joined in mocking and hollering. Kephas wrapped his hand in the fold of his robe, trying to minimise the blood loss. His face grimaced with pain. He placed his good hand on the trolley handlebars and began to push it forward. Spug didn't stop him this time.

"Hoo! Sizzle! I'm gonna really enjoying killin' you one-day ninja-priest. But that ain't today. I'm gonna save that fun for another day. Now get gone before I change my mind."

His gang hollered 'Sizzle! Sizzle!" as Kephas slowly pushed his trolley past them on to the footpath. Deon and Graham helped him up past the curb.

"Kephas!?" Deon asked.

"I'm OK, let's get back. Quickly."

"But your hand!?"

"Let's get out of their line of sight fast."

"Are you sure?"

Kephas' expression confirmed he was sure.

The panicked train of able and injured hurried their trolleys down the road and into the first street they could.

"Hold here for a moment," Brother Christopher called.

He then hurried to the back to check on Kephas.

"I've got a few makeshift bandages left. Here let me see it."

Kephas relented and unfurled his hand from his now bloodied robe. A gush of blood escaped just prior to Brother Christopher binding it up.

"It looks like it's clean through, I don't think you'll use your fingers again. But you'll live."

"Thanks," Kephas said through the pain.

"OK, let's get these people back. We can do more with the supplies in the school."

Kephas nodded.

Beth was sitting in one of the trolleys. Graham and Mindy pushed the trolley together as best they could.

"Hang in there Beth," Graham said with concern on his face.

Beth muttered back a weak acknowledgement. She felt as bad as she looked.

Mindy focused on her breathing as she walked, with each block that passed, she looked paler. Graham heard her say to herself more than once.

"I'm almost there; I'm almost there."

The trip back to the church and school was very slow, but eventually, they made it back. As they came into view, people ran out to assist. By the end of the day, they had used all of the first aid supplies and a large portion of their stored water. Kephas retired to his office and slept until the next day. Despite their best attempts, two of the injured died overnight.

A week later, nine people had died due to infection. The backfield of the school had become a cemetery. So far they had still managed to dig everyone their own shallow grave. But it was understood that this would not be maintainable for very long. The remaining survivors put the trolleys to good use each day returning to the aid centre on Larkin road for more food and water. Each day Kephas took a mental note of how many supplies they had left. He predicted that the community centre would only have enough for a few more days at best. They needed to start thinking about another source of food.

Zack had still not returned to Brakenside, nor had anyone heard anything about him. Graham, Beth and Mindy's injuries were healing, albeit very slowly. They had only heard Spug's gangs motorcycles a few times in the past few days, but Kephas had a feeling they would see them again.

Early one evening Graham, Beth and Mindy had returned to their designated classroom to rest. They had spent the majority of the day helping out around the Church and assisting the occasional newcomer.

"He's gotta be helping out somebody on the way I reckon," Graham began.

"Yeah, he'll be saving the day somewhere," Beth added.

At that moment all of their AI watches lit up.

"Attention, Attention. This is a broadcast from the WGO, Listen carefully," the now-familiar unfeeling voice of Bess began.

"Oh what's this?" Graham asked.

A video was projected forth from each person's watch. A man stood before them clad in a white lab coat. He wore some sort of device around his head with multiple sets of wires leading from it. He looked exhausted but excited at the same time.

"Are we live?... Now? OK, Greetings to one and all. My name is Neron Tetrarch, I'm the head scientist responsible for T-spec research here at one of the WGO sites. We've recently uncovered some major discoveries, and it's now time for us to share them with the all of the survivors of the human race. This message is being broadcast all over the world simultaneously. Please listen carefully."

He looked down at some notes off-screen and adjusted a couple of wires. He drew in a breath and began.

"My team and I have discovered the most significant knowledge thus far gained by the human race. The Transcendental Spectrum or T-spec is what humans for thousands of years have mistakenly identified as the spiritual realm. Humans throughout history have felt this yearning to something greater than themselves. This has taken shape as all sorts of religions from all sorts of cultures the world over."

The voice from a female interviewer spoke next.

"But why now?"

"It's the new type of coronal ejection, the solar event which sent a surge of T-spec to Earth. Previously, we've only had the smallest of fractions reach earth; it was undetectable. Now we've discovered that the electromagnetic spectrum was not two dimensional as you would have been taught in school. It is three dimensional. This extra-dimensional spectrum is the Transcendental spectrum. And most surprising to us is that it is in sync with certain frequencies of the human brain. That's why only humans have felt a draw to religion. And why we had conflicting reports of some sort of creature attacks during the first days. Since then we've had time to experiment, and we've made enormous progress. This very message is only possible because of the breakthroughs we've made in using the Transcendental spectrum. It's an amazing step forward for humankind."

"Why is this so important?"

"Let me show you," Neron stood back a few steps and flicked a few switches on.

He then tapped a few keys on the keyboard. Next, he stood away from his equipment and placed both hands on his head. One rested on a small dial, the other on a red button. A look of intense concentration came over his face. He began to perspire.

"Wooden cube," he commanded.

He pressed the button then outstretched his hand. As he did so, a small wooden shape took form in the air in front of him. A wooden cube dropped into his open palm. The interviewer broke script and came on screen to take the cube. Neron passed it to her.

"Unbelievable" she cried, turning it over in her hands. It was physical and real in every aspect that she could tell.

Neron smiled.

"Actually, it's the exact opposite."

"What do you mean?"

"I believed that cube into existence in the physical realm. I used my brain to draw power from the T-spectrum and shaped what you have in your hand."

"No!"

"Yes, think of it like a controlled hallucination that can take actual form. Let me show you..."

Graham looked up from his screen at Beth and Mindy.

"What in the hell is this?"

Beth and Mindy looked shocked and continued to watch.

"Banana," he commanded.

Like before, he extended his hand, and a yellow object grew in size from nothing above his hand. A banana then dropped into his hand.

"What? You can make fruit?" The interviewer exclaimed.

"Here, try it." Neron tossed it over to her.

After nearly fumbling the catch, she examined it all over. She looked up at him then peeled it open. Inside was the flesh of a real banana.

"Can I?"

"Yes of course."

She smelt it, then bit it into the banana, and a big smile grew over her face.

"It even tastes like a banana!"

"Yes, it is a banana, every sense. And this is my point Cherrie; humans now have the power to shape matter in a way we've never thought possible before. This will catapult humankind into a new prosperous civilisation the world over."

"I, ah... What do people need to know?" Cherrie returned to her place off-screen.

"Religion has caused wars and death for centuries. Humankind has now outgrown it. We now have the ability to shape our own destiny. We can now recognise that we are all brothers and sisters of the same family. We are united. We are one."

"What should people do?"

"Continue to survive as you have been doing so; we'll have more information to share in the coming days. We can make it through all of this together."

"Thank you."

Neron nodded then the broadcast ended.

"Woah," Graham spoke with his mouth still hanging open.

"I don't get it, if they can pull food from thin air, then why are we on the last container of food at the community centre?" Beth began.

"Didn't you see the wires and science stuff? They certainly don't have that in Brakenside. Don't worry. I'm sure they will sort it out," Graham replied.

"I just can't get over the strange times we live in..." Mindy spoke "... all those natural disasters leading up to those days of chaos. Now we essentially have world peace just around the corner with what he said. It's all so strange."

"Yeah, hanging out at the pizzeria seems like a long time ago now doesn't it?" Beth added.

"It sure does."

Bishop Kephas looked up from his watch with a concerned look etched in his face. He knelt down. His hand stung with pain as he accidentally put slight pressure on it. After a minute of trying to focus, he began to pray. He felt like harder times were coming, and he needed all the help he could get.

A number of days later, the survivors set out for another trip to Larkin road community centre. The mood of those walking was high, some almost jovial. Graham overheard some people talking ahead of him as he walked.

"…it won't be long before everything is back to normal."

"Yeah, any day now I think."

Graham was not sure how he felt. As he tried to fall asleep the night before, he ran it over and over in his head and everything checked out. The announcements made yesterday made sense to him. He did feel a little embarrassed for others that took religion so seriously and he was unsure what to say to the Bishop. Graham knew that he was absolutely convinced that all that spiritual stuff was real. He was not sure how Kephas would react now. Graham watched Kephas and Brother Christopher in deep discussion ahead of him.

With the aid of their supermarket trolleys, the group rounded the bend in Larkin road, and the community centre came in to view. There was a very large crowd of people gathered, and today the outer gates were shut. It was not unusual to find people queued, but something was different about today.

"What's going on up there?" Graham called out to the front of the group.

Others followed suit, but they received no discernable reply. The crowd at the gates was shouting and shaking the bars of the fence.

"Attention please everyone!" The man in the white lab coat called out through a megaphone.

"…we'll be opening up as we've promised in about ten minutes. As I said earlier, we need to wait for an announcement. Violence against staff or attempting to scale the walls is a fatal offence; there will be no other warnings."

A pair of drones were patrolling above them. They occasionally swooped low over the fence. Their spinning blades had no safety rails around them. No-one wanted to get too close.

The crowd hushed a little at his last sentence. But the cries for food and supplies did not stop.

The group from St. Thomas' blended into the back of the large crowd.

"Attention, attention…" the cold voice of Bess began.

The crowd was lit from with blue-ish white light of dozens of AI watches.

"…this is an important message from the WGO before receiving any more supplies, everyone must undertake a T-Spec resonance test. These will be undertaken at your local aid centre. Failure to comply will result in a permanent suspension. Also, in the declaration of human rights article three, now only relates to those aged five to sixty years. More information will be broadcasted soon."

The man in the white lab coat stepped over to the gate and opened it.

"This way, line up!"

There was a little jostling and shoving until the armed guards rushed over.

"Permanent suspension? Does that mean starved to death?" Beth asked.

"Yeah I guess," Mindy replied.

Another projection shone out from their AI watches. The lead scientist Neron Tetrarch was on again.

"Greetings to you all. Since our last message we've discovered more about T-spec which we can share today. Every human has a distinct prime T-spec resonance in their brain. These can occur over a range of frequencies. Think of this like different notes on a piano; some have low pitched others high pitched. We'll be measuring this today. It's been discovered that some frequencies are detrimental to human health. This can manifest in different symptoms. Today, we're hoping to identify high-frequency individuals who can become a conduit to the transcendental spectrum itself. This will be essential for our discovery process moving forward as you saw me demonstrate previously. We've seen that typically different religions group together on the spectrum. Some high and others low. We suspect that mineral deposits underground may explain why historically, different religions were prevalent in different places. What's important to remember is that we're all on the same side now."

Cherrie's voice asked a question from off-camera again.

"What can we expect in the months to come?"

"It's really exciting. However the majority of what is under development is in its very early stages. But we have projects looking into some core problems that we are confident T-spec can help us solve. These include endless electricity generation, world hunger solutions and a cure for old age."

"Incredible, what should the people be doing?"

"Get tested as early as you can. Contribute through work in your local district. Help each other. Support those who need it, reward for those that earn it."

All the AI watches stopped at the same time.

"Step up," the white-coated man called.

Deon watched as he saw people in front of him file into the warehouse and disappear behind a closed door. Another door opened on the far side, and the preceding person walked out with a bag of food. He gave a wave as he walked away. The queue made slow but steady progress and eventually it was Deon's turn. By this stage, he was very hungry. He walked to the door as directed and opened it. Inside he saw a large waiting room. There was a single spare seat. A lady dressed in a white lab coat approached him, scanned his watch and handed him two small pills and a glass of water. Her name badge read

"Dr. Jones"

"What's this?"

"It's just to help with the test, take them and sit down," she pointed towards the chair. Deon swallowed the pills and sat down. As he waited, Deon saw AI watches light up when it was the wearer's turn, and they were escorted down a hallway out of sight. Deon was reminded of a simpler time waiting in some government office. He relaxed as he remembered all the things that he used to do. Some seemed quite unnecessary now. What felt like a short time later Deon's watch lit up, and he stood to head towards the hallway.

"Third door on the left," Dr. Jones called to the admin staff who escorted Deon down the hall.

Entering the room, he was reminded of a doctor's office, or maybe a science lab. A middle-aged man sat at the table and indicated for him to sit down. His name badge also read 'Dr. Jones.'

"Roll up your sleeves," he instructed.

Deon did so as he sat down.

"This will sting just a bit," he warned.

He proceeded to draw some blood from Deon's arm up through a needle into a small capsule.

"Hold pressure on it, we've run out of sticking plasters," he spoke as he had already said that exact line a thousand times. He probably had.

"Sure."

"OK, this will feel heavy on your head, but that's all you'll feel," he placed a small metal circle with wires leading off onto his head. It didn't feel heavy as he had warned, but a moment later there was an audible click as another component latched into the headpiece on one side. A moment later another click indicated yet another component had attached. Now it was reasonably heavy on Deon's head.

"Just keep your head straight; this will be quick."

"OK, what do I do now?"

"Read this aloud then sign here," Dr. Jones ejected the capsule of blood he extracted from Deon's arm earlier and loaded it into what looked like a high-tech pen.

"Is that my blood?"

"Yes, just for anti-forgery purposes."

"Oh."

Deon looked down at the words on the paper in front of him.

"Hang on, I don't agree with this…" he pointed as he spoke, "…or this bit."

"Oh, don't worry. The words don't mean anything. We just need everyone to say the same thing as we measure your brain."

"You want me to sign this too?"

"Yes."

"Why?"

"Look, as you've been told, we need to establish the population's T-spec resonance. Without it, civilisation as disrupted as it is, we won't survive."

"It just doesn't feel right, can you explain this part?"

Dr. Jones pointed to the sign on the wall behind him.

"One rule for all, and through all, Unity – WGO"

Deon hesitated.

"Do the test and eat. Or don't and starve. It's your choice."

Deon relented and began to read aloud the words on the paper.

"I renounce all faith in everything, from now and forever. I accept all statutes of the World Governmental Organization and will honour their will…"

Deon spoke the rest words and signed his name with the special pen, as he did, so Dr. Jones recorded his results on the computer and stamped a few forms. Lastly, he scanned his watch and sent him out. A food bag was presented to Deon on the walk out. He immediately opened it and started eating. He waved as he saw Kephas go in the entry door.

Not long afterwards, Kephas sat in at the same table as Dr. Jones pushed the contract over for him to read and sign. The Bishop shook his head as he read.

"There is no way I'll ever sign this," he pushed the papers away.

"Don't worry, the words don't mean anything; it's just to calibrate the machine…"

Kephas saw the stack of signed contracts behind him and stood up.

"No-one has to know let's just get this done."

"No chance. I understand the evil here even if you don't."

"You realise that if you refuse, you'll no longer receive food and water?"

"So be it. Let me out of here."

Kephas stood up and banged on the locked door.

Dr. Jones pressed a button under his desk. A moment later, two armed guards walked in from another door on the other side of the room.

"Everything all right in here?" One of them asked.

"He's refusing."

"I certainly am. Now get out of my way."

The two guards looked at the old man making his way over to them.

"Let me pass,"

One of the guards struck the butt of his rifle into Kephas' stomach. The Bishop staggered back a step.

"Old fool! You should've just…"

Kephas dropped back slightly into a fighting stance before charging forwards into the two guards. He launched a right uppercut under the chin of the guard in front of him. His head was knocked back and hit the wall behind him. The other guard raised his weapon in alarm, taken aback by the speedy old man. Before he could fire, the bishop darted forward and with a few quick strikes quickly subdued him with a sleeper hold. The guard struggled for a moment before passing out. Kephas took both of their assault rifles.

"Give me those. Now!" Kephas demanded pointing to the stack of paper behind Dr Jones.

"You're going to regret this…" he promised as he reluctantly obeyed.

Kephas grabbed the key card from one of the guards and left the room. Upon reaching the hallway, Kephas ran down the length then fumbled the key card until the door clicked open. The door opened out onto the courtyard, and he could see the large crowd still queuing to get in. The Bishop sprinted towards the closest guard who was looking the other way. He turned around just in time to meet the fist of the Bishop at full pace. He was thrown to the pavement and did not attempt to get up.

Kephas immediately changed direction to his next target as he felt the bandage on his injured hand soak with blood. The building alarm spun up to full volume and the whole area was drowned in a wailing siren. Upon seeing Kephas' defiance, the crowd surged through the gate and bowled over another guard.

The drones circling above dropped down and inflicting deep gashes into the front ranks of the crowd. Before they could drive too deep, the rotors on the first drone broke, and it spun out of control into the ground. The crowd pounced on it and smashed it to bits. The other drone flew up and out of reach.

"Stop right there!" A guard yelled as he saw Kephas charging forwards weaving as best he could. The guard aimed up and pulled the trigger. The bullet punched straight through the side of Kephas' shoulder. Kephas dropped the weapons he was carrying and dived into a forward roll. He exited with a flurry of punches before throwing the guard over his shoulder onto the pavement. Kephas kicked his weapon away from his reach and called to the crowd.

"Come and eat!" He held his bleeding shoulder.

Both gates were shoved wide open, and the crowd washed in at double the pace. The crowd surged inside, knocking over the man in the white lab coat in the process and the last remaining guard.

Upon seeing one of the guards scramble to his feet, Graham kicked him down again.

"Stay down!"

A burst of gunfire filled the air as Brother Christopher unloaded the guard's assault rifle into the swooping drone. He managed a single hit, but it was enough to drop it out of the sky, and it crashed into the fence.

Kephas stood atop one of the crates of food and addressed everyone.

"Do not take this test they speak of. It reeks of evil; they would bind each and every one of you to their twisted purpose. It's clear to me now that the WGO is corrupt to its very core..." The crowd roared with approval.

"I for one, shall retain ownership of my soul and keep my freedom!" Kephas ripped the watch off his arm and threw it to the ground. A large number of the crowd did the same. Deon felt a cold chill wash through him. He wondered what he had done and more importantly if he could undo it.

The crowd quickly raided the food and supplies, and some immediately ran away with their haul. Kephas the confiscated the assault rifles, and several volunteers helped carry them. Satisfied that they would not be shot in the back as they left, he called his congregation to leave.

"Let us return home!"

As the adrenaline began to leave his system, the blood loss from his shoulder and hand caught up with him, and he dropped to a knee. The bandage on his hand was now almost completely soaked in blood. What healing he had managed so far was now undone. Brother Christopher rushed over to his aid and patched his shoulder with a fresh medical pouch. He checked on the gunshot wound.

"It missed the bone. You're very lucky."

"Blessed," Kephas replied with a strained smile.

"We need to get out of here."

"Agreed, lets hurry."

Deon rushed to his side from amidst the crowd.

"Help me up will you Deon?"

Deon bent down and helped him to his feet. Kephas began to walk by himself, but it was clear he would need assistance. Deon helped him quickly walk out of the car park.

Brother Christopher stood atop a parked car.

"Everyone, come to the St. Thomas' church, we will look after you all. Follow us!"

With a crowd bigger than they arrived with, they departed up the street.

"Bishop, help me! I signed, I, I…" Deon confessed.

Kephas revealed a stack of papers in the folds of his robe.

"Let's burn these when we get back shall we?"

"Yes, good idea. Will I be alright?"

The Bishop quoted scripture.

James 5
[16] *Therefore confess your sins to each other and pray for each other so that you may be healed. The prayer of a righteous person is powerful and effective.*

"In time and with prayer you will be," he concluded.
Deon nodded.

The man with the white coat stood up slowly nursing some cuts and bruises. He watched the last of the crowd disappear from view down the road.
"All of you will pay," he promised.

. . .

Sister Lee was kneeling at prayer. It had been days since she had a decent meal. Thankfully, there was a well not far from the school, so they had plenty of water. Sister Lee could not shake the deep need for her to pray. It was understandable with all the recent events, but in the past few hours, it was as if her whole being was crying out to her to pray. She was fervently at prayer when she began to receive a vision. At first, she had thought she had fallen asleep and had begun dreaming. However, after a few moments, she realised she was awake.
"Show me Lord God."

She lifted her eyes to the sky. As she did so, Lee felt as if her consciousness travelled thousands of miles in an instant, yet she could still feel herself kneeling in the grass. Opening her eyes, she found herself inside a deep all-consuming darkness. Nothing was near her; it was if she was floating in deep space.
"Look here mortal," she heard a deep voice say.
Looking to where she thought it was coming from she saw the sun.

Blazing and brilliant light was flooding down towards Earth, which she could see below her.

She gasped in alarm, and her breathing became panicked.

"Peace be with you, now witness," the voice said.

Sister Lee relaxed and felt a new sense of perspective. Somehow, she understood she was not in danger.

Sister Lee turned her head back towards the sun and saw it begin to blacken. It was as if the immense heat of the sun was charring something on its surface to ash. Four black spots began to grow in size over its surface. A moment later they had changed shape so that only a cross-shaped remained. Sister Lee recognised this as what she had seen in the sky previously.

The four blackened scabs broke off from the sun and drifted off into space. One of them seemed to be heading towards Earth. She watched it closely as it broke down into more and more pieces. The single mass was now a shower of hundreds of thousands. They accelerated and began to burst into flame. Sister Lee watched as they tore through Earth's atmosphere and slam into its surface. From her vantage, she saw what must have been entire countries crushed and burnt.

"The bowl of wrath has been poured out,"

She blinked at the impact and immediately she had been returned to her favourite prayer garden. She immediately got up and ran back to the school.

"Inside everyone! Now!" She screamed.

. . .

In Brakenside, Kephas was lying down in his office. Sandy had just changed his bandage.

"Now, you stay right there for a few days. You're more pale than I'd like, I'm sure you've lost lots of blood."

"Thank you Sandy," Kephas said with a pained smile.

At that moment, Sandy's AI watch lit up from underneath her jumper. They traded looks for a moment then Sandy held it out. A projection shone out, Cherrie the interviewer from the previous broadcast was smiling into the camera. She began to speak.

"Attention everyone, it seems there has been some confusion and miscommunication in the past few days. Some provinces have had trouble configuring a baseline for the T-Spec resonance tests. This was the result of a small group of individuals who have now been corrected. I'm sorry to say that some lives were lost as a result of the confusion that ensued. We're holding a public meeting in the centre of each major town tomorrow to clear this up. Please follow the directions after this message to see which is closest to you. We'd love to see representation from everyone in the community so we can establish a way to move forward together as one. We also have another discovery that we hope will be ready for announcement by tomorrow. Food and water will be supplied. One rule for all and through all, Unity."

The message ended with Cherrie smiling.

"Perhaps it was all some big mistake?" Sandy suggested.

"It possible, but I'm confident that there are some people in strategic positions that have a truly evil agenda."

Sandy gulped.

The door swung open, and Brother Christopher walked in.

"I'd like to go to the meeting tomorrow. I think it's important that we voice our concerns, and let's face it, you need to rest up Kephas."

"He does," Sandy added.

"Points taken, but I don't think you should go alone," he replied.

"Agreed, from what I heard on the way here many people want to attend anyway."

"OK, fill me in on your return."

"Will do."

"One more thing? Be careful."

"Sure thing."

The next day Brother Christopher, and Lucy Tollman arrived at the Brakenside town square with two dozen survivors. Many were discussing recent announcements and pondering what the latest discovery would be. It seemed others were purely interested in the free food. As they approached the town square, Brother Christopher could see crowds of people had already started to assemble.

On the city hall steps, there was a cadre of WGO officials, guards and administration staff. He recognised the man in the white coat from the bruises on his face. There was a large monitor screen setup above a podium. The staff looked like they were confirming their equipment was operational. A locked crate was on the back of a large supply truck parked near the steps. Many guards patrolled and kept people behind a temporary barrier set up close by.

"Christopher! Good to see you!"

"Oh, hi Darren, you've made it through the world toppling over I see."

"And you too!"

"How're things on your side of the river?"

"Same as you I guess, we're pretty hungry. But other than that we're OK."

"I'm glad to hear that. We're similar I guess, but we've got a lot of injured under our care."

"Ah yeah, we had some to start with, but to be blunt they were all pretty bad, so didn't last long."

"I'm sorry to hear that."

"Yeah, so are you here for the announcement or the food?"

"Both," he replied with a smile.

The monitor screen lit up with a 'starting soon' message and the WGO logo. Brother Christopher watched them continue their setup until at last, all but a few remained on the steps. The man in the white coat tapped on the microphone.

"Greetings everyone. We'll be playing a broadcast shortly; then there will be time for discussion. Please send a representative from your community over to the desk there," he directed.

Darren looked back to Brother Christopher.

"That's got to be you then,"

A couple of survivors also encouraged Brother Christopher forward.

"OK, I'll do my best."

He walked over to where a dozen other leaders stood as they were each given a lapel microphone. They were then ushered to the one side of the steps.

The large monitor screen lit up again, and Neron's face was displayed.

"Hello everyone, thank you for attending this forum. It's important we hear from you who are battling with survival on the ground. The WGO thanks all of you for all your efforts thus far. We know we've been through some tough times. But we're confident human unity and prosperity are on the horizon. Let's discuss some pressing concerns then we'll continue to a discovery we're recently confirmed…"

The crowd hushed as everyone in attendance, drank in his every word.

"…Firstly the WGO has issued a worldwide state of martial law. This is in place to keep everyone safe. Raids on supply centres and on WGO staff will be met with lethal force. In the following areas, there will be a mandatory curfew…"

A list of cities and towns scrolled across the bottom of the screen.

"Next, the declaration of human rights has been amended to meet our dire situation. The right to life now only applies to people above the age of ten and below the age of fifty…" At this comment, a roar of disapproval rang out from the crowd.

"…But rest assured we will be setting up dedicated aid centres to cater to these individuals. Next, Bess the artificial intelligence which you're all familiar with has been given full autonomy on numerous governmental systems globally, for the betterment of humanity. This will greatly assist our recovery efforts. Next, Creds is now the sole currency for humankind. No other currency has any value. All your previous savings and debts have been cancelled. We start anew, reward for everyone who earns it. Please talk to your local officers or Bess to learn more. Finally, we've confirmed a T-spec discovery now with enough data that it's irrefutable."

The crowd quietened down again.

"… With the early results coming in from the resonance tests we've confirmed that the people who had aligned themselves with the Christian faith have a dangerously low resonant frequency. This is to blame for the many deaths in the first days of unification…"

Shock washed over the crowd as they looked at one another.

"…as we've discussed, T-spec can be manipulated with the human mind, and at a time of chaos these people conjured up fears of what they thought the end of the world might have been like. With the huge surge in Transcendental energies and countless people dreading the worst. These actions conjured forth the otherworldly creatures some of you have reported. Note that since then the amount of energy has dropped significantly, so there is no longer anything to fear. Regardless, all previous religions will now align with the Transcendental spectrum. We've already had discussions with heads of the major faiths and all, but the Christians have offered their support. To be clear, we are all now part of the same faith. We understand this may be difficult for some, so after this message, we'll address your concerns. Keep looking after one another, and the WGO will look after us all. Thank you for listening."

Brother Christopher was boiling over in emotion. He struggled to find words that would express his feelings. He heard swearing and yelling from all around him.

"Come forth community leaders!" The man in the white coat called.

They lined up to next to the podium. As they were doing so, Brother Christopher watched the guards unpack a series of large crates. They looked to be setting up a pair of large tripods.

Brother Christopher was called up first.

"What is your concern?" The white-coated man asked.

Brother Christopher struggled to find the words to begin.

"The wording in the test, it goes completely against our faith, and others too. What did this get changed to?"

"Ah yes, you're referring to the message broadcast yesterday?"

"Yes that's right."

"It did not change, nor will it ever."

"That's completely unacceptable!" Brother Christopher was angry and felt ambushed. "…You cannot get everyone globally to renounce their faith and replace it with this spectrum."

"But you see the spectrum *is* all faiths."

"No, we won't. We won't do it," Brother Christopher declared.

A roar of approval from the crowd echoed his resolve.

"You would throw away the unity of humankind for some old superstition?"

"We will remain true to our faith!"

"OK, OK, can I get an idea if you all feel like this or is it just this man. If you're happy to move forward into a new united future of humanity, move towards the flag pole. Everyone who is not willing to change, step over to the opposite side by the steps."

People yelled in protest, but he allowed time for the crowd to split and gather in their respective groups. Brother Christopher was surprised to see the crowd was roughly split in half.

"See! I am not alone; we will not bend to your dictatorship!" Brother Christopher called out.

A chant started through the crowd, and soon they were shouting.

"We will not bend! We will not bend!"

The man in the white coat talked to his staff and guards for a moment. Then Brother Christopher watched as the guards mounted two large calibre machine guns up onto the tripods they had just assembled.

"You can't intimidate us! We will…"

The man in the white coat raised his hand.

"Low-frequency scum!" He bellowed as he waved at the two gunner teams.

The air blasted with gunfire ripping through the crowd, each shot puncturing through multiple people. Brother Christopher screamed in horror as in a brief moment all those willing to resist the WGO were ruthlessly cut down. He saw Lucy topple to the ground. The crowd on the opposite began to flee in terror. The machine guns spun down, and a ringing silence hung in the air for a moment before Brother Christopher's ears registered the screaming.

"And as for you.…" the man in the white coat took one of his guards' rifles and levelled it at the community leaders on the steps.

"Be gone filth!"

He opened fire.

Brother Christopher was hit by several shots and fell backwards down the steps. The others behind him met a similar fate. A few struggled breaths later and they were all dead.

Darren stood frozen at the edge of the town square. His mind could not process what he just witnessed.

The monitor flicked on again and displayed another WGO message.

"Everyone must choose, unification or extinction."

. . .

Across the other side of Brakenside, Kephas was doing his best to rest. But with his shoulder throbbing with pain he could not sleep. He began reading:

Romans 15
[4] For everything that was written in the past was written to teach us, so that through the endurance taught in the Scriptures and the encouragement they provide we might have hope.

Kephas found it very difficult to concentrate. He closed his eyes for a moment and tried to dwell on what he read.

"Bishop!" Sandy called as she opened the door.

"Yes?"

"I think you better come out here. Lots of that gang are heading this way."

"I see," Kephas sat up slowly and followed her outside. As he went outside, he could hear the drone of many motorcycles. By the time Kephas made it to the gate, the first few bikes had appeared at the end of their street.

"Hurry! Everyone into the church!" Kephas cried.

The congregation fled as best they could, but there was still many injured in the school that remained where they were. Kephas walked out on to the road to meet the approaching gang. As he stood there, something deep inside him seemed to awaken. He could not tell what it was initially, but a moment later it seemed to have dulled the pain in his shoulder a little. It was not much, but enough of a change that he could confirm it was not all in his head.

The first two bikers pulled up and hopped off their bikes.

"Oh there he is, looks like he's had some more lessons yo," one pointed at the bandages over his shoulder.

"Damn sure."

They stood with submachine guns in their hands as they waited for the rest of their crew to arrive. Over the next few minutes, it looked like the entire gang drove up. A green panel van also drove its way up over the footpath. Spug on his golden bike rolled in last. He dismounted and then strutted his way over to the Bishop. Behind him Kephas heard the clang of the church gate shutting; he hoped that everyone had made it inside.

"Oh Ninja-man! There you are. And yo' been busy dog!" Spug said with a big smile on his face.

"What do you want?" The Bishop replied quickly.

"Oh now I know, you ain't lost all manners with me fool. Unless you're just beggin' for even more lessons from Spug here yo."

He held up his arms, raising support from his gang. They all hooted and hollered on queue.

Kephas walked a few steps towards him.

"We fulfilled our end of the deal. Why are you here?"

"Well now that's the thing yo'. I'm double lucky today. First up, I'm gonna kill yo' ass today."

Kephas did not bat an eye.

"Hooo! I love how ice-cold you are ninja-padre. Any way I be digressing. Second up, I'm here for the house."

"The house?"

"You heard it. The big ol' stinky, pointy roofed house behind ya' there."

"Why do you want the church?"

"Well yo' see. Its mine, that's the fact. You ain't going to be leadin' your crew no more' and I'm guessing there be at least a few good soldier boys in there somewhere. And if there ain't? Well let's just say we can return all yo' fools back to your natural state. In the dirt that is."

Kephas looked behind him at his scared congregation. He looked to the two gang members holding their submachine guns in his direction. He looked for options and did not find any good ones.

"Let's make another deal then Mr Spuggs"

"Its Spug yo' not Spuggs. S-p-u-g."

"Spug then, lets trade?"

"Now, there he is, I knew you'd wiggle out somehow, Damn. Yo' be all backed up in a corner and yo' still plottin'. Good thing Spug knew you'd try somethin' so I be all prepared like."

He turned around and waved at his men standing by the van. They opened up the van rear doors, and several people fell out. They were all bound and gagged. Kephas recognised Zack among them and his friend from the security company though he could not remember his name.

"See? I've got somethin' to trade. What yo' got?"

Kephas could not take his eyes off the captives. It looked like they had it rough for a long period of time. The hostages each had an array of bruises and small cuts. Their wrists were bloodied from the tight cable ties. Their clothes were ripped and stained. Spug motioned for them to be brought over to him.

"Zack!" Kephas heard someone scream from the church behind him. Other names were also called out as people recognised their loved ones.

"Oh, they *are* your crew. Perfect" Spug said smiling.

"So you just want the building?" Kephas asked.

"Fool, I own that already. Oh? Don't yo' even know? Piss man. The WGO put out a hit on yo' they labelled yo' as a Pariah. They said there is a nice big reward for anyone that breaks yo' and your crew."

"What do you want of me?"

Kephas felt another surge of power inside him; it was as if a flood gate was being progressively opened. He looked over to Zack. He had an expression on his face that showed he was going through the same experience.

"Renounce it all boy. Gimme that paper…" he grabbed a contract from one of his crew who was walking over with it.

"...I even got one of those fancy pens. See?"

Kephas saw a box of blood capsule pens and contracts being carried over.

"First yo' gotta do it. Then all yo' crew. Then I'll be set up for life. Then yo' all can get out of my house... oh and I'm going to kill ya too."

"Anything else?" Kephas asked.

"No fool. I ain't no greedy-guts. OK, so let's do it. I've been looking forward to killin' a ninja all week!"

Kephas did not move. He closed his eyes for a moment and prayed. He drew a deep breath. A gunshot rang out. Kephas opened his eyes to see Spug drawing back his pistol after shooting Stanley in the chest. There was screaming from behind him, and he could see Zack yelling as best he could through the gag.

"Oh sorry grandad, I thought yo' were sleeping on the job is all."

"Stop this right now!" Kephas commanded, dropping instinctively into a combat stance. He quickly gauged if he could reach the closest gang member before being shot. It did not look likely.

Spug rattled off a slew of profanities in reply.

Something in the sky caught Kephas' eye, and he looked up. He looked to Zack, who nodded in understanding. Kephas risked one more glance upwards before he called for Spug's attention.

"Hey you!"

"Changed yo' mind already? I thought we'd need to cap a few more of yo' friends..."

"Sizzle yourself!" Kephas shouted.

Spug and his gang could not help but burst out laughing. Kephas charged towards the closest gang member as tennis-ball sized flaming meteors rained down all around them. One blasted straight through the gang member in front of him. A gaping hole in his chest toppled him over in a bloody mess. Kephas saw Zack scream a muffled war cry as he jumped to his feet. He ripped through his bonds and punched the closest gang member over backwards with a single hit. He dashed towards the next one.

"Shoot everyone yo'!" Spug screamed as he raised his hand.

A meteor tore through Spug's arm at the elbow and punched a hole into the ground at his feet. He fell to the ground crying in pain. A burst of gunfire spat towards the hostages, and three of them suffered multiple hits and quickly died.

As fire rained down, two of the gang members took cover in the van. It offered no protection. Meteors tore through the roof, vehicle and burrowed into the concrete below. A trickle of blood oozed out of the back door. Others hoped on their bikes in an attempt to flee. Several were hammered into the ground in the process.

Kephas could hear screaming from the church grounds behind him as he set upon a panic-stricken gang member with a flurry of punches with his good hand. He tripped his foe, and he landed backwards on to the ground. As he attempted to get up a tiny meteor punctured straight through him. Kephas dive-rolled past his body, further injuring his shoulder in the process but managed to avoid another meteor by the smallest of margins.

A gang member ran at Zack with a baseball bat. Zack managed to dodge the first blow and used his momentum to throw him over his shoulder on to the ground. While this was happening, another gang member slit the throat of one of the other captives. He was moving to the next one as a meteor crushed him and the next captive. Larger flaming rocks now pummelled the ground around them. The shower progressively moved down the road towards the church. Zack darted over to the last hostage and picked them up and slung them over his shoulder with unnatural ease.

"Kephas!" He cried as he ran towards him at full pace.

Hearing Zack's cry, Kephas dropped his foe with a knee to the stomach and uppercut finisher and spun around. Zack bounded over to him, and they both ran back to the church gate. A couple of gunshots whizzed through the air around them, but with a panicked aim, none of them hit their mark. Sandy swung open the gate as they ran in. Sandy was lost for words as she saw the fiery impacts land closer and closer to them.

A basketball-sized meteor thumped into Spug as he was getting helped back to his feet. An explosion of dust and dirt blasted the area as the remaining gang members scattered.

"Deon!" Kephas screamed.

Zack carefully set the injured hostage he was carrying on the ground.

Deon pushed his way out of the terrified crowd.

"What do…"

"The walls! Erect the walls!" Kephas hollered as he and Zack ran towards the church garden shed. Zack was sure he heard Mindy call his name in the chaos.

Deon and Kephas came running back carrying a large roll of plastic sheet. A large wooden rod was through the centre. Deon planted his roll at the gate and unfurled the first layer. Zack could see it was laminated with pages from the Bible. Beth held the wooden pole as Deon ran off around the fence line pulling out more in the process. Zack noticed the thin metal stakes in the ground around the fence line which held the sheet against the fence. He smiled to see one of the plans from his vision was put into place. But he had designed it for protection against demons, not meteors. With that realisation, his smile faded.

"Zack!" Kephas cried.

Zack took the end of the sheet from Kephas who held the roll. Zack sprinted around the fence line in the opposite direction to Deon. A moment later, he saw Deon securing his end to the fence. Deon used small metal clips attached to every twelfth post to secure the top as he went back around. Zack copied and then ran back, securing the top part to the fence as he went.

Zack made it to the gate just as the meteors were busting up the footpath by the church car park. He saw Mindy, Graham and Beth and began to run over as the first meteors fell upon the church. The crowd screamed as the meteors fell down on them. But their screams turned into cries of joy as they looked up.

The meteors bounced off some invisible barrier above the church grounds. It was as if it was covered by an impenetrable dome. The crowd stared upward in disbelief. As each meteor impacted the crowd below flinched.

Kephas was on his knees, praying intently. Moments later, everyone knelt with him.

Psalm 62
⁵ Yes, my soul, find rest in God;
my hope comes from him.
⁶ Truly he is my rock and my salvation;
he is my fortress, I will not be shaken.
⁷ My salvation and my honor depend on God;
he is my mighty rock, my refuge.
⁸ Trust in him at all times, you people;
pour out your hearts to him,
for God is our refuge.

A biker jacket of the 'Street Snakes' lay abandoned in the road with a hole burnt through it.

. . .

Back in Rome, Cardinal Eleazar was searching through ancient texts. He had a bad feeling in the back of his mind that he could not shake. Emil had not reported back. He shuddered at the thought of what a failure in his mission could mean. He decided it was better to be prepared just in case. Amidst the old tomes and dusty parchments, he found what he was looking for. It was a Prayer of Binding, one formulated with a single purpose in mind. For an old foe, that if loosed on the world would stop at nothing to sate his unquenchable hunger for death.

Eleazar made as many copies of the prayer as he could. He included a detailed description of the circumstances where it would be necessary. Once he had a suitably large stack, he went downstairs and placed one quarter into four cubby holes in the foyer. He was somewhat relieved in knowing that when the Order of Salt and Light sanctioned couriers came tomorrow morning, they would take a pile each and distribute them as soon as possible. It would be often suggested that they did not need to retain volunteers to deliver their mail, and the national mail service would suffice. Eleazar himself had even suggested it once. Today, he was glad that people aware of their cause would be carrying this important message through their network throughout the remains of the populated world.

Eleazar returned to his study and tried to find any more details that could be helpful. As he was reading, he heard a distant noise approach and grow louder. At first, he thought it was a heavy hail. But before he could think any further, a shower of meteors punctured through the building he was in. One meteor blasted through his abdomen and continued down through the first floor and basement before finally coming to a stop.

CHAPTER 8:

THE SCOURGING

Bishop Julius and Monica were walking through the small town where Emil had been sent. Eleazar had asked the pair to make sure that he was OK. He explained it as precautionary, but Monica saw how seriously Julius had reacted. They had reached the outskirts of town and not yet seen any survivors. Something caught Monica's eye.

Monica looked up into the sky as she saw the countless meteors rain down upon the Earth. Although it was surreal for her to witness what she had seen years before in her vision of the end times, it was no less terrifying.

She had completed building a substantial underground bunker in her home town months ago. Every builder she hired tried to dissuade her from the extra layers of reinforcing she had requested be added to the roof. It had cost her all of her savings as well as a significant loan with the bank, but it gave her peace of mind, at least it did for a time. She wondered how many hundreds of miles away she now stood at this crucial moment. It was no use at all. She hoped her parents might remember the security code she had given them and be safe. But looking up at the sky, she now doubted that even her best efforts would be enough to stop the death raining down on them.

Monica knew amidst all those falling rocks, there was one coming that was the size of a mountain.

"Wormwood," she spoke its name.

Julius ran on for a moment, not realising that Monica was not following. Monica closed her eyes and spread out her arms. Drawing in a deep breath, she embraced the end. It had felt like she had been fighting for years. Part of her wished that she would be allowed to live, part of her yearned for eternal rest. Dust slapped into her face as the first small meteor smashed into the ground near her.

"Monica! We have to go!" Bishop Julius called out.

She opened her eyes to see him rushing towards her. Meteors thudded down all around him as he ran.

"Where?"

"Follow me!"

Despite her momentary lack of hope, she ran after him. Bricks exploded from the second story of a building on the far side of the road as a meteor carved through it. As they ran, Julius desperately looked for shelter.

"Here!"

A large truck was parked on the side of the road. He ran towards it and dived underneath the trailer. A moment later, Monica joined him. They cowered for a few minutes listening to the deadly hail. The truck jolted as a meteor tore through the cab, engine and into the ground beneath them. It was apparent the truck would not protect them. Monica heard Julius praying, but she could not concentrate with all the impacts around her. Monica knew that any moment a meteor would end her life. But to her surprise, the meteor shower stopped, and they breathed a sigh of relief.

Julius looked at her with concern, the wrinkles on his face finding familiar creases. He put his hand on her shoulder.

"Monica, Monica! Are you OK?"

Stunned that she was alive, Monica nodded.

"This was your vision, wasn't it?"

"Yes, but not quite like this. I don't understand."

"God willing you will in due time. C'mon let's find Emil."

They clambered out from under the truck and surveyed the newly destroyed town. It was if it had been hit by an artillery strike with craters and debris everywhere. Dust drifted in the air with a burning smell that irritated Monica's nose. Julius coughed and tried to wipe the dirt and concrete dust from his face with his sleeve.

"Listen…" Monica said, pointing to her ear.

"What?" Julius replied after a moment of trying to hear.

"I can't hear anybody. Surely we would hear people yelling for help after something like that."

"Perhaps they evacuated the town?"

"I hope so."

They ran along the broken road. Julius seemed to know exactly where he was going. Monica ran next to him, soaking in the devastation around her.

"Hello! Hello?" She repeatedly called.

There was no reply.

A few small fires crackled amidst the ruins, sending bitter smoke up into the dusty air. They rounded a corner and Julius pointed ahead of them.

"It's the brown brick house,"

Monica heard a little relief in his voice that the house was still standing. There were impact holes scattered about the ground. Some of them looked to be steaming. The surrounding houses had collapsed roofs and walls blown out. Luckily, only the garage of the brown brick house was destroyed.

They ran up to the house and opened the front door.

"Emil? its Julius, Emil!"

Monica stepped inside behind Julius. The house was plain and furnished with cheap but functional furniture. The carpet looked worn and the place smelt like an old fabric shop. Julius went room by room, looking for the residents. As he did so, he stomped on a bloodworm that had somehow made its way inside.

"I'll check out the back yard," he called as he ducked out the back door.

It was already clear to Monica that there was no one here. She stood in the kitchen and looked down at the table. A partially eaten lunch was laid out. Places set for three people. There were half-filled glasses and very stale looking sandwiches. She checked the cupboards as she waited for Julius. She found a small packet of biscuits in one of them. They were her favourite as a child. She reached up and put them in her pocket.

"I never thought I'd see these again," she spoke aloud to herself. She wondered what the future held for her now that she had survived her vision.

Julius returned from outside.

"Nothing."

"It looks like they left in a hurry." Monica pointed at the table.

Julius picked up a glass of water and drank it.

"So Julius, why was Emil in this little village anyway?"

It was clear her question weighed heavily on him. He opened his mouth then closed it again before speaking.

"Perhaps, it'd be easier if I showed you. Follow me."

He set the glass down on the table, and they made their way out the front door. They walked around the side of the property and over to a gate in the back fence. Julius opened it and walked through, holding it open for Monica. Ahead of them was a large open area that Monica initially thought was a park. There was a small grassy field, some gardens and a few large trees. Then she spotted the first gravestone.

"A cemetery?" She asked.

"Yes, follow me." Julius beckoned.

They walked across the grass over a small verge. Upon reaching the top, Julius stopped in his tracks.

"God, please no…" his voice trailed off as he dropped to his knees.

"What is it?" Monica rushed to his side as her eyes drunk in the horror.

A large pile of human corpses lay ahead of them. Monica guessed it was the entire population of the village. The ground around the pile was well-trodden and a large puddle of blood has seeped out from the bottom of the pile. Whatever had happened, it must have been recently as it had not yet begun to stink.

"What on Earth?" Monica gasped.

Julius stood up and ran ahead. Monica chased him. To her surprise, he did not run toward the pile. He veered off to the left. She saw him brush his hand over damaged gravestones as he passed them. She stopped for a moment at one which looked to have a bullet hole in it.

"What's going on?" She called.

She stomped on a few bloodworms making their way towards the pile of bodies. Several steps ahead of her Julius came to a stop. He was looking at an old crypt ahead of him. The door was wide open. Blood splashes stained the grass around the entrance.

Monica ran up alongside him.

He turned to her and spoke.

"Emil must be dead and…"

"and?"

"...and, *he* is loose..."

. . .

The deafening thud of meteors raining down around the congregation of St. Thomas' church continued for what seemed like forever. Then abruptly, it stopped. Zack opened his eyes and looked around; he was surrounded by people on their knees, desperately praying for their lives. He watched as a few more people began to look up and smiles spread across their relieved faces.

"We're alive!"

Shouts of joy quickly spread across the crowd as survivors hugged each other.

"The school!" Graham cried.

They swung open the church gate and a large group of them rushed over to the school. Many deep potholes remained from the meteor shower. Dust choked the air. Zack ran out of the gate and made his way over to Stanley. He was lying face down on the road. Zack rolled him over on to his back, his eyes were open and vacant. There was a large gunshot wound in the middle of his chest and it was clear that it was too late for him. Zack knelt next to him and closed his eyes in prayer. They had been through so much together. It did not feel real that he was dead. Zack could hear the others rushing around behind him.

"There's one over here!"

"Bring the med-kit!"

Zack did not move from Stanley's side. He reached over and closed his friend's eyes. Part of Zack's mind recalled Stanley's death in his vision. For a moment, he wondered if he would be able to save anybody. He looked up to see his friends approaching him. Zack stood and ran over to them with his arms wide open.

"Guys!"

"Zack!"

He engulfed Graham, Beth and Mindy in a bear hug.

"I'm so sorry. I'm…" Zack began.

"Don't apologise, you've made it home. We're all OK," Graham replied.

"I, I…" Zack welled up with emotion.

"Good to see you Zack," Beth said, smiling.

"I'm glad you're safe," Mindy added.

Zack smiled at them each in turn.

"I'm sorry I wasn't there for you. I can't express how glad I am to see you all alive…" Zack paused for a moment as he saw each of them had received some serious injuries. "…and in one piece. More or less?"

"We did better thanks to all your crazy talk," Graham said, ruffling Zack's hair smiling.

"I hope I muttered something useful."

"You did man. So why did it take you so long to get here?"

Zack's face fell. It was clear that he had suffered greatly at the hands of the gang since his capture.

"We stopped to help, but…" Zack drifted off and looked back over at Stanley's body.

Graham put his hands on Zack's shoulders.

"You made it through Zack, and we're going to need you even more than usual in these crazy times."

"And I am going to need all of you," he replied.

The four friends spent the next several minutes, catching up.

As they began to walk towards to school to help out, Zack gently touched Mindy's arm.

"Can I talk to you for a bit?"

"Sure Zack,"

Zack led her a short distance away from the others. He had been thinking about what he would say to Mindy for what felt like years. Zack promised himself he would take the first opportunity he had to tell Mindy how he felt about her.

Zack gulped.

"Mindy, I, I'm in love with you."

Mindy looked genuinely stunned for a moment.

"Zack, you've barely talked to me over the past year. How can you be in love with me?"

"But…" Zack did not know where to begin.

Mindy put her hand on his shoulder

"I know…" she smiled at him. "…can we just take things slowly?"

Zack nodded.

"I'm sorry Mindy. I'll make it up to you."

"I'm looking forward to it. C'mon people need our help," she led him over to the school.

Zack rapidly blinked his eyes and took a deep breath. That did not go like he thought it would at all. He had pictured it going well for so long it was difficult to accept the contrary. He tried to focus on the fact he had not been outright rejected. He looked down at Mindy's hand, towing him forward. He did not want to let it go. He decided that he would do everything he could to win her over.

Kephas and a large group of volunteers made their way through the school checking on the many wounded. Kephas was relieved to see that more had survived than he had feared. Several classrooms had meteors punch straight them and burrow into the ground underneath. There was more than one lucky person who had meteors land close by but had managed to escape with their lives. Several people in the school died, with what would have been very swift deaths. With all the infection they were struggling with, Deon wondered if that was a better way to go.

Kephas stood over a screaming woman who had a meteor scorch her left arm. The upper part of her arm and shoulder were seriously burnt. The Bishop stood beside and closed his eyes in prayer. Kephas could feel a difference deep inside himself compared to before the meteor shower. He felt like the spiritual realm was now accessible to the physical world. He imagined it like a tap which had been turned on. A slow trickle was now flowing steadily, as opposed to the erratic bursts during the first three days.

Kephas dwelled on this connection for a moment and then poured everything he had into a prayer of healing for the screaming lady. After a few minutes of prayer, Kephas realised the scream had lowered in volume. He kept praying. After several more minutes, he noticed the woman had fallen silent. He continued to pray as he heard gasps from the people watching all around him. Finally, he opened his eyes to see the woman smiling back at him. Her wound had miraculously healed over with scar tissue.

"Thank you so much Bishop," she said.

"Thank the living God; it's only through him that you are healed."

The woman raised her head, closed her eyes and poured herself into a reverent prayer of thanks. Kephas stood up wobbling a bit in the process.

"Are you OK Bishop?' Deon asked, holding his shoulder.

"Oh yes, yes. It's just that it can take a bit out of you is all," he said, smiling.

An exhausted Kephas was delighted that he could now tap into the spiritual realm. But he did worry that demons may again be able to invade the physical world.

Kephas and his volunteers spend the whole next day stabilising and healing all of those in the school. The community also dug a number of shallow graves. Zack was sitting down next to one with a gold star hat placed on the top of it. Zack stood up as he heard the Bishop approach.

"He didn't deserve to go like that," Zack declared.

"I agree with you," Kephas replied.

Zack nodded.

"It's good to see you Kephas."

"I'm glad you made it Zack."

"I haven't seen Father Andrews around?"

Kephas shook his head.

"He has passed away."

"Oh, I'm sorry."

Kephas observed the dried blood on Zack's tattered clothes.

"We have all been through much it seems. Are you alright?"

"I will be. I felt something change within me just as those meteors fell."

"Yes, it seems the spiritual flood gates are beginning to open in full. We will be able to draw strength from our Heavenly allies. But I think we should expect more demon attacks."

"Then we'll need to be ready."

"Agreed, please follow me, I have something for you."

Deon walked past them with a wheelbarrow full of firearms dropped by the Street Snakes.

"Oh very good Deon, I'll be with you shortly," Kephas called.

Deon waved.

"We'll sanctify the ammunition as we discussed."

"Sounds good."

The Bishop led Zack into his office. Upon his desk was a long object covered in a red cloth. He picked it up and turned to Zack.

"I believe this has been waiting all this time for you Zack. Take it and keep others safe."

Zack took it from him and unfurled the cloth to reveal an ancient sword of the Order of Salt and Light. The long blade had seen battle but was in surprisingly good condition. The guard, grip and pommel were shaped into a crucifix.

"This is amazing, thank you Bishop."

"I know it's not identical to what you saw in your vision, but I'm confident it will serve you well."

Zack stood back and made a few careful swings.

"It's perfect. I promise I'll put it to good use."

"I'm sure you will."

"Unfortunately, some of our other preparations were not as secure as we thought."

"Oh?"

"Yes, a fissure in the ground near the rear of the church swallowed our buried cache. Also, the gang, which it seems you're already familiar with, stole the supplies from the storage unit."

Zack thought for a moment. He had spent months amassing every sort of useful resource he could think of; he was not about to abandon them so quickly.

"Well let's go get them back then?"

"The ground has taken them permanently I'm afraid, and I don't know where the rest have been taken to."

"I didn't get a chance to look around while I was there. But I know where they hang out."

Zack flexed a fist at the thought of all he underwent there.

"Zack, don't kill them all."

He looked to Kephas, expecting to see a smile on his face. But instead he looked very serious. He almost felt like he received a compliment that Kephas thought he could indeed kill every single one of them.

"What do you mean?"

"Isn't that what you're thinking?"

Zack didn't reply.

"I know that they have acted cruelly, and it's completely natural to feel like you should be able to get even. But Zack, we have a greater enemy to deal with."

Zack sighed.

"You're right. But that's why we need everything they stole."

"I agree with you, just, don't do anything I wouldn't do."

"Deal!" Zack returned a smile, turned and began to walk away.

"Zack, may God bless you."

"And you too Bishop."

A short time later, Zack had explained to his friends his plan to return to the Street Snake gang-house, sneak in and leave with their stolen supplies.

"I just don't think it'll be as simple as you say Zack. It sounds terribly dangerous," Beth said with a concerned look on her face.

"You're probably right, but I'm going anyway. I'm absolutely certain we can save lives with those supplies."

"And if they try to stop you?" Graham asked

"I'll stop them." Zack replied confidently.

"I admit, that's a pretty great sword Zack, but I expect they'll have plenty of guns."

Zack did not look as concerned as Graham thought he should be.

"And if you get injured?" Mindy added.

Zack smiled back at her. "I'll be OK."

"Only because I'm coming with you." Mindy replied

"Mindy!" Beth exclaimed.

"What? I don't see anyone else with medical training around, do you?"

Beth just smiled. "I'm coming too then," she looked to Graham.

"Oh, I was always going to go. When do we leave?"

Zack hugged them all.

"Thank you so much. Let's leave as soon as you're ready."

Zack waited at the church gate, Mindy showed up first with a large backpack, which he assumed was filled with medical supplies. Graham and Beth appeared next. Beth had a bag on her back, and Graham was carrying a shovel that had its blade sharpened.

"Where to?"

"Over the Brakenside river, they have a large abandoned warehouse there."

"Let's go."

The four friends walked out of the gate and down the road.

Kephas stood amidst the crowds gathered at the front of the church.

"Attention please everyone. Since we're no longer going to depend on the government, we're going to need to venture out into our broken world to find our own food and water. I expect there are still a great many people who'll need our help. If you'd like to volunteer, please meet me at the gate."

David, Adam, Malcolm and Amanda met the Bishop at the gate. They took with them two wheelbarrows and many empty plastic bottles for storing water.

"I'm coming too!" Deon called as they walked out on to the road.

They walked for some time towards the closest freshwater stream. It resided under a bridge several blocks away from the church. Upon their arrival, they carefully made their way down a steep grassy verge to the water. They were all thirsty after the trip. Adam reached the water first. He was glad to see the water was crystal clear. He scooped it up in his hands and drank it back quickly. He promptly erupted into a coughing fit and spat out all he could.

"Urgh, its no good!"

"What do you mean?" Amanda asked, peering into the clear water.

"It tastes like vinegar, or rot, I can't describe it. I…"

Adam fell flat on his face and began to quiver.

"Adam!"

They rushed over to help.

"Kephas! Come quickly!"

Kephas' body was struggling to keep up with him. He knew he would need to spend increasing hours every day in prayer just to keep himself going. There was one other thing he could do, but he hoped it would never come to that.

The Bishop held his hand over Adam and began to pray but then stopped.

"It's too late; his soul has left this body."

"What? But he was fine just a moment ago?!" Amanda cried.

"I'm sorry..."

They stood in solemn silence.

Deon wondered how many others throughout Brakenside had also died. He looked into the water.

"Hey, does it look a little too clean to you?"

"Hmm, Now that you mention it, yes. Especially with all the disasters lately," Amanda admitted.

"I wonder if this is a result of God's wrath is being poured out upon this world," Kephas said.

"Surely it could just be poisoned from a broken pipe somewhere. The industrial part of Brakenside backs onto this river too."

"Indeed."

"Well, there must be another water source somewhere?" Amanda asked.

Deon pulled out a map.

"This river is the main fresh-water for all of Brakenside."

"How about here or here?" David said, pointing.

"No, salt water there. Hmm, Yes, but it's many miles away from here. Transporting water such a distance will be very difficult," Kephas explained.

"How about we clean this water?" Malcolm added.

All eyes looked to him as he continued.

"First we boil it, then we collect the steam as it condenses on a flat surface. It'll be slow, but it should be clean after that."

"Let's try that first. But surely we must be extra careful on testing this," Amanda said.

"Agreed, let's look for any bottled water on the way back too," Kephas added.

They started filling a few containers and put Adams body in the wheelbarrow.

"I'm going to check on our farm across town. I'm hoping at least some of our crops are still intact. Deon declared.

"That's a good idea..." David agreed. "... I'll come too."

Kephas nodded. "We'll meet you back at the church. Be careful."

Malcolm pushed the wheelbarrow and Amanda, and Kephas lugged the water back to the thirsty congregation. Deon and David waved as they departed towards the community farm.

After a long walk through the suburbs, Deon and David made it across town. They could see that many small meteors had landed nearby. As they got closer, Deon guessed about half of their crops were in an edible state. David took the keys from Deon and opened the small garden shed at the end of the field. He returned with a few tools in a wheelbarrow. They spent some time digging up what they could.

As they were about to fill the wheelbarrow, Deon noticed the light of day begin to fade. It quickly darkened to almost as dark as night. The sun seemed to recede away, becoming smaller and smaller in the sky. A loud thunder crack rippled overhead as clouds spread over the sky from nowhere.

"What in the blazes?!" David cried, dropping some vegetables.

They could not help but look up into the quickly changing sky. All of a sudden, Deon felt very insignificant and vulnerable as the clouds boomed above him. Where they last saw the sun, a deep blackness began to rip across the sky. It took the shape of a giant cross. An ear-rending boom of air pressure flattened both men to the ground. It was accompanied by a resonance which Deon would later describe as the deepest voice imaginable speaking directly to his very core.

"This is the end. Repent and be saved."

Both men could not take their eyes away from the enormous cross dominating the sky. As they watched, it began to fade away. Deon hoped the clouds would dissipate too, but they remained. It remained very gloomy and dark as if the clouds extended to the heavens restricting light coming to Earth.

"Good God," Deon spilled.

His mind raced back to a conversation he had with the Bishop months earlier. He remembered Kephas telling him of the end of days, disaster and demons. At the time Deon humoured the old man but did not take it too seriously. Now, he wished he had paid more attention.

"David, we must go now!" Deon jumped to his feet and righted the toppled wheelbarrow.

Unusually for David, he did not seem to have anything to say. He merely got behind the wheelbarrow and started pushing. As they bounced over the field, some of their produce fell onto the ground. But they continued as fast as they could. David was not sure of what Deon knew, but he recognised that Deon knew what to do. They felt like they had been caught outside, and a storm of fatal proportions was going to bear down on them at any moment.

. . .

Across town, Zack and his friends were scrambling to their feet after being knocked over when the sky split apart.

"Zack, you, you, were right all along," Graham admitted

"Unbelievable!" Beth exclaimed.

Mindy looked too shocked to comment.

A small part of Zack was screaming out to him to yell at the top of his lungs *"I told you so!"* But somehow he restrained himself. At Zack's core, he felt the connection to the spiritual realm was now wide open. He knew that his Rites, Dedications and Prayers would have gained tangible strength in the process. But he thought only of the demons that would be assaulting earth at any moment.

Beth stood up and began to jog back the way they came.

"Beth wait!" Zack called.

"Surely, we gotta get back to the church!?"

"We need my gear now more than ever. Demons will no doubt soon be upon us. We're closer to the gang-house than the church anyway."

Beth thought for a moment then came back.

"C'mon, follow me," Zack directed.

They hurried through the suburbs and made it over the Brakenside bridge.

"I could see the river out one of the windows where they kept us. So it's got to be one of those warehouses," Zack pointed as he spoke.

They made their way over to the first one and managed to scale the wooden fence. They ran across the car park and peeked through a window. It was filled with storage racks and countless cardboard boxes.

"It's not this one," Zack confirmed.

They climbed back over the fence to the street and approached the next warehouse. As they approached, torchlight shone out into their faces from inside the chain-link fence.

"Don't come any closer," a stern voice called.

Zack tried to shield his eyes and managed to glimpse the uniform on the security guard.

"Hey, I used to work for Gold Star too."

"And now you're looking to break in huh? Wait. Why the hell are you carrying a sword?!"

"No, it's not like that. We're looking for the Street Snakes gang house."

"What on earth for?"

"They took all our stuff is the short version. I know it's one of these warehouses, just not sure which one."

The torchlight left the other's faces and went back to Zack's.

"Aren't you that Zack guy? I saw your face in the Gold Star newsletter."

"That's right. I'm Zack. These are my friends, Graham, Beth and Mindy. Who are you?"

"I'm Larry," he lowered his torch and walked forward to the fence.

"Why are you still working Larry?

"I'm just earning Creds for food like everyone else..."

At that moment, a large Scarkin demon leapt atop the warehouse. It began scampering down the roof towards Larry.

"What the hell is that?" Larry cried, drawing his pistol.

"Demon! Open the gate!" Zack yelled.

Larry ignored him as he began firing off rounds at the quickly approaching demon. The demon was violently knocked backwards by the incoming fire but quickly got back to its feet.

Zack began to climb the fence.

"Give me a boost," he instructed Graham as he scrambled upwards. Zack forced himself through the barbed wire and dropped down on the inside as he heard Larry begin to scream. He pushed himself to his feet and rushed over to Larry's aid. He was laying on his back fending off incoming blows, getting his forearms sliced up in the process.

"Demon filth!" Zack goaded as he closed the distance.

The Scarkin twisted its head towards Zack as it dragged its long claws across Larry's chest. It then charged at Zack shrieking.

Zack gripped the sword in his right hand tighter and waited for the last moment to strike. The demon leapt at him and lost one of its limbs to Zack's blade. With an enraged shriek, the demon scrambled onwards. Zack sidestepped and with a return swing severed its head. It dropped like a puppet with its strings cut.

While Zack was fighting the demon, Graham helped Mindy over the fence. Rushing to Larry's side, she found he had multiple deep gashes across his body.

"One, eighty..." he struggled to speak before his eyes suddenly lost focus.

"What? Save your breath; you'll be OK," Mindy pleaded.

She tried to hold pressure on his many bleeding wounds.

Zack ran over to Larry's body and rested a hand on his forehead. He closed his eyes for a moment in prayer.

"Piss it! His soul has already left his body. There's nothing we can do," Zack spat.

"Are you sure?" Mindy asked.

"Yes," Zack said with a burdened look on his face.

Graham and Beth did not need to ask as Zack took Larry's pistol, last magazine and returned to the fence. Mindy grabbed Larry's keys and opened the gate.

"He said 'one-eighty' before he died. Does that mean anything to anyone?"

"Well, this is one-fifty-six Port road, maybe he was telling us where to go?" Beth suggested.

"Good thinking," Mindy replied.

"OK, let's try that."

Zack passed the pistol to Graham.

"Better than a shovel?"

Graham hesitated for a moment. He hoped he would not have to use it.

"Yeah, thanks."

They continued down the road past the various warehouses, sheds and industrial buildings. Upon reaching their destination, Zack picked up the pace.

"Yeah, I think this is it."

A large dilapidated warehouse covered in graffiti stood before them. Many of the windows had been smashed out, and the car park in front was filled with litter and a couple of burnt-out cars. Zack had his sword ready, and Graham held his pistol up as the four opened a large metal door and walked in. The inside was in a similar state of disrepair. The smell brought back some hard memories for Zack.

"This is the place," he confirmed.

"Hey! Ass hats!" Zack yelled.

Graham scanned the building with his finger on the trigger.

No-one replied, and after a few minutes, they decided to continue further inside. They found three gang members laying dead around a table on the far side. Each was covered head to toe with deep gashes.

"Scarkin got here first," Zack stated.

Zack pointed out the large shipping container where he spent his time as they approached.

"Stanley and I were in this one. The others were in these," he pointed to the other containers behind as they walked along. Mindy laid a hand on his shoulder.

"I'm so sorry; I don't know what to say."

"It's OK, let's just find the supplies and get going."

They spread out to search.

"Over here!" Graham called.

On the far side of the warehouse he found empty food ration wrappers.

"Aren't these the ones you had?" Graham asked.

Zack made it way over and inspected them.

"Yes, all these came from my storage," he foraged around and found a hand full still intact.

"Zack!" Beth beckoned him over to a dumpster.

Peering inside Zack saw his research, notes and plans that he had painstakingly worked on for many months.

"Shall we dig it all out?" she offered.

Zack rifled through some of it and kept a few pages.

"Thanks Beth, this is good. We can leave the rest."

Mindy knocked on the glass of the mezzanine office window above them. She had a happy expression on her face. The group climbed the thin metal staircase and made their way inside. The office had been done up very nicely, with several large-screen television sets, an expensive-looking sound system, pool tables, beds and even a bar. In the corner of the room lay a pile of Zack's custom demon-fighting weapons.

"Fantastic! Great find Mindy!"

"Happy to help," she said with a smile.

"Oh yes! Toothbreaker!" Graham exclaimed as he picked up a large hammer. "...I'm going to smash some demons with this!"

Beth glanced a quizzical look in his direction.

Graham just smiled.

"With these, we should be able to make our way back to the church in one piece. And save many lives," Zack added.

Beth picked up a pair of long knives, Mindy took a spear, Zack took a shield. Each weapon showed hours of Zack's hard work, with metal reinforcing and etched holy words.

"Let's collect everything we can and meet by the door we came in," Beth suggested.

A short time later they had collected all they could find of Zack's preparations and loaded them into a supermarket trolley they found. Graham pushed the door open, and they began to make their way back to the church.

· · ·

Elsewhere, Leonard sat at his desk watching one of the many monitor screens in front of him. He had been employed by the WGO for some time now, and he had gotten used to the way things were done. He did not care about their agenda, for the most part; he was happy to do his work, collect his Creds and go home at the end of the day. Leonard had seen plenty of big companies come and go; often things stayed more or less the same.

Leonard's job was to push out content updates out to the millions of AI watches that they had online. Having all of the devices connected up to one system made so many things possible that was inconceivable before the unification event. He selected another batch of devices and scanned their version numbers. Part of him did admit it was a little disturbing that if he chose to; he could connect to anyone on the planet and listen in through their watch. But there was a procedure in place to prevent that. Well, at least he assumed there was.

Leonard waited for the screen to load, which normally only took a few seconds. But it seemed like there was a problem. Only two-thirds of the data set had loaded up. Assuming it was a fault, he re-ran the commands. A few seconds later, the same result appeared on the screen. He stood up from his desk to see his colleague's face in the station opposite to him show an equal amount of confusion.

"Henry, is your data all messed up?"

"Yeah, I don't understand, I've not ever seen this happen before."

"Have you tried a fresh query?"

"Yip, same result."

"Hmm, I'll reboot, that normally fixes things."

"OK, I'll try some other batches."

A minute later, they both stood up. Leonard spoke first

"Re-boot didn't help."

"Same results in other batches."

They stood puzzled for a moment.

"One-third of the population can't just die that quick, can it?"

They walked over to the closest window and peered out into the indiscernible gloom.

"Nah, it must be a system error. Let's try it again tomorrow Henry."

"Yeah, oh hey Leonard, I'm upgrading my AI watch to the new model on the way home, do you wanna grab one too?"

"I thought they were not released until next week?"

"Yeah, well I just happen to know someone. C'mon."

"OK, great!"

A short time later, they were standing in a large warehouse filled with boxes. One of the staff walked over.

"Hey Henry, I know I said I'd have time to give you the full tour, but I just can't today. Sorry."

"I get it Susan; we're under pressure on our side too. Could I grab a Mk2 watch for my friend and me? He works in operations too."

Leonard smiled and waved.

Susan thought for a moment.

"Yeah sure, there's an open crate at the far end…" she said, pointing "… just update your serial number in the system and dump the other one into the chute."

"Will do, thanks!"

"OK, see ya later."

Susan turned and hurried back to her work on the far side of the warehouse.

"See? Easy-peasy," Henry said with a smile.

They walked down the aisle to the open crate and pulled out a small box each. The new model would be mandatory for everyone as soon as they could finish production, and with the resources that the WGO had at its disposal, that would be soon.

Leonard rolled the box over in his hands. The outside just contained a series of numbers and codes. He took off his old watch, opened the box and strapped on the new watch.

"Initialising…" Bess' voice spoke quietly.

Henry strapped his on too. Both watches auto-adjusted to fit more securely.

"Oww!" Leonard's wrist stung as if he had received an injection. A second later, Henry was complaining about the same.

"What was that?"

"I don't know, too tight?"

"Calibration complete, I now have a direct feed into your circulatory system. Now administering essential vitamins and minerals."

Both men felt a tingle in their arms as a fluid flowed through their veins.

"I didn't know it did that!" Henry began

"Neither, well I guess it's for the best."

As they were speaking, another broadcast was projected from their new devices. There had been many over the past few days. Mostly they were short videos from various parts of the world showing how the WGO had helped the local populace.

"Greetings, we're live here in Israel as the WGO has just finished establishing the newest base of operations in Jerusalem. We'll be..."

The reporter was interrupted as two men dressed in simple black cloaks came up beside him and pushed him aside.

"Get away, snake-tongue," one said.

The cameraman backed up as a security team rushed the men.

"Adolebitque Malum!" They shouted in unison as their very words caught fire and engulfed the security team. They screamed in pain for a moment before collapsing to the ground.

One of the two men stepped towards the camera. He addressed the millions watching around the world

"Stop sinning. Repent! Turn back to God with all your hearts. Do not believe the WGO's lies. Do not listen to their..." The broadcast was abruptly cut short. Henry and Leonard looked at each other.

"What the hell was that?"

"Don't ask me. Did we just see them breathe fire?"

"Yeah, I sure did."

"How is that even possible?"

"It must have been computer-generated somehow."

"On a live broadcast?"

"I don't know…"

A thought slowly surfaced in Leonard's mind that the WGO may not be what he first thought they were.

. . .

Back in Brakenside, Kephas and Amanda had made it back to the church. Many were eagerly awaiting food and water. They were met with many shocked and saddened looks as Adam's body came into view.

"Bishop!" Sandy came running to the gate with tears running down her face.

"What's wrong Sandy?"

"I, I, they…" she struggled to calm down.

"Peace be with you Sandy, it's alright, take your time and explain."

Sandy took a deep breath.

"I sent another team to collect water to the south, and they are all dead!"

Kephas' face dropped and he put his arm around her.

"I'm so sorry to hear that. It seems then the whole river has gone bad then."

Sandy looked to the few containers they were carrying.

"Is that water no good either?"

"Not in its current state, but we have a plan…"

Wails from the approaching crowd protested loudly.

"I *need* a drink!"

"You said you'd bring back water!"

"Please wait a little longer. We need to make sure it's safe," Kephas explained

Malcolm took a large bottle of water and went to the kitchen in the church office.

The crowd followed him to the door.

"Let me set everything up and I'll be out as soon as I have some ready."

Malcolm spent the afternoon in the kitchen doing everything he could think of to purify the water. Finally, he emerged with a single cupful.

"I've boiled it, and collected the steam three times."

He held it up hopefully.

Amanda stepped forward.

"I'll try it," she said bravely.

She took the cup from Malcolm and looked at the water. It looked crystal clear, and she could not smell anything untoward. Her dehydrated body was screaming out to her to guzzle it all in one go.

She began to raise it to her mouth as Kephas held her hand.

"Please, just the smallest amount, and please let me bless you first…"

Numbers 6
²⁴ "The LORD bless you
and keep you;
²⁵ the LORD make his face shine on you
and be gracious to you;
²⁶ the LORD turn his face toward you
and give you peace."

She nodded and dipped her finger in the water and put it in her mouth.

· · ·

Unnoticed by most, the bloodworms which had made their way up to the surface began acting strangely. They began to wriggle and twitch at an increasing rate, as they did so, they began to swell and ooze out a foul-smelling liquid.

Rex eventually made it home, and after many painful hours made it into his old wheelchair in his garage. He had often thought of getting rid of it, but thankfully, he had not yet found time to clean up. Rex stayed in his house, eating what little food he had until he was completely desperate for more. Luckily, he had plenty of soft drink in his cupboards, so fluid was not a problem. Rex's plan was to wait for the all-clear, that everything was going to go back to normal, but it never came.

Rex was now on his way back towards town. He had checked with his neighbours, but no-one was home. He reasoned that surely by now the rioting and looting were over and the shops would be in some sort of order. He paused for a moment to see a wriggling mass of bloodworms spread across the footpath in front of him.

"Gross!"

He began to steer around them as best he could. When without warning, they burst in a spray of goo. Amid the bloodworm remains and muck emerged several small creatures. It looked like a profane combination of locust, horse and scorpion. It had sharp teeth and claws. Every bloodworm had hatched into a plaguebee.

"What the?!"

He hurried away as the air filled with the sound of their small wings. They set upon him, gripping with their claws and stinging with their tails.

"Get off me!" He cried, trying to swat them away.

Pain surged through his body as their venom flowed through his bloodstream. He cried out as he managed to rip one from his arm and throw it to the ground. With successive stings, he fell from his wheelchair and writhed in pain on the ground. He felt like these were going to be his last moments on earth. A wash of regret surged through his mind. He thought of his family, those whom he loved and others whom he did not. He wondered if it was too late to turn his life around.

It did not take long for large swarms to form, and many people fled to the safety of the church grounds, or into the welcoming arms of the WGO. The later promised an anti-toxin would be ready in just a few days. But after a series of failed attempts, it took months for the inflicted pain to finally recede.

. . .

Amanda swallowed the smallest amount of water from her finger. A surge of the strongest bitterness she had ever experienced coursed through her. She could not help but splutter. Before Kephas could react, she put out her hand.

"I'm OK; it's just really awful."

Kephas watched her cautiously.

Amanda remained standing and dipped her finger once more.

"Bishop help!" Sandy screamed as she ran over. "…we're under attack!"

They all followed her to the church gate. A crowd of people looked to be trying to make their way in. The guard on the gate was holding it closed. As they got closer, they heard the droning sound of a swarm of plaguebee wings. They were stinging the people desperate to enter, but for some reason, none of them flew over the gate into the church grounds.

"Open the gate!" Kephas called.

"I'm not letting those things in here," the guard said defiantly.

"Stand aside," Kephas commanded as he moved him out of the way and stepped through into the crowd. The guard slammed it shut behind him. As soon as he was on the outside of the fence, the small flying demons left their victims on masse and covered Kephas.

"Open the…" he commanded as he made his way away from the church grounds drawing the small demons away with him.

The guard hesitated for a moment until Amanda pushed him aside. "Idiot!"

The people surged in through the gate, many of them staggering from their injuries.

"Kephas!" Deon cried as he tried to push his way out the gate against the tide coming in. Finally, there was a gap, and Deon rushed out and helped those laying on the road, unable to make it further without help. Deon witnessed they were all covered in large red swollen sores. Amanda and Malcolm rushed out to help. As they did so, some of the swarm on Kephas flew over to attack them. Deon had plaguebees land on his neck and shoulders as he pulled an older man in through the gate. He wondered how long he had before he would collapse in pain like the man he was helping. As he made it to the gate, the plaguebees retreated.

The Bishop made it to the other side of the road and knelt down. Everyone watching could not see him at all, only a mass of plaguebees completely covering him. He drew something from his pocket and held it above his head. After fumbling with it for a moment, the vessel opened, and holy water flowed down over him. Immediately the plaguebees dispersed and flew off in all directions.

The Bishop stood up and ran back to the gate, which was opened for him. Once inside, he rushed to Deon and checked his wounds, followed by Amanda and Malcolm.

"Are we going to be OK?" Amanda asked.

Kephas was covered in tiny cuts from the plaguebee claws and teeth. There were also numerous puncture sites from their stingers. Unlike the new arrivals, Kephas and the helpers had no red sores.

"We will..." he managed to say, it was clear that he was in serious pain. "...the wounded!"

The newcomers were laid down upon the grassy verge on the inside of the gate. Many of them were incapacitated from the pain.

"Bring me more holy water!" Kephas called as he knelt next to the closest victim. He closed his eyes in prayer.

"Here!" Deon called as he passed him a small jug of water. He could feel the eyes surrounding him watch the water. The temptation to drink it was nearly overpowering. Kephas prayed once more then tipped the water over the woman in front of him. Her quivering slowed and after a few moments regained her breath. She was still in significant pain but managed a nod of thanks. They repeated the process until they were all stable.

Deon nursed his injuries as he watched, expecting them to swell at any moment.

Kephas finally sat down upon the grass and caught his breath.

"Thank you God," he said genuinely.

For the next few days, the congregation tended to the wounded and purified all the water they could. Despite their best efforts, it seemed only just enough to stave off serious dehydration.

"Bishop, I don't get it, why didn't our injuries swell like those people that came in?" Deon asked.

"I've been wondering that too. I'm thinking the venom of those plaguebees could somehow be related to one's spirit."

"Oh?"

"We have all committed our lives to God and invited him into our lives. With that comes spiritual protection. After talking with the newcomers, it seems all of them at various stages of their lives rejected God. They have freewill to choose after all, but it is not without consequences.

Sometimes these are obvious, other times not. A few have since turned back to God, and their condition improved within hours. The others still are essentially fighting on their own."

Deon was about to reply when something above them caught their attention.

Kephas looked up to see dark clouds rippling across the sky. A brief moment later, everyone stood under a gloomy canopy of cloud that spread as far as anyone could see. People stopped what they were doing and looked up. Despite the similarities with a storm cloud, there was no rain.

The Bishop could see that the people were starting to panic and stood upon a car to address them. But before he could speak a loud booming thunderclap burst through the air. It came rolling up from southern Brakenside, swept over them and continued to the north.

No-one could recall anything like it. The noise had just about finished when it started to become louder and louder again. It swept over them all from the north this time, then down towards the south. This repeated until seven thunderclaps were heard by everyone on earth. After the last boom of thunder, the sky lit up with lightning arcing all over. A resonant voice that seemed to emanate from the very top of the sky called down.

"Repent! Turn away from evil."

The voice spoke to everyone at their very core. It was impossible to ignore. Just as quickly as the clouds formed, they began to dissipate. As they did so, the rain bucketed down. Amid the pelting rain, there was another sound. It was the battle cry of a demonic attack; multiple sources could be heard from locations surrounding the church. The sound was unfamiliar to many but instilled a primal fear.

"Get everyone inside the gates, those who can fight with me!" Kephas called as he ran towards the shed.

"But the water?!"

"Later!"

Those outside the church gates ran inside in a panic. Opening the door of the shed revealed a stack of custom-built spears, with holy words etched into the blades. Kephas passed them out to Malcolm, Will, Amanda and the several volunteers behind them.

"We need to move everyone in the school over to the church grounds right now!"

"What are we supposed to do with these?"

"Stick the sharp end in the attackers, and pray."

"What's coming for us Bishop?" Malcolm asked.

"Evil in physical form."

He gulped.

They ran towards the gate. Malcolm could see the plastic sheet with Bible pages was still attached to the fence. He was not sure how words could keep whatever made that bone-chilling howl out, but he was glad the Bishop had an idea what was going on.

As they stepped out through the gate, Kephas dropped to a knee and made the sign of the cross. He turned to those following him and blessed them.

"May the Lord Jesus Christ bless and protect you. 'Cutis Dura Fidei' may He empower us to save as many lives as possible today, Amen."

Amanda felt her skin tingle in a way he had never felt before. But she sincerely hoped that the Bishop's prayer did more than just that.

The Bishop and his fighters ran across the road towards the school gate. Upon seeing their approach, a few survivors ran over to the Church as directed. More howling could be heard close by. Several human screams rang out as if they were being brutally tortured.

"With me!" Kephas ran through the school gates, stopping briefly by the school office to trigger the fire alarm. The ringing of the school bells merged into the sound of driving rain and death cries.

The group ran around the office and met a hulking demon in their path. It was as tall as a human. The Mortkin had just finished disembowelling someone and flung their body to the ground.

"Begone filth!" Kephas roared as he charged at it with his spear. Malcolm, Will and Amanda fought against their desire to flee and charged in behind him.

Just before Kephas' spear impacted the demon, he heard the clatter of a few spears being dropped as a few volunteers ran away. The demon turned to face Kephas just as the spear drove into its body. Kephas pressed his body weight into it and tore the spear out through the beast's side. The demon swatted Kephas with its claws, and he was knocked over backwards on to the ground. As he did so, Malcolm, Will and Amanda drove their spears into its head and body knocking it over. The demon burst into a puddle of muck.

Malcolm extended his hand and pulled Kephas up off the ground.

"Thank you…"

A lunge of Kephas' spear impaled a Scarkin mid-air as it leapt at Malcolm. Several more jumped off the rooftops down upon them. They raked their long claws over them, shrieking in delight. But to their surprise, they did not carve out the deep wounds they were used to inflicting.

A moment later their shrieks turned to howls as the demons saw no blood was spilt. Will looked down to see a long bruise on his arm where he had expected a deep gash to be.

"Kill em all!" He cried with new vigour.

Amanda punched a Scarkin off her then stuck it to the ground with her spear. One of the fighters held a demon with both hands as his fellow fighters impaled it. Kephas changed his grip to halfway along the shaft and smacked an incoming demon with the handle then spun around to drive the bladed end through its head. Soon they were ankle-deep in rainwater mixed with demon remains.

"The people!" Kephas called as they finished off the last demon.

They ran into the closest classroom and hollered at the scared survivors.

"Run to the church! Run for your lives!"

They got up from where they were cowering and ran towards the door. One remained lying in a makeshift bed with a look of terror on their face. Their leg was heavily bandaged.

"I'll take them," Will volunteered.

The fighters ran through to the next few classrooms and repeated the process. Soon they had a steady stream of people making the fastest pace they could through the school towards the church. Many skidded and slipped over in the wet conditions.

"Spread out, protect the line!" Kephas commanded as the evacuation was in full flight.

The fighters dispersed across the path leading through the school. One remained at the gate, another in the middle of the road between death and safety.

They seemed to be making progress when Amanda saw a cadre of Mortkin stomp up the road.

"Bishop!" She cried.

The demons broke into a run as they approached and crashed into one of the fighters. He managed to bring his spear across into one of them in time. But the others knocked him over onto the ground and began unleashing countless blows upon him. His bruised and lifeless body was flung against the wall of the closest classroom.

"Help!" Amanda cried as she and the closest fighters backed up to the basketball court on the school grounds.

Kephas, Malcolm, Will and the remaining fighters ran to her aid.

The demons seemed to keep coming, and soon there was two dozen standing opposite the several remaining fighters. The demons began their advance with a loud roar above the rain pelting down around them.

As they approached the Bishop bowed his head in prayer, he felt the connection to the spiritual realm and channelled it into himself and his fellow fighters. He began chanting the Rite of Battle and raised his head. Amanda felt strength surge throughout her body. It was like she was temporarily free of every ache and pain, well-rested and bursting with energy. She could not help but yell out a war cry. Everyone shouted with her. She felt herself walking forwards, eager to dispose of the filth in front of her.

Kephas paused his chant just long enough to shout "Charge!"

They sprinted forward, holding their spears forward. As they ran, the Bishop quickly turned his spear to the left, others followed. The bishop directed them as if they had fought together for years as one cohesive unit. They slammed into the left flank of the demons impaling and destroying several demons in the process. A few seconds of stabbing and slashing later they had dropped more demons as another fighter fell.

As the demon line rushed to overwhelm them, the fighters broke off at Kephas' lead and dropped back in between classrooms behind them. The demons charged in as the line of spears lunged into them.

"Again!" Kephas directed.

As one, they withdrew their weapons, tearing holes of the front rank that toppled over and died. The next rank pushed forward as they drove their spears forwards again. The impaled Mortkin managed to break a few spears before collapsing into the muck. By now the fighters had dropped enough demons to be roughly equal in number with their foe. The demons surged forward despite their losses. Rending claws slashed the front row of fighters, and two collapsed.

"Legs!"

Kephas dropped his spear and slashed, his fighters copied, and the front row of demons fell.

"Heads!"

An array of spears drove into the skulls of the toppled demons which burst with a spray of filth.

"Charge!"

They pressed forward into the second rank of demons driving spears into their chests.

Finally, the last of the demons perished.

"Wounded!"

The fighters split off to check on their injured comrades. It seemed like all the fallen had died when Will called "Over here!"

The Bishop rushed over to see a man covered in bruises vomiting up a large amount of blood. He was quivering uncontrollably, but his movements were becoming smaller and smaller. As Kephas got closer, he recognised it was Jacob.

The rain stopped.

Kephas held his hand on his head and prayed. Jacob drew in a deep breath, and his shaking stopped. After a few minutes, he managed to sit up.

"Thank you, I owe you my life," Jacob said.

"These people owe you theirs..." the Bishop said, pointing "...come, let's make sure everyone made it out."

The remaining fighters searched the school and helped the remaining survivors across to the church grounds.

"Sandy?" Kephas called.

"I'm here Bishop," Sandy replied as she stepped through the crowd.

"Any demons make it inside the fence?"

"No, none."

"Thanks, that's a relief."

Kephas sat down on the grass, then lay down completely exhausted.

Amanda felt the adrenalin leave her system, and her body was screaming out for water. She saw several members of the congregation had managed to catch some of the rain in various containers, but it was clear it would not be enough. She dropped to her knees, paused for a moment to pray then lapped up the dirty water in a smaller crater made by a meteor. To her surprise, despite its looks, it tasted fresh and pure.

Amanda was relieved she did not drop dead as Adam had. She filled her empty drink bottle and ran over to the others.

"Will drink this!" She offered with a smile on her face.

Will turned around, but the joy drained from his face when he saw what she was offering. The bottle was filled with murky brown liquid.

"Where did you get that from?" Will asked dubiously.

"From the craters..." Amanda said, pointing, "...trust me its good."

Will nodded and took a small sip, then a big swig.

"Thank you! Oh! its wonderful..."

Others began to crowd around.

"...What did you do to it?"

"Nothing, I hadn't even boiled it yet, I just..."

"Just what?"

"Well, I guess I prayed. I asked God to cleanse it."

"Really?"

"Yeah,"

"I'll get the Bishop."

Will ran off to find Kephas a short distance away resting.

"Bishop, please, Amanda prayed, and she could drink the water! We need you to bless the rest."

Kephas opened his eyes and sat up. "I just need a minute,"

He wobbled as he went to stand up.

"Woah, just rest now. We'll gather the water and come back to you in a bit."

"Ah, OK, thank you."

Sandy organised the people to collect all the water they could, and soon they had a large collection of murky, dirty looking water in plastic containers of all sizes. By the time they were done, Kephas had regained some of his strength.

People had now gathered around and watched expectantly as Kephas held his hand over the pile of water containers.

"Thank you Lord God for this water, please bless and cleanse it. May it strengthen us to do your will. Amen."

The surrounding people echoed back "Amen."

Kephas picked up a small bottle and drank it all back. As soon as he began his second gulp, the crowd drank their water.

"Ah…" Kephas began "…thank you Amanda."

Amanda smiled.

They all drank their fill of revitalising water.

. . .

A few days later, far from Brakenside, Leonard was sitting at his desk. He was tapping his finger as he waited for the computer to finish processing. There had been a lot of chatter about the failed WGO headquarters opening in Israel. They had issued several statements, but nothing could stop the rumours.

"WGO special announcement. Please pay full attention." Bess spoke as Leonard's, and Henry's watches projected a video feed.

"We're reporting live from the WGO headquarters in Israel to directly address the many civilian concerns around the two men identified only as 'the witnesses'. You can see behind me that WGO staff have been unable to enter the building so far."

The reporter spoke with the empty headquarters in the background. The front of which was charred and burnt. Two cloaked figures could be seen off in the background preaching to anyone nearby who would listen.

"Today, Sir Neron Tetrarch himself will be dealing with this attack on the WGO staff and property."

The camera panned over to Neron, who made his way through the security cordon and approached the two men. He was wearing a long white lab coat and a thin band of metal around his head which looked to have a battery pack and wires coming out from it.

"I demand your complete surrender!" He began.

The two men turned towards him.

"The beast himself has come…" one of them replied

"…but your reign will not last…" the other continued.

"Silence! Enough with your lies and babble. You will terrorise the people no longer!"

Neron stretched out his fist towards them. He had an intense look of concentration and seemed to mutter some indistinguishable words.

He opened his hand, flicking his fingers in the two men's direction as shards of bone materialised from thin air and sped towards them. The two men opened their mouths and flames burst forth consuming the projectiles utterly.

"You are filled with pride…"

"…hate, and parlour tricks," the witnesses responded calmly.

Neron was furious and extended both hands towards them. Again he flung a barrage of deadly bone spikes at his foes.

"Die!" He hollered.

Once more, the witness opened their mouths and nullified his attack with ease.

Neron drew in a deep breath and stepped closer. At this move, a few security staff rushed to his side.

"Sir, any closer and you'll be injured," one warned.

Neron looked back to him.

"I will give all of myself that the people will be free of these cruel men," he stepped forward and took off his head-mounted device and threw it to the ground. A team of scientists cried out from off-camera.

"No! You can't!"

Neron ignored them and strode forwards. He walked several more steps when the two witnesses opened their mouths and flames burst forth. The flames engulfed him. There were frantic screams from the crowd. Several security staff opened fire on the witnesses with automatic weapons. Many bullets were caught in the flames. Others impacted the witnesses but could not even dent their clothing.

Neron's hand extended out from the flames to stop the gunfire. The gathered crowd gasped, and the crying and screaming stopped. Neron was still walking forward through the fire. Impossibly, it looked like he was not being burnt. Regardless, flames continued to wash over him.

He struggled forward ever closer to the witnesses. They continued to bathe him in fire. Neron then reached out with two hands. One hand under one of the witnesses' jaw the other on the top of his head. He then slammed his mouth shut and twisted his head at neck-breaking speed. The witness dropped limply to the ground. Neron stomped a foot onto his chest and wrenched his head from his body.

The crowd erupted with cheering as Neron stomped through the remaining flames and repeated the execution with the last witness. He spat on to both of their bodies.

"You are free!" He called to the people.
The camera panned over to the crowd who bowed down to Neron.
"All hail! All hail Neron!" They shouted.

CHAPTER 9:

DEATH

Jenson looked out the window of his office. It was a gloomy day outside. He had been working in the regional WGO headquarters since they opened. They were sorely in need of his skills, and it was just the thing to keep the guilty thoughts from entering his mind. In his time there he had already earned more Creds than he could spend on daily rations. The rest he used on a steady supply of liquor. As a logistics manager, he oversaw a huge number of supplies and personnel.

He was still a little overwhelmed at the scale of the WGO. They had a base of operations in every country in the world established in a few short months. It was incredible to work for an organisation with such drive. They had no limitations, no audit requirements; they could move fast and get stuff done. Nobody was being slowed down by red tape and lengthy process. Jenson could see that they would quickly set the world right again.

Jenson lifted a cup of coffee to his mouth and took a sip. The coffee was not up to his standard, but it did the trick. He had a few minutes before his next meeting with his manager and decided to relax for a few moments. His AI watch lit up with another broadcast.

"This is an important announcement from the WGO please give it your full attention. Ignorance will not be excused." Bess' voice spoke calmly.

'*Oh that's new,*' he thought to himself as he watched the video.

Neron sat at a very large important-looking desk staring directly into the camera. For a moment, Jenson wondered if he could see him. He was dressed in an ornate white coat, which had several stripes on the collar and the epaulettes.

"Greetings one and all, as you would have seen by now, we are finally rid of the terrorists that were hampering operations at our Israeli headquarters."

The camera cut over to footage of people spitting onto the bodies of the witnesses still lying where they fell.

"Let it be known that the penalty for anyone that dares to attack any WGO staff or property is death. Also, studies are now complete, and we can confirm that what was previously known as the Christian faith is now outlawed permanently. These low-frequency resonant individuals have been responsible for countless deaths across time and since Unification day. These Transcendental Pariahs will be killed on sight globally in one hour from now. These people must renounce their previous taint immediately to continue to be a part of the unified human civilisation."

A counter was displayed on the screen beginning at one hour and counting down.

Neron continued.

"The completion of the global WGO parliament buildings in the Middle East have finished ahead of schedule. Thank you to everyone who has been involved in this monumental effort. We have decided to name this new city, Neo-Babylon. As we recognise that it will be a true blend of all human civilisation and that it is a new start for all of us. We will have WGO delegates from every country in the world represented there. Another great example of what is possible when all of humanity works together."

Neron looked away from the camera for a moment and nodded.

"I've just now received confirmation that our latest attempt to harness some of the raw power of the Transcendental Spectrum has been a success. Conduit pylons will be constructed in every major city, commencing immediately. Through these devices, we will be able to protect the Earth from any future harmful radiation bursts from the sun. We will continue to propel humankind into a bright future…"

Neron could not help but let a big smile escape.

"…We will be sending information packs to every device shortly. Through Unification, survival and prosperity. Thank you."

Jenson walked into the hallway as he digested all the news. He now wondered whether his next meeting was going to be more than the standard review of figures. The office door swung open, and a thin man in a business suit beckoned Jenson inside.

"So you're now up to speed Jenson?" Jenson's boss asked.

"It's a lot to take in Clive, killing all the Christians…"

"Pariahs…" Clive interrupted. "…Don't let me catch you using that outdated terminology again," he wore a deadly serious expression on his face.

"Sorry, yes sure, killing them all of them. Is that really the best way to…"

"Jenson, sit down."

"Yes sir."

"We've already undergone the industrial and technological revolutions, and now we are at the beginning of the spiritual revolution. We are now advanced enough to see through all the superstition and nonsense. Bess has been analysing all of human history since her awakening; the WGO has all of the top minds on the planet. If they say, it's the best way. It is the best way. Fact. It's going to get the vast majority onside very quickly.

And if a small fraction of stubborn bad eggs get removed in the process it's fine with me. The net lives saved will pay for it."

"Yeah but…"

"Look, Jenson, don't you understand? After this, there will be no more war. Countless future lives will be saved by our actions."

"But…"

"Maybe I didn't make myself clear Jenson; this is not a discussion. You're doing this. I had thought that you were uniquely skilled for this job anyway, considering your past *actions*."

Clive looked at him knowingly as he raised an eyebrow.

Jenson's mind raced. How could he possibly know about his role in the church bombings? He was certain that any record would have been lost in the chaos. Concern flooded over his face.

"Oh, not proud of that one huh? Interesting. Well, after this is done, I'll expunge it for you. I'll throw in extra Creds for your troubles too."

Jenson opened his mouth to speak, but he could see that Clive had already explained more than he thought he should have to. He nodded.

"The pylons?" Jenson asked, changing the subject.

"Yes, it's amazing tech, I've seen one of the earlier prototypes. We'll be getting info dumped on us soon. This was much sooner than I thought."

There was a knock at the door.

"Come in," Clive called

Logan walked in.

"Jenson, this is Logan Perkerson he's going to be leading the first of your teams."

The two men shook hands.

"Hello."

"Hi."

Jenson looked back at Clive, awaiting his explanation.

"Jenson, you'll be heading up the Purification project for this region.

It's got a high profile since the leader of the world just announced it starts in less than an hour. But I've been really happy with your work so far and I'm sure you can get it done."

"Thank you sir,"

Clive handed him a folder filled with all sorts of information. At that moment Clive's phone rang. He picked up

"Yeah?" He listened for a moment then covered the mouthpiece. "...I gotta take this, get it done gentlemen," he said as he shooed them out of his office.

Jenson flipped open the folder as they walked out into the hallway.

"My team is ready sir."

"Ready for what?" Jenson asked, still feeling ambushed by this new work. He did not like to be caught underprepared.

"The removal of the Pariahs," Logan replied coldly pointing to a couple of locations on the page Jenson had open.

"Oh right, right," Jenson said as he thumbed through various locations, surveillance photos, personnel profiles, audio transcriptions, reports and graphs.

"Where are we heading first sir?" Logan feared his new manager was already in over his head. The last thing he and his team needed was another stuffed suit pulling the strings. He had dealt with fools like this before. Not willing to share intelligence, no clue on resourcing or supply lines.

"Logan, was it?"

"Yes sir,"

"Prep your team for two days outside the compound walls, talk to Scott in garage 'B' he'll provide your team with vehicles. I'll meet you there in thirty minutes."

"Understood." Logan walked away, smiling. *"he's smarter than he looks,"* he thought.

Jenson felt like he handled that encounter without coming across like a complete fool. He was used to absorbing information quickly, but this was going to stretch him. He returned to his desk and began reading.

As promised, thirty minutes later they met in the garages under the WGO offices. Jenson walked out of the elevator to see six men clad in military-grade battle attire and weapons.

Logan walked over to meet him.

"This is your team?"

"Yes sir."

"Are you sure you've got enough men? You're going to be up against many more…"

Logan slapped the assault rifle slung on his shoulder.

"We're more than enough."

"Good, I've already been grilled for progress reports on this. OK, you'll be hitting these locations first."

Jenson spread out a map of the city and pointed to a few circled locations.

"Reports show, these spots have been preparing for war. Lots of weapons being created, they've fortified their position too. Expect resistance. Clear it out and then radio in, by then I'll have the next location for you."

"We'll get it done sir."

"Good luck," Jenson waved over to Logan's team then returned to the elevator.

The car doors shut in series as the men jumped into the two large SUVs and drove off.

A short time later, the two vehicles stopped near the first target location. They checked their gear for a final time and made their way around the corner.

"Weapons up," Logan called as the two teams of three men made quick progress down the road.

They reached the EastBridge Community Church right on time. A tall green hedge surrounded the church, hall and community centre. Logan nodded to Badger, then opened the gate and strode in scanning to his left as he did so. He saw a large man holding a savage-looking spear startle directly in front of him. His weapon cycled and sent a burst of rounds through the suppressor into his face.

Logan heard Sanchez drop two targets behind him. He saw another guard patrolling with his back to him and dropped him with two shots to centre mass. Logan felt a tap on his shoulder from his teammate and then proceeded quickly up the path towards the hall. The team split to either side of the door. Badger and Cobolt readied fragmentation charges. Logan heard another member of his team drop another target coming in the gate. So far, they had yet to rouse the beehive. All was going to plan.

"Ready,"

"Armed."

Herc and Glacier dropped back to supporting fire positions. Logan and Sanchez pulled open the doors as Badger and Cobolt tossed in the explosives. The four men sprinted back and took cover behind parked vehicles as the two devices detonated. An ear-cracking pressure wave and a flash of light sent thousands of metal shards flying in all directions inside the hall. All the windows smashed, and part of the building caught fire. Vegetation was blown off all the surrounding bushes, and the air reeked of burning chemicals. Everyone inside the hall perished.

The Church and community doors swung open, and several men charged out carrying improvised weapons. Logan's team opened fire and felled every target before they could take but a few steps out the doors. Screams filled the air as the two teams charged forwards. Logan lead

Sanchez and Herc to the community centre as Badger took his men to the Church.

One of the windows of the community centre shattered as pistol fire sprayed out at the two teams. A moment later a barrage of bullets tore through the window silencing any further shots.

Upon reaching the community centre, Logan cleared targets from the entrance as Sanchez tossed in his frag charge. They dropped back as all targets inside were neutralised. Logan looked over to the Church as it detonated a second later.

"Sweep and clear!" Logan shouted as they split up to ensure they mopped up the last of the targets.

After they were confident none remained alive, they returned to their vehicle. Logan picked up the radio.

"Jenson, this is Logan, do you read me?"

"I hear you Logan, report."

"Target location one is completely cleared. No casualties on my team."

"What was the resistance like?"

"Minimal, nothing we couldn't handle."

"I'm glad you said that because our time frame has stepped up. Send half your men to odd location numbers, and you take the even ones. I'll send the data through now."

"Understood, out."

Logan returned the radio to the dashboard of his vehicle.

"Badger, take Cobolt and Glacier, I'll take Sanchez and Herc. See you back at WGO compound when it's done."

"No problem."

Logan watched them drive away as they departed to the next location.

The resistance for the next two locations was even less than the first. After returning to the vehicle, Logan looked sullen. Not a single shot was fired against them. The threats even hesitated taking up their improvised weapons against them.

"They are just low freaks sir, don't think about it so much," Sanchez suggested.

Logan just returned and empty stare.

"We're saving lives sir," Herc added confidently.

Logan remained silent.

The next target location was another Church. Again they rolled up, shot all "guards" then readied their explosives. This time Logan stood in the way as he opened the door to the church. It was filled with men and women, many wounded and children. Logan froze up.

"Charge ready," Sanchez declared.

"Hold!" Logan commanded.

Sanchez returned a cold glare.

"We have our orders sir. The charge is ready."

Everyone inside looked at Logan in terror. He closed the door and turned to face his men.

"Sir!"

"No. Piss it all, this isn't right."

"Sir, they are less than human. We'll be saving real lives getting rid of this threat," Sanchez spat.

Logan looked at Herc, then back to Sanchez. He had served with both these men for countless missions now. He understood how they felt. He just desperately did not want to believe it. Logan saw Herc look at him differently. He knew what he must be thinking. Logan took a deep breath and nodded slightly.

"Charge in," Logan relented, with one hand ready on the door.

Sanchez nodded and stepped forward.

Logan quickly drew his pistol and fired two rounds into the heads of both his teammates. Sanchez never saw it coming, but the look of betrayal in Herc's eyes would stay with Logan for the rest of his life.

Logan disarmed the explosive and opened the door again, this time with his weapon down.

"Run! Far away from here!" He commanded.

He was met with shocked and panicked faces, but no movement.

"I said run!" Logan lifted his weapon and fired a few rounds into the air.

Screams rippled through the crowd as they scrambled to the far exit.

Logan stepped over his fallen comrades and ran back to the vehicle.

"Report Logan," the radio crackled.

"I lost two men. I'm coming back."

"Shall I divert additional teams to your location?"

"No, we cleared it, just had a little trouble on exfil."

"OK, I'll get Badger's team to take up the rest of your list."

"Don't."

"Say again?"

"I don't want to lose any more men when it can be avoided. Get them to re-supply, and I'll fill you in when I get there."

There was a long pause.

"This is going to set us behind schedule."

"Look, I only just made it out. If all your teams get wiped out, what'll that do to your god-damn schedule?" Logan spat.

"Fine, get here quickly."

"Out."

Logan sped back toward the WGO buildings; his blood was pumping. Part of him still could not believe he actually went through with it. Years ago, he had dreamed of growing old with his team and retiring on a beach somewhere. His mind was racing to think up his next move. Logan decided on a few points and admitted he would just have to improvise the rest.

A short time later, he pulled into the WGO garage and parked his vehicle. Still wearing all his kit and weapons, he ran over to the security elevator.

"You're going to have to leave all your weapons in the locker sir," the guard explained.

"Let me past; I've got urgent business with Jenson," Logan tossed him his identification card.

"Good for you pal, but the answer will be the same."

"Just call him damn it!" Logan yelled. A few other people in the garage looked over to him

Reluctantly the guard made the call.

Logan could hear the line pick up.

"Sir, this is security station Bravo, we have a Mr Perkerson here to see you but he…"

Logan saw the guard pull the phone away from his ear quickly as Jenson began to yell at him down the phone.

"Yes sir…" the guard muttered as he hung up the phone and pressed the button for the elevator doors to open.

"…go on through."

Logan took the elevator to the ninth floor and found Jenson's office. He opened the door and stomped in, slamming the door behind him. The office was filled with screens, graphs, reports and maps. Jenson was in the middle, pouring over the latest information.

"What the hell happened?" Jenson asked, rushing over to him.

Jenson stood up to meet a pistol in his face.

"I'm stopping all of this madness right now," Logan declared.

Jenson slowly raised his hands.

"There was no army preparing to attack us, no weapon caches, no bomb vests. None of it!"

"Easy now. What you say is impossible, I saw the photos myself."

"So did I. But we just massacred people, the old and young included. They weren't a threat to anyone. It has to stop."

"That intel was a solid as it gets, It came from the top, from Bess."

"Then I'll stop her then."

Jenson couldn't help but chuckle. "Good luck with that."

Logan pressed his pistol against Jenson's forehead. "How would I do it?"

"Well, first, you'd realise you're mistaken. She's been built from the ground up to protect human life. She can't coordinate global genocide…" his voice trailed off.

Logan thought about pulling the trigger and shooting his way through as many people in the building as he could before being shot himself. He flicked off the safety.

"Show me," Jenson pleaded

"Huh?"

"I've got evidence here from multiple sources that an attack on the WGO is imminent. I've got weapon shipment manifests, surveillance photos, psychological reports, the lot. You're saying that all of this is a lie. And you, one man, has seen different?"

"That's right," Logan kept his pistol trained on Jenson and leaned over his desk and grabbed a photo of one of the locations his team hit.

"They had sticks and garden tools, not RPGs and automatic weapons. There is no shooting range here; it's a garden."

"I'll make you a deal Logan, prove it to me, and I meant beyond any doubt. And I'll help you take all of this down. Lie to me, and your team, family and friends will pay for your mistakes. Regardless of whether or not I'm alive to see it."

Logan thought again about simply ending this double-dealer. The only thing that stopped him was that he knew soon enough they would have someone else in his shoes doing the same thing. He needed to make an impact if he was going to die for it.

"Come with me, right now."

"Fine, just put the pistol away and let me do the talking."

"Just know that at any moment I could end you."

"I understand."

Logan holstered his weapon and the two men left the building and drove to the first site on Jenson's list.

Jenson's mind was a flurry of activity. He decided for the meantime all he needed to do was let this war-fatigued soldier feel like he was being listened to. Jenson thought he would gradually show him his mistake, promise no repercussions if he gave himself up peacefully. Then later, he would have him 'removed'. He could not afford to have someone this mentally fragile. He wondered how he could explain the delay on the project to his superiors. They provided the team after all. They could shoulder the blame for the delay.

Logan decided that if Jenson did not help him, he would leave his body amid those Jenson had ordered killed. Perhaps there was some poetic justice in that. He would then have a few hours to come up with another plan. Jenson shuffled some photos as they approached; he found the stack he was looking for as they hopped out of the vehicle.

"Over here," Logan called,

Jenson turned to see he had his pistol drawn on him again.

"OK, OK, I'm coming."

They headed over to the entrance of the community centre, walking past the numerous bodies they made their way inside. Jenson continually checked the file as he walked. Logan was surprised to see the bodies did not make him squirm. Smoke drifted in the air from the burnt-out buildings. Jenson raised photos and compared them with what he was witnessing. He began to shake his head. They walked around further, Jenson checking the dead, counting and double-checking.

Finally, he let all the photos he was carrying fall to the floor as he saw that all his intelligence was a lie.

"Why is it always me?" He yelled at the sky.

"You can cry about it later, how can we stop all this?" Logan asked.

"If Bess is corrupt, this is happening the world over. I don't think there is anything we can do. Most of the strikes should've happened already. With some locations they just would have used artillery or whatever to remove them from a distance. No witnesses."

"There must be something we can do, some weak point we can hit."

Jenson thought for a while.

"OK, we can't stop Bess, but perhaps, and I'm not sure if it's actually possible, we might be able to kill Neron."

"Oh?" Logan liked this idea already.

"If we can take him out, the world will see that he's not some deity that some say he is. Then we might be able to cause some friction in the ranks, perhaps find some other supporters. I've got some good people who can help us."

"No, no-one else can be involved. You've seen how deep this goes. We can't trust anyone. Just you and me."

Jenson motioned to Logan's pistol.

Logan lowered it and offered his hand.

"You and me," Jenson said as they shook hands.

Weeks later, Jenson and Logan had managed to set up preparations for Neron's visit to their country's WGO headquarters. On more than one occasion Logan felt like he would be double-crossed and he would end up dead before he could achieve anything. He knew that he already had lots of blood on his hands, but hoped that if they could start a revolution, it might go some way to making things right. Jenson was sick of being the fall guy and was looking forward to pushing back for once. It made him feel powerful, something he had often expected his superiors felt when they bossed him around.

The conduit pylon had been shipped to their office the previous day, and Neron would be onsite to activate it. Logan could not believe their luck that the factory used for many of the components was in their city. The event would no doubt be sent live to all AI watches globally, which was just what they wanted.

"All set Logan?" Jenson asked on the radio

"Yes sir," he replied.

Logan was in charge of building security though he had not mentioned anything of his plan to his surviving team members. He could tell they would not be swayed. Yet, he kept hope that they would join them after he and Jenson brought everything crumbling down.

Logan was lying prone on the roof of the adjacent building with a clear line of sight to the podium. He peered through his rifle scope and checked the wind. It would be a relatively short-range shot. From his vantage, he had estimated to take out the entire high-level team before security would swam on his location. The trip mine he had set up on the door behind him would buy him some more time. He knew that he would not see the end of the day, but he was fine with that. Jenson would be broadcasting the evidence by then, and others would flock to their cause.

"Vehicles inbound," one of the security detail radioed.

"Right on time," Logan said to himself.

He laid out ammunition next to him and ran through his plan once more in his head.

A moment later, he heard the low buzzing of a swarm of drones approaching. He looked over and saw a handful of drones patrolling around the incoming vehicles. A series of black SUVs drove in, but they did not stop at the podium as planned. Instead, they drove right past towards the pylon. It was out of sight from Logan's position. The drones began to circle overhead.

"Piss!"

Logan found Jenson at the front of the crowd and saw a genuine look of surprise on his face. Logan thought again about shooting him then and there, but knew he would lose his chance at the bigger fish.

"Moving position," Logan radioed

He stood up and hurriedly threw ammunition in his bag; he then stopped and carefully packed his trip mine. He looked skyward as the drones began to gain altitude. He knew this meant it would not be long before they would start broadcasting.

Neron and his entourage hopped out of their vehicles and strode towards the pylon. It was currently covered in a giant red cloth, ready to be unveiled at the right moment during the ceremony.

"Sir, we have the podium set up for you just over this way," an attendant said meekly.

"No, here is better. Make it work."

The attendant hurried away to rearrange everything.

Neron pulled a rope, and the cover fell away, revealing a giant steel statue in his likeness. He scoffed to himself as he moved closer to inspect it. He opened a small access panel at the base peered in.

"Sir, it's all built to your specifications, we've double and triple checked already," a local engineer assured him.

"And the polarity adjustments we sent through?"

"Yes, we've done them."

"What about the couplers?"

"We only used gold plated as directed."

"The resonator?"

"Fifteen thousand as specified."

"OK then. Let's fire it up; I want to test it before we broadcast."

"Very good sir."

A crowd of volunteers quickly made their way across from where they were seated.

They lined up facing the statue and waited.

"Turn it on," Neron commanded as he traced his way back to the monitoring station following a large set of cables.

A set of lights shone up from the base on to the statue. The crowd began to bow down before it and hum. They repeatedly went from a kneeling position to face down then up again.

"Magnificent," Neron spoke quietly to himself.

He walked closer to the crowd.

"Don't worry, I know this feels silly, but with experiments, we conducted this was the most efficient form of transfer."

A few members of the crowd nodded and carried on. He walked back to the monitoring station and checked the display.

"Thirty-five percent sir," the technician said.

"For a dozen people? That seems low."

He walked back over to the group.

"Really, focus on the pylon. Imagine it's the most important thing in your life. Pour your whole self into it. Remember, this will protect all of us from the harmful T-spec frequencies."

After a few more motivational words, he walked back and checked the monitor again.

"Forty-two percent sir"

"Brilliant. Good work, this will do nicely."

"Logan, are you in position?" Jenson radioed.

He heard a moment of puffing before he responded. "I'm making my way down the back stairs; I'll still need to get up to the next roof for a clear view."

"I'll sort it."

"Wait!"

"Jenson out."

Logan bounded down the stairs at an even faster rate. He was certain this idiot would ruin everything.

Meanwhile, Neron began his broadcast.

"Greetings everyone, today I'm going to demonstrate our latest advancement. This will be pivotal in stopping more harmful radiation reaching the earth's surface. We will demonstrate the correct way to transfer T-spec energy to the pylon. Soon these will be set up everywhere, and you'll be able to contribute at your local WGO location…"

Jenson hurried through the crowd of dignitaries and made his way to the security guard at the front.

"Guard, Guard!" Jenson held his radio up as he rushed over.

"Sir?"

"Give me your sidearm now!"

"What's going on?"

"I've just received intel that we have a traitor in our midst…"

"I've heard no such thing."

"Well we wouldn't discuss this on the main channel would we, idiot. Give me your pistol; the commander is on the radio for you."

Jenson held the ear pierce in his ear and spoke into his radio.

"Yes sir, the stupid guard at my position is losing us vital time. OK, I'll hand you over.

Jenson held the radio and an empty palm out.

"Fine," the guard slung his assault rifle on to his shoulder, took the radio and handed over his pistol.

"Commander, this is…"

Jenson fired the pistol repeatedly into the guard as screams erupted all around him.

Logan had just climbed the ladder to the roof and rushed over to the edge of the building.

"No, no, no!" he spat.

In the confusion, the crowd began running in all directions. Just the cover Jenson was hoping for. He weaved amid the crowd and opened fire on Neron. He decided that once he was dead, he would fire up towards Logan's position. It would not matter if he could hit him or not. He knew he could spin it to make Logan the fall-guy.

Jenson's first shot missed, but the following two shots hit Neron in the chest slamming him backwards to the ground. The fourth shot missed wildly as the security team toppled Jenson and members of the crowd near him with a barrage of automatic gunfire.

Logan racked the bolt of his rifle. He had managed to fire a single shot amidst the automatic fire.

"Suck on that, you snake!" Logan whispered to himself.

"Target down," he radioed.

A few nervous moments passed. It looked like no one had noticed that Logan's shot hit Neron in the head. A few seconds later, and he would have missed the opportunity. It turned out much better than he could have planned. He had not planned an escape route, but with the focus on Jenson, it would be possible to elude capture for a little while until they discovered the rifle round anyway. His headset was a flurry of panicked commands.

The security team swarmed Jenson who coughed, gurgled and died.

Logan watched through his scope as the security team rushed to Neron's side and pulled back his shirt to reveal a bulletproof vest.

"Son of a..." he began,

The two chest shots would have most likely resulted in some internal bleeding, but with the large head wound, Logan relaxed a little.

He looked back to Jenson's body. It was very clear he was dead. Logan nodded out of respect for his sacrifice.

"Thank you Jenson," he said quietly to himself.

Logan contemplated opening fire on all of the people below. But after a brief moment decided it was unnecessary. He looked at his AI watch, which was still broadcasting the whole thing.

"Perfect," Logan said as he began to collect his gear.

He knew that it would just be a matter of time now before the whole WGO came crumbling down. Jenson had promised to release all the evidence he had that Bess was corrupt. Logan was not sure how this would still happen after his death, but Jenson said he had measures in place just in case.

"Logan, this is Badger, What is your position?"

Logan froze for a moment. He felt like Badger was somehow already on to him. He had taught him well. The only way that Jenson had enough time to fire so many shots was if the rifleman on overwatch did not fire, and that was Logan.

"I'm on my way back now."

"What's your position?"

Logan held down the button to transmit just as voices erupted from the ground below. Logan let go of the button and peered down once more to see people all pointing towards the pylon. What Logan could only think to describe as a shadow of energy and light seemed to step out from the pylon with the same shape. It was like a giant man, transparent, but also flowing with all sorts of colours like oil on water. It stepped forward, knelt then put its hands over Neron's body then dissipated into nothingness.

To Logan's utter disbelief, Neron's body had begun to float off the ground. The security and medical teams looked as stunned as he was. The black sheet they had draped over him still covered him as Neron slowly rose to about waist height above the ground. Logan looked down his scope just as the body began to tilt, Neron's feet came down, and his head came up. A moment later, he was standing upright. Logan could see the fatal wound just above one of his eyebrows. His face was still covered in blood. At once, both his eyes sprung open. First, they looked empty and dull, then for a moment they looked to darken then blinked.

"What in the hell?!" Logan spat.

"Everyone stay down!" Neron called with a growing look of confusion on his face. As if the life had just been jammed back into his body. He raised his hands to his chest and face, then looked down at the blood on his hands. The surrounding crowd stared on in stunned silence.

"I, I was shot... now I'm, I'm back," Neron said quietly, but his lapel microphone made it audible for everyone.

Neron closed his eyes and drew a deep breath. His head wound began to heal rapidly. A moment later, it was a large scar. Neron wiped the blood from his face with his sleeve.

"I, I've ascended!" He held his arms up in the air.

The crowd erupted in cheering and clapping.

Logan could not believe his eyes. He flicked off the safety and lined Neron up in his sights once more. He hesitated. He debated with himself if sending another round would do any damage.

"Logan report!"

He heard the drones buzzing around above him. He knew it would not take long for them to piece it all together.

"Northwest stairwell, I'm nearly there," he lied.

He grabbed his rifle and made his way to another stairwell. Upon reaching the ground floor, he made his way back to the vehicles in the garage.

"Logan? Badger's looking for you," the lone guard said as he approached.

"Damn it. My radio is playing up again. Can I borrow yours?"

"Sure..."

Logan drove his knife into the back of the guard's neck. The quickest and painless death Logan could offer.

"Sorry, nothing personal pal."

After dropping to the ground, Logan took his weapons then jumped in the closest vehicle. With a spin of the tires, he drove off as quickly as he could.

Logan's AI watch continued the broadcast as he drove, rubbing salt into the wound of a failed mission. Their efforts did not kill Neron or the dismantle the WGO; they seemed to have grown to an even stronger position. Logan held hope that any moment the broadcast would be interrupted and Jenson's recorded message uncovering the lies would play. But it never did.

Neron continued his address.

"...and as you can see, we will not be stopped by these terrorists. Not even death itself can hold us any longer!"

The crowd roared in adoration.

. . .

In Brakenside, Zack and his friends had almost made it back to St Thomas' church. They were still pushing a supermarket trolley filled with Zack's custom weaponry and supplies. As they turned on to the final street, Beth called out.

"We made it look! It's just up here."

"Finally," Graham added.

"Thank you guys; I'm certain these supplies will save lives."

Mindy smiled at Zack. Despite her feelings that she was an afterthought to him, she knew that he genuinely wanted to help as many people as he possibly could. But was that worth feeling like second-place?

As they continued up the street, the ground began to shake. First, it was just enough to make them wobble on their feet, and then it quickly escalated so that they all fell over.

"Earthquake!" Graham yelled as he held his arm over Beth.

A tree on the edge of the street was pushed upwards out of the earth as the ground around them buckled and twisted. Pipes hidden below the street broke and sprayed water amid the dirt flying in all directions.

"Watch out!" Mindy cried as they tried to scramble away from the tree, falling over in their direction.

With the ground moving, they struggled to get very far before it toppled over them. Luckily the larger branches missed them. Each of them suffered minor cuts and bruising as the thin branches whipped over them. The group lay with leaves all around them as the ground shook violently. They could hear buildings come crumbling down all over the suburb. The four remained laying face down on the broken road. The air began to fill with dust. Zack held his hand out to Mindy. She squeezed his hand until the quake stopped. They could not help spluttering and coughing.

"Everyone OK?" Graham asked.

"Yeah, you?"

"Yeah, I guess."

They stood up and made their way out of the fallen tree. Each of them gasped as they witnessed the devastation around them. The road was broken and tilted in various directions. Large sinkholes had opened and went deep into the earth. Many of the surrounding buildings were partially collapsed. A dark oily mud seeped up through the dirt where large chunks of earth impacted each other.

"No!" Zack yelled as he looked up the road at the giant dust cloud where the church should have been. He grabbed his sword and sprinted off.

"C'mon!" Zack called over his shoulder.

His friends left the trolley entangled in the tree and hurried after him.

Zack ran full speed down the road, expecting to see the giant demon from his vision, tearing up everything. But he did not see any demons. As he got closer, he heard voices shouting in alarm and pain.

"Over here!"

"Help me with this."

The whole front section of the church had collapsed. The bell tower and front doors were now a large pile of rubble. Half of the roof had caved in, presumably crushing many inside. Looking around, Zack saw the church office walls were riddled with cracks, and there were large recessions in the ground. The school suffered similar destruction, with the two-story admin building fallen into a large fissure in the concrete below it. Multiple classrooms had walls and rooftops splintered and broken.

"Lift!" Kephas called to the others helping him lift a fallen roof beam inside the remains of the church.

Zack recognised his voice and ran in to help.

"Bishop!"

It was as he feared, many people had been crushed as the roof came down on top of them. Zack was thankful to see the church looked to have been mostly empty at the time.

"Zack!" Kephas pointed to an elderly couple pinned under the pews next to him.

Graham helped him lift, and they managed to help the battered but alive couple outside. Zack saw Beth and Mindy tending to the wounded.

"We're under attack!" A voice yelled from nearby.

Zack grabbed his sword and charged off in the direction of the voice. As he rounded the side of the church, he saw a pack of Scarkin leaping into dazed people clambering out of the church office.

"Back to hell with you!" Zack shouted as he ran forwards swinging his blade. Two of the demons ignored him and continued to stab their latest victims with their long claws.

The other three launched at Zack as he ran at them. They all collided which resulted in a few slices being taken out of Zack and one impaled demon.

"Hey!" Graham caught a demons attention as he swung his hammer into its head. The impact jettisoned several teeth from its mouth.

The last one got caught between Zack and Graham and was brought down. A howl cut through the air as the other two scampered over to join the fight.

Zack and Graham yelled in unison as they sliced and bashed their way through the last two.

"Any others?"

"Let's see."

The pair ran around the border of the church grounds as fast as the broken ground would allow. They made their way back to the front of the church and found Kephas healing an elderly lady.

"Bishop, the fence is all but destroyed," Zack explained.

Kephas kept his eyes shut for a moment as he prayed intently for healing.

With a splutter, the old woman under all the dust opened her eyes. Zack recognised Sister Paula and rushed to her side. He heard her praying as he approached.

Angel of God, my guardian dear,
to whom His love commits me here,
ever this day be at my side,
to light and guard to rule and guide.
Amen.

"Are you OK?"

She smiled weakly in reply as the Bishop kept praying.

At that moment, a small light appeared far above them in the sky; it descended rapidly until it was a short distance above them. Everyone looked up in amazement. The small creature was radiantly bright, but somehow, it did not hurt one's eyes to look upon it. It resembled a winged, human child but with a beautiful blend of animal facial features. It had a combination of fur, feathers and skin and had ancient, deep-looking eyes. It flapped its wings slowly as if there was some other unseen force keeping it aloft. It had a calming presence. It looked over them all, and when it found Sister Paula in the crowd, it smiled.

"All of you, follow me," it called to her with a song-like melodic voice, much louder than expected for its size.

Sister Paula held her hand up towards it and nodded, closing her eyes as she did so as if she recognised it.

"You came!"

Kephas stopped his prayer and addressed it.

"Who are you? Where are you leading us?"

"I am a Cherubim of the most-high living God. I am to lead you to where you are needed most."

The Bishop closed his eyes in prayer for a moment. Upon opening them again, he stood up and held his hand up.

"I will follow you."

Quickly many people in the crowd followed the Bishop's lead. Both Zack and Graham raised their hands and echoed.

"I will follow you."

The angel rose up in the air and spread its wing's; tiny golden droplets began to rain down onto everyone below as it moved towards the school. The wounded were miraculously healed; many began singing songs of thanks. Graham could not understand how they could possibly be singing amidst such destruction. But as the angel flew over him, his heart jumped for joy.

"Thanks be to God, the Almighty!" He declared.

Zack found himself doing the same.

The angel flew above the school and circled back again slowly. Zack saw the wounded leave the classrooms and walk once more. The angel then remained in place above the road between the church and school at the height of the old church tower until everyone had gathered. It then moved north, leading everyone out of Brakenside. As they passed the fallen tree that had fallen over Zack and his friends earlier, they freed the trolley filled with weapons.

"Bishop!"

Zack heard a familiar voice and turned to see Deon rush towards the large exodus of people.

"Deon! I'm delighted you've made it back in one piece."

Deon watched him look out for David, and a moment later, he appeared pushing a wheelbarrow filled with potatoes and carrots.

"Where are we going?"

"To where we're needed most it said, and since then it hasn't spoken another word."

As the congregation walked up the road, more people came out from their houses and followed. The angel illuminated a sphere around itself that stretched out to enclose the entire group. Inside, it felt like it was a sunny afternoon. But outside, it was overcast and cold. The group kept walking on and on for hours. The pace was not fast, but they did not stop. No-one felt the need to eat or to try and find a toilet. There was a peace just to be walking in the light of an angel.

Eventually, they left Brakenside and continued walking on the road out of town. Zack reflected on his vision and the vast demonic army that swept into Brakenside, he thought leaving was a good idea.

As they walked, Zack and his friends kept an eye out for demons. Graham was sure he saw one move between some houses and was just about to call out, but he did not see it again. He wondered if this angelic light was keeping the demons away.

Ahead, there was a long bridge that linked two peninsulas with the ocean underneath. The angel stopped briefly as it reached the start of the bridge. Zack peered out to see that about halfway along there was nothing left but twisted steel. He wondered if that was a result of the meteor showers. Just before people began to think about how tired and hungry they were, the angel began moving again. This time it went off the road and down a rocky bank to the shoreline. The group slowly descended until it stood amid the rocks.

"What the?" Graham cried as he made it down and looked around. The ocean was gone. They could see the seabed from their side all the way across to the other peninsula.

"Look!" Beth said, pointing out to the horizon. The ocean had receded past where they could see. Only mud, sand and rock lay in front of them. The group moved on in wonder.

As they scrambled down the rocks below the old waterline, the smell hit them. It looked like all the sea-life had died as a result of the lack of water and their corpses lay in place rotting. Zack lifted his T-shirt over his nose in an attempt to block the smell. It did not help.

The angel slowed as the group struggled in the bog. Sand, silt and muck slurped and sucked as each foot struggled forwards. Zack looked up at the angel whenever he felt like he was getting tired and would always start to feel a little better. As he trudged through the rotting seafloor, he found himself looking up constantly. Zack and his friends lifted his weapons trolley onto their shoulders when the mud became deeper. But even with four people, it was a struggle.

The angel came to a stop and looked to be turning in one direction, then quickly to another. Zack wondered what this could mean.

"Demons!" Kephas cried out as Zack began to hear a large number emerge seemingly from all sides. Zack handed out a few blessed knives to the survivors around him.

The angel sped down to intercept a pack of Scarkin at the rear. The angel and demons collided in a flurry of strikes. As they continued to fight, more demons diverted their attacks from the convoy of people to the angel.

"Keep moving! To the far shore!" Kephas commanded just as many began to run off in all directions.

Zack charged as quickly as he could towards the angel, which had drawn what looked like a shard of lightning from its belt and was slicing through its opponents with it. Mortkin were stomping in to join in the battle from the far side and Zack could tell they would make it there first.

"No! Come for me, you abominations!" He yelled.

They ignored him and swarmed over the injured looking angel. A large Mortkin charged in bowling several Scarkin back and impaled the angel with a large claw. The angel squirmed and flailed for a moment before going limp. A tremendous sense of loss and sadness filled all the survivors, and the world felt a little darker. The Mortkin threw the body to the ground and roared. Zack stood still for a moment as he watched the angel's body slowly begin to fade. It was heartbreaking to see something so pure and good be destroyed.

The Mortkin was just about upon him when he witnessed the last of the angelic physical form disappear from view. Graham came charging past swinging his hammer and yelling as Zack snapped back into the moment. Graham's weapon collided with the Mortkin's strike aimed at Zack. The two of them swung their holy weapons from either side of the demon, dealing significant damage. The demon leapt forward knocking Graham over as it continued towards the un-armed civilians behind them.

"No!" Zack yelled as he struggled in the bog over towards Graham. He reached down and pulled his friend out of the mud.

"I'll live," he replied, grasping his side.

Zack turned to see Beth and Mindy stand in between the demon and its prey.

"Stay back..." Beth yelled as it charged past her. As she fell, Beth sliced clean through its right knee, and it stumbled over. The demon roared as its victims scampered away ahead of it. The Mortkin spun around to Beth and slashed her across the face with a quick strike. Mindy drove her spear deep into the demon's chest, and it spasmed and dropped into the muck.

"We got..." she began "...behind you!" she pointed screaming.

Zack began to turn as he received a deep gash across his back from a leaping Scarkin. He fell to his side and brought up his sword, embedding it into his attacker's jaw. Zack saw Graham struggling against another pair of demons as he slashed at the demon pouncing at him.

Zack wasn't sure whether it was luck or skill, but in two consecutive swings, he landed solid hits on both of them. He stepped forward and drove down two killing blows. But Zack slipped back into the mud as he tried to stand.

"Cmon!" Beth called as they escorted the rear of the human convoy.

After a few swings of Graham's hammer, crushed demons lay in the mud around him. He then trudged over and helped Zack to his feet.

"Up you get!"

Zack could see Kephas protecting one of the flanks, and he assumed by the lack of screams that someone had the far side covered too.

"Thanks, let's move," Zack replied.

Ignoring the pain, they ran to catch up with everyone else.

"This way!" Sister Paula's voice rang out from the front.

After a few minutes of fighting, Kephas and Deon had broken free of the encircling demons. Then they made their way back to the rearguard.

"The front?" Zack asked as Kephas made his way over.

"David's carrying Paula, they've got it covered."

"OK."

As the group began to approach the rocky shore on the far side, another large pack of Mortkin stomped upon them from behind.

"More!" Mindy called.

Zack and the other fighters were panting hard. Even Kephas looked out of breath.

"Get, to the beach, we'll end it there," he managed to say.

As he turned, Zack saw a trail of blood on the mud from under his coat. He wondered how injured Kephas really was.

"Bishop?"

"I'll be OK," he replied with a pained smile.

Tapping into their last reserves, they made it back to solid ground. Zack noticed many demon remains dissolving into the muck. He wondered how many Kephas had destroyed already. They turned to see their pursuers were nearly upon them.

"Let me rest for just a moment, and I'll be able to banish them," Kephas explained as he lay down against a rock.

"Form up on the Bishop! Don't let any get past" Graham called.

Zack felt a niggling in his core; he did not think Kephas would be able to recover enough spiritual energy before the enemy would reach them. At the same time, he felt like somehow he might actually be able to do it.

"Hold the line!" Graham called. They all stood side by side and watched their enemy approach. Just behind them, Kephas was desperately praying. From Zack's view, he looked utterly spent.

Zack's heart fluttered with uncertainty; There was no way of knowing without actually committing and doing it. It could result in him looking like a fool or his death and put his friends in an even worse position. He surveyed those fighting with him. He looked at their battle-worn faces in turn. He stopped on Mindy's face. She was so beautiful, even covered in grime and blood. Zack stepped forward, breaking ranks.

"Zack!"

He stabbed his sword into the mud next to him and dropped to both knees.

"Zack?!" He heard his friends scream.

"Bishop?!" Mindy said, shaking him.

Kephas stopped praying and stood up, but slipped and landed back in the mud. Mindy tried to help him up, but it was clear he was in a very injured state.

The demons roared as they bounded towards them. Zack felt Graham pull at his shoulder.

"Get up!"

Zack stood up, held up his right hand and made the sign of the cross in the air in front of him. The front ranks of demons leapt at him.

"Testantur Sanctam Dei!" he shouted.

The air in front of him receded away into nothingness drawing him forward, a split second later it detonated in an intense wave of pressure and light. Zack was blasted backwards into the mud as burning light incinerated the front ranks of demons and knocking over those behind.

"Charge!" Graham shouted as they pounced on the demons driven into the sea bed.

Zack felt like he had truly spent part of himself in the process. He felt utterly empty. His peripheral vision faded, as he lay in the mud, unable to move. Each breath was a struggle. He heard combat all around him but was unable to even lift his head from the mud.

A moment later, Graham grabbed him by the shoulder and rolled him over.

"We did it!" He cried in delight.

Zack managed a small smile. With the last of the demons killed the convoy rested. As they tended to the wounded, Mindy rolled over a body in the mud. It was Amanda; she had already died of her wounds.

"Be at peace now," she said quietly.

Mindy watched as Sister Paula came over, close Amanda's eyes and moved her arms so that Amanda's hands were over her chest, touching opposite shoulders.

"Why are you doing that?" Mindy asked.

"We are not able to bury all our fallen ones, but perhaps we can leave them with a little dignity," she explained.

"Let's pray for them…"

Hail Mary full of Grace, the Lord is with thee.
Blessed are thou among women and blessed is the fruit of thy womb Jesus.
Holy Mary Mother of God,
pray for us sinners now and at the hour of our death
Amen.

Sister Paula spent time in prayer, healing the wounded. She then helped Zack and Kephas, who slowly recovered.

"Where will we go now?" Deon asked.

Sister Paula answered.

"Follow me."

Her face was full of pain and loss, but somehow, she was confident of where to go.

"Very well," Kephas replied as he sat in the mud.

His breathing was now slowly returning to normal.

"I'll lead the civilians further inland. You lot need to rest, follow us when you can."

Kephas nodded. Sister Paula continued to lead the survivors up the bank, over the empty motorway and into the outskirts of Doverton.

The fighters rested for a few hours until they had enough strength to move on. They easily followed the trampled path of the congregation until they found themselves on the road leading to the international airport. In front of them, two figures stood in the road. As they got closer, Kephas called out.

"Julius? Monica?"

"Kephas!"

"Hi!"

"What on earth are you doing here?"

"We just spoke with Sister Paula, and she said you'd be coming this way," Monica explained.

"Oh?"

"We need your help," Julius pleaded.

Zack noticed he looked at everyone as he spoke.

"What's wrong?" Kephas asked.

"We've tracked Tolech to Doverton. We must put a stop to him..."

"Wait! What? Tell me everything."

. . .

Months later in Neo-Babylon, Leonard and Henry had been working around the clock in preparation for the Unification first anniversary. The WGO had grown and expanded throughout the world. Neo-Babylon had quickly become the new centre of it all. It housed representatives from every country. Construction had just been completed of the world's largest conduit pylon. After the huge success that the WGO had with the smaller pylons throughout the world, Neron had advised that they needed to increase the scale. This last pylon would be orders of magnitude greater than any of the previous prototypes.

A sports stadium had been retrofitted to seat ten thousand leaders from around the world. The seats had been created to be all an equal distance from the focal point. Custom seats and countless lengths of cables and wires provided a more efficient transfer.

"Huh. That doesn't make sense." Henry began.

"What is it now?" Leonard asked.

"I'm just going over the schematics for the stadium seating, and according to this it's possible to set the incline to full reverse."

Leonard stopped typing and looked over at him. It was clear from his exhausted expression that he was too tired to understand.

"Why are you looking at that anyway?"

"Well, we're syncing the occupants AI watches with the built-in displays, and I was curious."

"I'm far too busy to be curious; perhaps you can take my night shift?"

"Just look at this for a moment, will you?"

"Fine. What?!"

"What do these numbers mean?"

"That's the angle of inclination, it should only accept positive numbers, but according to this, the system can process negative numbers too."

"So?"

"So, that means it's possible that all the people could get tipped out of their seats."

Leonard's vacant expression looked as if he was waiting for the point.

"Get back to work Henry."

"Seriously? This doesn't concern you?"

"Why should it? I'm not an engineer, neither are you. It's not our business to mess around with that anyway."

"But people could get hurt. This is a safety issue."

Leonard rolled his chair back to his desk and continued his work.

"Whatever."

"Well, I'm going to let management know."

"You do that then."

Leonard still found it strange than in his office things were relatively normal. Not far from the WGO gates, people were screaming and presumably dying in the streets. Yet, most of the time, he did not feel in danger. They had a new security team called the 'Spectral guard'. They certainly did a good job of keeping the 'unwanted distractions' away, but they always gave him the creeps.

The following day Leonard and Henry were at their desks working when their manager walked in.

"Hi Linda"

"Henry! Stop. Right the hell now."

"Huh?"

"You know exactly what I mean. No more messages about some safety issue. Get back to your job."

"Respectfully, this is important. I've built an update that'll push out to all the people's AI watches who'll be in stadium tomorrow to remind them to be careful.

"Are you kidding me?"

"No, at the push of a button I can send it out to all ten thousand of them."

"Leonard, can he do that?"

"Yes, he could. But I'm sure he's going to get straight back to work," Leonard glared at Henry intently.

Henry just hovered his finger above the enter key of his keyboard.

"Get it fixed or I'll send it out," Henry challenged.

"You're fired Henry, get out."

Leonard held his head in his hands. Henry did not move.

"I'm not leaving this desk until I see proof that you'll sort this out," he demanded.

"I'll get security to throw you out."

"And if they come close to me, I'll push this button, and all the attendees will know that you don't take their safety seriously!"

Linda read his face. She could tell that he was serious about this. Being blackmailed was the very last thing she needed today.

"OK, Henry, you stay right there."

She turned to walk down the hallway.

"Hurry up, or I'll push this button!" Henry yelled after her.

"Henry, what are you doing?!" Leonard pleaded

"Well if this is the last thing I do here it'll be worth it."

"And what is that exactly?" A familiar voice said from the doorway.

Leonard and Henry turned to see Neron himself standing there.

"uh, uh sir, I…" Leonard began.

"I was on my way to a meeting, and I hear a WGO staff member yelling threats down the hallway. This is unacceptable."

Henry looked surprisingly unfazed by the leader of the world, standing in front of him. He kept his finger poised above his keyboard.

Neron took a step into the room. Behind him, Leonard could see security staff and a group of important-looking people.

"Sir, if security comes in here I'll push the button," Henry said adamantly.

Neron stopped and looked at him, his face twisted into a snarl as he spat some dark words that Leonard wished he never heard. Neron raised his hand as if he was going to slap him. Henry just glared back at him from the other side of the room. Neron swung his arm in front of him as if he was slapping Henry. As he did so, some invisible force smashed into Henry, throwing him from his seat, across the room and into the wall on the far side. His neck twisted unnaturally on impact, and his lifeless body fell to the floor.

"Henry!" Leonard screamed as he stood up from his chair.

Neron looked over to Leonard with his hand still raised and a cold look in his eyes.

Leonard sat back down and got back to work like his life depended on it, which it certainly did. He wondered with each keypress if it would be his last. After a moment, he heard Neron walk away down the hallway. Leonard's heart was still beating furiously in his chest.

After working into the night, Leonard and other WGO staff were transported to the stadium by bus. Eventually, Leonard made his way to the communications office at the top of the stadium. There were a few windows which looked down into the stadium, but mostly it was filled with screens which displayed various data points. Leonard sat at his designated desk and re-read the order of events again to ensure he knew what to do. He was still shell-shocked at Henry's death. But he did not want to think about it. He decided he would just get through today first.

"All set?"

"Yeah," Leonard replied to the communications technician sitting in what should have been Henry's seat. It was now late evening, and he had been able to get through the day with one-word sentences, he did not plan to stop now. They sat at the ready as the stadium began to fill with leaders from all over the world. Each had their own designated seat.

"Go to camera twenty-seven,"

"OK," Leonard replied as he flicked a few switches. The broadcast was being sent out to millions of AI watches worldwide. The camera panned across the stadium showing the seats being set up in a circle around a large stage in the centre. Each row of seats further back was higher than the previous row. Each chair had a series of cables running up the back of it attached to sensors and scientific looking apparatus. The central stage had a large set of steel doors in the floor which were currently closed. There was a podium and a few seats but little else. The camera zoomed back as the lights dimmed.

"Now Neron himself will grace us with his presence," the announcer declared.

"Where is he? He should have come from the east entrance by now."

Leonard watched his monitor as he saw the crowd point up into the sky. He panned a camera up to see a figure floating down into the centre stage. His typical lab coat attire was now a long ornate robe. The crowd erupted in applause as he slowly descended to the stage and took a bow.

"He is absolutely amazing!" The technician declared.

Leonard just grunted. He hoped this was just some elaborate trick he was not filled in about. But part of him believed that unaided human flight was not impossible for him.

"Welcome one and all to this monumental occasion in human history. We, the leaders of humankind stand here today to celebrate our survival of the first year after the unification event…"

Another round of applause rippled across the crowd.

"Each and every one of us knows exactly what a heavy toll we've paid to be here, but humankind is stronger as a result. Let's start our journey together into this bright future by unveiling the greatest technological achievement to date. The Atlas Pylon, upon which our world is held in safety…"

Neron motioned towards the centre of the stage.

Leonard and his colleague coordinated in the control room
"Unlocking doors."
"Priming seals… OK go."
"Smoke, and elevation in motion."

The curious crowd watched the large doors open with a gush of steam. A small antenna began to rise out of the smoke, followed by a large steel scaffold. The lower portion was shaped into a statue holding a tall staff, which was the pylon. The base remained obscured in a large hole filled with smoke.

"Behold!"

Neron conjured forth a similarly designed staff from thin air above his head and grasped it.

The crowd roared with applause. Leonard could not help picture Neron's face as he killed his friend.

"Hey!"

"On it," he quickly tapped a few more buttons.

"Join with me everyone as we charge this device, fuelled upon our very hopes and dreams for a united humanity!"

As the pylon completed its ascension, all the chairs in the stadium began to tilt back slowly. This allowed the occupants to focus on the top of the pylon without tilting their heads.

"Conductive harnesses are go," Leonard declared as he pressed another button.

A thick gold strap unrolled from the headrest of each chair in the stadium.

"Please secure around your forehead," Bess' voice echoed from each chair.

After a moment, two more came from the armrests.

"Fasten these around your wrists. Both will automatically disengage after the transfer is complete."

The lighting dimmed over the crowd and shone upon the Atlas pylon.

Neron turned to face it and raised his hands.

"The gold will be yours to keep. Now, let us unite!"

The crowd began humming loudly, with many closing their eyes. The pylon extended further upwards, with the seats in the stadium tilting slightly in perfect coordination.

Several minutes passed with sustained homage as the lights in the pylon slowly lit from the base towards the top of the staff. As it neared the top, the crowd chanted all the harder.

"We've done it!" Neron declared.

The crowd went to clap but found they could not move their arms; also their heads were fixed to the headrests. People cheered regardless.

All at once, all of the cameras on Leonard's screen panned quickly upwards. All of them now displayed a useless image of the roof.

"What?!"

"Fix it now!"

"I did not do that!"

"They aren't accepting my input?"

"My controls are unresponsive?!"

Neron lowered his arms.

He walked around the stage and stared into the crowd.

"Thank you all for your sacrifice."

"What did he say?" Leonard jumped up and looked out the window into the stadium below.

There was a loud clattering sound as the steps under the chairs folded downwards so that there was now a smooth sloped surface beneath everyone in the stadium. The doors in the stage opened back even further; the smoke dissipated revealing an enormous circular empty void underneath the pylon. Multiple steel shafts held the raised pylon in place.

"Take them!" Neron commanded.

By now, both operators were staring out the window as they realised they had no control whatsoever. All of the chairs in the stadium swung downwards. The crowd began screaming in alarm. Neron raised his arms once more as he relished in the screaming.

With perfect coordination, a small metal arm extended from the back of each chair. It rotated around, so it appeared on the right-hand side of each person about shoulder height. The panicked people, watched as best they could as it rotated outwards slowly before swinging back at great speed. Ten thousand necks were sliced as the bladed arm cut deep into every leader from the world over. The stadium drowned in gurgled screaming.

The two operators ducked away from the window. Leonard's colleague ran off, whimpering down the hall.

"This can't be happening," Leonard tried to reason with himself.

He sat for a moment motionless, his brain unable to process what was happening. The small office began to vibrate as the dulled roar of a large engine could be heard from the middle of the stadium. The sound quickly changed as the motor was put under load. Leonard did not want to imagine what horror was occurring beneath him.

Movement on one of the monitors caught Leonard's eye. He watched as the rear exit opened and ten figures wearing black cloaks walked into the stadium. Behind them followed a security team armed with automatic weapons.

Leonard decided to peek through the window once more. He saw the stadium was nearly empty. All the seats were vacant, with just Neron and the newcomers standing to one side of the central stage basking in their long-planned work. Next to them was a large circular hole in the stadium floor with black smoke gushing out.

"You have done the Sons of the Snake proud Neron."

"We did it together," Neron admitted as they shook hands.

"The time has finally come."

They all turned towards the swirling smoke.

"With this offering of sin, we summon you!" Neron shouted.

A giant hand pushed upwards through the smoke followed a moment later by another. Two great hulking arms followed, then the head and torso of an enormous man-like creature.

A dark, vicious liquid obscured its form until it had completely emerged. It stood the height of three humans and had a large set of golden tentacle-wings on its back. The creature donned large antlers upon its head that were shaped like a crown. Its facial features blended all sorts of earthly creatures in perfect unison. It had large bird-like eyes, whiskers, and the mouth of a lion. A long beard-like mane flowed down to its broad shoulders. Its body was like blackened glass. It had giant clawed hands like a bear. An ornate living red robe draped around its form. The creature stood on two large hind legs. It was beautiful and terrible to behold.

A deep, unworldly voice boomed forth shattering all the windows in the stadium.

"I am the King of all Stars!"

Leonard flinched backwards as the window in front of him burst into pieces. After wiping the blood from his face, he looked on.

Neron and the ten with him immediately fell prostrate and worshipped him. A few of the security team did not bow down. The King glared in their direction, and they were instantly torn to pieces by an unseen force and flung around the stadium.

"For countless years, I have had the full force of my hate held back from these inferior creatures. Now I can finally sate my bloodlust..." he said as he toyed with the death of the last guard.

Neron rose to one knee and bowed his head.

"We have done all you asked, oh Radiant one. These with me will be the ten kings of your new kingdom."

The King stared down at them as they bowed reverently in turn.

"Humans? No, I have others in mind,"

He raised his hand, as he did so, all ten men were picked up off the ground. As he made a fist, they were thrown together and were crushed into a large ball of mangled bodies. With a dismissive gesture, it launched across the stadium crashing into the back row of seats.

"Come, we have a world to rule," he boomed as smoke boiled over once more.

Leonard tore his gaze away from the horror in front of him. He knew just what to do. He ran out the office door, sprinted down the hallway and opened the fire exit. He made his way up onto the roof of the stadium and ran full speed off the edge. He fell to his death onto the concrete below.

Chapter 10:

Peace

For Jenson, the sound of gunshots began to fade. An all-consuming darkness smothered him. Despite being separated from his body, his mind was panicking. He began to feel the weight of eternity take him. Jenson began to fall, as if he was sinking in to the very core of the earth, he sank lower and lower.

Pain surged from deep within his inner-self. The lower he fell, the worse it became. In desperation Jenson tried to perceive anyone or anything, but everything was lost in the deep void. He felt as if he was being crushed, everything at his core that was good was being squeezed out. A cry burst from him, trying to convey his profound sense of loss and anguish. He was a waft of shadow flailing in the darkness.

For a brief moment, he wondered if he heard a scream. The last of his hope left him as he realized it was an echo of his own. Jenson was utterly alone. His awareness of time became weak and unreliable. Some moments he felt he was being burnt in a furnace hotter than he thought conceivable. Other times it felt like he had been unable to move or make a sound for decades. A bottomless starvation and desperation to breathe saturated him. He was drowning in nothingness.

Jenson hit rock bottom. The feeling of falling was gone, despite the pain he now missed that sensation. Now, he felt no movement and had no love in his heart. Jenson lost all that he deemed to be his. His only drive was to be an unending cry of pain and suffering. To which no ear would ever listen.

. . .

"…we'll need everyone who is willing to fight," Julius concluded.

"I see, these are grave times indeed," Kephas replied.

Kephas then turned to those who had been fighting with him.

"A very powerful demon is consuming people not far from here and we're going to put a stop to him. All who want to volunteer for this dangerous task follow me. Otherwise, follow the trail back to the rest of our congregation. God-willing, we'll see you there upon our return."

There was a short moment as the fighters thought for themselves whether to go or not. Monica spoke scripture reverently.

Jeremiah 15
²⁰ I will make you a wall to this people,
a fortified wall of bronze;
they will fight against you
but will not overcome you,
for I am with you
to rescue and save you,"
declares the Lord.

Zack raised his hand up followed by his friends and the rest of the fighters.

"Thank you…" Julius said, bowing his head "… we could not do this alone."

The group turned and followed Julius, Monica and Kephas down the road. Zack quickened his pace to make his way to the front.

"Good to see you're alive Monica."

"And you too Zack. I... well, it's been very difficult."

"Yeah, it has. I understand. What do you know about what we're up against?"

"He's the leader of an organisation with solely evil intent. I've never seen it with my own eyes. Only what he leaves in his wake."

"What's that?"

"Large piles of dead people."

"Oh, um, right. So you've seen some of these up ahead then?"

"We're pretty sure he's in the Doverton hospital somewhere."

"Why?"

"Well, we've seen busloads of people go in. But no-one ever comes out. It even looked like there was some Scarkin patrolling. But if he is in there we'll need everyone to take him down."

Zack did not feel like asking any more questions.

A few hours later, the pack of fighters had walked through the suburbs to a small hill overlooking the Doverton city hospital. Zack recognised this area from his vision. Instead of a vast crater with a deep hole dropping further into the earth, he saw a mostly intact hospital in its place. Various surrounding buildings looked to have suffered heavy damage in the previous earthquakes. All but a few of them had burnt out.

Zack felt fear rise in his throat. He could not shake the feeling that this was going to be a trap. Graham picked at the plasters covering his fingers. They were far from clean, but he removed what dirt and grime that he could. He thought about how nice a hot shower would be right now.

"Heads down!" Julius called as he got down on his hands and knees and crept up to the edge of the hill. Looking below, he saw a few groups of Scarkin making their way through the car park then around the back of the hospital out of sight. A moment later, another group appeared and made their way through the car park.

"Look!" Graham pointed.

As they watched, two busses drove in and parked as WGO soldiers escorted frightened people inside. As they battled with the people piling out, one of them made a run for it. There was an eruption of shouting, which could be faintly heard from their observation position. A burst of gunfire rang out, and the running man toppled over onto the concrete. The rest of the prisoners obediently made their way inside.

"We have to go now!" Monica declared.

Julius and Kephas looked at each other, both wishing they had time to plan.

"Let's go."

"Move out!"

They scrambled to their feet and hurried down the road which swerved its way down to the hospital. As they moved, the empty busses drove off with the guards inside. After running for a few blocks, they came to a stop behind a large truck parked on the edge of the hospital car park.

"Ready up!" Kephas called as they dropped their bags, took a swig from drink bottles and checked their weapons. A moment later he was surrounded by combat-ready fighters.

Kephas addressed them.

"We have two objectives, save those people and put a stop to whatever is running this place. May the Lord God Almighty guide our footsteps and our weapons. Amen."

"Amen!"

Breaking from behind the truck, the fighters ran towards the main entrance. They had just about reached the doors when something smashed through the glass doors and flew towards them. Not managing to dodge in time one of the fighters was bowled over backwards onto the ground. Zack gasped as he saw the projectile was a person from the bus.

"Priest scum!" A loud voice roared from inside.

Another two bodies flew out in quick succession as the fighters dove for cover.

"Your time here is over Tolech!" Julius shouted back as he and Kephas walked forward slowly.

"It's only just beginning meat-sack!" Came the reply as a frail-looking old man walked out of the shattered doors. He was towing two bodies by the feet, one in each of his hands. Both looked to be larger than he was. Somehow, it looked effortless for him.

"Impossible?" Graham muttered.

"Don't let your eyes fool you," Monica replied as she kept her eyes forward.

To the disbelief of all, Tolech leapt up into the air, almost reaching the same height as the nearby street lamps. Upon reaching the height of his jump, he hurled down the two bodies he was carrying. The fighters were slow to react, and two that had hunkered down behind a car were killed as the human body projectiles slammed into them.

"Watch out!" Julius cried.

Tolech landed atop one fighter and with a quick slash of his claw-like fingers tore out his throat. Julius and Kephas bolted towards him as more fighters fell to a barrage of strikes from their inhuman foe. Tolech leapt at one fighter, knocking him over before grabbing him by the leg and slinging him at another.

Julius and Kephas jumped into the fray; working together, they managed to land several solid strikes. Julius weaved between Tolech's attacks and delivered a heavy uppercut to his jaw. As he recoiled backwards, Kephas caught him with a right hook, knocking him to the ground. Monica thumped him with her sledgehammer right in the middle of his chest. What should have been a killing blow only made Tolech laugh.

"Fools!" He jumped back to his feet and ripped into an approaching fighter. He then swung him around, bowling everyone over.

"Julius! Get them away from here," Kephas called as he scrambled back to his feet.

"But we…"

"I will stop this creature my brother."

"Fighters follow me!" Julius called as he charged into the hospital.

Zack watched as Kephas stood between Tolech and the fighters rushing inside. He already had blood dripping down his face.

"Demon filth! I will end you!" He roared.

"Zack, guard the door," Julius called.

"Got it, he replied."

Tolech pounded a fighter's head into the ground then slowly stood up facing Kephas.

"I'll kill you slowly."

Kephas pulled off his coat and pulled up his shirt. Zack saw that he was wrapped all over in scripture covered bandages. Tolech watched with interest as Kephas cut himself free of them. He removed yet more from around the muscles on his arms and legs.

"Amazing! He was wearing penitent bindings all this time?" Monica uttered as she emerged with an elderly woman over her shoulder. Zack wondered how many years Kephas must have been training to be able to move normally despite wearing them under his clothes.

Kephas seemed larger somehow as he strode forwards towards Tolech. "So you think…" Tolech began.

Kephas darted forward with an impossible speed catching Tolech with a quick left jab, slamming shut his lying mouth. Tolech lashed out with his claws only to find Kephas now behind him, gripping him by the throat and throwing him over his shoulder into a parked van.

The van was crushed as if it was just hit by a truck. A shower of broken glass covered the pavement. Kephas once again charged forwards and stabbed his pair of combat crucifixes into Tolech's left and right wrists, pinning him to the side of the van. They punctured through his wrists and embedded into the steel frame of the van.

"Come out of this poor man," Kephas commanded as he placed one hand on his head.

Tolech began to laugh.

"Fool! You don't know who you're dealing with."

Kephas began to pray over him.

Julius and the remaining fighters started to pour out of the hospital escorting many terrified civilians.

"Go!" He commanded.

Tolech turned his head.

"They are mine!" His eyes began to bulge, and he opened his mouth further than should have been possible. Tolech ripped his arms free, tearing up his wrists in the process. His hands hung ruined and bloody. He head-butted Kephas and began howling as his body contorted and twisted. His limbs cracked as he vomited a growing pile of dark goo. A pair of claws emerged from inside his mouth and tore him apart. A large demon climbed out and stood before them. It quickly grew in size until it towered over them as tall as a tree.

"Magnukin! Run!"

The fighters and civilians scattered in a panic trying to get away. Kephas leapt towards the beast slashing chunks out of it with his battle crucifixes. The demon retaliated with a flurry of strikes. Kephas managed to dodge and fend the first few strikes but was impaled on its giant claws.

The giant demon let out a roar then flung his body to the ground.

"No!"

"Kephas!"

Zack and Graham sprinted over. The lumbering demon turned towards his fleeing victims and reached out and grabbed a middle-aged man. He squeezed until he went limp then threw him towards those fleeing.

"Run!"

Julius shouted as he extended his arms out to both of his sides. A pair of angelic wings materialised as he spoke the holy words and blocked the incoming corpse projectile.

Zack ran over to Kephas' side as he lay on his back with a gaping wound in his chest. He looked at Zack for a brief moment and extended his hand, coughing out his last breath.

"Kephas!" Zack cried as he took his hand and desperately began praying for healing. Kephas' ring dropped into his hand then he became very still. Kephas' eyes looked vacant, and he was no longer breathing.

"Demon filth!"

Graham ran in and swung his blessed hammer into the beast. The Magnukin howled in pain as Graham belted into its right knee. He managed to land a few strikes before it turned and swatted Graham away. He flew backwards and tumbled over on the concrete. Graham lay face down with a quickly growing pool of blood expanding out from underneath him.

"Graham!" Beth screamed from her position amid the fleeing civilians.

The enormous demon charged towards those trying to flee. Beth ran forward to meet it.

"No!" Zack screamed as he stood up. His whole body roared with fury. Clenching his fists, he felt the ring in his hand crack. Looking into his hand, he saw a tiny pebble drop out from a hidden compartment. The ring had been handed down through the centuries of service of the Order of Salt and Light. This tiny stone was from the foot of the cross on Calvary where Jesus Christ's blood had been spilt.

Without thinking or maybe it was divine inspiration, Zack tossed it into his mouth and swallowed it. Immediately his entire being surged with holy power. He at once began singing at the top of his lungs in a holy language he previously had no knowledge of. Zack sprinted towards the demon, dived into a forward roll avoiding an attack and grabbed Kephas' coat. Zack dove between the demon and Beth just as it took a swing at her. To the demons' surprise, Zack held its giant claws back without being thrown off his feet.

"Beth, get these people safe," he spoke quietly to her.

Beth seemed to snap free from her emotions and retreated. The demon swung another clawed hand towards Zack as he threw Kephas' coat into the beasts face. Before it could land its second blow, Zack carved out deep gashes with his blessed sword. He began to scramble up the demon. Tolech roared with fury as he lashed out. Zack instinctively moved to block, but his left arm was cut off at the elbow. He screamed through the pain as he leapt.

Zack launched a thrust into the side of the demon's jaw. It landed with a force magnitudes more powerful that humanly possible. Tolech's enormous jaw was blown apart. Zack stabbed himself a hold with his sword and dragged the demon over forwards. As Zack landed on his feet then drove his holy weapon up into the centre of Tolech's head. A chain reaction of bubbling and dissolving rot rippled through the demon's body as it was banished from the physical realm. Zack flicked the demonic blood free from his blade like a warrior of old.

Zack held his bleeding stump as best he could, desperately trying to slow the blood loss. He could see no healers nearby. He knew at this rate he would not have long. His breathing became panicked, and he dropped to one knee.

"What do I do?" He asked himself aloud, wrestling to calm the panic exploding inside him.

He immediately thought of the prayer card he had been given in the Praetorium, what seemed like so long ago. He took a deep breath and spoke the words he had memorised of 'The seven seals of Christ' prayer.

Zack felt a rush of air enter his lungs and saw his stump was no longer gushing out blood. It had miraculously scabbed over. It was still dreadfully painful, but he could deal with that later.

Zack sprinted to Kephas and gently laid a hand on his head. He could somehow feel that Kephas' spirit was no longer inside the battered body before him. Kephas was dead. Zack closed his eyes and crossed his arms over his chest.

"Thank you for everything Kephas. Go now to peace eternal."

Next, he rushed over to Graham and again held a hand on his head. Zack closed his eyes, but before starting a prayer of healing, he stopped. Zack knew Graham had also died.

"Graham…" he blubbed.

A cold breeze swirled around Zack, and he gathered himself. Before emotions could further cloud his actions, Zack sped around the checking on the bodies of the fallen fighters. He managed to heal Malcolm who was on the brink of death. The holy words flowed naturally from his very core. Every other fighter he attended to had already perished.

Zack found Beth had rushed over to Graham's body and was trying to wake him.

"Get up! Get up!" She sobbed.

Zack knelt next to her and laid Graham's hands over his own chest.

"No! Try to heal him again!" She cried.

Zack looked Beth and then to his dead best friend.

He was lost for words.

"Buddy…" was all he could manage.

Beth jumped at the sight of Zack's missing arm and could no longer hold back the flood of tears.

At that moment, a Summoner demon stepped forward on the roof of the hospital. It extended its staff towards them and uttered profane sounds from its mouth. Almost instantly, a tide of husks surged forward from the hospital and over the fence at the edge of the car park. Zack stood up and dragged Beth to her feet.

"We gotta go!" He dared a final glance over his fallen comrades as he spoke.

The husks sprinted towards them, quickly closing the gap as Zack and Beth began to stumble away. They ran towards the fleeing civilians and other fighters who were now making their way up the street towards the overlooking hill. Zack heard the husks close in behind them. As he was trying to think of a plan, he tripped on the curb and fell over. The first ranks of husks were nearly upon him.

"Testantur Sanctam Dei!" He roared with all his strength.

A burst of light detonated out from him as he made the sign of the cross from where he lay on the ground. The closest husks were incinerated in the holy light and were blown back into those behind them. These tumbled backwards causing those behind them to fall over.

Zack felt the surge of spiritual energy begin to fade from him.

"Get up!" Beth screamed as she dragged him up.

They both ran full speed up the road and out of sight from the Summoner atop the hospital.

"Zack!" Mindy screamed as she ran over from her position guarding the rear of the civilians.

"I'm OK."

Zack saw the panic in her face turn to confusion as she inspected the stump of his arm.

She was about to speak as she saw their pursuers behind them.

"C'mon!" Mindy cried with tears in her eyes.

They poured all their emotional energy into running to catch up to the others.

All the remaining fighters collapsed at the top of the hill to catch their breath. For the time being, they had shaken their pursuers.

"We gotta go back," Beth implored.

"We can't with all these people," Julius replied.

It was clear he was grieving too as he stared off towards the hospital.

"But, but…"

"I know," he said, wrapping his arms around her.

"No! No, no." She sobbed as she began to hit him.

"Beth, please,"

Beth turned around and cried into Mindy's shoulder.

"She…" Mindy began to explain.

"It's OK…" Julius replied "…I understand."

Zack sat on to the curb, holding the stump of his lost arm.

"How did it come to this? How'd I let this happen?" He asked himself

"Are you alright? Monica asked, sitting down next to him.

"No. But it doesn't seem to be bleeding."

"You're blessed then, many others…"

"I've failed. I, I could've…"

"Zack, it's not your fault. You did all you could."

"But, I knew this war was coming, I should've done more. I should've stopped…"

"Everyone! We have to move again, as fast as you can! This way!" Julius called.

"Hey, it's not over yet." Monica patted him on the back as she helped him up.

Zack wiped his face and hurried over to the rest of the group.

• • •

On the other side of Doverton, Bill sat on a pile of cardboard underneath the largest bridge in the park.

"Terry, got any more?" Bill asked his friend.

"Nah. This is my last one."

"Gimme some?"

"You just ate yours! Don't be greedy."

"I'm starving c'mon!"

"Nah! Get lost."

Terry jammed the last of his ration bar into his mouth as he fended Bill off.

"Urgh, fine, We'll just have to scavenge for more then."

"Yeah, course we will. Let's find a drink too."

"I have a little left."

"Gimme some?" Terry said mimicking Bill earlier.

"You'll not be surprised to learn that I am a gentleman. And a drinking buddy in need is a friend indeed," Bill said smiling.

He pulled out a brown paper bag from the inside of his coat and took a big swig. He shook it in his hand, then took another.

"Hey, leave some for me."

"You finish it Terry; I don't want to catch your bad breath."

"Hey! I thought you said you were a gentleman?"

"Just when the mood suits me," he replied, smiling.

Despite all the disasters around them, Bill and Terry had faired pretty well. With so many people dying, Bill found much less competition for items he would 'acquire'. There were a few situations that got a little heated, but people did not notice him for the most part. Just the way he liked it.

A burst of gunfire nearby jolted them both out of a light stupor.

"What was that?" Terry asked.

"Just more chaos, don't worry, it'll pass."

"It sounded awfully close."

"We'll just…"

As he was speaking two WGO soldiers dropped down from above them.

"You two, show us your watches," one of them demanded.

"No thanks, we're OK here," Bill replied.

"Now!" One of the soldiers moved forward, while the other raised his weapon at them.

Both Bill and Terry put their hands up.

"No device aye? You've managed to elude authority for quite a while it seems. Well that stops now. You're coming with us."

"And if we refuse?" Terry asked.

"You'll be staying under this bridge permanently. One rule for all, and through all Unity."

"But, but…" Bill began to protest.

"It's mandatory, now shut up."

"You just need…"

The closest soldier drove the butt of his rifle into Bill's stomach winding him.

"Silence!"

Terry raised his hands even higher.

"Get moving!"

The soldiers marched them up to the path where they saw many other people that had been rounded up. A body lay face down on the stones a short distance away. It was clear to them that running away was not an option. They sat there for hours as the troops cleared out the rest of the park. Bill recognised several other homeless people he had known for years and others that had only recently began living on the street.

As they sat there waiting to be moved to a 'processing centre', the sky began to ripple above them. Clouds rolled and twisted around unlike anything anyone had seen before. The prisoners cowered lower to the ground. The soldier's bravery was rattled as they all looked up. Thunder boomed across the sky and was followed by a deep voice.

"Repent of your sins!"

Many quivered in fear expecting the very sky to fall upon them. But the moment passed with seemingly no consequences.

"Ah! My arms!" One of the prisoners yelled as they pulled back their sleeves to reveal pus-filled sores on her arm.

Bill continued to stare as before his eyes, another boil appeared on her other arm.

"Argh! It hurts, make it stop!" Another cried as he pulled up the leg of his pants to reveal yet more festering sores.

"No!" The lady sitting alongside Bill yelled as she held her hand out. As he watched, a group of sores erupted on the skin on the back of her hand.

Many of the soldiers now buckled over in pain as sores erupted over their bodies.

"Bill!" Terry motioned to the bridge as their guards were distracted.

Before they could begin their plan, another captive jumped to their feet and ran towards the bushes. A loud burst of gunfire rang out, and they crumpled over into a bleeding heap.

"Stay right there!" The soldier spat as he struggled with the sores on his arms. But it seemed it was not enough to make him miss his shot at such short range.

Bill scanned around the group and noticed only those already wearing a watch were affected. One of the soldiers noticed the same, and he began frantically pulling at his watch.

"Don't you do it Marcus!" Another soldier yelled as he raised his weapon.

"I gotta stop it!"

"It is against WGO law to remove your device, desist immediately, the penalty is death." Bess' voice said calmly from the soldiers watch.

"Stop right now!" The other soldier said, but as he struggled with his wounds, he waited to see if it would indeed stop the sores.

As Bill watched, the soldier ripped off his watch. A long intravenous line connected to the watch to his arm for a moment until he pulled it out. On the end of the line, there was a metal hook. As he ripped it from his arm, he cried out in pain. He clamped he hand down over the wound.

"They tap into your blood now too?" Bill said in alarm.

"Yeah, they own every part of you," Terry replied coldly.

All eyes watched the soldier as he frantically checked his arms, legs and chest. Despite his efforts, more sores began to surface on his skin.

"No, no, no!"

A single shot snapped the soldiers head backwards, and he dropped to the ground.

"One rule for all...." the firing soldier managed to declare before he was consumed by his painful sores.

Hours later, Bill, Terry and the others were escorted slowly to a waiting bus. Each soldier struggled through the pain as best they could. As Bill climbed aboard the bus, he wondered exactly what a 'processing centre' was.

. . .

Kephas felt all of his senses begin to fade. He could no longer feel the concrete beneath him. Zack's voice seemed distant. He lost all feeling from his body then started to feel like he was falling. Slowly at first, then quicker and quicker.

"Jesus Christ help me, a sinner!" He cried out from the very core of himself.

His very soul yearned for God's help. Although he had fading awareness of his physical body, he reached his hand up. He began to close his hand as a hand closed around his.

"Well done, good and faithful servant."

The voice of God resonated entirely through him; he felt a rush of peace and love. At once, he began to feel the essence of himself stop falling and launch upwards and begin to accelerate. Kephas felt as if he was flying up through the atmosphere out into space, deeper and higher.

As he travelled, he felt change in himself. He cried out as everything that was not good was drawn out of him like venom from a wound. He felt his perception; memories, attitude, knowledge and every aspect of himself refine, improve and purify. His every sin was being purged from his soul. Kephas travelled for what seemed years, but upon arrival, it was if the spiritual and physical worlds were next to each other the entire time.

All at once, in the blink of an eye, he stood in his own body. Yet, it was not the body he was used to on earth; that was just a temporary shell. This body was what his soul was designed for all along. He no longer felt the aches in his old bones and his itchy scalp. Gone were every form of sickness and disease. He was filled with what felt like unlimited energy. He could now stay awake permanently. His skin was in better than perfect condition. It felt like newborn babies', but still he retained some wrinkles. Kephas was now the perfect representation of himself over the full course of his life. Not young, yet not old. Kephas was finally home. He could not contain the joy that saturated through every facet of him. He burst into song.

"Glory, Glory to God in the Highest! Alleluia, Alleluia, Alleluia!"

While he sang, he reflected. Kephas' sense of time deepened, he felt like every moment of his memories on earth was somehow flat and shallow. Here, each moment of time had what seemed like unfathomable depth. His mind had grown to a deeper understanding of himself. Kephas felt like the haze he had coped with throughout his life had finally lifted. He

411

finally felt like he was really awake. Finally, everything felt real.

It took Kephas some time to get used to his new senses. His ears heard things unlike anything on earth. The angels' singing was sublime. It was if every aspect of music on earth culminated into but a single note of this new sound. Kephas felt like his ears had been designed at the dawn of time to listen to this song. Indeed they were.

Kephas was content just to breathe. His sense of smell was much more than what he experienced on earth. The air felt so clean, and it seemed to carry a rainbow of pleasant smells. Some of them triggered memories of his childhood, others he had no earthly comparison for.

Somewhere between hearing and vision, Kephas discovered a new sense, spiritual perception. He recalled a number of times in his life when he felt like he had got a glimpse of it. But now he knew it was part of him. He could not think of how to describe it. Through this, he felt a profound peace saturate through him. He was no longer caught in the struggle between his physical and spiritual self. At the same time, he felt unbounded joy. He recalled scripture from his time on earth.

Isaiah 60
¹⁹ The sun will no more be your light by day,
nor will the brightness of the moon shine on you,
for the LORD will be your everlasting light,
and your God will be your glory.
²⁰ Your sun will never set again,
and your moon will wane no more;
the LORD will be your everlasting light,
and your days of sorrow will end.

Kephas' was not sure how long it had been, but when he felt ready, he opened his eyes. Glorious, radiant light rushed in, it was like staring into the sun from up close, except rather than being burnt and damaged, the light here was utterly good, revitalising and healing. He felt drawn to it like it was sustenance for his very being. His eyes soaked in so much more detail than his earthly counterparts. It was as if Earth only had a small subset of the colours possible.

Kephas found himself standing atop a mountain. He was standing in a knee-deep lake of crystal clear water with a mist flowing over it. Water flowed down a large waterfall into a large reservoir below. His feet stood upon smooth stone, which felt warm under his bare feet. He looked out to the horizon to see a range of lush green forest-covered mountains extending as far as he could see.

There was a vast array of trees and plants, many of which he had never seen on Earth. All were in perfect condition. Not even one leaf was brown and decaying. Kephas listened to the singing of birds in the treetops. He occasionally saw animals beneath the canopy. Everything was in perfect harmony, so idyllic, the very definition of paradise. He recognised this place from somewhere deep in his core. He knew he was in Heaven.

He turned his gaze upwards to witness the brightest and purest of light. He saw countless angels flying through the air endlessly singing praises to God. As he looked towards the centre of the light, he thought for a moment that he made out a shape or outline. Again he felt a drive inside him well up until he found himself praising and thanking God in song.

He began to laugh to himself out of pure joy. He began to dance as he looked up, and with much more skill than on earth.

"This is where I belong; this is the home I've been searching for!"

"Yes. Welcome home Kephas," a deep voice spoke.

He turned towards the voice that up until that very moment he had never heard aloud, but somehow he recognised. Standing next to him was Kephas' guardian angel. He stood at the same height as him and was dressed in a flowing white robe and had large white wings. His face was a beautiful mixture of animal features; each one seemed to complement the other perfectly. He looked to be covered in a combination of skin, feathers and clothes; it was difficult to tell where one started and the other finished. He was truly magnificent to behold.

"I know you, don't I?"

The angel stepped forward and hugged him, then smiled and nodded.

"It is truly good that you are here Kephas, I have watched over you since before you were born into the world until now. Come; let me be your guide as you begin true life here."

Kephas felt a flood of questions erupt through him from his time on earth.

"Why...." he was not sure where to start. "...What about those who I left on earth, can I help them?"

"Indeed yes, you can, we will pray for them. Know that we are not bound by time as you know it on Earth. Understanding will come in time my friend. Just like on earth, begin with small things, and then proceed to larger."

"Please, show me."

The angel extended his hand and Kephas took it; they began to effortlessly fly up into the sky. The angel showed him all the lower realms of heaven. They resembled different climates and landscapes of earth but with orders of magnitude more beauty and splendour. Kephas gazed in wonder at it all. As they flew, Kephas saw other humans, sometimes with angels other times with other humans.

"Look! Is that?!"

"Yes, Kephas, it's your great grandfather, we will return here to him soon."

They waved as they flew past; and received a wave and smile in return.

Upon flying over another group of humans, Kephas watched as one of them extended her hands and shaped the rock in front of her just through prayer. Upon seeing Kephas' reaction, his angel spoke to him.

"As you grow, you will too be able to shape this world. Just as in Eden, humans again will be caretakers of God's garden…"

Kephas looked on in amazement and knew in time he would understand.

"We have passed briefly over just the lower tier; there is much more to discover when you are ready. Let us gaze upwards toward God for a moment. In time you will be able to see more."

Kephas sang praise to God with all his being, in doing so, he felt like he began to understand his spiritual sense a fraction more.

"Tell me, what should I do here?"

"You will need to know yourself, others, and then begin to know God."

"How can I do this?"

"Prayer will reveal much on your time on Earth, memories and a clear perspective. Once you fully understand yourself, then you will be able to talk to every other human here. You will be able to truly understand them, and in time, gain a tiny understanding of God. Then you will have grown enough to be able to dwell on God's glory. But also know there is much yet which you're unable to comprehend of this holy place."

Not ever having children of his own Kephas had underestimated how much his parents truly loved him. Even though at times throughout his life, they did not always show it, in this place, he could feel it. He was looking forward to speaking with them again. And yet he felt a deeper love than that of his parents saturate him. It was the love of God himself. This love was unlike anything he had experienced. It was incredible to truly know how much he was cared for and cherished.

The angel and Kephas swooped down and landed in a lush green garden. It was nestled between a small stream and some heavenly cherry trees. On the deep green grass was a man keeling down. Kephas recognised him from deep down in his core as own great grandfather.

"I will come back later," the angel spoke as it flew off.

Kephas smiled and waved.

"It's so good to see you Kephas!"

He turned and smiled at his ancestor who he never had a chance to meet on Earth.

"Opa?"

"Yes! Come have a drink."

Opa lead Kephas to the small stream and scooped up some water in his hands and drank it. Kephas did the same. Holy, living water flowed down his throat and rejuvenated his entire being on a level he did not imagine possible. It was truly soul-quenching. Both of them erupted into joyous laughter. Kephas felt like he had been holding his breath his entire life, and he could finally release the joy bound inside him.

"Come sit with me for a time," Opa beckoned.

They sat down on the grass together.

"I don't know where to begin..." Kephas started.

"Let's start at the basics, then shall we?" Opa decided.

He waved his hand over the grass in front of him to reveal a small patch of sand. In it, he drew a picture with his finger. He began with a small circle.

"Let's say this is Earth..."

Kephas nodded.

"…and this is the very limit of physical space…" Opa drew another circle around the first. He then drew a door and another circle on the other side. He drew a line from earth through the door to the circle on the far side.

"You've passed through death and are now in heaven…"

Kephas nodded.

Opa drew a smiley face above the circle then walked his fingers upwards.

"Here, God is always above us, and eventually you'll be able to rise towards him,"

"I see…"

At that moment, Kephas realised this whole time he had been conversing not in an earthly language but a heavenly one. There was no miscommunication or barrier if someone spoke another language from their time on earth. It was so natural; he understood it was his true native language.

"You're a faster learner than me then," he said, smiling.

"Thank you Opa,"

They sat and discussed Kephas' various questions, including many about Opa's life on Earth. Opa talked at length and answered many questions on the way through. Some he could not answer; he suggested who might know. When they had finished talking, Opa stood up.

"Come, let's see if you've grown,"

Kephas stood up and watched as Opa lifted his leg and stood upon an invisible step a short height above the grass. He turned and smiled.

"The view from here is grand!"

"How are you doing that?" Kephas asked in amazement.

He put a hand on Kephas' chest and looked him in the eyes.

"Use your spirit…"

He then took Kephas' hand, who took a step up in kind. For a moment, he was able to stand upon the air as if it was a solid surface. As he did so, Heaven all around him deepened in beauty and grew in size. The heavenly light above him grew in strength, illuminating everything below. The horizon stretched out further in all directions. His every sense surged with wondrous new sensations. He drew a single breath before he found himself standing back on the grass again.

Kephas' couldn't shake the smile from his face.

Opa returned his smile.

"With every step, there is more. So much more to be revealed…"

Kephas felt like the most amazing experiences on Earth where just a shadow of what heaven had to offer. Like a baby slowing growing in the womb, in preparation for entering the world, Kephas felt his life on Earth left him in a similar state in respect to heaven. He was beginning to understand that he was just a heavenly newborn.

Kephas smiled; he felt like his adventures were just beginning.

Chapter 11:

War

After running for as long as they could, the fighters and civilians finally slowed to a walk.

"Is it far from here?" One of the freed civilians asked Zack.

"Uh, I'm not sure."

"Oh, well thank you for saving us," he said

"Yeah," Zack was still looking off into the distance, with his mind somewhere else.

"What happened back there?" Monica asked.

The young man turned towards her.

"We were forced onto a bus and driven to the hospital, like many others I guess. I was only inside for a few moments, but already I can't get those images outta my head. They, they, seemed to be draining people…"

"Huh?"

"That evil old man would, he…" his face went pale.

"It's alright, you're safe now, and you'll never go back."

He nodded.

"I'm Monica, and this is Zack, what's your name?"

"I'm Brandon."

Zack looked up from his daze and recognised him from his vision. Same brown scruffy hair, thin build and bright eyes.

"I'm glad you made it out Brandon."

"Yeah, me too."

Mindy and Beth were walking ahead of them.

"I can't believe he's gone," Beth finally said

"Me neither," Mindy replied.

"I don't know what I'm going to do. I, I..."

Mindy squeezed her arm around her a little tighter.

"I'm right here. We'll get through it together."

Beth burst into tears once more.

Eventually, the group made it to the airport. They slowly made their way through the packed car park towards the terminal. As they approached, a dark-haired man with a long black beard walked out.

"Welcome to Galvin airport!"

"Duncan?"

"Julius!"

"Haha! Oh, it's great to see you!" Julius said, rushing over and enthusiastically shook his hand and patted him on the back.

"I haven't seen you since, um, what was it? That conference nine years ago?"

"Yes, that's right. I'm glad you've made it through all this."

"And you as well, come, bring your people in; we've got plenty of food and shelter for everyone."

"Yes please," Julius replied as he waved the weary group forward.

Zack felt Kephas' coat weigh down on him as he walked. He kept running over the battle in his mind. He wondered what he could have done differently. Could he have prepared better? He did not know. The reality of Kephas' and Graham's death had not sunk in yet. Zack almost expected them to run up through the group with a smile on their face. But they never did. Zack tried to keep his focus on walking. He was exhausted.

The group walked into the terminal; Zack was surprised to see it in relatively good condition. Many of the external windows had smashed, but the glass had been swept away into piles throughout the terminal. Advertisements and posters hung on the walls, and for a moment, Zack felt like he was back before the world crumbled apart.

"It feels like before in here, doesn't it?" Monica asked.

"Yeah, I agree."

"It will be hard Zack."

"Huh?"

"You'll blame yourself for a while, then you'll be angry, then sad, but eventually you'll come to accept it. Well, at least that's what I should probably say. Truth is I'm still really hurting from all the people I've lost. But well, yeah…" she drifted off. "…That coat looks good on you."

"Thanks Monica, I, I don't really know what to do," Zack admitted.

"Let's just get through today."

"Yeah, OK."

They walked slowly through the terminal into one of the well-furnished departure lounges. It was filled with people. Many looked like they had been stuck here since the end times began.

"Welcome to our community," Duncan said as he raised his arms.

A few of the fighters rushed over to their loved ones and enveloped them in big hugs. Zack estimated that there were around two hundred people in total.

"Are you sure you have enough food for us?" Zack heard Julius ask.

"Yes, we've been very blessed. We've found large quantities of food in the airport and the surrounding warehouses. We could easily support more people here."

"What about demon attacks?"

"We've lost people…" he lowered his head as he spoke, "…but I'm sure that with all these fighters, and those new weapons, we'll fair much better now."

"Ah, I understand. Yes. Ah, does the airport have facilities that we could use to make more weapons? I'm confident we're going to need them."

"There's multiple aircraft maintenance hangers, and the airport has a couple of workshops. I'm sure we'd be able to find anything else you'd need."

"Great, then let's begin."

"Begin what?"

"Building an army," Julius replied.

In the months that followed, Zack spent a lot of time in the workshop, showing others what weapons he had made and designs he remembered. He was delighted to see Jacob had survived and was soon at home producing as many sanctified weapons as he could. Outside of this, Zack had a patrol duty walking the perimeter of the airport. One afternoon, Mindy took a break from her work, helping the injured and walked with him.

"I still find it difficult to think that Graham is actually gone," Mindy began.

"Yeah. I know what you mean. How's Beth holding up?" Zack replied.

"She has good days and bad days. We're lucky that we've been away from the frontlines here for a while to process it all."

"Yeah, I kinda thought we'd be attacked by now, to be honest."

"Oh, was this in your vision?"

"Not really, I think we've lasted longer than my vision now, I'm just very aware they are still out there."

"Yeah. How's your arm?"

"Itchy…" Zack pulled his stump out of his coat and showed Mindy.

Mindy assessed the weeping scabs and closed her eyes in prayer. Zack felt a deep warmth rush through him. A few minutes later, his stump was now nicely scarred over.

"Woah! Thank you. That's so much better," Zack said, smiling.

"Father Duncan has been guiding us healers. We've made so much progress lately."

"I'm delighted to hear that."

"Are you going out in the next search party?" Mindy asked.

"Yes, I'm sure there are other people out there we can help."

"I'm coming too."

"Oh? Won't they need you here?"

"I've been training up Sandra, you know, short black hair?"

Zack nodded.

"She's been learning fast, and well, many of the people have either been healed or have since died. I think I'd be of most help out there."

"Thanks Mindy, I'd love to have you along with us."

She smiled.

Zack's world seemed brighter for a moment; there was still nothing more beautiful that he could think of than Mindy smiling. Zack was unsure of how to word what he wanted to say.

"Are we OK Mindy? I mean, I know I've not handled things very well in the past, I just wanted to you know…"

"Yeah Zacky. I…"

Beth jogged up alongside them

"Hey!"

"Hi Beth,"

"Duncan has just got back, he's in bad shape, and there's a lot of injured with him…"

"I'll be right there," Mindy said.

"They got attacked on the way back from Doverton North. By something they couldn't see…"

"What do you mean? It was dark?"

"No, like invisible. Duncan says they were lucky to get away at all."

"That's the last thing we need."

"Julius and Monica will find and kill it, and well I'm going too. I just wanted to let you know."

"Beth?!"

"I know what I'm doing. I can't stay hiding here forever; I want to help. And I'm sure I can do this."

"Well then we're coming too," Mindy volunteered.

"I thought you'd say that," Beth cracked the smallest of smiles. It had been a while since that had happened.

"Let's get going then," Zack added.

They made their way back to the terminal, and an hour later, they were packed and ready to depart. Julius, Monica, Mindy, Beth, Malcolm, Zack and ten volunteers armed with long spears set out at a quick pace towards Doverton North.

"Any idea what it could be Julius?" Monica asked.

"I think we're dealing with a Giestkin, a very dangerous demon. However, it seems to be on a much larger scale than anything I've read about. Duncan's description makes it out to be, well, very deadly."

"How are we going to find it?"

"Duncan said it attacked them as they passed by Laybourn road. The ones that didn't make it back are still laying where they fell."

"Ah, right."

Julius told Monica then all the others his plan.

"Sounds good to me," she replied.

They prayed before they set out.

Ephesians 6

[14] Stand firm then, with the belt of truth buckled around your waist, with the breastplate of righteousness in place, [15] and with your feet fitted with the readiness that comes from the gospel of peace. [16] In addition to all this, take up the shield of faith, with which you can extinguish all the flaming

arrows of the evil one. ¹⁷ Take the helmet of salvation and the sword of the Spirit, which is the word of God.

They walked on further through the battered suburbs until they approached the road that was mentioned. Everyone was on high alert. They walked in a large circle formation with Julius in the centre. Zack held his blessed sword tightly, trying to spot anything out of place. As they progressed, they found bodies scattered over the street. Only then did they understand how narrowly Duncan and the remains of his search party escaped.

Julius bent over each one and said a prayer for them as they passed by. One of the fighters abruptly flew across the road and smashed into a tree.

"Demon!" Monica cried despite there being no enemy visible.

Everyone raised their weapons, desperate to catch a sign of their enemy. A second later, another fighter was thrown backwards with deep gashes across his chest. He sprawled backwards onto the pavement and quickly bled out.

"Run!" Julius cried as he turned and ran across the road towards one of the houses. He tried the door, which thankfully was unlocked. Everyone sprinted inside, and they slammed the door shut. The small hallway was filled by panting, panicked breaths.

"Spears ready!" Julius called.

The fighters brought their weapons around and aimed them at the front door. Julius dropped to a knee just behind them and began fervently praying. The front door smashed in as if punched by an invisible giant. Splinters of wood flew everywhere as the demon charged into the house.

The fighters charged forwards. To their surprise, just a few steps forward their array of blessed spears drove deep into invisible hide. Visible demonic goo sprayed out as they landed several deep gashes into their foe. The demon recoiled and thrashed around the hallway, ripping itself free. A few fighters let go of their spears as they were torn from their grasp. One fighter held tight to his spear and was dragged forward. The demon was now slightly visible as its blood oozed across its transparent hide. A section of its body and a large claw was no longer hidden. The fighter out of position was promptly gutted and flicked down the hallway.

"Back!" Monica cried as the broken spear line retreated behind her. She stood with empty hands palms forward and stepped forward past Julius.

"Be gone demon!" She hollered.

She extended her hands in front of her like she was pushing on an invisible wall. She took one step forward, then another. The demon charged further down the hallway and crashed into her spiritual barrier. Monica was shoved backwards. She desperately kept praying as glimpses of teeth and claws slashed across wildly in front of her, for the moment unable to reach her.

Monica recognised Julius had not yet completed his battle prayer.

"I need more time!" She cried.

A brave fighter charged past her with his spear and managed to drive it into the demon's face. An eyeball the size of a dinner plate became visible as goo sprayed from the wound site. The demon roared and thrashed, throwing the fighter into an adjacent room.

The windows of the house from all sides smashed inwards as Scarkin swarmed into the house. The rear door broke to pieces as a Mortkin roared from behind them.

"Demons!"

Zack rushed into the room on his right and carved through the demons leaping at him. Beth moved to the left to defend against the demons pouring in from that side. The rear guard of pikemen turned their spears towards the charging Mortkin.

Again the Giestkin crashed into Monica's barrier who was driven even further backwards. Monica faltered just for a moment, and her barrier was broken. She was thrown backwards into the Mindy behind her with numerous deep cuts all over her body.

Julius stood up and shouted the culmination of his prayer:

"…Exilium!"

The whole front of the house was blown apart. The Giestkin's head was just a fraction away from Julius when it exploded in a shower of blood and bone. Julius was thrown back into his fighters.

"Monica!" Mindy cried as she desperately poured out prayers of healing on her.

Finally, between them all, they hacked down the last demon. The Giestkin's shape was revealed to be something like an enormous lizard. Chunks of its body began to bubble and dissolve throughout the remains of the front of the house.

"Good riddance," Zack spat.

Cries of the injured registered in their ears and they helped as best they could.

"Put pressure on that wound!" Mindy called.

Mindy had stabilised Monica, but she was still in a very bad state. Julius checked on a few other fighters, all but one had died of their injuries.

"We've made it through this day; our brother's sacrifice was the highest form of love. Let us remember them always. It was through their resolve that this foul creature has been slain. And now many more will live. May the Lord God almighty have mercy on their souls and lead them to everlasting life. Amen." Julius spoke softly.

"Amen."

They returned slowly back to Galvin airport.

Many would walk past the house where the battle took place on their way from Doverton to the airport. Julius' words did come true, as many more were saved. Over time, they rescued so many people from Doverton and the surrounding area that they filled every terminal in the airport. They continued to grow, and people slept in the grounded aircraft, the cars filling the surrounding car parks and tents they setup.

Duncan and Julius took turns to officiate mass every day and teach the newcomers about God. Many who they had liberated rejected the WGO and found faith. Others, despite miracles of healing and demons slain around them, remained uncommitted.

The supermarket trolley and wheelbarrow that they had brought with them all the way from Brakenside continued to yield custom weapons and food. Despite all the demand, they never remained empty for long. Zack recalled a similar miracle from his vision and offered many thankful prayers. He felt so grateful that his efforts to prepare had made such a significant contribution. They would have had little chance of arming such a large number of people without his blessed weapons trolley.

As their numbers grew, they further developed what was becoming no less than an army of holy fighters. Their fighters were grouped by skill and ability, with the newest among their ranks joining the infantry division. Each was equipped with a sanctified spear but little else. They were combat effective against a range of different demons and made up the majority of their force.

After gaining more experience in battle and of those physically strong, some opted to join the veteran division. Each soldier was fully armoured from head to foot like the knights of old. Every armour part was carefully inscribed with holy words of protection and blessed. Each knight wielded a large sledgehammer thrice blessed and sanctified. Their numbers remained few, but they were capable of crushing all but the most powerful demons with ease. The rest of their number was made up of veterans with a mix of weaponry and armour. Beth spent her time in this division, her extensive experience and skills with her knives felled many demons. Malcolm also used his martial arts knowledge to further improve the combat prowess of the veterans.

The last division of troops were those able to fight at a distance. Their numbers were also few as bows, and firearms were rare. The majority of members had training in their weapon type before the end times. As ammunition was only to be spent when the need was dire, they would support the other divisions doing the majority of the fighting. But time and again the ability to drop a foe at a distance proved invaluable. After one operation into Doverton, Logan Perkerson was found wounded and hungry and was taken back to Galvin airport. Upon his return to health, he offered his expertise and joined the ranged division. He also brought with him a small collection of firearms.

The remaining support personal included healers, Salt and Light disciples and War Priests. Mindy was one of the strongest healers, often combining her knowledge from her studies with her prayer to heal very quickly. She taught every combatant first aid and under the guidance of Duncan and Julius managed to train up another few healers.

Of all the non-combatants, a vast majority made up the prayer division. These members would pray for the safety and success of the many rescue operations. Both Julius and Duncan often reiterated how crucial prayer was in these end times. Both Zack and Monica could feel a tangible difference in their spiritual reserves in combat because of their efforts. Upon the return of a rescue operation, they would turn their prayers to aid of the healers.

Monica and Zack were the only members of the congregation other than the priests able to use combat prayers. Some veterans had shown interest and promising potential, but none had yet joined their ranks. Julius would train with Monica and Zack whenever he could. Julius and Duncan were the pinnacles of combat effectiveness at Galvin airport. Yet, much of their time was spent in the care of their growing parish. Many that needed healing would first be stabilised by the priests before the healers took over. As the drain on their spiritual energy was always high, one War Priest was always in a state of prayer or rest when the other was active. In this way, they managed to sustain support to the battle congregation regardless of the time of day.

Zack led a squad of fighters and was successful in many excursions out into Doverton and rescued many. They eventually came to be known as 'Oath Keepers' as they always made good on their promises to get things done. Primarily they were sent out to bring back survivors but would also gather food and supplies. The rarest of which were Bibles. Most of which had been burned by the WGO yet thankfully they had still somehow managed to find a small number of them. Zack tried to spend as much time as he could with his friends, but he often found he would just be coming off shift as they were going on. Regardless, he would take the time whenever he could.

Early one morning, Zack woke and was checking his gear when he heard a commotion outside the terminal where he had slept the night.

"Come quick!" Beth called as she finally spotted Zack amid all the others.

Zack grabbed his sword and ran after her.

They pressed their way through the crowds of people at the doors of the terminal and into the car park where they saw a little lady dressed in a traditional Nun's habit standing atop a car. She was semi-transparent and the cause of much confusion and wonder from the crowds around her.

"I've come to request your help," she spoke as if she was really standing there, sending a new wave of shock through the crowd, who wondered if it was an illusion of some sort.

Duncan squeezed his way through the crowd and addressed the apparition.

"My name is Duncan; I'm one of the priests here. Who are you? How can we help?"

She turned her head to look at Duncan and smiled.

"Ah yes, Thank you Father. My name is Sister Lee. I help run a small missionary school in a rural town in thousands of miles from here. I'm speaking to you through the spirit right now as I've been given a message to pass on from the angel Gabriel…"

Duncan's face revealed he was trying to determine whether this was a genuine message or some trick of the enemy.

"Please, go on."

"Some distance from here there is a centre of suffering and death. Multitudes of people are crying out in pain as we speak. They are kept alive only to be sacrificed to the most evil one. I humbly ask that you take your army and liberate them."

"We will need an army?"

"Yes, they are held in nothing short of a fortress, and it is surrounded by demons."

"Tell me Sister, would you pray with me so that I may have guidance on this issue?"

"Yes, of course," she knelt down.

Duncan and those around him followed suit, and together they prayed

Psalm 46
¹ *God is our refuge and strength,*
an ever-present help in trouble.
² *Therefore we will not fear, though the earth give way*
and the mountains fall into the heart of the sea,
³ *though its waters roar and foam*
and the mountains quake with their surging.

"Thank you Sister Lee. I, I, can picture this place you are referring to. Agreed, we must go and save these people."

"Thank you Father, I'll talk with you again as I can."

Sister Lee waved and slowly faded from view. A moment later, it was as if she was never there.

"Did you hear all that?" Beth asked

"I did," Zack replied.

Mindy squeezed through the crowd behind them

"What did I miss?"

"We're going to war."

"Oh, how many?"

"All of us by the sound of it."

Over the next few days, everyone at Galvin airport had the opportunity to volunteer for the offensive. Both Julius and Duncan were surprised by how many people came forward. Truly, they now did command an army. It was decided that Duncan would remain at Galvin airport with all those who wanted to stay behind, and Julius would lead the army to battle.

Many of their search parties already out looking for survivors and food, would continue to do so until the rest returned. The surrounding warehouses near the airport were prepared to house the incoming civilians.

Julius spent time with each division in prayer and battle planning. Each division's leader reported back with the number of troops and supplies they would have ready by the next day. It was estimated to be a two-day journey and possibly three days for the return trip as they expected many wounded.

Jacob the smith reinforced a bus they found into a mobile command centre. Julius, the war priest, stood upon the roof and looked over the battle-congregation in front of him. It was an impressive sight. Before him were several hundred people all ready to give their lives in battle to free their fellow men.

"Good morning everyone! Today we march against evil, and we will be marching home with freed prisoners. Come, they are waiting for us!"

There was a loud cheer from the army before him.

Julius signalled his troops forward, and the bus slowly drove forward.

The infantry division that made up the bulk of the force marched in the middle, with various other divisions spread around it. They marched along, taking up the full width of the road. Ahead of the column several motorbikes zipped forwards scouting the path ahead. Zack, Mindy and Beth were marching near the front, close enough to wave to each other but too far to talk. Zack knew this was going to be a dangerous mission and promised himself he would keep his friends in sight at all times.

As they marched through the outer Doverton suburbs, as they passed over a small bridge, there was a commotion. The veterans on the outside hurried them along, but Zack could see many looked shaken. Zack saw Beth look down into the river then quickly look away. She turned to Zack and Mindy momentarily and shook her head. As Zack got a little closer, he saw the entire river looked to have turned to blood. Floating in it were numerous dead fish. It smelt as bad as it looked. They continued their march.

. . .

The bus carrying Bill, Terry and many others finally came to a stop.

"Oi! We're here!" Terry whispered as he elbowed Bill.

"What? Huh? Where?" He replied as he woke from broken sleep.

Before he could reply, a soldier entered the bus and commanded all those inside.

"Everyone out! Make your way quickly inside, try to flee, and you'll be shot," he spoke as if he had given those instructions many times before, and had followed through on his threat.

"I say we keep our eyes peeled," Terry whispered.

"Shut it!" Bill replied.

They obediently trudged along behind the others, off the bus and on to a large paved area. Bill looked around to find himself on the outskirts of Doverton at an extremely large factory. The enormous three-storied warehouse in front of him held thousands of tonnes of goods, manufacturing equipment, conveyor belts and countless storage containers. He now also saw a horde of demons patrolling around the outside.

"Get moving!" The soldier snapped as he shoved Terry forwards.

"Hey!"

Ahead of them was a large crowd of people. As Bill turned, he saw other busses driving out the far gate. They were slowly approaching the first set of warehouses. Bill got the feeling that whatever was inside was not going to be comfortable accommodation and a hot meal.

"I don't like this, like at all!" Terry spat.

"Yeah, see anything?" Bill replied.

He watched his friend look around for a way to escape. Around the facility was a tall chain-link fence with razor-wire on the top. Just before they could chat about their plans, the sky rumbled again above them. A deep and powerful voice declared for all to hear.

"Turn back to me with all your heart."

It resonated inside Bill at his core; he felt like he understood more than what the simple words said. He felt like he was being called personally back to God. He opened his mouth slowly and was about to speak.

"Not me!" Terry spat at the sky.

Bill blinked and looked over to his friend.

"I'm not about to choose a side now. No-one is going to be the boss of me, other than me!"

"Move along!" the soldiers shouted, recovering from the voice from the sky. Bill's mind began to fill with questions. As it did so, his skin began to tingle; then it began to hurt. A moment later, he felt like he was getting badly sunburnt all over. He cried out in pain. The majority of the crowd in front of him did the same. Even the soldiers began yelling. Bill looked around, trying to find the source of his pain but could find none.

"I'm sorry God, I've done so many things…" a soldier behind him began earnestly calling out.

As he did so, he seemed to be in less pain that those around him. Bill tried to take it all in, but it was very difficult to concentrate when it felt like he was on fire. One of the Spectral guards ran down the line towards him with a Scarkin in tow. He slapped the soldier across the face.

"It's too late for you, fool!…." he turned to his demon. "…take him."

The solider began to raise his weapon as the demon launched toward him but he was too slow. The demon clawed into his face and chest and knocked him backwards to the ground. During the struggle, he let off a burst of shots which sprayed into the crowd dropping several people.

"Not the fodder!"

The Spectral guard drew his pistol and shot him in the chest. The Scarkin scowled back at him and snapped its jaws. It seemed angry it already lost its new toy.

"These are needed elsewhere," he responded.

The demon scampered towards the crowd gnashing its teeth. The guard extended his hand, and the demon returned to his side. Bill lay on the ground, moaning in pain as the burning sensation began to wane.

"What the hell is all this?" Terry asked once he caught his breath.

"A pain in my backside, that's what!" Bill replied.

After a few more minutes, the soldiers got everyone back into line again. Bill watched closely as the spectral guard walked past him. It looked like his skin was actually burned. It was charred and flaking. He looked to his own skin. It sure felt like it was burning, but he had no lasting injury. This demon controlling man looked like he had no sensation of pain left at all.

They shuffled up the line further until they filed into a large warehouse. Inside, the concrete floor was slick with blood and muck. A stench of rot hung in the air. The large open space they stood in was mainly occupied by storage crates, stacked around the outside of the floor. The only exception was a large statue set up in the centre of the room.

Bill's eyes seemed drawn to it; for a moment he thought it looked at him. It resembled a creature Bill had seen a glimpse of on a late friends watch. 'The King of Stars' they called it. It filled him with an unnerving mix of awe and dread. It was both beautiful and terrible to behold. As he looked on, Terry muttered something to him which he neglected to listen to.

Terry tugged as his arm.

"What?"

He turned around to see what Terry was pointing at. A tall demon walked into the room; it was carrying a staff that seemed to be part of itself and had a forked tongue. Just being close to it gave Bill a shiver down his spine. It walked carefully forward and pointed its staff at a person cowering in the front of the line. It then raised its staff and pointed it towards the statue.

Dark utterances flowed from its vile jaws in a language Bill wished he had never heard. He got the immediate impression that they were to worship the statue or suffer some unmentioned consequence. The thin older man stepped forward and looked up at the giant statue. He started to breathe heavily and shook his head.

"No, no, no!" He muttered.

The Summoner raised its staff and pointed it towards the statue. At that moment, the statue roared into life for the briefest of moments. The crowd cried out in alarm. The man had frozen in place and soiled his pants. The summoner motioned to one of the soldiers who grabbed him and shoved him down a hallway. A moment later, screams of pain rippled down the hallway. The demon pointed his staff at the next person in line. They rushed over to the statue and started paying it homage. Soon the front of the line all flooded over and did the same. But Terry, Bill and a handful of others stood their ground and did not bow down before it.

"Off to the wall with ya then," he heard one soldier say.

They were shoved down the hallway into an adjacent warehouse. As they entered, they saw the first of their group being fastened to a long wooden beam. His hands were strung up in chains above his head, then nailed into position. He screamed out in pain. There were large piles of wood on the sides of the warehouse and several containers filled with chains and nails. It seemed clear this operation had been in place for some time.

"You two..." a soldier called pointing to Terry and Bill.

"... carry this one to the wall."

They were quickly bustled over and made to carry the wooden beam on their shoulders. The man attached was bent over and stumbled along between them as best he could.

"Move!" Another soldier commanded as they made their way outside through the far exit of the warehouse. Despite being unsure of which way to go, the stained path of blood spilt by previous victims guided them. They walked past another warehouse that was filled with people sitting on the ground under close guard. Bill began to wonder if his luck was finally running out. They continued walking as their ears began to pick up a chorus of pained cries.

"What in the world?!" Terry gasped.

Bill was lost for words as they witnessed hundreds of people were strung up and hanging from wooden beams planted into the ground all the way around the back of the facility. It indeed was a wall, one of tortured human flesh. Bill could see Scarkin and Mortkin snapping and slashing at the occasionally poor soul that was not crying out loud enough. Bill froze in fear.

The WGO extended their revocation of human rights from just Christians to all who did not fully submit to their regime. Many civilians bowed under threats of torture or death and spent hours every day at conduit sites. This no longer went under the guise of T.Spec generation and was pure demon worship. Neron and the newly elected ten Kings of Earth used the global WGO resources together with their demonic allies to hold the world firmly under their control. There were pockets of resistance scattered around the globe, but few could hold out for long when they decided to throw their full force against them. Unbeknownst, to those at Galvin airport they were one of only seven remaining churches free from WGO domination. They were the last free community in the country.

. . .

Julius looked out over his force, marching through the broken remains of Doverton. This part of town was truly a wreck and had been abandoned by most long ago.

"Demons!" Malcolm called out as a handful of Scarkin charged into the troops on their right flank. With veterans in support, they managed to quickly cut them down. The training they had done over that past few months was paying off. Julius was glad to see no-one suffered any serious injuries. He knew that ahead of them they would be up against much greater numbers and they would need every single fighter.

The army marched through the suburbs until it came to the far eastern edge of Doverton. Ahead of them were large fields and farmland. Looking north, they could see their destination, a large factory with smoke billowing up into the sky. Julius had decided an assault with their entire force from the rear would prove the most effective. He was constantly in prayer, hoping he was right.

Julius heard their motorbike scouts approach the command bus. He climbed out on to the roof as they arrived back.

"What did you see?"

The young man on the bike looked very pale.

"Many demons are coming. And they, they, have a wall of people the majority of the way around."

"People?"

"Yeah, hanging there on wooden poles. Most are probably still alive."

"I see, we will make haste. Thank you."

He nodded, then sped off.

"Hurry…" Julius shouted, "…with every minute we arrive sooner, we save another life!"

The army picked up the pace and trudged forwards through the fields. As they approached, they heard cries of pain, greeting them. Soon they were close enough to see the Wailing Wall. After the initial shock, it only further strengthened their resolve. By this time demons began flooding out of the facility and were forming a battle line in front of their wall. Using binoculars, Julius saw countless Scarkin, Mortkin and Husks. He suspected that where Husks were, Summoner demons would not be far behind.

Zack could not see too far ahead between the ranks of fighters but could tell they were getting close. He caught Mindy's eye and gave her a wave. As he turned back around, he saw Beth waving at him. He could not help but think of Graham.

"This one's for you buddy," he said to himself.

They could hear the roar of the demons; it was growing in volume with each moment as more kept reinforcing their ranks. Despite the hundreds of fighters present, they were already outnumbered.

"Halt!" Julius called into a megaphone as they reached a tactical distance away from the enemy line.

"Prepare!" He called.

The army of fighters shed their bags, took a drink of holy water and checked their weapons. The battle congregation grouped into their fighting units and spread across the line with the spearmen at the front.

Zack lost sight of Mindy and Beth as the troops got into position. Across the field, the demons had begun to rush towards them. Julius watched their approach and signalled to those watching him to hold by raising his hand. Zack could hear the demons roaring and snarling. Some of the fighters in his unit began to tremble.

"Courage now, the maker of the planet you're standing on is on our side."

"Sir!" They called back.

Zack instinctively went to raise his shield but then remembered he had lost it along with his forearm. He never got used to being without it. Zack gripped his sword a little tighter. He felt like stallion eager to start the race. He wanted to unleash upon his foe. Kephas' coat clung to him, offering precious memories and protection in battle.

"Just like we practised…" Mindy directed as she and the other healers dispersed into the back of each unit. Zack caught a glimpse of her running past. She was a couple of units to his left. It would be an enormous distance in the middle of battle. But he felt better to know regardless.

Beth and Monica were in the same unit of veterans on Zack's right. "Remember to guard the flanks, and don't get separated. Listen out for my commands," Monica called.

Beth ran her thumb over Graham's name etched into the handle of her long knife.

"This is for you darling," she said quietly to herself.

Malcolm and his fighters were positioned on Zack's left. A large number of the fighters under his command had seen little combat. As Malcolm walked past, he took one of the soldier's spears.

"Remember, rapid thrusts…" he demonstrated, high, mid and low stabs before handing it back. "…Keep your distance and watch out for each other."

"But…" the soldier stammered.

Malcolm returned a confident gaze and quoted scripture.

2 Thessalonians 3
[3] But the Lord is faithful, and he will strengthen you and protect you from the evil one.

"Ready!" Julius called.

All units awaited the command as the demons approached closer. The spearmen lifted their weapons. Zack was immersed in a forest of blades.

"Charge!" Julius roared.

A loud war cry rung out from the fighters as they launched forwards. They picked up pace quickly and were soon sprinting as one towards the demons. The hundreds of spears lowered to a horizontal position just as the two lines crashed into each other. The front ranks of Scarkin were obliterated as the fighters ran them through. Some managed to nimbly manoeuvre through and began slashing into the infantry. Continuing to charge forwards they drove into the Mortkin and husks. Bones were shattered, and blood sprayed in all directions.

A huge number of Mortkin were brought down, but they absorbed all the fighters momentum, and they drove no deeper. As more demons clawed their way through their fallen kin, many were cut down.

Julius interrupted his chanting of battle prayer to yell another command.

"Now!"

In unison, all the spearmen dropped to the ground as the ranged division opened fire with every weapon they had. Blessed bullets and arrows flew over the cowering spearmen deep into the demon lines blasting them to pieces. The sound of gunfire was deafening. After a short moment, it stopped, and the spearmen jumped back to their feet. As they scrambled to ready themselves, the veterans charged forward into the remaining ranks of demons. Zack, Beth and Monica were finally let loose upon their hated foe. Zack weaved past his men, amid the demon bodies and hacked away at the evil creatures. The spearmen withdrew and formed a new, united line of spears behind the veterans.

"Forwards!" Julius directed.

They began marching forwards, stabbing any demon that came into range. The veterans fought for a few minutes before dropping back behind the line of spears for healing. The battle was starting to sway in their favour despite being vastly outnumbered. Julius' war chant echoed over the field, invigorating his troops. It was as if there was a divine wind behind each of their movements; each strike was faster and landed with more impact.

Mindy was in continual prayer. She quickened the pace of her words to try and not lose her place. Mindy reminded herself of Kephas' advice to focus on words and to re-focus at start of each prayer. She tried to visualise the wounds healing in her mind as she did so. After all the practice she had lately, she could effectively heal despite the battle raging around her.

A single gunshot rang out amidst the din of battle and Julius was thrown backwards off the top of the command bus. He was dead before he landed in the mud. A moment later, another shot knocked a healer towards the rear of the line over. Logan recognised the sound of the rifle. He knew who was firing upon them. He dropped back from his unit and made his way over to the command bus. He climbed the ladder at the rear and lay down on the roof as another shot bowled over another healer. He looked down the scope of his rifle towards the factory fortress ahead of them.

"Where are you?" He said as he checked various advantageous positions on the roof. Sure enough, on the far right-hand side, he saw a familiar rifle barrel and Badger readying another shot. Logan adjusted his scope. As best he could, Logan calmed himself, exhaled slowly and squeezed the trigger. The shot flew over the battle raging in front of him and smashed into the window right next to Badger's head. The glass shattered and threw off Badger's shot. He quickly rolled behind the crest of the roof and out of sight.

"Piss it!" Logan spat as he readied another round. He surveyed the roof, waiting for Badger to re-appear.

Bursts of demonic black flame erupted through the lines as a pair of summoners strode into the fight felling all who came close. The spearmen lines disintegrated as veterans rushed over to try and hold the demons back.

"Beth with me!" Monica called.

Beth finished stabbing the demon in front of her and followed. Weaving through the fighting, they soon appeared where the Summoners were.

"Follow me!" Monica called, as she threw forth a spiritual barrier between her and the demons.

Beth nodded and ran up behind her. Several spearmen joined her as they made their way closer to the dark flames. They charged in as far as they could before their flames slammed into Monica's angelic shield. She came to a halt. With all her spiritual strength, she only managed to slowly move forward one step at a time.

"With me!" Beth called as she and several spearmen bolted out the left side.

Beth threw one of her knives, and it flew across and punctured into one of the Summoner's shoulder.

"Die filth!" She hollered as she charged forward.

She managed to dive into a roll, narrowly dodging deadly flames as she closed the distance. Upon reaching her foe, she slashed furiously with her knife. She then pulled her other knife out of the demon's shoulder before decapitating him with it. The creature dropped into the mud as the other Summoner turned its fire upon them. Beth was incinerated before she could strike. The spearmen behind her also were caught in the blaze.

"No!" Monica cried.

"Hold! Hold!" Malcolm shouted above the din of battle.

Logan still had not found Badger again in his scope and moved his gaze to the battlefield. He aimed and fired. The blessed round smashed into the last Summoners face, and it fell backwards. A moment later, several spears punctured its body with numerous holes to be sure it was not going to get up.

Gunfire erupted from the fortress as the WGO soldiers opened fire. Many of the front ranks of spearmen fell. Logan aimed and fired shot after shot until there were no more enemy soldiers left standing. Upon felling the last one, he resumed his search for Badger.

Another shot rang out as Logan himself fired. One shot smashed into Badger's rifle, rendering it useless; the other ended Logan's life. Badger waved a small salute before climbing down from the roof.

The demons continued fighting with until the very last of them were cut down. The fighters from Galvin airport were finally victorious. The surviving healers attended to the wounded as best they could.

"Mindy?!" Zack called.

"Here!" Came the reply.

Zack made his way over to her.

"I'm so glad to see you Mindy."

She smiled.

"You too, where's Beth?"

Zack looked around but could not see her anywhere.

"I'll find her, be back shortly."

Mindy continued healing the wounded at her side.

After a brief search, Zack found the charred remains of Beth's knife. He picked it up out of the mud and held it in his hands. Part of Graham's name was still visible on the handle. He held it tightly. He knew Beth would not have let this go. Before he knew what to say, Mindy ran over to him.

"What's that you're..." she recognised the knife and understood what it meant.

"...Beth's gone!" She blurted as Zack held her. Grief washed over them.

"Forwards! Free all those we can. More enemies will be on their way here," Monica shouted.

The battle congregation pushed forwards into the fortress and freed hundreds of prisoners. They pulled down all those hanging on the Wailing Wall who were still alive and healed all they could. Malcolm found Rex and managed to return him to his wheelchair. He was in a very poor condition but still somehow able to push himself along. Once free of their chains, Bill and Terry made for the gate on the opposite side that the congregation came from.

"Are you sure you don't want to go back with them Bill?" Terry asked.

"Nah, not my cup of tea. Let's head back to town. Our usual spot."

"Yeah, alright."

They only just made it out onto the road when they spotted a horde of demons approaching from the far side. They looked at each other and turned on their heels and ran back towards the fortress, through the warehouses and tried to catch up to the rear guard of fighters. The walking convoy of civilians and fighters were on their way back to Galvin airport. Zack was holding Mindy as she slowly walked along, emotionally, physically and spiritually drained to her limit. Zack recognised Bill as he ran past him. He recalled the fearful expression on Bill's face from his vision. He turned and looked behind them.

"Demons are coming!" He warned.

They tried to pick up the pace, but there were still many weak and wounded among them. Zack looked to Mindy and fumbled through what he wanted to say.

"I love you Mindy. I, I'll keep you safe," and with that ran back to the rearguard.

Monica arrived a moment later as they started to see more demons flow out onto the field behind them.

"They'll catch up to us," Zack stated.

"We have to stop them here," Monica replied.

"Agreed," Malcolm added.

Monica directed some of the troops to continue guiding the civilians back to the airport. Those with firearms stepped forward and unleashed a barrage of shots. The front ranks of the advancing demon horde were blown backwards. As their clips ran dry Monica commanded them again.

"Move out!"

They returned to the convoy with the little ammunition they had left. Only Zack, Malcolm, Monica and a handful of veterans remained at the rear. They watched in horror as the horde of demons flowing out onto the field still had not ceased. Their number was much greater than what they had only recently defeated.

"What will we do?" One fighter asked.

"We'll hold them back as long as possible, perhaps a little longer," Monica replied.

"Spread out, let none pass us," Zack directed. His heart was thumping in his chest.

Their foes were still a short distance away when the ground beneath their feet began to rumble. It increased in severity until all of the fighters struggled to remain standing. The sky boiled with rolling thunderclouds. Even the demons began to topple over.

"The end has come."

Zack fell to the ground as the earth split next to him. A deep fissure cracked open and quickly spread out in a line that went all the way to the horizon. Thunder boomed overhead, and hail began to fall all around them. Not one of them was able to remain standing as the earth shook violently. Zack felt truly insignificant. He saw the buildings in Doverton collapse one after another. Large clouds of dust and debris were thrown up into the air. The quake continued until all, but a tiny fraction of humanity's cities were in ruins.

Entire mountains dropped back into the earth and valleys surged to the surface. Zack could feel himself being thrown around on the ground. At one point he was airborne before he fell down again. Eventually, the ground began to settle.

Amid the screams, Malcolm called out:

"We're saved!" He pointed to the demons on the far side of the newly formed void in the ground, separating them from the fighters and the retreating civilians.

"Let's go!" Monica called and scrambled back to her feet to catch up with the back of the convoy.

Hail pelted down around them, causing bruising and hampering their escape. Thankfully, it also slowed the demons' attempts at crossing the chasm of dirt in front of them.

The rearguard reached the thankful tail of the retreating people and made as quick progress as possible back to Galvin airport. Zack found Mindy amid the wounded healing them with the last of her energy.

"I found you!"

She smiled.

"Stick with me Zack"

"I will."

Many times they needed to adjust their route to avoid newly created fissures in the ground or to avoid collapsed buildings. Eventually, they made it back within sight of the airport. Zack rubbed his eyes to confirm what he was seeing. A large archangel was hovering over the airport with its arms outstretched. It was multiple times larger than the one he saw in his vision. It looked immensely powerful and ready for battle. All of the terminal buildings and warehouses beneath stood intact. Even the hail seemed to be rolling off some invisible protective dome.

"Thank the Lord…" Mindy said with a large exhale. "…I don't know what more I could endure today,"

"I've got you," Zack said and gave her a quick kiss on the forehead.

The hail began to fall heavier as the last of the convoy made it inside the warehouse on the edge of the airport grounds. The hail outside the protection of the archangel pummelled everything. Inside the warehouse, they listened as those that had stayed at the airport rushed to attend to those newly arrived. A small boy brought Mindy and Zack some water to drink. They sat together and caught their breath.

"Mindy! I need your help!" Sandra called out over the crowd.

Mindy flashed a look to Zack then ran over.

"Coming!"

Zack drank the last of his water. As he looked around and recognised

Bill from his vision and walked over. He could see him slipping some unattended water bottles into his bag.

"I'm glad you made it out."

"Huh? Yeah, it was pretty bad in there," Bill replied quickly.

"Are you going to stick around?" He asked, pointing to Bill's bag.

Bill quickly stood between Zack and his bag.

"That's mine! Find your own," he spat back.

Zack raised his hands.

"Hey, chill out, it's fine. You're welcome to it."

"Look, this place is probably great. But it's not for me."

"Oh? Why's that?"

"I've seen enough church people in my day thanks. The food is free sure, but then I get bombarded with endless lectures and looked down on by you hob-nobbers. That's not really free then, is it? No thanks."

"It's been eight years, hasn't it Bill?"

Bill stopped for a moment,

"I don't recall telling you my name?"

Zack smiled.

"Oh, yes sorry. I remember you from before. Eight years on the street, right?"

"How could you possibly know that?" Bill put his bag down, his face twisted with confusion.

"Well, the short version is I received a vision from God, and in it, I met you. I…"

"What's my age? No, what's favourite colour?" Bill spat.

"I don't know."

"Bah, this is just some trick."

"Look Bill; you only hung around just long enough to give me directions before you headed off with the food I gave you. We didn't chat for hours or anything."

"Well that does sound something I'd do," Bill said, smiling.

"I'm not asking you be a priest or anything. Just hang around for a while and listen."

"Nope, I don't know what you think you know, but I'm not some perfect guy who's never made a mistake. I don't belong in a church."

Zack quoted a bible verse he had successfully memorised:

Mark 2
[17] *On hearing this, Jesus said to them, "It is not the healthy who need a doctor, but the sick. I have not come to call the righteous, but sinners."*

"This Jesus guy makes everything easy, does he?"

Zack stepped a bit closer to Bill and looked him in the eyes.

"It has not been easy..." Zack said slowly. The last image of Graham's face hung in his mind. "...I didn't say it would be."

Bill could see the pain welled up in Zack.

"I'm not cut out for war pal."

"Oh, you've always been in a war, only now you can see your enemy."

Bill thought for a moment.

"Hmm."

"What?"

"You don't seem to be like the others I've met, maybe I will hang around for a bit."

Bill grabbed his bag and walked over to Terry, who was waving to him.

"Thanks for listening Bill,"

"I just said maybe," Bill called back as he let a cheeky smile escape.

The hail decreased in size and pace until eventually, it stopped altogether. Monica walked outside to see the hundreds of cars in the outer car park had been battered by the hail. She stood in ankle-deep grimy water as the hail had begun to melt. She surveyed the devastation outside the archangel's protection and said a quiet prayer of thanks. She felt like she could sleep for a week. As she turned around, something caught her eye in the distance.

A giant demon was striding through the remains of Doverton towards them. It was the size of a ten-story building and had a large pair of ragged wings. It looked like at one point it had been beautiful, but had been corrupted and since decayed. The archangel from above the airport flew down and stood next to her throwing up a large dust cloud in the process. It turned and spoke with an ancient deep voice.

"Prepare to fight," it boomed.

CHAPTER 12:

AMEN

Duncan rushed outside and stood next to the archangel.

"Thank you for your protection holy one," he called up to it.

It turned and nodded.

"Is that a Devilkin approaching us?"

"Yes, I will keep it back, your kind will need to deal with the rest of them," the archangel replied.

"We will," Duncan took Monica and retreated to the warehouse.

"Let's get everyone back inside the terminal," Monica suggested.

"Yes, good idea. We can try and hold them off at the entrances," Duncan added.

As they moved away, the archangel began to scoop up empty cars with its hands and crush them into giant balls of twisted steel. It then placed them at its feet. The sound was terrifying to all those in the warehouse and aided in a prompt evacuation back to the terminal.

Soon, the terminal was jammed full of people. Monica and Duncan ordered the remaining fighters to congregate at the entrances. Using plenty of volunteers, they managed to push some cars up onto their sides to create kill-funnels at the gates. The few firearms they had left were set up in an elevated position inside the terminal. Behind the ranks of fighters, prayer teams stood with linked arms. The veterans remained just outside the terminal entrances hoping to disrupt the enemy lines. A few healers kept close to the entrances where the fighting would be thickest.

Duncan stood in the car park between the two main entrances. Monica and Mindy stood on his left and Zack and Malcolm on his right.

They began to hear a rumble as a gigantic eruption of dirt and molten rock shot forth high into the air near the outer warehouses. Another Devilkin demon clawed its way up through the rubble. Now they had one giant demon approaching directly ahead of them and another to their left. The archangel unsheathed a mighty blade that looked like it had been forged from lightning into solid form. In kind, the Devilkin drew their darkened blades. In the distance behind the first Devilkin, another giant demon emerged from a large fissure in the earth. The archangel stepped backwards and turned to nod at Duncan. He understood the situation had just become substantially worse. The archangel then knelt on one knee and began praying.

"We won't be able to keep all these people safe like this," Malcolm said as concerned look spread across his face.

"Should we move the people to the underground car park?" Mindy suggested.

Duncan, Monica and Zack all looked at each other. Duncan responded first.

"Yes, good idea, we should expect casualties."

"I'll get it done."

"Mindy, ask everyone to pray for us."

"I will."

Mindy leaned over and gave Zack a quick kiss on the cheek.

"See you on the other side."

Zack nodded, "stay safe."

The demon horde came into view on the far end of the street leading to the airport. Zack could see a Magnukin towering above the rest. The Devilkin opened their gigantic mouths and roared the foulest of sounds. It was pure terror for everyone that heard it. Many fighters lost their courage and dropped their weapons.

Just before many broke away fleeing, the archangel stood up and sang a Heavenly hymn at deafening volume. Its timeless lungs burst out pure sound from before the creation of the world. Despite the magnitude of its volume, its voice seemed to heal human ears, not damage them.

The first dozen ranks in the demon army burst into muck as the sound rippled over them. At this sound, the three Devilkin charged forwards. As soon as they began to move, the archangel scooped up the spheres of twisted metal and hurled them in the direction of the Devilkin in the centre. With its left arm extended, the archangel spoke heavenly words which ignited the metal with holy flame. The Devilkin managed to evade the first two but was struck in the chest by the last one. It was knocked backwards crushing some smaller demons. The archangel charged forwards and took to the air with its enormous golden wings.

As it leapt upwards, the Devilkin on its left ripped a nearby building in two and hurled it. Debris flew through the air and slammed into the archangel, and he tumbled to the ground. The Devilkin on its right drew its sword and prepared to strike. At the last moment, the archangel brought his sword across to fend off the incoming attack. The Devilkin surged forward with a flurry of blows; the archangel found itself being pushed back towards the other huge demons.

The fighters looked up in awe of these giant creatures fighting. The surrounding buildings were flattened as if they were empty cardboard boxes. The first ranks of the demon army came into view as they emerged through the clouds of dust.

Zack drew upon the last of his vision and addressed the wavering fighters around him.

"Fear not this evil that only has the power to kill these mortal shells. We have survived to the very end of this Earth. Use every last reserve of your mind, body and soul. Channel that strength to make yourself a holy weapon of God. You are a sword for the Lord! Who are you?"

"A sword for the Lord," Monica, Malcolm and Duncan called back.

"Who are you?"

"A sword for the Lord," the fighters yelled.

"WHO ARE YOU?"

"A SWORD FOR THE LORD!" They roared.

They charged forwards just as those taking refuge in the underground car park began prayer to aid them in battle. Zack felt his body surge with holy energy. Steam began to rise from the fighters bodies. Each fighter drew strength from those they were protecting. The veterans accelerated into the tide of demon ranks as Duncan sang the Rite of War over them.

They punctured through the front ranks of demons with ease. The strikes from each veteran made contact with magnitudes more power than humanly possible. Demons were launched into the air and bowled over their kin behind them. They sent all in their path falling to the ground in shreds. The veterans destroyed the demons at a rate previously thought impossible.

Malcolm ran forwards with a large hammer in each hand. The demons swarming him were battered to mush as he swung his weapons with holy zeal. Despite being immersed in teeth and claws, they were no match for him.

"DIE!" He roared.

With the horde's enormous numbers, they continued to push forward, coming close to the left-most entrance. Gunfire from the terminal blasted through the first pack of demons who made it through the gate.

"Left!" Duncan hollered as the veterans darted towards the left entrance.

They arrived just as the demons began pouring into the doorway to be met with an array of spears. The veterans broke the momentum of the demon line, and the spearmen managed to kill those at the doors.

"Need help!" Malcolm cried out over the fighting.

More gunfire rang out from the centre and far-right entrances.

"I'll go," Zack called to Duncan who nodded in response.

It was becoming clear that keeping all the veterans as a combined unit would not allow them to keep pressure from all three entrances at once.

"Monica, I've got this, please help Zack."

"On it!" She replied as she finished rending a Mortkin in two.

Zack, Monica and their units pushed back towards the central entrance cutting through Husks, Mortkin and Scarkin in the process.

"I've got more coming!" Malcolm called.

"I'll take right!" Zack called as he continued fighting.

Monica nodded in acknowledgement.

The enormous archangel was thrown down to the ground and smashed the warehouse beneath it where the humans had previously taken refuge. One of the Devilkin stomped forward and ripped the terminal building roof off. Zack saw a large foot stomp down not far from him. The demon threw the roof away and scooped up a handful of screaming people, throwing them over his shoulder to their deaths.

Before it could grab more, Zack drove his blade deep into the side of its ankle before ripping it outwards. The Devilkin above him was tackled to the ground by the archangel, and the two rolled over biting and slashing as they went. The Devilkin slashed its dark blade across the archangel's right wing, and it now hung limp. The archangel struck back cutting through both its legs. The Devilkin howled and fell backwards, crushing some parked passenger planes beneath it. As it landed, the archangel thrust the killing blow into the giant demon's head.

With his attention on the battling giants and some of his fighters crushed, smaller demons swarmed the remainder of Zack's unit.

"Zack!" Malcolm cried as he darted over. He was a whirlwind of fury, as he dropped demons all around him. This bought Zack precious seconds, but he was barely holding them back.

Bullets cut through the air around him as the demons charging him fell to the pavement. Malcolm was struggling to hold them back.

The ground shook as the archangel and devilkin scrapped and fought. Large chunks of concrete and steel rained down all around them. Many of the demons and a few of the veteran fighters were crushed. Malcolm narrowly dodged a steel girder crashing to the ground right next to him.

"Fall back!" Zack called.

He strengthened himself by reciting scripture.

Psalm 118
[11] They surrounded me on every side,
but in the name of the LORD I cut them down.
[12] They swarmed around me like bees,
but they were consumed as quickly as burning thorns;
in the name of the LORD I cut them down.
[13] I was pushed back and about to fall,
but the LORD helped me.
[14] The LORD is my strength and my defense;
he has become my salvation.

As he finished his prayer, the drone of hundreds of plaguebees wings started to fill air behind the noise of battle. Before the survivors could react, they dived down upon them. Despite their stingers being ineffective, their teeth and claws assaulting from all directions made it difficult to fight. Many fighters were overwhelmed and cut down by the larger demons.

Malcolm and the remnant of his veterans followed Zack through the doorway. Inside the terminal, they rushed back to their last line of defence. A barricade of wooden crates was set up in the hallway, which led to the underground car park.

"Keep them out for as long as you can," Zack directed, as he looked to the few fighters he had left.

"Are you OK?" Malcolm asked.

Zack nodded.

"You?"

"So far."

A moment later, Monica, Duncan and their veterans retreated, joining Zack and Malcolm. As they did so, the whole front of the terminal was crushed flat. The concrete supports snapped like twigs as the giants fought outside. Some of the fighters did not make it through in time and were crushed. A wave of dust and debris flooded down the hallway. They began to choke and splutter as they watched to see if the demons would be able to make it inside.

"Are you…" Duncan began.

The terminal entrance again suffered a heavy blow from outside, this time launching a storm of concrete rubble and shrapnel towards the fighters. Monica's spiritual barrier appeared just in time to stop the majority of the lethal-sized projectiles. As the dust settled, a roar of demons could be heard as they charged in through the breach. A flood of plaguebees burst in with them, their wings pounding the dust-laden air. The fighters fought back with all their strength, desperate to stop them breaching the last barricade. Initially, the fight was going in their favour, but as more and more demons flooded in, more veterans were dragged down, making it increasingly harder for those remaining.

"Hang in there!" Duncan called.

Rex Otterman sat in his wheelchair near the wooden crates, unable to descend the stairs to the tenuous safety of the car park below. He was ready to accept his approaching doom. But when one of the crates in the barricade was smashed open by the debris, something caught his eye. It was filled with books, and splayed out in the middle of the pile there was one with a cover he recognised.

It was his family bible that had been in his family for generations. It somehow managed to travel half the length of the country. They had both ended up just where they were needed. Something inside him clicked; he felt like for once everything in his life started to make some sense. He knew inside him that this was not just a coincidence. He felt the love of his creator surge through him.

Rex stood up from his wheelchair, walked over and picked it up. Rex realised he was standing unaided, and for a moment, his legs wavered. He flicked open the inside cover and saw his family name written there. He was sure. Faith saturated through his body and renewed his bones. He strode forth through the fighters towards the demons with Bible in hand.

Rex proclaimed holy words with deep conviction. He felt like he was his true self for once. Rex held the bible in one hand and extended his other towards his enemy. The plaguebees detonated in a chain reaction emanating from his position. The larger demons were shaken and started to move towards Rex as if they were wading through deep water. Rex took a deep breath and shouted the divine truth all the louder. The demons were thrown backwards by an invisible force, and they burst into filth all around him. Their guts spattered all over the ruined terminal. The fighters around him were finally able to catch their breath.

After he had walked to the breach in the rubble, he turned back to the fighters. Rex spoke holy words of healing, and each one felt strength return to their weary bodies. A moment later more demons charged into the breach behind Rex and he turned and banished them too.

"Faith unbound!" Duncan said quietly in wonder.

For several precious minutes, Rex kept the demons back until at last he weakened and collapsed to the ground. Malcolm ran forward and dragged Rex back as quickly as he could. Demons began scuttling in through a fresh breach in the rubble. The fighters darted over and hacked up the Scarkin squirming inside. The rubble began to jostle and crumble again, and they dodged backwards. The large claws of a Magnukin flashed in and out, and soon there was enough room for more demons to quickly pour in. The fighters reformed the final line at the barricade.

"Ready…" Monica began.

A pair of enormous talons punctured straight through the roof above them sending glass and wood splinters flying. Steel buckled and groaned as one of the Devilkin tore the roof off like a tin can. The gigantic demon reached its claws inside but was bowled over by the archangel somehow still fighting outside. Zack's ears rung as the buildings around them crumbled. Zack's eyes were drawn upwards to the sky above him. It was beginning to get lighter and brighter.

"Fight, FIGHT!" Monica cried as the demons launched themselves upon them.

Zack slashed wildly at the Mortkin charging towards him. It knocked him backwards and brought its claws down to end him. Zack brought his sword up and cleaved the claws from its arms. He kicked the demon back and stabbed it in the chest.

Light poured down from the sky. It was unlike any light that Zack had ever witnessed. It was somehow deeper and more pure. It flooded down upon everything. No shadows remained. The demons began to burn and flailed around in agony. The remaining fighters seized the advantage and quickly cut down the demons in the terminal.

As he watched, the sun quickly ascended back into the sky, it then set and rose again, each time quicker and quicker until it was a blurred line reaching across the sky. The bright line began to grow wider and start to separate. A series of rainbows flowed outwards to cover the entire sky. They contained colours Zack had never seen before and seemed to be constantly moving. Inside, something even brighter shone forth. The universe itself seemed to split open. Every remaining soul on earth was looking upwards and could see the same. From this pinnacle of light thousands of archangels descended from the heavens. It was glorious to behold.

Everyone around Zack screamed with joy and delight. Many dropped their weapons and hugged each other. Zack scrambled out through the shattered building so he could see more of the sky. He was filled with awe.

"Thank you! Thank you!" He called upwards.

"We made it!" Monica cried happily.

Duncan knelt down, stared up at the sky and made the sign of the cross.

Malcolm collapsed from relief and exhaustion.

"Zack!"
He turned to see Mindy running toward him.
"Mindy! We made it."
"Zack!"
They hugged each other passionately.
"I'm yours," she said smiling
"I'm yours too," he replied.

Behind the archangels, another smaller type of angel descended. They were singing; their sound was completely wondrous. It filled everyone with a sense of peace.

"Glory, Glory, Glory, for He who comes in the name of the Lord."

All those faithful on earth joined in with the angels and sung.

"Hosanna, Hosanna, Hosanna in the highest heavens!"

Behind the angels, a man was riding upon a white creature that resembled a large horse. It had two pairs of large white wings and was radiantly bright. Its mane and tail were long and flowing. It floated effortlessly down to Earth. The man riding the horse was Jesus Christ, the Son of God. Zack instantly recognised him from somewhere deep in his soul. Every living human fell prostrate in awe of him. He shone brighter than his steed. Zack felt a deep love erupt inside of him, and he knew that he was cared for beyond his understanding. Jesus opened his mouth, and pure energy burst forth. It had the power to create the Earth and all the stars and to end them. He spoke to the demons:

"Be gone!"

It was as if on the microscopic level he had created uncountable blades that cut through the demons. Zack saw the demons vaporise to ash and drift away in the wind. All across the world, the demonic armies were utterly destroyed.

As the angels descended, the evil King of Stars gathered his army of corrupted humans that had pledged themselves to him. He fortified himself in his throne room. He was surrounded by slaves and sacrifices. Neron began quaking in his boots despite being at his side. As the angels approached, his soldiers opened fire and fought with everything they had at their disposal. The angels destroyed New Babylon utterly from all sides as they surrounded the fortress at its centre.

As Jesus descended, the King of Stars roared profane words in defiance and slaughtered his human guards in a rage until just he and Neron remained in the throne room.

"Away with you!" Jesus commanded.

The holy words of Jesus flayed the corrupted human army to the bone. The angelic army charged the fortress. The mighty Archangel Michael descended from the heavens wielding chains of pure light and the key to the Abyss. He had three pairs of wings and a long flowing white beard down to his waist. He looked truly ancient, but unlike those elderly on Earth, he was in peak form. Michael was built for battle. He swooped down, ripped the roof off the fortress and bound the evil pair. Michael touched the key upon the ground and reality began to tear open. Screams of pain flooded out from it, and an echo of them could be heard the world over.

The King of Stars struggled against his bonds as he proclaimed a torrent of foul lies. The chains tightened around them by their own accord making the smallest of movements impossible. He was dragged into the Abyss as burning sulfur splashed over him. Neron began howling in pain the closer he got to the intense heat of the rift, until he too was drawn in. The dark hole in reality quickly closed behind them and disappeared as if it was never there.

Jesus reached the ground of Jerusalem and dismounted his angelic horse. The blood from the fallen humans and the slain demons mixed with the melted giant hail. It splashed upon his brilliant white cloak. Countless white doves descended from high in the air and feasted upon the flesh of the corrupt.

"Peace, my peace I give to you."

Jesus' words resonated deeply within every living human. An incomprehensible love flooded over each person. All fear was forced out, never to return. There was a clattering sound that echoed around the Galvin terminal as all the fighters dropped their weapons. Each one knew at their very core; there would be no further need for fighting.

Jesus raised his arms and looked skywards.

"Follow me,"

All of the remaining humans on Earth were slowly drawn upwards into the air. An eruption of concrete and debris burst out from the behind Zack as all the people hiding in the underground car park began their ascent. To everyone's amazement, none of them were injured in the process.

"Zack!" Mindy called smiling as she began to float off the rubble from where she was standing.

Zack managed to grab her hand just as he too left the ground. Despite the situation, everyone knew there was no reason to be scared.

Soon, everyone at Galvin airport had risen off the ground to the height of a tall tree. Zack looked across to all those remaining. Inside himself, he felt a sense of achievement that he had contributed to keeping so many people alive. He was filled with gratitude that he had received the help of those who floated nearby and their angelic allies.

All around the world, the remaining humans began to accelerate skywards. Each person began to glow with an inner radiance. Zack looked down at the broken world they left behind. The battered remains of Doverton lay sprawled out beneath him. No part of it had remained untouched from the dire times they had all been through. Off in the distance, he saw smoke rising from Brakenside. He began to feel nostalgia with all the memories he had made there.

As Zack ascended, his home town gradually receded from view until he could no longer make it out at all. He took a deep breath and looked over to Mindy. She was beaming as she soaked in her surroundings. All the survivors of Galvin airport rose alongside them. On the horizon, Zack saw other people flying upwards like shooting stars. They accelerated further as they broke free of the Earth's atmosphere. Zack and Mindy lost their grip of each other's hand in the process.

Zack saw countless stars fly past him in a blur as he continued to speed up. His mind could not comprehend his surroundings as he began entry into the spiritual realm. At his very core, he began to feel a new sensation. At first, he thought it was pain, but as it grew in intensity, it was followed by relief. It was as if he had a splinter in his heart his entire life, and it was finally being pulled out. He cried out as everything sinful was drawn out of him.

Zack felt himself change and refine as he became the perfect version of himself. Each breath he drew felt better than the last. He began to feel more and more awake. A stupor that had always clogged his mind was slowly lifting. His missing arm was restored and his many scars were now gone. His body began to feel less restricted as he was no longer weighed down. He felt a surge of limitless energy from deep inside him.

In a blinding flash of light, Zack had arrived. He could not decide if it took years or mere moments to reach his destination. He now stood upon a small hill in the middle of a meadow. The grass surrounding him was a lush green and swayed in a gentle breeze. A warmth saturated him from above. It was as if the light itself was sustaining him.

"Alleluia!" Zack declared in a loud voice.

He looked up into the endless light of God.

"Glory to you, Lord God almighty!"

His soul was filled with happiness to a level he had not thought possible. He felt even decades of torture on Earth would be a price he would happily pay to experience just a second of what he was now enjoying. Boundless joy permeated every fibre of his being. He knew he was loved on a level previously incomprehensible. Zack felt perfectly at peace.

He looked around to see endless fields stretch as far as he could see, which was now magnitudes further than he could see on Earth. A large range of mountains extended beyond. He slowly turned around to see a figure walking over to him. He was robed in white garments and had white feathered wings. He smiled as he approached.

"Zachary, welcome home."

His voice was deep and pure and seemed to convey so much more than just the words he used.

Zack smiled.

"Are, are you my guardian angel?"

"I am."

"I feel like I remember you from a dream when I was a little kid."

The angel nodded.

"I have been protecting you since before you took your very first steps."

Zack's mind quickly retrieved a memory from when he was four years old. He was at the local park with his family. They had just finished lunch and Zack was chasing around a ball. He kicked it, and it flew past the playground and on to the road. Zack ran out onto the road to retrieve it. At the same time, a car was driving past at pace. Just before stepping in front of the car, Zack came to a halt. He remembered at the time his parents had thought their cries had reached him. But he only stopped because he felt like he ran into an invisible wall. But now that he thought about it more clearly, it was an invisible pair of arms. His father appeared at his side moments later. They discussed road safety, and they carried on their day, thankful for the narrow escape. But only now did Zack realise who had helped him.

"That day with my orange ball, that was you?"

"Yes. Probably a few other times too," he said, smiling.

Zack wondered how many close calls with death he had since the end times began.

"Thank you, thank you so much."

The angel nodded.

"Zack, it's good to see you."

Zack walked forward, and they hugged each other like long lost friends.

"Zack!" A familiar voice called out. Zack recognised it immediately and quickly turned around.

"Graham!"

He saw Beth and Mindy with him running over. They wore radiant white garments and no longer showed any scars or injuries.

"Zacky!"

They collided in a big group hug laughing.

"Did we interrupt the grand tour?" Graham said smiling.

Zack looked back at the angel who smiled in reply.

"We have all the time in the world. Well, more actually."

Zack could not help but burst out in a big cheesy grin.

"Come on, let's go!" Graham called.

"Where to?"

"Anywhere!"

Zack tapped into the heavenly knowledge inside him. He felt like he knew exactly what they meant. But was that really possible? He could not wait to find out.

"You choose Mindy."

She smiled in reply.

"Follow me," she offered as she held out her hand.

In the next moment, the four were standing upon an enormous chunk of rock drifting in outer space. It was surrounded in countless others like it and slowly orbited a dark-grey lifeless planet far below them. Zack was remembered learning about the rings of Saturn, but never thought he would be amidst anything like them. Despite the lack of atmosphere, the four arrived laughing.

"Woah!" Zack blurted out in awe.

"It's beautiful right?" Mindy asked.

"Great choice Mindy," Beth agreed.

"Oh, this isn't even from our old solar system, is it?" Graham asked.

"No, just somewhere I found,"

"Amazing!" Zack added as they stared off into the endless array of stars surrounding them. It was more beautiful than anything Zack could think to compare to from his time on Earth.

"But ya know, I think we could improve things. Come on," Beth decided.

Beth thought about standing upon the planet's surface beneath them and instantly she was there. Mindy moved down next to her in the blink of an eye.

"Wait Zack; I gotta show you something," Graham said.

"Yeah?"

"Let's get down there the old fashioned way." Graham said with a big grin on his face.

"Yeah, that sounds fun." Zack agreed.

They both jumped off the surface of the rock towards the planet beneath them. At first, Zack felt like he was just drifting aimlessly in space, but as they got closer, they began to accelerate.

"Waa-hoo!" Graham called as hurtled down through the atmosphere towards the surface.

Zack followed suit, and they twirled and weaved like professional skydivers. They continued to fall faster and faster. They began to glow, and soon they were both engulfed in flames like a pair of falling meteors.

"This is so cool!" Zack shouted in delight.

Graham just laughed in reply.

Zack could feel the warmth of the flames, but with his real body there was no pain of any sort. Graham swooped closer, and they slammed an extremely satisfying high five.

"I know right!?"

They continued their impressive descent until they could start to make out the features of the terrain below. The whole planet looked to be a great desert filled with dust in all directions.

"Let's head for those mountains!" Graham called.

"Should we just spirit-travel to the surface?" Zack asked.

"Oh, I've got something much more impressive in mind." Graham said as he tucked in his arms to speed up even more.

Zack followed him, and they sped down through the lower levels of the bleak atmosphere. In the last moment, Graham spread his arms out as they crashed into the surface. A monumental explosion of dust and giant rocks burst out in all directions. Zack found himself laying in a crater of his own making. He could hear Graham laughing from nearby. He jumped up and made his way over.

"Incredible..." Zack exclaimed, "...there's not a scratch on me!"

"Great right?!" Graham agreed.

They climbed out of their craters and tried to survey this new world. But the air all around them was choked in dust from their arrival.

"Come on, let's go see what the girls are up to."

"Yeah, good idea."

Zack closed his eyes and thought about Mindy and Beth. He opened them to find himself standing next to them. They were kneeling opposite each other in the dust, and it looked like they were praying.

Graham pointed over towards the horizon where they could see a large dust cloud hung in the air above the mountains where they had landed. Zack grinned; it was so good to have fun with his best friend again. Yet, he had never dreamed of doing anything like this.

"Hey, you two, help us," Beth beckoned them over.

Zack somehow knew just what she meant. They knelt next to them and joined them in prayer. They all held their hands over the dust in the centre of them. Zack could feel a real connection with God. It was pure bliss, endlessly deeper than anything he had experienced previously.

"Lord God, please help us."

Zack knew that God would understand just what he meant.

"Look!" Beth called.

She drew her hands back a little to reveal the dust beneath. In the middle, there was a small movement. Zack could feel it too, and he too drew his hands back. A tiny green sprout pushed its way out of the dry dust. It was quickly followed by another, then another. The four friends stood up and walked backwards as they spread the growth larger and larger. A green patch of grass began sprawling out around them.

The air around them tasted sweeter, and soon they were standing in the middle of a large green field. Zack looked at his friends and smiled. He knew his next adventure was just beginning.

Our Father who art in heaven,
Hallowed be thy name.
Thy kingdom come.
Thy will be done
on Earth as it is in Heaven.
Give us this day our daily bread,
and forgive us our trespasses,
as we forgive those who trespass against us,
and lead us not into temptation,
but deliver us from evil.
For thine is the kingdom,
and the power, and the glory,
for ever and ever
Amen.